# MY SOUL TO TAKE

# THE OCULUS GATE SERIES

BOOK ONE: HEAVEN CAME DOWN
BOOK TWO: INVADING HELL
BOOK THREE: MY SOUL TO TAKE
BOOK FOUR: ON EARTH AS IT IS IN HELL
(BOOK FOUR RELEASE - APRIL 15, 2023)

# MY SOUL TO TAKE

## BOOK THREE IN THE OCULUS GATE SERIES

### BY

# BRYAN DAVIS

MOUNTAIN**BROOK**FIRE

My Soul to Take
Published by Mountain Brook Ink under the Mountain Brook
Fire line
White Salmon, WA U.S.A.

The website addresses shown in this book are not intended in
any way to be or imply an endorsement on the part of Mountain
Brook Ink, nor do we vouch for their content.

This story is a work of fiction. All characters and events are the
product of the author's imagination. Any resemblance to any
person, living or dead, is coincidental.

Scripture quotations are taken from the King James Version of
the Bible. Public domain.

Hymn - "It is Well with My Soul" (UMH 377) Words: Horatio G.
Spafford, 1873.

ISBN 9781943959-87-7

Published in association with Cyle Young of Cyle Young
Literary Elite.

The Team: Miralee Ferrell, Alyssa Roat, Kristen Johnson, Cindy
Jackson
Cover Design: Indie Cover Design, Lynnette Bonner
*Mountain Brook Fire is an inspirational publisher offering worlds you can
believe in.*
Printed in the United States of America

# Chapter One

Ben climbed the ladder leading to the top of the swaying Alaska transport tower. Wind-driven snow buffeted his body. Even the parka and gloves he had found among the surrounding corpses couldn't stave off the stabbing chill.

Above, the tower's pair of dish antennas combined their radiant streams to create a multi-colored triad of wriggling lights that snaked east and west around the Arctic Circle. Somewhere beyond the horizons, the streams connected with those of three other towers on the same latitude, forming the boundary of the conduit that could transport a person to another world through the Oculus Gate portal high in the sky.

Below, the ground quaked, making the structure's sway worsen. With each step up the ladder, he searched the tower's lattice-like framework. Dr. Harrid had said he would destroy the tower after Winella transported herself and her son home to Viridi, but so far, there was no sign of explosives or any other means of destruction among the structure's supports.

His gut tossing like a ship in a storm, he paused at the ladder's halfway point and called through his earbud's embedded microphone. "Trudy, this tower's wagging like a puppy's tail. I hope you have something in your medical bag of tricks when I come back down. I'm ready to barf my breakfast."

Her voice entered his ear, barely audible against the whistling wind. "Don't be a wimp, Ben. The poison from that bullet in your head should be long gone by now. Are you going to let the queen of hell get the best of you? Now get your butt up there and stop this earthquake."

Another hard tilt forced bile into Ben's throat—hot and acidic. He swallowed it down and climbed on. For some reason, the rungs felt weaker than before, bending under his weight, but they seemed strong enough. "Easy to say when you're not riding this rollercoaster a hundred feet in the air."

"Hey, macho man, you're the one who volunteered. But I'll give you another dose of nausea meds when you come back. I can grind the tablets into apple juice in a sippy cup for you."

"You're so funny, Sis."

"Glad you noticed. Seriously, though, I can give you something stronger, but it'll have to wait till I get back to the tower. Jack and I are checking out the radio relay station to see if we can make a longer distance call for help if we're stranded. Leo and Iona are heading toward the spot where you left the SUV you drove here ... What was it now? A couple of days ago? Anyway, Kat's the only one left at the base of the tower."

"Copy that." When Ben reached the top of the ladder and climbed onto the wooden platform, he kept a firm grasp on a side rail while tightening the shoulder straps of a parachute he had found below on a dead giant. The huge man was one of several bestial giants from Viridi who wore parachutes in case the conduit picked them up off the ground during a recent tower network activation. The chute's pack was too big, of course, but perfect for wearing over a parka. It would serve as a safety precaution if the wind tossed him over the side or if the Oculus Gate conduit somehow drew him into its upward pull.

He trudged through accumulated snow to the platform's edge and looked down. Kat stood at ground level, barely illuminated by the antenna streams and the pad's glow in the never-ending darkness of an Arctic winter. As horizontal sheets of flakes whipped her parka's hood off, exposing her pageboy-style hair, she tapped on a computer tablet screen, her feet planted firmly to battle the ongoing quake. She pulled her hood back in place and called through their

2

earbud connection, shouting to overcome the whistling wind. "I've got this tablet synced with the tower. I'm reading the data now."

Ben adjusted his earbud, but the new position failed to block the competing noise. "Good. Let me know what you find while I try to figure out a safe way to shut this thing down."

"Go ahead, and I'll see if I can do it from here. Either way, we've got to stop this quake. It's getting worse by the second."

"We'll stop it even if I have to tear the antennas down." Ben again eyed the pair of antenna dishes—too far above his head to reach. He would have to find something to stand on. "But it makes no sense that Harrid would leave it running. He told Winella that it would shut off with a timer, and then he would destroy it."

"True, but I don't see a timer function. I'll keep looking."

"Keep me posted." His grasp still on the railing, Ben leaned closer to one of the antennas. No snow had accumulated on the dish's concave surface, probably melting on contact with the warm metal. "I think this thing's been running quite a while." He turned and looked at Kat again. "No wonder the quake's so severe."

She brushed snow from her tablet's screen. "The data records show a transport through the Oculus Gate exactly fifty-seven minutes and five seconds ago."

Again battling the wind, Ben shuffled toward the ladder, searching for something to boost him to one of the dishes, Kat still barely in view. He mentally recalled their recent chores since arriving from Viridi through the Oculus Gate—finding Winella's computer tablet in her and Caligar's lair, borrowing the clothes from the corpses, and warming the oversized garments in the lair's fireplace. "Didn't we get here about an hour ago?"

Kat glanced at her wristwatch. "Yep. Almost to the second. Which means someone probably shot out of here the moment we showed up."

"Maybe we're the reason he took the leap. He must've been standing well north of the Arctic Circle boundary, out in the launch area. He could probably see us arrive from there." At the edge of the platform near the ladder, Ben's boot struck something solid. Crouching, he brushed snow away from a metal container the size of a large toolbox, not big enough for the boost he needed to reach an antenna. "I found something. It wasn't here last time. Some kind of gear box, I think."

"What kind of gear?"

"Hang on." Ben flipped the latch open and lifted the lid. Inside, several unlabeled spray cans lay in a haphazard pile. He picked one up—lightweight and nearly empty. He cleared a spot on the platform and sprayed the wood with some of the can's remaining contents. A clear liquid soaked into the fibers, but it had no apparent effect.

He aimed the nozzle at a metal plate connecting two boards and released the spray until it sputtered. The plate sizzled, and smoke shot up from tiny bubbles on the surface.

Images flooded in—dozens of similar connection plates throughout the tower, including many in the weakened rungs he had climbed minutes ago. Rushing down them now might make them break, and the ladder would collapse, giving him no time or room to deploy the parachute.

A brief gust tore through the area. The tower leaned once more and stayed tilted at a precarious angle. "Kat." Ben slowly straightened, battling the wind and the tilt. "The tower's been sabotaged. I have to deploy the chute and jump."

Kat shouted, "Jump toward me. There's a big snowdrift to my right. Wind's going that direction."

"On my way." A firm hand on the parachute's ripcord, Ben crept across bending boards toward the platform's edge, ducking low under the radiant stream connecting the two antennas. A new gust blasted through. As the tower's tilt worsened, the antennas swung downward, and the streams shot into Ben. Light erupted in blinding flashes. Intense heat coursed across his skin. Then, he blacked out.

# Chapter Two

"Ben!" Kat adjusted her earbud and scanned the dark sky for a parachute. "Ben! Can you hear me? Are you still up there?"

The tower toppled to the right. Kat scrambled back, barely avoiding the massive structure as it crashed to the ground, the midsection only a few feet away. The framework shattered, and the antennas exploded in a shower of sparks. Kat ducked under the hurtling shards and stared at the wreckage. Her heart racing as the light dimmed further, she scanned the area for any sign of Ben. The moment the sparks vanished, darkness shrouded everything, and the earthquake died away.

"Ben!" Kat grabbed a flashlight from her belt, flicked it on, and sprinted toward the wreckage. "Jack, Trudy, get back here! The tower crashed with Ben on it!"

"On our way," Trudy said into Kat's earbud. "We're five minutes out." Her words shifted to barked commands. "Leo! Iona! Abort the search for the SUV. All hands to the tower."

"Making tracks," Iona said. "Two minutes."

Kat leaped over a broken tower support, skidded to a halt at the point where the platform had struck the ground, and swept the flashlight from one shattered lattice beam to another. The antennas sat nearby—ripped, blackened, and sparking. The platform's boards lay strewn about, a few protruding straight up from the drifts.

Ben was nowhere in sight.

Fear spiked. Kat shivered hard. She waded into the snow, shouting for Ben while snatching boards and tossing them to the side as she cleared a wide path. After trudging to the far end of the wreckage, she pivoted and began clearing a new swath. "Ben! Where are you?"

Only the whistling wind responded.

She bit her lip and waded on. "Ben! Talk to me."

Something rustled. Kat spun and pointed her flashlight toward the sound. Upwind, Iona appeared, her red hair poking out from under a parka hood as she ran with high steps through the drifts, her flashlight swinging. Leo trudged behind her, pumping his much longer arms and legs as the wind blew back his hood and shoulder-length hair. It seemed odd that he wouldn't be blazing a trail for Iona, but she was probably too quick.

As Iona drew closer, Kat shouted, struggling to keep her voice steady. "I can't find Ben anywhere. He's not answering my calls."

Iona halted within reach and scanned the site with her flashlight beam. "He had a parachute, right?"

"Yes. Taken from a dead giant. But I didn't see it deploy."

"Since the parachute belonged to one of the giants, it had to be huge."

"True, but it got dark real quick. I might've missed it."

"I'll search where the wind would've taken him." Iona jogged from the wreckage in a leeward path, her flashlight beam bouncing ahead of her again.

When Leo arrived, Kat pointed at him. "Get your nose in gear. You know Ben's scent. Find him."

"Yes, of course." Leo inhaled. "The wind will make it more challenging, but I will do my best."

Jack and Trudy ran into view, their feet pitching up snow behind them. They halted in front of Kat and puffed thick clouds of white. Jack's parka hood had blown back, revealing his scattered curly hair. He set a hand on Kat's shoulder. "Quick rundown."

Kat gave them a short summary of the tower's crash and Ben's disappearance. When she finished, she added, "He has to be close. This area is where the platform landed."

Jack nodded. "Gotcha."

Trudy laid her gloved hands on her narrow face, trying to warm her cheeks. "I see where you've already searched. We'll cover a different section."

While she and Jack pushed through drifts, Kat continued her back-and-forth march. She glanced at Leo from time to time as he meandered in the area, sniffing every few seconds. Then she caught a glimpse of Iona. No longer on her earlier path, she stood next to one of the scorched antennas.

"Kat?" Iona touched the edge of the dish with a gloved hand. "Did any of the light streams strike Ben?"

Kat resisted another hard shiver. "I don't know. But I was on the ground, and the storm was ..." Shaking her head, she let out a long sigh. "I just don't know."

Iona set her flashlight beam on Leo's chest. "I'll bet you're not getting even a whiff of Ben's farm smells, are you?"

His shoulders sagged. "I'm afraid not. If he were in the vicinity, I would have detected him by now, even in this wind."

Kat blinked away flakes that tried to adhere to her eyelashes as she looked at Iona. "Are you saying the streams sent Ben through the Oculus Gate? Just like they did to you?"

"I can't be sure, but ..." Iona shrugged. "What else could've zapped him clean out of here?"

"I don't know, but having something so bizarre happen twice seems impossible." Cold wind still buffeting, Kat marched in place and waved for Jack and Trudy to join her. When everyone had gathered around, she stood in the middle of the group. Battling panicked mind fog, she forced a take-charge tone. "Okay. What does everyone think? Is Ben here or not?"

"Not a sign of him," Jack said, bouncing on his toes. "I'm going with the zapped-through-the-Gate theory."

Trudy pointed. "Jack and I came from the direction a parachute would've taken him. I don't think we could've missed him."

Kat pinched her chin. "Let's think about this. If Ben got transported to Viridi, he'll plunge like a rock because the tower crashed, and there was no reverse pull. But he's wearing a parachute, and it's a big one, so he should be able to land safely if the zapping didn't knock him out, which might be a big *if*. And since he's been there before, he'll know his way around, but that's only if he lands on Viridi close enough to where he landed before."

"Not to be a pessimist," Jack said, "but that's another big *if*."

"All right. *When* he lands close enough to where he landed before." Hoping to affirm her words of confidence, Kat steeled herself against the wind and again firmed her tone. "God rescued us from hell only an hour ago, and before that, he sent us an archangel to help us battle aliens that had taken over the world. I'm not about to be a pessimist. We're going with *when*."

Iona raised a finger. "And that includes *when* he dodges the man-eating giants on Viridi."

"True. Another good *when*." Kat set her hands on her hips and looked at the sky. Shrouded by darkness and thick clouds, the Oculus Gate, that glittering, evil eye in the sky, looked down on them, a portal they thought they wouldn't have to deal with again. She inhaled deeply. "Okay, let's say Ben's on Viridi. I can't go there to find him because our tower's in pieces." She pivoted toward Jack and Trudy. "Give me an estimate. How long to repair it?"

Jack whistled, but the wind tore the sound from his lips. "Oh, man. Weeks. Maybe more than a month. We can salvage a lot of the materials, but we need tools and manpower. And the antennas look like they're shot. When Trudy and I repaired the Russia tower, I learned a lot about the technology, so I could replicate it, but with bitter cold and constant darkness ..." He pulled his parka's hood back and scratched his head. "It'll take a lot of time. With just us, one month minimum. Obviously, the more helpers we can get, the faster it'll get done. I mean, twenty skilled workers could get it done in a few days."

8

Kat surveyed the wreckage in the glow of their flashlights. "Rebuilding is probably our only option. Caligar said he was going to destroy his conduit mirror after he sent us home. So Ben can't use that."

Iona bundled her parka close to her body. "Caligar didn't say how long after. Maybe Ben can find him in time."

"In time." Kat balled a gloved hand into a fist. "Time is our worst enemy right now. Who knows what the Refectors have been up to while we were gone? I'm sure Damien hasn't been idle. He wanted my blood for a reason, to get something only I, that is, Queen Laramel, had access to. If he got it, he could be trouble."

"That reminds me," Iona said. "Alex spilled a lot of intel about Refectors. You know how hard it is to extract an angel? Well, it's a lot easier to kick a Refector out of a person's brain. You can do it with electrical shocks. Alex said the jolts need to be pretty strong, but they don't have to be deadly. Shocks even work against Radiants, strangely enough."

Kat narrowed her eyes. "Why would Alex tell you that? The Refectors are on her side."

Iona shrugged. "Showing off her smarts, I guess. You saw how cocky she is. She probably thought I wouldn't make it out of hell to tell anyone."

"Good intel. I'll keep it in mind." Kat set a hand on Jack's arm. "Listen, since I'm probably the only person who can stop Damien, I can't spend a month here rebuilding the tower."

"Say no more." Jack patted her hand. "You go home and see what's up. The rest of us will stay here and start rebuilding the tower. But we still need transportation to get you home."

"Agreed." Kat looked at Iona. "Any sign of the SUV?"

Iona glanced behind her. "That's something else strange. I didn't mention it before because of the Ben's-missing emergency, but the SUV was gone with tracks leading north past the Arctic Circle."

"Into the conduit launch zone?" Jack asked.

"Definitely looked like it. With snow covering the tracks so fast, I can't be sure. But I know it started out heading north."

"So maybe whoever stole it took it to Viridi."

"Maybe." Iona gazed at a line of snow-laden evergreens for a moment as if trying to decide what to say. "But there's good news. The angel cruiser is sitting next to where the SUV used to be."

"What?" Jack drew his head back. "I would've shouted that news right away. We can use the cruiser to sweep the area for Ben."

"And we will," Kat said as she gave Iona a long look. "Let's pile into it. Now."

Iona aimed her flashlight at a path in the snow. "It's not far." She took off at a trot.

Kat followed at the same pace, staying close behind while the others trailed. Iona seemed to be acting strangely, even for her. Waiting so long to mention the cruiser didn't make sense, even in an emergency. Like Jack indicated, since the cruiser could hover over the area, it was the perfect search vehicle. It could mean the difference between Ben getting rescued or freezing to death.

When everyone had boarded the cruiser, Kat hustled to the pilot's chair and started the engine with the press of her thumb on a scanner. A light flashed, reading her print and recognizing it as belonging to Laramel, the angel queen. The motor purred to life. She turned the interior heater on and fired up the propellers, but when she pushed the throttle to lift off, the ship stayed on the ground.

"Cruiser," Kat commanded, "throttle report."

A computerized voice emanated from the control panel. "Throttle is locked."

"Unlock throttle."

"The cruiser is moored. The throttle cannot be unlocked."

Jack slid into the copilot's chair next to Kat. "These transports have a mooring cap that twists off a threaded valve. If you remove the cap, the ship won't take off. That's so the pilot can walk away with the cap in his pocket. No worries that someone will steal the cruiser."

Kat scanned the area around her, looking for the cap. "I never knew that, and I don't see it here."

"Is this it?" Iona asked as she withdrew a dark metallic disk from her coat pocket. "I saw it on the ground outside, so I scooped it up."

Jack rose from the seat. "Yep. I'll put it—"

"I got it." Iona shot up, bundled her coat, and pressed a button next to the side door. The moment it slid to the side, she leaped out. Bitter wind gusted in, prompting Kat to close the door from the control panel.

Kat looked at Jack, again seated in the copilot's chair. "When I was in Russia, I left the cruiser running so Winella could fly it back here. Maybe she parked it where she knew we would find it. And since I'm the only one who can start it, whoever stole the SUV couldn't take the cruiser instead."

"Makes sense." Jack turned toward the door. "But something's not sitting right."

"What?"

Rapid knocks sounded at the cruiser's side.

"Tell you later." Jack buckled in. "After we search for Ben."

Kat pressed a button that opened the door. Iona hopped in, closed the door, and shivered, her hands in her coat pockets as she bustled back to her seat. "Done. Let's fly this bird out of here."

"Thanks." Kat pushed the throttle again. As they lifted off, she guided the craft slowly out of the clump of trees toward the tower site. Snow-laden gusts blasted the windshield, making the cruiser lurch. "Belts on?" she called as she twisted in her seat toward the spacious passenger compartment.

Seated in plush chairs with a wide aisle down the center, Trudy, Iona, and Leo buckled their lap belts and shoulder harnesses with a chorus of clicks.

"All set," Trudy said from the front row across the aisle from Iona.

Kat flicked on a front-mounted searchlight and guided the cruiser toward the wreckage. When they arrived at the area, she manipulated the light's controller and swept the beam across the debris. "Look out the side windows. With snow beating against the windshield, I'm flying kind of blind. I might miss something."

"Turn on the heat sensor," Trudy said. "Look for a signature."

Kat found the infrared scanner and flipped its switch. "Got it." A two-foot-wide screen on the control panel showed the bleak ground below—nothing but snow and broken tower parts. Twin orange blobs indicated where the antennas lay, but there was no sign of any living humans.

Iona spoke up, out of Kat's view. "While we're searching, we can talk about our plans. I was thinking Kat could fly the cruiser home and run a command center from there. You know, send construction materials, maybe hire more workers."

Kat glanced back, but only for a brief second. "Maybe." When she turned toward the front again, she let her eyes dart between the heat sensor and the windshield and back again. So far, no significant signatures except for the dishes. "I can't focus on anything but finding Ben right now."

"No problem. I'll keep searching out my window."

As Kat made slow sweeps across the area, hovering about thirty feet off the ground, she tried to ignore chatter from her passengers, but the words drilled in anyway.

"I think it's a good idea," Trudy said. "Kat's the only one who can access whatever Damien's trying to get. The rest of us can work on the tower."

"She shouldn't go alone, though," Iona said. "Leo and I should go with her."

Trudy huffed. "Kat doesn't need protection. She's kicked more butts than most battalions have."

"Not for protection. I could be a … a project manager, I guess. While you and Jack scope out the repair project and Kat looks into what Damien and the Refectors are up to, Leo and I will collect the supplies we need, including portable heaters, fuel, and food. And I have contacts from the angel temple who can round up some workers for us. Once that's all done, we'll fly the cruiser back here with everything on board, maybe with some helping hands. Whole lot more efficient than Leo and me staying here and working with what we've got."

"Gotta admit, it's a good plan." Trudy shivered. "I don't like the idea of staying here and freezing my backside off, but Jack and I have experience with repairs, so we can get started with the technical stuff. And the radio relay station is running, so we can update you with a supply list as we figure out what we need."

Kat spun her chair toward them, her cheeks hot. "How can you possibly be concentrating on the search for Ben while you're clucking back there like a bunch of brooding biddies?"

Everyone stared at her, their mouths agape. After a second or two, Leo raised a hand. "Kat, I would like to apologize on behalf of the group. Chatting while we should have been focusing on the search was insensitive at best and a dereliction of duty at worst." He gestured toward the windshield. "Please. Let's continue. And I will personally enforce silence while we concentrate on locating your beloved husband."

As Kat gazed at his sincere expression, his thick eyebrows wet from snowmelt and his skin reddened from exposure to the whipping wind, every molecule of anger drained away. A tear dripped to her cheek, and she heaved a sigh. "I'm sorry." She brushed the tear away, turned toward the front, and eased the cruiser down to a landing.

When the landing runners settled, she faced the others again, her jaw firm. "The search is over. Ben's not here. He's either dead or marooned on Viridi, and we can't go there until the tower is repaired." She nodded toward Iona. "We'll go with your plan. Jack and Trudy will stay at Caligar and Winella's cave with all the supplies we have here in the cruiser, then we'll head home as fast as this ship can travel."

Jack unbuckled, rose from the copilot's seat, and stood next to Kat, a hand on her shoulder. "You know Ben. He's a survivor. We'll find him. You can count on it."

She laid a hand over his. "Yes, I know. And thank you."

He turned toward the others and clapped his hands. "All right, you three. Go to the cargo hold and collect whatever we can use. I'll join you in a minute."

While Trudy, Iona, and Leo unbuckled and headed toward the rear of the cruiser, Jack crouched and whispered into Kat's ear. "Have you noticed a change in Leo and Iona?"

Kat spoke in a low tone as well. "Kind of subtle. Iona is acting like the boss of the two, which isn't overly odd, but she's leading with her brain instead of her mouth. And Leo hasn't said much at all until that little speech he gave a minute ago."

"That's what made me wonder. Leo has always been great with words, but that speech was … I don't know … more eloquent than usual. And he hasn't pegged anyone with one of his trademark nicknames. Not only that, Iona hasn't even mentioned her helmet. She was practically glued to that thing."

"Do you know what happened to it?"

"When she and Leo came up out of the abyss, I took it off her and set it on the ground. It's probably still there. And I don't think she's wearing her cross necklace anymore. I glanced at her neck a few times to see if I could spot it, but I don't think it's there."

"It could've fallen off in hell with all the climbing and crawling she said she had to do."

"True." Jack sighed. "I'm just trying to put all the clues together."

Kat nodded slowly. "The simplest explanation is that they were in the abyss. A shock to the system, maybe."

"Not likely. In my experience, a shock to the system usually makes people quiet or causes a stress disorder. I don't see that in either of them."

Kat looked him in the eye. "What exactly are you trying to say?"

"I'm not sure." Jack firmed his lips as he watched the trio sliding crates out of the hold and into the aisle. "They were in hell a long time. Way longer than we were. And in the abyss, the deepest part.

14

No telling what might've rubbed off on them, if you know what I mean."

Kat narrowed her eyes. "No. What *do* you mean?"

"Bad stuff. Evil things that should've stayed in hell."

She laughed under her breath. "The fact that they picked up eloquent diction and smart strategy led you to that conclusion?"

"Yeah. I know. It's a stretch. But I can't shake the feeling that something's off." He patted her shoulder as he rose. "Just watch them. That's all I'm saying."

"I can do that." Kat glanced out the windshield. The snow had diminished to flurries, and the wind had eased. "Storm's passed. Flying should be smoother now."

"Good. Fly us to the cave, and we'll get this plan moving." Jack strode to the rear of the cruiser and began helping with the cargo.

Kat turned to the controls and lifted the cruiser from the ground. As she flew toward the cave, only a one-minute trip, Jack's words returned to mind like a distant echo. *Evil things that should've stayed in hell.* At first, the idea sounded like fearful nonsense, but Jack was right about one thing. Leo and Iona had been acting strangely— not patterns of speech or the birth of a solid plan, something else. Something deeper ... darker.

She shuddered. That topic would have to wait for a smooth cruising altitude and a dose of daylight. Pondering the dismal fortunes of the damned would only distract her from her one and only mission—to find Ben and bring him home. Damien and his schemes could also wait. Ben came first. Always.

# Chapter Three

Iona stepped out from Alex's castle and onto its drawbridge. Leo walked at her side, holding the violin and bow they had found in the basement. Dense mist hovered over the marsh, the water motionless. Black algae floated on the surface, as dead as everything else here in hell, including every tree in the surrounding forest—gnarled, leafless trees with no undergrowth, only black soil with protruding knobby roots, nothing but death and desolation as far as the eye could see.

Iona inhaled, a strange sensation considering she was now a disembodied soul trapped in the underworld. The air smelled mildewy, tinged with a hint of sulfur and infused with the odor of decaying flesh. And the reason for the latter stench was easy to find. At the far end of the drawbridge lay piles of dead trolls, for the lack of a better word. They looked more like piggish bipeds with hairy bodies.

Her clothing also seemed odd. She still wore a soldier's camo outfit, complete with boots, belt, and tactical vest with an attached handgun holster, though the gun was no longer there, tossed to the side after she emptied the rounds defending herself against the trolls. Yet, she had her body then. Did her soulish self keep everything she had on when she lost her body?

She touched her cross necklace. Good. That was also still there. And Leo wore his usual long, dark cloak and rugged huntsman clothes, perfect for tracking fugitives in the wilderness, the same outfit he had on before losing his body. The mystery added to the eeriness of the place.

"Ah," Leo said. "I see you spotted your necklace. I found it on the castle floor and put it on you before you woke up."

"On the floor?" She crossed her eyes and looked at it again. "I wonder why I wasn't wearing it."

"Maybe it's real. Physical, I mean." He patted his cloak pocket. "Like the little box I found with the mirror inside."

"So it fell off my body in the healing pool?"

"I suppose so." He shrugged. "Maybe it's a sign we're still being looked after."

"Works for me." Iona fingered the cross for a moment. Real or not, it seemed to have no power to alter the dismal mood. She lowered her tone, though no one but Leo was around to hear. "Hell feels a lot different now that Alex is gone."

"Yes, dethroning the self-proclaimed queen of hell is bound to change the place." Leo furrowed his brow, lowering his bushy black eyebrows. "But what does *gone* mean? She was already dead. I don't think you can get deader than dead."

"True. But there's a lot we don't know about being in hell. Like how can we feel so ... so solid, I guess, not to mention breathing and—"

A loud pop sounded from within the castle. Iona and Leo peered through the entry into the dimness within. A sizzling noise followed, growing louder and louder.

Leo prodded Iona's back. "Run!"

They sprinted away from the castle and leaped off the drawbridge near the pile of dead trolls. Iona looked back. Black smoke erupted from a hole in the castle's roof and crawled along the angled rooftops and down the walls like a coat of sooty fog. After several seconds, the smoke began dispersing, starting from a pair of spires protruding from the top floor and moving downward, leaving nothing behind, as if stripping away matter along the way.

The shredding progressed to the second floor. The outer façade disappeared, though the basic inner layout remained—blackened floor, stairs, and columns. None of the furniture and other trappings remained, leaving a burned-out shell instead of an exquisite castle fit for a queen.

Finally, the smoke cleared completely. A black cauldron sat at the center of the first floor, a curl of smoke rising from its mouth. All lay quiet again. Whatever had happened appeared to be finished.

Leo ran a hand through his thick mane and breathed a single word. "Witchcraft."

"Maybe." Iona squinted at the remains. "Bart called Alex a sorceress. But why would she brew something that would destroy her own castle?"

"Did she?" Leo stared at the ruins for a long moment. "Maybe she destroyed the illusion."

"You mean, the stuff that disappeared wasn't really there?"

"That's exactly what I mean. It made no sense for all of those luxuries to exist in hell. Maybe some of them were real, things she created herself, like the healing pool, but it seems that she left behind an anti-hex bomb of sorts to disintegrate the phantom images."

Iona looked deeper into the ruins. "Yeah. Not much left. Even those creepy portraits on the wall are gone."

"But that isn't gone." Leo strode to the castle's entry arch and picked up the violin. "I dropped it so we could run faster."

When he returned, she looked the violin over. The beautiful black instrument Alex had played from within the mirror appeared to be perfectly polished, without a nick or worn spot. Since it seemed to conjure images in the mirror, apparently some of Alex's tools had power while some did not. "Why would Alex have a spell to get rid of the phantom stuff?"

Leo shrugged. "It wouldn't make sense unless she knew she was going to leave and no longer had need of it."

"You mean ..." Iona scowled. "That conniving witch planned everything, and we were part of her scheme. Retrieving the mirror, getting stabbed, using the healing pool. She *wanted* it all to happen."

"If so"—Leo tapped the violin bow on his shoulder as he thought—"Alex's soul still exists. She wouldn't have planned her own demise."

18

Iona glanced from side to side, but silence and calm still ruled the bleak forest. "Then where is she? What's she up to? And why did she purge our souls from our bodies?"

"That's a quixotic quiz, indeed. I have no answers."

As Iona scanned the ruined castle, Alex's words returned to mind, as if the mirror were still speaking from the abyss. *Disembodied souls are another matter. They are designed to inhabit any human body, and some of the abyss dwellers have the knowledge to penetrate and inhabit you, though they would first have to purge your soul.*

"Leo!" Iona clutched his arm. "I think I know the answers. Alex purged my soul so she could possess my body. Ben and the others left hell thinking I was with them, but it wasn't me. It was Alex."

Leo stroked his chin. "Which means that Bart probably possessed my body. The diabolical diva wanted to take her henchman with her."

"Most likely. And I'll bet it happened in the healing pool. Alex staged the stabbing so we would have to go there to keep from dying. Our souls got purged, and Alex and Bart possessed our bodies."

Leo whistled. "It's a wild stretch. In fact, it sounds insane, but I can't think of a better theory."

"Same here. It's crazy, but it has to be true."

"Then it's an ingenious plot. The scheming sorceress pulled it off, even though we were watching for any kind of devilish move."

Iona spread her arms. "Then what are we going to do? Alex is crafty enough to pretend to be me. Ben and the others won't be able to figure out who's really inside my body."

"Perhaps our allies are more perceptive than you think. In any case, I suspect that Bart won't be as adept at being me. Maybe we can count on him to tip them off."

Iona lowered her arms to her sides. "Good point. Bart's intelligent, but he thinks he's smarter than he really is." An odd sound filtered into the forest, like garbled voices—blending together in an indecipherable mass. "Do you hear that?"

"If you mean a low murmuring, then yes." Leo rotated in place, his brow low as he scanned the area. "I hear your voice in the mix."

"My voice? How is that possible?"

"Shhh. Listen."

The voices continued, though they seemed different from normal sounds—fragile, without a source, as if they weren't coming from people at all, more like emissions from air particles. A few distinct words penetrated the murmurs—*not for protection ... project manager ... repair project.* The voice did seem to be her own.

Iona whispered, "This is so weird."

"I heard you mention Kat," Leo said. "Not much else."

After a quiet moment, Leo's voice entered the murmurings, clearer than Iona's. "Kat, I would like to apologize on behalf of the group. Chatting while we should have been focusing on the search was insensitive at best and a dereliction of duty at worst. Please. Let's continue. And I will personally enforce silence while we concentrate on locating your beloved husband."

"Leo," Iona said. "It's Bart speaking through your mouth. I'd know his puffed-up jargon anywhere. And Alex is speaking through my mouth."

Leo nodded. "And it seems that Ben is missing again."

"Right. Not good at all. But maybe we can learn more. Somehow we can hear what's going on with our bodies, like there's some kind of strange attachment."

"It is strange, but this is a strange situation. Maybe it's because our souls belong inside our bodies. We're not supposed to be separated from them until we die."

A growl rode the motionless air, coming from somewhere in the forest beyond the moat. Another followed, deeper and closer.

Iona swallowed. "That was a real sound. Here in hell."

"Agreed." Leo inhaled through his nose. "I smell a stench, something even more foul than these two-legged swine."

Iona picked up a hefty branch. "We never saw any other beasts in this forest before."

"Considering the timing of their arrival, maybe her witchcraft kept them at bay, and that smoke bomb stripped her refuge of its protection."

"Good theory." Iona glanced around. The stillness felt ready to erupt with danger at any moment. And the murmuring voices had quieted, at least for now. "We'd better find shelter."

"Agreed again. But we should leave a message in case someone returns to hell to rescue us."

"Return to hell? Why would anyone do something as crazy as that?"

"Like we talked about. Someone will notice how different the Bart version of me is. They'll know he's an imposter."

Iona took on a sarcastic tone. "Okay. Sure. I'll buy that. Someone will say, 'Hey, you're not really Leo. Let's go to hell, find Leo's soul, and get him out. Easy peasy.'" She rolled her eyes. "Talk about wild stretches."

"Maybe so, but I can't think of any other option to—"

Another growl emanated from the forest, louder and closer.

Iona clutched the dangling cross. It might be just a symbol, but holding it brought some comfort. "Okay," she said as she searched the trees for the source of the growls. "Leave a message. But make it fast."

"One fast message coming up." After handing the violin and bow to her, Leo dragged one of the troll corpses to a nearby tree and propped it in a sitting position with its back to the trunk. "No scavenger has eaten these foul beasts during all this time, so I think this one won't go anywhere."

Iona took a step closer. "How will you leave a message on a troll?"

"I'll scratch words in its hide." Leo reached up and broke a twig off a branch. Black goo oozed from the break and dripped onto the corpse's head. "Even better." He dipped one end of the twig into the goo and used the tip to write on the troll's forehead, speaking the words as he wrote. "Seeking shelter. Look for signs. I and L."

He slung the gooey twig to the ground and took the violin and bow from Iona. "Let's go. We'll head for the portal at the abyss. Easy to follow the sulfur odor."

Leo and Iona jogged toward the abyss side by side, slowing every several steps for Leo to poke a hole in the ground with the end of a branch. During each pause, Iona scanned the forest again. The thought of the prowling beasts sent a surge of tingles up and down her spine. Maybe a distraction would help. "Okay. Let's think about this. Since disembodied souls like us can't use the portal, we need to find a different way to escape. But as smart as Alex is, she would have found it if it existed. That's why she hatched that insane plan. I know it worked, but my point is that there's no easy way out."

"For her," Leo said. "We're not Alex."

"You mean, maybe we can do something that she couldn't?"

"Exactly. There are differences between her and us. For example, she's as evil as the devil himself, and we're not."

"Right." Iona dodged a dead winged creature, probably one of Alex's pets. "And she was condemned, and we're not. We're not even dead."

"True." Leo kicked a fallen branch out of the way. "But how does it change our fortunes?"

"Well, for one thing, God knows we don't belong here."

"Ah. Divine help. Fair point from our theological theorist. Yet, any path of escape might be a harrowing journey. Even one God provides."

Iona chewed on her bottom lip. "Okay. You're right. But I'm not going to let that get me down. We've been through harrowing journeys before. We can do it again. I mean, I'd do anything to get us out of here."

"Agreed." Leo halted to make another mark and inhaled again. "I no longer smell those growlers, and the sulfur odor is getting stronger."

Iona sidled to him. As they both stood silently, moans drifted across the air, sad and tormented. "And I hear the souls," Iona said. "We're getting close."

22

When she took a step forward, Leo grasped her wrist. "I suggest we maintain silence until we reach the abyss. I smell an unusual aroma. It's familiar, but I can't place it yet."

She whispered, "No problem."

They walked on, slowly now. Soon, a call came from the direction of the abyss. "Who walks in the witch's woodland?"

Iona and Leo halted, both holding their breath. The caller sounded like a woman—commanding, confident, though not threatening.

She called again. "If you think you can fool me with your sudden silence, you're wrong. Come, now. Answer me. I heard two of you, and I know the footsteps and gait of Alexandria and Bartholomew. You're not those evil vermin."

Leo mouthed, "Evil vermin?"

Iona nodded. If this person thought Alex and Bart were vermin, maybe she wouldn't be an enemy. Still, she was a resident of hell. She couldn't be trusted, at least not yet.

"If you want help," the woman continued, "you have to come to me. I can't go into Alexandria's forest. Her sorcery is powerful."

Iona lifted her brow, hoping to signal Leo with the obvious question. *Should we go out there?*

He nodded and whispered barely audibly, "If she tries to assault us, we can run back into the forest."

Iona replied in a similar low voice. "Yeah. I'm no coward, but here in hell, running's a good strategy." She tapped herself on the chest. "My turn to go first."

"True, but—"

"No buts. We've done this before. I'm way less intimidating than you are."

"All right. I'll be close behind."

Iona called, "We're coming," then strode toward the abyss, her muscles flexed and her face firm. She had to show confidence, fearlessness. A rival to Alex might try to be intimidating in spite of her helpful invitation.

With Leo at her heels, Iona broke into the clearing and halted. A woman stood a few paces in front of the abyss. Average height with hands on hips, she wore a hooded cloak, reddish-brown and open in front to reveal military camo garb. A belt wrapped around her narrow waist, holding various gadgets, too distant to identify. Red hair flowed from under her hood, framing a freckled face—lovely, yet mysterious. She seemed familiar somehow.

Leo gasped, then quickly stifled himself.

Iona swiveled toward him. "Are you all right?"

"In a manner of speaking." He cleared his throat. "I'll explain later—that is, if I can."

The woman gazed with piercing blue eyes. "I don't understand. The witch's forest is locked to all outsiders. How did you enter? And it's obvious that you're new arrivals. How could you escape the abyss so quickly?"

Iona crossed her arms. "I'm not sure how much information to give away."

"A fair response. I am a stranger to you. My name is …" She glanced at Leo for a brief second before continuing. "Charlie."

"Iona." She gestured with a flick of her head. "He's Leo."

"Leo?" Charlie narrowed her eyes. "Interesting."

"His name is interesting?"

"Oh. I was referring to the violin. I have not seen one in hell before."

Leo, a fist around both the bow and the violin's neck, held them up. "Alex left it behind. We thought it might have some power."

"Perhaps it does. I have heard the witch play it from time to time." Charlie wrinkled her nose. "I find it interesting that you call her Alex. Is that a nickname you chose, or has she told you to call her that?"

Iona touched her chest. "My choice. She prefers Alexandria, her queenly name, so I'm sticking with Alex."

24

"I see. Then I will do so as well." Charlie walked into the forest a few trees deep. When she pivoted back, she set her hands on her hips again. "How strange. The warding is gone."

Iona scrunched her brow. "Warding? What do you mean?"

"I'll explain later. For now ..." Charlie marched back out. "Come with me. When the beasts sense that the warding is gone, they will emerge from their holes. They can't destroy you, but they can make you suffer." She strode to the edge of the abyss, turned right, and continued at a brisk pace around the perimeter, her cloak flowing behind her.

Iona looked at Leo. "Should we follow?"

The moment he opened his mouth to answer, another growl came from the forest, closer than ever. "Go. I'll guard your back."

Iona spied her helmet on the ground. Jack must have dropped it there earlier. She scooped it up, set it on her head, and took off at a jog with Leo's footsteps pounding to the rear. Charlie, now about fifty yards ahead, also broke into a trot. Her strides seemed effortless, like those of a gently loping gazelle.

As Iona skirted the abyss on barren, rocky terrain, lamenting cries rose from the depths. She cast quick looks into the pit. An amorphous mass of souls meandered at the bottom. A few tried to climb the walls, only to fall back into the moaning mix.

Trying to shake off the tragic scene, she accelerated. Their situation was horrible, but there was nothing she could do about it. She had to move on, though guilt dragged at her like an attached ball and chain.

When she and Leo caught up with Charlie, they slowed to her pace. "Where are we going?" Iona asked, now jogging at Charlie's side while Leo lagged a few steps behind.

"To my refuge." Charlie's words broke with her tiring breaths. "It's not much farther."

Iona listened to her own respiration. Although her breathing felt different in this disembodied state, running hadn't altered it at all, as if physical exertion made no difference to her stamina. Maybe that would change over time as it had for Charlie.

After nearly a minute, they entered a wooded area. Charlie veered away from the abyss and continued jogging for about half a mile before halting at a huge tree with a thick trunk and hefty limbs that spread to the sides, just out of reach. Like all the other trees, it had no foliage, though a mass of twisted, thorny vines fashioned a cocoon-like shell in the midst of its branches a few feet above their heads.

More growls emanated from deep within the new forest. Leo sniffed the air. "I smell something foul, like cat urine mixed with fecal matter."

"Hellcats." From a spool on her belt, Charlie pulled a line with an attached hook. With an underhand motion, she tossed the hook into the tree. When it failed to catch anything and dropped to her feet, she muttered something unintelligible.

More growls rode the air, closer now. Iona scanned the trees for the approaching hellcats, but so far nothing moved. "Can I help somehow?"

"No. I've got it." Charlie tried again. This time the hook caught something unseen within the cocoon. She jerked down on the line. A ladder made of leafless vines and crude wooden rungs unreeled until the bottom rung swayed at knee height.

She unfastened her hook from the ladder, pushed a button on the spool that reeled the line back in, and began climbing. "Careful. I cut the thorns off the vines, but some of the stubs are still sharp." When she entered the cocoon, she turned and poked her head out. "And a few of the rungs are unsteady."

From around a distant tree, a dark, catlike creature appeared, the size of a cougar, with a coat as thick as a lion's mane and pointed teeth overlapping its lower lip. It crept closer, snarling, its hackles raised as several other cats joined it from behind.

"They're ready to attack." Charlie reached a hand down. "Get up here. Hurry!"

# Chapter Four

Leo stepped between Iona and the hellcat and jabbed a finger toward Charlie's cocoon. "Go! I'll hold it off."

Iona leaped, caught a ladder rung, and climbed as she shouted, "Hurry, Leo!"

"I'm right behind you."

From within the cocoon, Charlie grasped Iona's wrist, hauled her in, and thrust her onto a bench that lined the circular wall of vines. More feline snarls erupted below, then a squeal. Leo's arms protruded through a hole at the bottom of the cocoon, then his head as he climbed. Iona and Charlie grabbed his arms and helped him scramble the rest of the way in.

Leo and Iona sat hip to hip on the bench with their backs against the cocoon's inner walls while Charlie pulled up the ladder. "I see you left the violin on the ground."

Leo nodded. "Made climbing easier."

"Smart move. It's a beautiful instrument but not as important as your health. I don't think the cats will bother it." When she finished reeling the ladder into an awkward coil, she sat next to Leo. The trio, along with the coil, nearly filled the entire space. Below, more cats growled, though their rage-filled snarls stayed low to the ground.

"They don't climb." Using both hands, Charlie pushed the coiled ladder into the hole and plugged it, muffling the noise. "Their claws can shred your skin, but they break off with pressure."

"Then why plug the hole?" Iona asked as she removed her helmet and set it on her lap.

Charlie nudged the coil with her toe. "Bats. As big as hawks. They've flown into my hideout a few times."

"They're dangerous, I assume."

Charlie nodded. "Venomous teeth and claws."

"How can venom hurt souls?"

She shrugged. "I don't know, but it does. A few years ago, I saw a bat bite a soul who had escaped from the abyss. He shriveled into a wrinkled shell before the bat carried him away. And a bat scratched me as I was climbing into my hideout. I was sick for three days."

"Wow. Scary." Iona shook her head. "I don't get this whole disembodied thing. I feel physical. I have weight. I breathe. My heart beats. How can our state be called disembodied?"

"Did you notice how easily I hauled you into my refuge? You're much lighter as a soul. If we cut you open, I'm not sure what we'd find inside—a heart, probably, maybe a physical brain. Obviously souls have minds, but they might be like an imprint of the brains they had when they were alive. Metaphysical, I guess you might call it."

"What do you eat?" Leo asked. "I haven't seen a green plant since we arrived. And the beasts look like walking botulism—rotted meat with legs and claws."

Charlie laughed. "That's a good description. But I eat what the birds deliver."

Iona drew her head back. "Birds bring you food?"

"Yes. Ravens. Most of the time it's berries the size of a pebble. Tastes and feels like moist bread. And sometimes they bring a brown nut, like an acorn, but not as hard. Kind of chewy inside." Charlie shrugged. "It's not much, but at least it keeps me from starving."

"Starving?" Leo narrowed an eye. "That's an odd concern. The souls in the abyss have no food source that I'm aware of. How do they keep from starving? And what about water? You obviously keep yourself clean. I detected no odor from you except a hint of sulfur."

"I have a well not far off, and I am supplied with soap and other essentials when needed, but enough about that." Charlie folded her hands in her lap. "We're getting off topic. I promise to tell you everything quite soon." She reached into a hole in the wall, withdrew a gray sphere about the size of an apple, and rubbed the surface

28

against her shirt, as if polishing it. Within a couple of seconds, it glowed with a yellowish aura. She set the orb on her lap. "This light will last an hour or so."

As the glow illuminated the area, she lowered her hood, fully revealing her face for the first time. Her smooth, rounded cheeks and full lips made her look younger than before, maybe in her mid-twenties. Yet, her serious dark eyes seemed older, at least forty. A small birthmark on her throat, although brown on the surface, glowed with a purplish tint in the orb's aura.

Iona studied every detail. Again Charlie seemed familiar, like someone she had seen in a fleeting dream.

"Since I saved you from the beasts …" Charlie eyed Leo and Iona in turn. "I think you should answer my question first. How did you break Alex's warding and enter her forest?"

Iona gave a light shrug. "I don't know anything about a warding. We just walked right in. Well … I did. Then Leo came later."

Charlie tilted her head as she studied Iona. "Did you enter alone?"

"No. Bart … I mean, Bartholomew, Alex's toady, was with me. We went through a dense, thorny hedge, but that was the only real barrier I can remember."

"Interesting. Did Bartholomew go through the hedge first?"

Iona nodded. "The thorns didn't seem to affect him."

"Then he must've removed the warding somehow."

"Maybe he did, but I didn't notice. I just forced my way through." Iona tapped on her helmet. "I was wearing this, so most of the thorns didn't hurt me, though one did stab my arm. I bled a little, but not much."

"Wait a minute." Charlie narrowed her eyes. "You bled?"

"I was physical then. Alive. In my body."

"Then how could you be here as—"

"Wait," Leo said, lifting a finger. "I have a theory about the warding. While we were with Alex, she wondered how Ben could break the warding and enter the forest, and she put the warding back in place. Then Iona broke it, and Alex didn't bother to restore it later. What did both Ben and Iona have in common? They were both alive, and they both bled. At least I assume Ben bled. He had blood smears on his face."

"Interesting." Charlie tapped a finger on her chin as she stared at the floor of her cocoon. "So if blood breaks the warding, that means ..." As she continued staring, her smile quivered, maybe from fear or maybe from excitement.

"Is something wrong?" Iona asked.

"No." Charlie shook her head as if casting off a shadow. "So you were here while you were alive, and then you died and came back?"

"Not exactly." Iona took a deep breath. "Okay. I'll spill my story." She gave Charlie a summary of their adventures, including Alex conjuring images in the mirror by playing the violin, though she left out her discovery of her past, that she was likely adopted and Leo was somehow related to her.

When she finished, Charlie offered a thoughtful nod. "Interesting. It's happened before. I mean, someone coming here in physical form." She opened her cloak in front and touched a hole in her pants, revealing an oozing cut on her knee. "As you can see, I bleed."

Leo's mouth dropped open. Iona gasped. "Then you're alive?" she asked.

"I am. I didn't tell you at first, but now that I know you're not in league with Alex, I decided to trust you." Charlie looked at Leo, her brow lifting high. "I'm trying to read your expression. Are you shocked? Frightened? Relieved?"

He closed his mouth, then murmured, "I ... uh ... all three, I think."

She set a hand on his knee. "Have no fear, Leo. I understand. Souls like you are the reason I am here. To bring you comfort and make sure you are taken where God wants you to be."

He stared at her hand, saying nothing.

Iona glanced between Charlie and Leo. This cloaked woman's presence was having some kind of weird effect on him. "Okay,

Charlie ..." Iona hardened her expression. "Your turn to spill. Exactly why are you in hell?"

Charlie drew back from Leo and again folded her hands in her lap. "I am a Reaper."

"A Reaper?" Iona blinked at her. "I thought they were extinct."

"Not extinct. Merely rare."

"Ah," Leo said. "Now you're talking history, one of my specialties." He looked at Iona. "How familiar are you with the history of Reapers?"

"Not familiar at all. My history teacher treated them like a myth."

"They're far from mythical. At one time there were many Reapers. More than two centuries ago, souls of the dead roamed the earth, trapped under a radioactive layer that surrounded the globe because of a nuclear meltdown. Eventually, a heroic pair of Reapers eliminated the layer and set the souls free."

"Phoenix and Shanghai," Charlie said. "Reapers were always named after cities that were destroyed during the government fire purges, but the details would take far too long to tell. Suffice it to say that as the radioactive shield dissipated, the number of Reapers dwindled because they were no longer needed. As far as I know, there are only two left—myself and another Reaper in hell who has similar responsibilities."

"Are you named after a city?" Iona asked.

"Yes. Charlie is a nickname. My city name is obscure, destroyed years ago, so I go by Charlie. Again, it's a long story, and I've told you what you need to know, but maybe this will help you believe me." She touched her birthmark. "See the purple glow? It's the identifying mark of a Reaper, a sign of my power. I am a shepherd of souls."

Iona gazed at the mark. The glow did seem odd, but it didn't prove anything. Still, it might be better to drop the proof topic and move on. "Why is a shepherd of souls needed in hell?"

"If I were to try to explain it, you would have many more questions. It would be better if I showed you a place where everything will become clear."

Iona nodded. "Okay. A picture's worth a bunch of words. But what about the hellcats? I can still hear them growling down there."

"They will be gone by morning. And I understand your concern. Our encounter with them was frightening." Charlie reached into the alcove again, withdrew a lyre, and set it in her lap. "Would the two of you like some music to settle your thoughts?"

"Um ... sure. I guess that might help." Iona looked a Leo. "You?"

"I will be glad to listen. I had a close friend who played the lyre." He gave Charlie a boyish smile. "It will bring back memories."

"A *friend* played it? Interesting." Charlie set the lyre on her thigh and strummed the strings with her fingers and thumb, creating beautiful notes that echoed in the cocoon. "Very few play this instrument these days, and even fewer play it well."

Iona let the notes filter into her senses, soft and lovely. As Charlie said, the music did massage the senses in a soothing way. "Then obviously you're one of the people who play it well."

"I have been a musician since the time I could walk. I hope that my gift brings joy to others." Charlie closed her eyes and began a new melody. "This is part of a psalm of King David of Israel that I set to music. Before I became a Reaper, I was a professor of Middle Eastern antiquities with a keen interest in their arts, especially music." She took a deep breath and sang. "I will call upon the Lord, who is worthy to be praised. So shall I be saved from mine enemies. The sorrows of death compassed me, and the floods of ungodly men made me afraid. The sorrows of hell compassed me about. The snares of death prevented me. In my distress I called upon the Lord and cried unto my God. He heard my voice out of his temple, and my cry came before him, even into his ears."

Charlie gave the lyre a final strum and opened her eyes. "That song always brings me comfort."

"It's beautiful," Iona said. "Really, really amazing."

Leo gazed at Charlie with glistening eyes. "Your talent is extraordinary."

"Thank you, but although the psalm is comforting to me, it can cause others agony. I learned that the hard way. I composed the music soon after I arrived in hell, and I was foolish enough to think that the song might bring comfort to the souls in the abyss, but I quickly learned my mistake. The song enraged them. One soul who had escaped from the abyss even attacked me."

Iona winced. "Wow! That's extreme."

"But understandable. In their hopeless condition, the words were like rubbing salt in a fresh wound. Their lamenting calls to the Lord were fruitless, and that will never change. For all eternity."

"But you sang it for us."

"Because I believe there is hope for you." Charlie gazed at Iona for a long moment, her own eyes glistening. "Do you ever sing, Iona?"

"Me? Um ... Sometimes. Not lately, though. I used to sing to our lambs when I was little. I think they liked it, and I sang 'Jesus Loves Me' to my baby brother when he was sick. He cooed at first, but then he got sicker and I couldn't tell if he liked it or not." Iona's throat narrowed. "And ... and then ... well ... he died." She swallowed, then took a deep breath. "I don't think I've sung ever since. Not that I stopped believing in God. I just didn't feel like singing anymore."

"Your heart was broken." Charlie offered a trembling smile. "But your singing was a precious gift to your brother. His cooing proves that he loved your singing. His later suffering wouldn't allow him to tell you so."

"Yeah." Iona averted her eyes. "Maybe."

Charlie touched Iona's chin and turned her head, forcing eye contact. "Will you sing with me now?"

"Sing, now? Why?"

"There is another song I sing to myself for comfort, and I always wanted to sing it to the souls, but I never did for fear of enraging them once again. But it's perfect for a soul who is filled with light, a soul such as yourself."

Iona resisted the urge to look away again. She certainly didn't feel like she was filled with light. "Then go ahead and sing it. You don't need me."

"But I do. It is meant to be sung with two voices, and my solos don't do it justice."

"Why would you write a song for two voices?"

"I didn't write this one. It is a very old composition by a man who lost everything, and he wrote a song of comfort for his soul. Since you are a soul who needs comfort, I was hoping you would join me. I will lead. Your part will be small. I promise."

Iona concealed a sigh. "All right. I'll give it a try."

"I'll help you when it's your turn." Charlie began singing with a beautiful alto voice as she strummed the lyre. "When peace like a river attendeth my way, when sorrows like sea billows roll; whatever my lot, thou hast taught me to say, it is well, it is well with my soul."

Iona shivered. So lovely. So moving. The sorrows were, indeed, billowing. Leo brushed a tear from his cheek, his stare riveted on Charlie, obviously spellbound.

"Now the refrain. I'll sing a phrase, and you answer like an echo. I'll help you the first time." Charlie sang slowly. "It is well …" She nodded at Iona and played the notes on the lyre, then they sang the words together, matching the notes.

"It is well…"

"Good." Charlie sang the next phrase. "With my soul …"

Iona echoed it, this time on her own. "With my soul."

"Perfect." Charlie played the next few notes. "Now together again."

They sang as one. "It is well, it is well with my soul."

Charlie set the lyre in her lap and clapped. "Wonderful! You matched the lyre perfectly. Have you heard the song before?"

"I don't know." Iona shrugged. "Maybe I heard it before and didn't remember it until now."

"Then the words might come back to you when we sing the second verse. Its message is important. It relates to how we'll eventually get you out of hell." Charlie played the opening notes and began singing while Iona concentrated on Charlie's lips and repeated the words the moment they came through.

"Though Satan should buffet, though trials should come, let this blest assurance control."

The words began flowing into Iona's mind before Charlie sang them as they continued singing together. "That Christ hath regarded my helpless estate, and hath shed his own blood for my soul."

Charlie began the refrain. "It is well ..."

Iona echoed, "It is well."

"With my soul ..."

"With my soul."

Then they sang together, their voices in perfect unison. "It is well, it is well with my soul."

Charlie clapped once more. Iona smiled, her heart overflowing. She hadn't felt this good in so long.

Charlie slid her hand into Iona's. "It seems that it is well with your soul, even here in hell."

Iona gazed at their clasped hands. The touch felt as good as the song's uplifting message. "I ... I guess it is. I mean, I'm okay with being here, at least for now. I don't feel like God abandoned me or anything like that."

"A courageous statement." Charlie looked at Leo. He sat with his mouth partly open, as if stunned. "And you? Is it well with your soul?"

Leo shifted uneasily. "I ... uh ... well ..."

"No need to answer. My question caught you unprepared." Charlie let out a wide yawn, put the lyre back in the alcove, and withdrew a set of headphones that matched her camo gear. "It's been a long day. Since you two aren't alive, you don't need any sleep, but I do. We have a long journey ahead."

Iona gazed again at this remarkable woman—so mysterious, so talented, so attractive. No wonder she was having a powerful effect on Leo. "Where are we going?"

"To a potential exit portal, but that is all I will say for now." Charlie set the glowing ball in Leo's lap and put the headphones on. "These cancel the noise. I wear them when the hellcats are prowling outside." She leaned her head against his shoulder. "Wake me at dawn. You will know it is time when you hear the ravens cawing." She closed her eyes. "I hope you don't mind, but I always pray out loud before I go to sleep. It's a child's prayer, but it always helps me, even as an adult, especially when hellcats are prowling close by."

"No problem," Iona said. "Please do."

Her eyes still closed, Charlie spoke in a sing-song cadence. "Now I lay me down to sleep. I pray the Lord my soul to keep. If I should die before I wake, I pray the Lord my soul to take." She inhaled deeply, then whispered, "Amen."

Iona echoed her whisper. "Amen."

Leo did the same. "Amen."

Within seconds, Charlie's breaths grew slow and even.

Iona stayed quiet, waiting for Charlie's sleep to deepen. The ball dimmed slowly, as if signaling the night's advance. After a few minutes, Iona whispered, "Leo, what's your take?"

"On what exactly?" he whispered in return. "The singing, the praying, the potential exit portal?"

"Anything you want to comment on."

"The singing was extraordinary. You have a beautiful voice. I think it would be called pitch perfect."

"Um ... thanks. I guess I inherited it from my mother. She was really good, and she sang a lot."

"Yes, a genetic link is likely. In any case, regarding a potential exit portal, the prospect sounds good, and the news that blood counters the warding seemed to spark an idea in her mind. That's a positive sign."

"Right. I say we stick with her. She might be our only chance to get out of hell."

"Agreed, though we don't have any other obvious options." Leo craned his neck to glance at Charlie, shifting his body while trying not to disturb her. "I think we can trust her."

"Yeah, but you're not sure, are you? You've been acting strange. One minute you look at her like she's a goddess, and the next minute like she's going to turn into a werewolf. What gives with that?"

Leo waved a hand. "It's nothing. Being in hell has me spooked."

"Leo …" She stretched out his name in singsong. "It's me. Remember?"

"How can I forget? You're the scarlet seer." He heaved a deep sigh. "Okay. Confession time."

Iona pressed her lips together and remained silent. Apparently Leo had something to say that weighed heavy on his mind. He needed a few quiet moments.

"It's like this …" Leo's whisper became almost inaudible. "Charlie said that Reapers get their names from cities that were purged by fire."

Iona gave him an affirming nod. "Right. I remember."

"Okay. Now, do you remember a city in the east that the angels burned soon after they arrived?"

"Sure. Charlotte. The home of the first big rebel base. They burned it to smoke the rebels out."

"And Charlie is short for …" Leo gave Iona a prodding nod.

"Charlotte, I suppose."

"Do you remember where you heard that name recently?"

Iona's cheeks warmed. "The woman who jilted you when you were young? Charlie is that Charlotte?"

"The very same."

Iona gritted her teeth. "So she's the conniving—"

"Shhh." Leo glanced at Charlie again. She slept on, undisturbed. "I recognized her immediately, but I didn't want to say anything to you until we had a chance to talk privately."

"Okay. I get that. But now you're ready to trust her to lead us through hell? After what she did to you?"

"People can change. You know that. Both of us have changed. Even quite recently."

"Yeah. They *can* change. But how do you know she *has*?"

He shrugged his unladen shoulder. "I don't. I'm just hoping."

"Hoping? We need certainty. We're talking about eternal damnation. We can't hope Charlie's changed. We have to be sure."

"We can't be sure unless we give her a chance. She can't change unless we let her change."

Iona narrowed her eyes. "Are you sure you're not blinded? You know, still in love with her?"

Leo huffed in a lighthearted way. "I'm not a starry-eyed schoolboy anymore, if that's what you mean" He let out a wistful sigh. "I did love her deeply, and I still do in a way. I mean, I always hoped the best for her regardless of what she did to me. But does it matter? Blinded or not, we have to give her a chance to redeem herself. Besides, what else are we going to do? She's the only guide we've got."

Iona sighed as well. "True. And she's not Alex's ally. That's another plus on her side."

"Exactly."

Iona poked Leo with a finger. "But I'm keeping my eye on both of you. She charmed you once before, and I'm not going to let it happen again. Changed or not, she's still in hell. Someone sent her here for a reason. Reaper or no Reaper, this has to be a punishment job."

"As you wish, my steadfast skeptic, but remember that we're in hell, too. We should be the last ones to rush to judgment about being here. And you heard her singing. How could anyone sing with such conviction unless it came from her heart? We were both enraptured. Our spirits soared. But then when you heard about her past, you turned an about-face against her, almost giving me mental whiplash.

Her sins are in the past. Or do you insist on being a judgmental jurist, willing to condemn her for something she did more than a decade ago?"

Leo's words hit hard. He was right. She had done a crazy-fast about-face—one moment in blissful worship with Charlie, then ready to skewer her the next moment. It wasn't fair at all. "You're right. I was being judgmental. I'm sorry. I think this place is really messing with my mind."

"Understandable. This is a land of condemnation. A wilderness of shadows. It's bound to cast darkness into our minds."

"Like I said, you're right. She's changed, and I promise to look at her that way." Iona gazed at Charlie. In the dimming light, her face and red hair took on a fuzzier aspect, similar to the view in the mirror when Alex played the violin and conjured the image. No wonder Charlie's face seemed familiar. In Iona's recollections of her own life, Charlie looked like the woman who gave baby Iona to a nun. Later, that baby grew up to witness the deaths of her adoptive parents. What could it all mean?

The ball of light in Leo's lap dimmed further, allowing darkness to veil his face. Since he seemed open to revealing secrets, maybe now was a good time to probe further. "Leo, while I was in the abyss with the mirror, I learned something about us. You and me."

"Oh? What might that be?"

She curled her arm around his and paused for a few seconds before answering. "We're related."

"Ah. We have speculated about that possibility. The resemblance between you and my sister is uncanny. Are we cousins somehow?"

"That's just it. I don't know. I didn't have time to find out from the mirror. But I did learn that I'm adopted, and my adoptive parents never told me. Not only that, they were killed by a fake angel, and I blocked the memory."

"I see. Both revelations must've been quite a shock."

"They were a shock, but for some reason I got over it quick. I'm not sure why. Maybe being in hell is such a big shock, any other shock feels kind of secondary."

"So we're likely related through your birth parents. Even if we leave this place, it might be impossible to find any records that reveal the relationship. Adoption agencies are often secretive about such things."

"True. I was hoping you might know something you haven't told me yet."

"Only guesses," Leo said. "My mother had eight siblings. My father, five, and I didn't care to keep track of how our family tree sprouted branches. And I have four siblings myself that, much to my sorrow, I left behind when I started huntsman training. I hope when this is all over to return to my hometown and make amends for my wandering ways. Maybe then I can track down how you and I are related."

"Yeah. I guess we're both on a path of ... um ..."

"Atonement?"

Iona nodded. "That's a good word. We're on a path of atonement."

"Then maybe we're exactly where we're supposed to be."

"What? Do you think we're supposed to be in hell?"

Leo tapped a finger on Iona's knee. "Hear me out. Maybe we're seeing the end result of the previous road we were on, at least the one I was on. Destruction. Ruin. Sorrow. As the old saying goes, you reap what you sow."

"But you chased criminals," Iona said. "That's not a bad thing. You said yourself that you turned down jobs you thought were unjust. That's honorable."

"I told myself that. But it wasn't honorable. I was trying to polish my reputation, pin a badge of honor on my chest. My real goal was money. Well, money and adventure. I was a phony." Leo inhaled deeply, then let the breath out slowly. "I see that now."

"Yeah. Same here. My big mouth was a scam. A way to prop up a scared pipsqueak. I was a little girl trying to act big."

Leo chuckled softly. "Well, Mournful Munchkin, whether or not our dark self-evaluations are accurate, we should be thankful that we might have a second chance. Or a third or fourth chance in my case. My sins have been many."

Iona quieted herself. Leo's mention of sins hit the mark once again. Mother and Father talked about God once in a while, enough to keep her in line as a child—commandments from the Bible along with their punishments and rewards. She believed some of it and longed to know more. But getting betrayed by the fake angels injected bitterness that shattered all trust. Maybe this path of atonement would provide the answers she needed.

She leaned her head against Leo's shoulder and listened to the silence, broken only by Charlie's deep respiration and the cats' growls outside. Soon, the strange murmurs returned—Kat's voice, Leo's, and her own—too warped and blended to understand. Whatever Alex was up to, Kat could figure it out. She was smart enough. Yet, Ben's disappearance might distract her, keep her from seeing through the scheme.

The orb blinked out. Blackness veiled everything. The cats quieted. Even Charlie's breathing settled to a nearly imperceptible hum. Iona, her arm still around Leo's, slid as close to him as possible. His presence felt good, though his body emanated no warmth. A sense of coldness permeated everything—lonely, bitter coldness.

Here she sat in a fragile fortress, suspended by a rickety tree rooted in the soils of hell, while Alex walked freely on Earth, wearing an Iona mask, hatching an evil scheme that no one would be able to stop. Only the real Iona could pull the witch's mask off and expose her.

And speaking of masks, what kind of mask was this mysterious Reaper wearing? Although she seemed familiar, that could be a mirage, borne of a hope to latch on to anything familiar in this eerie place. Could she be a wraith that had taken on a human form, a phantom who would lure them toward greater misery? It made sense that a sentinel in hell would be here to punish souls, not to help them.

Iona clenched her eyes shut. Her mind was wandering too deeply into darkness. Maybe this place had warped everything. She had to push the troubles out of her mind and listen for the call of the ravens. Maybe morning would bring a ray of hope, something more than meager food fragments for a mysterious Reaper—a woman with a treacherous past whom they now had to trust to lead them on the next leg of their dangerous journey.

# Chapter Five

"Benjamin."

Ben winced. Everything hurt, from the top of his head to the soles of his feet. And someone was calling his name—a woman with a familiar voice.

"Benjamin."

Something cool and damp covered his forehead. It felt good, refreshing.

"You need to wake up."

Wake up? He blinked his eyes open. He lay on bare, rocky ground, pain at every point of contact. Dressed in her usual pioneer-style leather, Winella knelt at his side, an archery bow over her shoulder, a quiver of arrows attached to her back, and her long sepia braid dangling near his face. Barely able to move his mouth, he whispered, "Where am I?"

"If you wish to know which planet you are on, it is Viridi." She removed a rough, gray cloth from his forehead and set it on the ground next to her knee. "To be more precise, you are near the precipice above our observatory. I found you in the forest close by and carried you here to see if sunlight would awaken you. Water from the forest stream was not enough of a ... stimulus?"

"Yeah. Stimulus is a good word." He looked into the giantess's huge eyes. "How did I get to Viridi?"

"I was going to ask you that. Caligar told me he sent you home to Earth."

"He did." Ben closed his eyes again. Images flashed—the Alaska tower, the snowstorm, preparing to jump before the tower fell, then the blazing light stream stabbing his body. "I got transported back. The Alaska tower was still operational."

"How odd. Dr. Harrid told me he would destroy it."

Ben reopened his eyes and focused again on Winella. "He sabotaged the metal connectors with some kind of acid. The tower gave way while I was on the platform. I was transported the moment it toppled."

"If the tower fell when you transported, how did you land safely without a reverse pulling mechanism? You had no parachute."

"I didn't?" Ben pushed himself to a sitting position in spite of the pain. He felt his shoulder for the pack's strap. It was gone, along with the parka, leaving only the dirty camo clothes he had been wearing for far too long. His earbud was also gone. "I had a chute when I transported."

"Let me help you up." She set her bow on the ground and grasped Ben's wrist. "Are you ready?"

He nodded. "Slowly, please."

After she pulled him gently to his feet, he shook each limb, trying to cast off the tightness and aches. Within seconds, he felt more limber, and his head began to clear. The new clarity brought the reality of where he stood roaring to mind. The only way to get home was to use Caligar's mirror, but he said he was going to destroy it. Had he already done so?

Ben gave Winella a nod. "Thank you. Now, can you tell me where Cal—"

"You are welcome." Her skin darkened, as if heated by a blush, a deeper shade of brown instead of red. "I am pleased that you are not angry with me for my part in the … plan … scheme … against you and your friends."

He waved a hand. "All is forgiven. Really. Now, I need to find—"

"I am truly sorry for what you suffered, and I am thankful for your mercy." She grasped his wrist again and set her braid in his hand. "Here on Viridi, we have a tradition. We consider our braids to be sacred, yet they are also a … a weakness, I suppose. A vulnerability. An enemy can snatch it and pull its wearer into submission, which is why we tuck them away in battle. Placing it in your hand means that we are ... allies?"

Ben nodded. "Yes. Perfect word."

Winella smiled. "Since you are my ally, I trust that you will not use my braid to harm me, that you will not betray me as Caligar and I betrayed you. Your forgiveness is a gift that I can never repay. This token of my alliance is all I have to offer."

Ben closed his hand around the braid. Going through this ceremony with Winella was proving to be quite a delay, but it was necessary to heal her guilty conscience. He gazed into her eyes and spoke in a solemn tone. "I accept your gift with gratitude for your trust in me."

As she withdrew the braid from his hand, her beaming face turned serious. "I assume you wish to know where Caligar is."

"I do. Has he destroyed the mirror yet?"

"He has begun the process of dismantling it, but he has been occupied by other priorities, and he is not there at this time. We were hunting for food with Bazrah when we heard a strange noise. I left them to investigate, and that is when I found you."

"A strange noise?"

She nodded. "Similar to a motorized vehicle, such as the buses we saw on Earth, though we have nothing like that on Viridi."

"Interesting." Ben looked into the nearby forest. "Can you show me where you found me?"

"Of course." As they walked away from the precipice and into the woods, Winella gestured toward Ben's back. "The parachute must have given you a safe landing, or, at least, a ... a safer-than-death landing, though you likely struck hard enough to render you unconscious, then someone stole the parachute."

Still somewhat dizzy, Ben looked at the ground as they walked next to the creek that spilled over the precipice, careful to keep from stumbling. "I'm guessing maybe Harrid came here. Not sure why yet, but he could've stolen the parachute."

"That is a good guess. If anyone else had found you, besides myself, Caligar, or Bazrah, you would have been killed and eaten."

"Right. The savage giants consider humans a delicacy."

Winella muttered in a derisive tone, words too quiet to hear. After nearly a minute, she stopped and pointed at the ground. "There. Where the ferns have been flattened." She looked upward. "The forest ceiling is too dense for a parachute. Maybe a branch caught it and stripped the pack from your back. Then you hit the ground with enough force to knock you unconscious."

Ben scanned the tree canopy, void of anything but lush foliage. "I don't see any remnants of a chute."

"Nor do I. My speculations are likely unwarranted."

Ben studied the forest floor. A path of flattened ferns led well into the distance. "Maybe I landed somewhere else and Harrid dragged me here."

"Why would he do that? My impression is that he is no friend of yours."

"Good question. Another is, why would he come back to Viridi? From what I heard, he desperately wanted to return to Earth." Ben crouched and lifted one of the crushed ferns. A tread pattern covered the leaflet. "Tire marks."

Winella crouched with him. "Perhaps it was made by the motorized vehicle I heard."

"Maybe Harrid brought my SUV here." When Ben rose, his head pounded, a remnant of his violent passage through the Oculus Gate, yet, not as bad as earlier.

Winella joined him and looked him over. "You are not completely well."

"Getting better. It'll take a while." He concealed a wince and looked at her. "Is the conduit's pull strong enough to lift a vehicle through the Oculus Gate? Something the size of a small truck?"

She gazed at the sky as if imagining the process. "At full power, I think so. Once an object leaves the ground, its size and weight are not critical. Before departure, its attachment to the ground is the most important factor."

"I think Harrid and the SUV went through the portal, and he left the tower network running so it would slow the plunge, but his timing was interesting. He left at almost exactly the time I returned to Earth, like he was waiting for me to arrive."

"Why would he do that? To make sure you were safe?"

"I doubt it." Ben scanned the forest for more clues. The flattened path continued toward the giants' soup cauldron. Exploring in that direction might bear fruit, but that could wait. The transport mirror was far more important. "How do we find Caligar?"

"I will signal him." Winella lifted her head and released a warbling whistle that lasted four or five seconds. A moment later, a similar whistle called from deep in the forest. She strode toward the sound. "Come. He is this way."

Kat eased off on the lower thrusters and let the cruiser's dual landing runners settle onto the temple's vacant parking lot. The moment she killed the engine, Iona unbuckled at the co-pilot's chair. "Whew! That was a super-fast thrill ride."

Kat unbuckled from her seat, rose, and attached her computer pad to her belt. "Most drones don't have jet engines like this one. They would've taken a couple of days to get here instead of a few hours."

"Yeah. Well, thanks for the flying lesson. I'm sure I can handle picking up the supplies while you set up the command center."

"Oh. Right. Since you're flying, I need to start it up again." Kat set her thumb on the control screen's scanner. When it beeped, the engines roared back to life. "Now put your thumb in the same place, and it'll allow you to start it. I found that setting on our way here."

Iona did so. The control screen beeped again, and a robotic voice responded. "Secondary pilot registered."

Leo called from his passenger seat, a step or two behind the cockpit. "Shall I assume that I should stay put? The onboard restroom and snack-filled refrigerator have fully prepared me to travel with Iona right away."

Kat gazed at him. Like Jack had said, his manner of speaking wasn't quite right—more polished and without a hint of his occasional joking manner, especially since he never once used a clever nickname. Yet, Iona was definitely her old self, not a hint of change in speech. Maybe being in hell had affected Leo and not her. "Sure. You can stay put."

Iona gestured toward the rear of the cruiser. "And the onboard weapons cache should give you all the firepower you need to handle the temple control center by yourself. Damien might've looted the weapons in the vault."

"I don't think I'll need a huge arsenal. According to the computer pad, Damien tried to access the main computer but couldn't get past the new passwords, and it looks like he and his minions left the temple."

Iona bent her brow. "I wouldn't trust that intel. Snakes hide in the grass, not out in the open. I'd go in locked and loaded. Can't hurt."

Kat scanned Iona's stance, a fist on her hip—cocky and self-assured, as usual. Yet, for the first time, something was off. Had she forgotten about Ben's disappearance? She normally wouldn't take on this tough-girl persona without prefacing it with some kind of condolence. Her fondness for Ben had become more and more obvious. "You're probably right."

Kat strode to the rear wall, opened the door to the cache, and withdrew an automatic rifle and several ammo magazines. She attached the mags to her belt along with a few grenades, several smoke bombs, and a handgun.

When she grasped the door to shut it, a label on a shoebox-sized container caught her attention—*Communications*. The wooden box sat on a head-high shelf between a spool of black cable and an array of wiring tools hanging from hooks. She opened the box's hinged lid. Inside lay several earbuds and a switch that looked like a control on the console. She lifted the switch and looked it over. Its peel-off, adhesive back meant it could attach to the cruiser's control panel—a dummy toggle switch, a surveillance device. Printed specs on the back of the peel-off label provided contact instructions.

Kat palmed the switch, grabbed three earbuds, and closed the cache's door. "That should be enough."

Iona scanned her and smiled. "Yep. Warrior mode looks good on you."

"We need a secondary way to stay in touch." Kat set an earbud in Iona's palm. "Just in case."

Iona inserted the bud. "In case of what?"

"Someone might be listening in on our shortwave frequencies. The earbud channel is encrypted." Kat walked to the control panel and looked at the radio's tuner as she stealthily peeled the dummy switch's label from the adhesive. "Keep the cruiser's comm tuned to the ham frequency we've been using. Let me know if you hear from Jack and Trudy. And especially Ben. But if we have to talk about something we need to keep secret ..." Blocking Iona's view, Kat turned the control panel's communications channel dial, at the same time attaching the dummy switch to the panel. "Change the radio to this setting." She shifted to the side and pointed. "The earbuds will transmit to the cruiser from up to a mile away, and the cruiser will relay it through a channel I can pick up at the temple's bunker."

"Got it." Iona sat in the pilot's seat and pushed a button. The cruiser's side door slid horizontally into a panel. "Our first stop is the hardware store. Jack's list is pretty long, but most of the stuff will probably be there."

"Good. Once I'm holed up in the bunker, I'll let you know if I find anything unexpected." Kat exited and stepped down to the pavement. When the door closed, she turned toward the cruiser and backed away. The engine noise strengthened, and blasts of air swirled, batting her clothes and hair. Seconds later, the ship lifted off and flew away.

When the breeze diminished, Kat looked at the slip of paper she had peeled from the spy bug's adhesive. Tuning in to the bug would have to be a high priority. She spun toward the temple and broke into a quick jog, clutching the rifle at her side. Lacking trust in Iona and Leo felt like treachery, but she couldn't take any chances. Their roles, like everyone else's, were vital. The tower could never rise unless they could get the needed materials. And without the tower, Ben might stay marooned forever—if he even made it to Viridi, or survived at all.

Alexandria flew the cruiser to a point a thousand feet or so above the temple, set it in hover mode, and looked at Bartholomew. He sat in the co-pilot's chair and shifted nervously in Leo's body while drinking from a flask of angel tea that Leo had left in his cloak pocket.

"Now, Bartholomew." She resisted the urge to wince at the sound of Iona's voice. Even after all these hours, it seemed impossible to adjust to the childlike tones. "It's time for us to—"

"Iona or Leo," Jack called through the cruiser's radio. "I need to add a few more items."

Alexandria sighed and pressed a button to activate the transmitter's microphone. "This is Iona. What do you need?"

"Another cordless drill like the one on the list, and two battery packs that'll charge from a standard outlet. And we redid the math. Better add another two hundred screws. Same length and diameter. And fifty more flanges."

"Consider it done. Anything else?"

"Yeah. Remember that handgun you took to hell? You said you shot some of Alex's goons with it. What was the brand name? I'd like you to get one for me if you can. Easier to carry than a rifle. I talked to Kat. She said there aren't any handguns left in the cruiser's cache."

"The brand name. Let me think." Alexandria gave Bartholomew a prompting glare. He shrugged, obviously clueless. "I'm drawing a blank. Sorry."

"No problem. Trauma does that to you. But it was a nine-millimeter, right?"

Alexandria rolled her eyes. "Does it matter? I'll get you a handgun that'll put down a grizzly."

"Great. Thanks. I'll call back if I think of anything else we need."

"No hurry. We have to stop and refuel the cruiser. That might take a few hours. And I have to recruit some laborers."

"Copy that. We need all the help we can get."

"Talk to you later." She deactivated the microphone and stared at the console. "That should give us enough time."

Bartholomew set the flask on the dashboard. "If Jack is familiar with this cruiser's fuel capacity, and if he checked the level before we left Alaska, he'll know that it doesn't need refueling yet."

"That is highly unlikely, but even if so, it's too late for him to do anything about it."

"You're concerned about something else."

Alexandria nodded. "Jack was fishing. He knew the gun's brand name. He wanted to see if I knew it. It was in Iona's brain, but I didn't have time to search for it." She closed her eyes and scanned her memories until she located an image of the gun's label. "Toger. The gun was a Toger forty-five." She reopened her eyes and looked at Bartholomew. "Not a nine-millimeter."

"Then you're safe. You never took the bait."

"I didn't, but my plea of ignorance was insufficient. Iona would have known the gun's brand right away. Otherwise, Jack wouldn't have brought it up. His team is smart enough to figure out who we really are."

Bartholomew pointed at her. "But, as you said, it's too late for him to do anything about it. We're in the clear."

"Perhaps. Even if they deduce our identities, they can't possibly know what my plans are. And stopping us will be impossible."

"Yes." Bartholomew shifted nervously in his seat, fiddling with a clasp near the neck of Leo's cloak. "Well, speaking of those plans, perhaps it's time to tell me what you have in store."

"No, it's not time. I can't trust you to keep my secrets."

Bartholomew scowled, the angry lines on his Leo face looking more menacing than he could ever be with his own face. "Trust? Who are you to talk about trust? You shot me, you conniving witch."

Although he deserved to have his tongue pulled out by the roots, she kept her voice calm. "I had to dissolve your soul into the healing bath. It was the only way you could enter Leo's body. Would you prefer to be in hell?"

The anger lines in his brow eased. "You could've told me. Given me some warning."

"And risk having you accidentally leak the secret to Ben or one of his allies? Nonsense. It was my plan and mine alone. Your part was to believe and obey. And that must continue. I will tell you only what you need to know at the proper time."

Bartholomew sighed. "All right. You win. Let's hear what I need to know."

"Very well." She concealed a smile. As usual, she had conquered this fool. Now it was time to feed him a seed of truth, enough to be believable. "Damien has contacted our influencers, and they were able to find the tower schematics where Dr. Harrid said they would be. They are at this moment sending laborers to take over the reconstruction of the Alaska tower and begin the enhancements at the other three towers."

"Influencers. You mean the one hundred who got the obedience payload in the vaccine."

"Correct." She allowed the smile to break through, one he would recognize as the coverup for a lie. Believing in his own skill to detect falsehood would give him unwarranted confidence, a potentially fatal mistake. "My influencers are the best and the brightest in every needed discipline, from tech workers, to healthcare professionals, to heads of state. Since the angels pummeled the populace into willing submission, and since their departure left the world in a chaotic state, my team is well positioned to exert control over the world. Being immune to the contagion, they can use the threat of a new plague to instill fear, and fearful people are easy to dominate."

"If you're so intent on controlling Earth, why do you want to rebuild the tower?"

She pursed her lips, another sign he would recognize, this one communicating her surprise that he detected the lie, again giving him false confidence. And a defensive answer would boost his bravado, especially since he would see himself as bigger and stronger than the diminutive girl before him, an estimate that would soon lead to his downfall. "You don't need to know. My team will see to rebuilding the tower while we attend to more urgent business."

Bartholomew retrieved the flask and took a long drink, obviously feigning casual comfort. "Resurrecting your body, I assume."

"Correct again. I didn't rescue your soul from hell so you could fill Leo's belly with angel tea."

Bartholomew rolled his eyes. "You keep switching between sweet, naïve Iona and your devilish self as easily as a foul wind turns a weathervane."

"An interesting analogy, but I don't need to hear your commentary." Alexandria toggled the control screen to the flight-control map and used a finger to change the map's magnification level. While he watched, she feigned scratching her lower back to detach a hidden tube of paralysis ointment from her belt. Now to force his hand. "No more chatter. Put the location in the guidance system immediately, or I will jerk your soul out of your body and cast it to the wind."

Bartholomew sneered. "That's big talk from such a small girl. You have the knowledge of a Reaper but not the genetics. You're not Alexandria, the great Owl, Reaper extraordinaire. You're just little Iona. Therefore, your threat is an empty one."

"Is it now?" She whipped a knife from a belt sheath and set the blade against his throat, pricking him just enough to draw a trickle of blood. At the same time, she squeezed a dollop of ointment onto the nape of his neck and rubbed it in with his collar. "Don't move a muscle, or I'll slice your jugular. Obey me, and you will live. Disobey me, and you will die. If you understand, blink twice."

He blinked once, clenching his eyelids tightly, then again. When his eyes reopened, they focused on the control map.

"Oh, I see," Alexandria crooned. "Now you're willing to enter the location, exactly as I requested."

He again blinked twice, sweat beading on his forehead.

"It's so gratifying to have your enthusiastic cooperation." She slid the blade a bit deeper. Blood oozed down into his shirt. "Now reach over and enter the coordinates."

Bartholomew extended an arm and tapped on the map's screen.

"Good." She drew the knife back and cleaned the flat of the blade on his pant leg, then retook her seat in the pilot's chair. "I'm sure you can find the first-aid kit. It will be enough to patch that tiny scratch."

Bartholomew lunged and backhanded her across the face. She toppled off the chair to the floor and dropped the knife at her side. Lying on her back, she glared at him as she held a palm over her stinging cheek while using her other hand to stealthily hide the tube behind her belt. "So you're resorting to mutiny? How low of you." She glanced at the console. Now to set the final hook to make him think she was clueless. "Let me guess. You entered fake coordinates."

"No, witch." He stood over her, one foot next to each hip. He reached down, snatched the knife, and straightened, pointing the blade at her. "I entered your body's location, but I'm in charge now. I watched you and Kat enough to fly this vessel myself. And when I get there, I'm going to slice your body into pieces. You have no power to stop me. Alexandria the Reaper must not rise from the dead."

She huffed. "Oh, how dramatic."

"Perhaps so, but I had to do something." He backed away a few steps. "If God really exists, maybe he'll change his mind about sending me to hell. It takes a hero to save the world from the vilest devil the world has ever known. Am I right?"

Alexandria pushed up to a sitting position and applauded slowly. "Bravo. Well done, hero. You have conquered a child, a mere wisp of a woman. If I were back in my body, you would be cowering in fear."

He sighed. "I admit, probably so."

She spread her arms. "So what are you going to do? Kill poor little Iona?"

"I was thinking I would tie you up until I can figure out how to expel you and give her back to her people."

"Ah. Good plan." She looked past him at the digital clock on the control panel. Close to a minute had passed since she applied the ointment. "Now, to proceed with my own plan. It's time for a countdown."

Bartholomew squinted. "A countdown? What do you mean?"

"You will soon see. Ten ... nine ... eight ..."

He shook a finger. "Oh, no, you conniving witch. You can't fool me. You're trying to goad me into a mistake."

"Seven ... six ... five ..."

He swiveled his head, glancing around as his hands trembled. "What did you do to me?"

"Four ... three ... two ..."

He lunged to the dashboard, grabbed his flask of tea, and sniffed the contents. His eyes widened. His face now bright red, he glared at her. "Did you drug me?"

"One ... zero."

They locked stares. Alexandria kept her expression perfectly blank, making him squirm. After several seconds of silence, he snorted. "Ha! Maybe your potion isn't as potent as you think. Spiking my drink failed."

She smirked. "Do you think I would be fool enough to risk detection by your talented nose? I didn't spike your drink."

Bartholomew's mouth dropped open. His eyes rolled upward, and he collapsed next to her.

She shifted to a sitting position on his stomach and patted his cheek. "My timing was a bit off. It seems that Leo's body is more resilient than I expected." She rose, strode to the pilot's seat, and shifted the propellers to send them forward. "I know you can still hear me. The paralysis affects only your gross motor skills, not your ability to see or hear. Also, you should be able to speak, though with difficulty."

After setting the cruiser to follow the course on the map, she swiveled in her seat and looked at him. As sweat trickled into his eyes, he blinked at her, muscles in his face twitching. "Now we can discuss the next step, Bartholomew. The point on the map is a general area, not the precise location of my body. If you cooperate, I will give you an antidote to the paralysis. If not, I will kill you. The choice is yours."

Kat typed on the temple computer's keyboard and reopened the communication channel to the Alaska station. "Jack, can you hear me?"

"Yeah. Our plan worked. Something's definitely wrong with Iona. I gave her a test. Remember the gun she had in the holster of that tactical vest she was wearing?"

"I remember. Attached at the front."

"Right. I found it in Alex's castle. A Toger forty-five. I asked if it was a nine-millimeter, and Iona couldn't remember. She prides herself on being an expert sharpshooter. No way she wouldn't know."

"You're right. She would know. And it all adds up. The angel spawn said Alex needed a vessel to get out of hell. I think Plan A was to possess Ben, but when Iona showed up, she was a better option."

"So Iona is really Alex, and Leo is probably really Bart."

"Yep. I was suspicious before. Now I'm certain." Kat tapped her chin, imagining the conversation between Jack and Alex. "Did Alex cover up her ignorance about the gun?"

"Not very well. I think I caught her off guard."

"Then she probably guessed why you asked. She's no fool."

"So she knows that we know."

"Exactly. And she will adjust. Count on it."

"Any plans to figure out what they're up to?" Jack asked.

"I've been trying to listen in on a spy bug I planted on the cruiser, but there's too much interference." Kat leaned back in the chair. "Do you have any experience with bugs? It's the adhesive kind. Looks like a control switch."

"Yeah, I saw that in the cache. Those bugs are pretty great unless another transmitter is interfering with the signal. Some frequencies will do that."

"The cruiser's radio. I told them to keep it tuned in to the ham frequency."

"There's your problem. The ship's normal communication frequencies probably wouldn't interfere, but the shortwave signal is giving it headaches. Unless you can figure out how to get them to turn that radio off or change the frequency, your spying trick won't work."

"Okay," Kat said. "But we made progress. We know Iona's not Iona. We won't trust either her or Leo."

"Got it," Jack said. "Iona is now enemy number one."

# Chapter Six

A hint of light seeped into the cocoon. Leo's outline clarified, along with Charlie's as she continued leaning against his shoulder. Her hand lay over his, both resting on his stomach.

As more light illuminated their refuge, Iona gazed at the two hands. Charlie might have unintentionally moved hers there during the night, an innocent act, but Leo didn't bother to object. He could have guided hers back or slid his away. Obviously, he was still smitten with her. A certain steadfastly skeptical soul would have to keep an eye on that.

A moment later, a low croaking sound pierced the motionless air. Iona craned her neck and imagined a bird making the noise. Although deeper and coarser than usual, it could be a raven.

"Leo." Iona nudged him with an elbow. "It's time to wake Charlie up."

"Yes, I heard." He grasped Charlie's wrist, pushed her hand to her lap, and lifted one of the headphones away from her ear. "Good morning, if a morning in hell can be good. I think breakfast is served."

"Thank you." Charlie straightened, took the headphones off, and rubbed her eyes with her knuckles as she spoke with a yawn. "We should hurry. It's not far to our destination, but dangers along the way could delay us."

"Like the hellcats?" Iona asked.

Charlie nodded as she blinked, apparently still drowsy. "I'm sure they're gone by now, but once they pick up the scent again, they'll return, even in daylight. We have to stay ahead of them until we get to the lake. They won't follow us there."

"The lake?"

"The Lake of Fire." Charlie clipped the headphones to her belt. "All beasts stay away from it. And for good reason. It's the most dangerous place in hell."

Leo frowned. "From the frying pan into the fire, it seems."

Iona glared at Charlie. Maybe last night's dark thoughts about this strange woman were true after all. She really was leading them into danger. "Why didn't you mention that before?"

"It wasn't an issue then." Charlie shifted over to the exit hole and moved the ladder coil out of the way. "I was going to take the long route, bypassing the lake, but I had a dream that reminded me of a newly forming lava trench that would keep us from going that way. We already have to cross a chasm, and it's dangerous enough."

"Whatever you say. Obviously you know better than we do."

"You might not think so when we go directly across the lake." Charlie crawled through the hole and dropped about ten feet to the ground, bending her knees to absorb the impact. She looked up into the cocoon. "Come. And don't worry about jumping. It won't hurt you."

Leo stepped to the hole, dropped to the ground, and landed softly. When he moved out of the way, Iona looked down at him. "Are you sure about this?"

"When did the ginger giantess start acting so gingerly?"

"Don't try to shame me. I have good reasons to be careful. I mean, it's the Lake of Fire, probably the worst place in the universe." Iona glanced at Charlie as a raven landed on her shoulder, a purple berry in its beak. "And other reasons."

Leo glanced that way as well before stepping closer to Iona and whispering, "I understand, but hiding in a cocoon like a cautious caterpillar isn't going to get us out of hell. So spread your wings and—"

"No butterfly references. I'm coming." Iona jumped and landed softly on the ground, as if butterfly wings softened the impact, but there was no way she would mention that to Leo, not with the way he was grinning.

Charlie took the berry from the raven and popped it into her mouth. After chewing and swallowing, she looked at the raven. "Thank you, Horace. That will be enough for today. I have to go on a journey, and I'm in a hurry."

The raven cawed, leaped from her shoulder, and flew to a high tree branch. From there, it cawed several more times.

"Horace is giving my message to the other ravens." Charlie pulled a patrol cap from her back pocket, put it on, and lifted her hood, partially hiding her eyes. "You have a choice. You can either run with me or ride in my cloak."

Iona blinked. "Ride in your cloak?"

"Yes." Charlie grasped the cloak's clasp. A brilliant shimmer ran along the sleeves and down to the hem before dimming to normal. "I have the power to absorb you into the fibers. It's a bit uncomfortable for you, but you would be safe, and I could run faster if I didn't have to worry about you keeping up with me."

Leo leaned close to Iona and whispered, "More doubts?"

Iona cupped a hand over her mouth and pressed close to his ear. "Lots of doubts. I'm not getting absorbed by a Reaper from hell who can't decide on a route unless she dreams about it."

"Agreed. It's too soon to trust her. She needs to prove herself."

"Glad your head's on straight."

When they looked again at Charlie, she released the clasp. "Your answer and lack of trust are obvious. Come. We have already lost precious time." She took off at a jog, her cloak flapping at her feet.

Iona and Leo ran side by side several paces behind her. The trees grew denser. Protruding roots multiplied, some with ends that looked like snake heads, ready to strike at anyone foolish enough to venture into the forest.

Vulture-like creatures perched on leafless branches, leering at the newcomers with shining black eyes. One opened its mouth and spewed greenish liquid that splatted inches behind Charlie and burned an exposed root. The sizzle emitted orange fumes that curled upward toward the darkening canopy. Yet, she ran on, either oblivious to the dangers or counting on their speed to keep them safe.

Iona and Leo jumped over the root and continued giving chase. Leo grimaced. "That bird's spittle smells worse than vulture vomit. I'd wager it could burn through metal."

Iona held her breath until they ran out of range. "Vile stuff."

"I also smell the hellcats. Apparently they caught our scent, and they're gaining on us."

"Let's catch up with Charlie." Iona accelerated, eyeing one of the huge birds and its iridescent eyes as it kept its stare on the passersby.

When Leo matched her pace and ran at her side, she focused straight ahead. In the distance, a gap in the ground appeared, maybe the chasm Charlie mentioned earlier, too deep to see the bottom from their angle, but she neither slowed nor shouted a warning. She leaped, extending a foot as if making ready to land on the other side. Then she vanished.

Leo and Iona skidded to a halt and stood at the edge of the chasm. Far below, a river of orange flowed, probably lava. Above, leafless tree branches arched over the chasm, intertwining with branches of trees from the other side, growing near the rocky ledge that lay at least thirty feet in the distance—much too far to reach with a jump. Charlie apparently thought she could make it, but she stood nowhere in sight.

"Did she ditch us?" Iona asked.

Leo peered into the chasm's depths. "If she's the woman I knew years ago, it's possible, but I'm not ready to believe it." He inhaled though his nose. "I smell her. She's close by."

Iona shouted, "Charlie, can you hear me?"

A warped voice returned, more like an echo than a reply.

"Leo, could you make that out? Was that Charlie?"

"I think so. She said something about a rope.'"

61

"Rope? I don't see a—" Something brushed against Iona's nose. She swatted it away. "Are there bugs here?"

Leo snatched at the air. "I caught it." He pushed a transparent, fibrous line into her hand. "Feel it?"

"Yep." Iona tugged on the line. It felt secure enough. "But I don't see Charlie over there. What's up with that?"

"No time to guess. The cats are coming." A nearby growl punctuated his warning. "Go!"

"But it's your turn to go first."

"Hush and hang on!" He gave her a shove. "Send it back when you get there."

Clutching the rope with both hands, she sailed across the chasm. The moment she set her feet on solid ground, she turned toward Leo. Three huge hellcats stalked toward him from less than twenty feet away, their dark hackles raised as he watched them, his back to the chasm.

"Leo! Here it comes!" She swung the rope toward him.

When it reached the opposite side, it smacked him in the back of the head. He spun and grabbed it. Just as he leaped toward the chasm, one of the cats lunged and lashed at his back with a swiping paw. Its claws snagged Leo's cloak and ripped him away from the line. The cloak, still in the cat's claws, stripped off his arms, and he plunged into the darkness without a sound.

"Leo!" Iona screamed. The rope sailed toward her but not quite within reach. She bent her knees and leaped for it, but something dark wrapped around her body and pulled her back with a strong grip. She thrashed to no avail.

"Be still, Iona."

She rested, panting. "Charlie? Is that your cloak around me?"

"Yes. Don't fight me. I can't let you jump into Lucifer's Gorge."

Iona struggled against her powerful grip. "But I have to save Leo!"

"Stop it! There's only one way to save him, and I'll need your help to do it."

"Okay. Okay." Iona rested again. "I'll do anything to help him."

"Of that, I am certain. First, I need to absorb you into the cloak. We have to run like the wind to save Leo, and you're too slow on your own."

Iona nodded as she tried to settle her breaths. "Go ahead."

"Brace yourself. There will be some pain, but it won't last long."

Iona closed her eyes. A slowly increasing vacuum pressure flattened her against the cloak. Her limbs stretched, and her eyes bulged, like they were about to pop out of her head. Pain rippled along her body, then warmth followed, a soothing sensation that coursed across every inch.

She opened her eyes to darkness, though something glimmered. Her own body? It seemed so, as if her essence had transformed into a spray of radiant particles that glittered as she tried to move.

"Are you all right?" Charlie asked, her voice muffled and far away.

"I think so." Iona tried to inhale, but air entered slowly. "Kind of stuffy though."

"That's normal, and you'll adjust. You're not really breathing now. A different kind of respiration. It's difficult to explain."

"Just go. We have to save Leo."

"Trust me, I understand—I love him, too. But no more about that." The surrounding material shifted. "I'm putting the headphones on and a mask over my face. The noise and stench for a living person are unbearable near the lake. I'll still be able to hear you through the cloak, but save your questions for later. I'm going to run as fast as I can until we arrive."

A sense of wavering movement entered, probably the flapping of the cloak. Iona settled herself and rode with the undulating flow, though shocking pulses spiked in her mind—snapshot images of Leo flailing as he plummeted into Lucifer's Gorge. How could he possibly survive, especially if the river actually was lava?

Yet, Charlie seemed to think rescue was possible. Since dropping from the cocoon proved to end in a soft landing, maybe a bigger drop wouldn't be harmful either, and maybe lava couldn't destroy a soul. Still, Charlie was in a huge hurry. Apparently Leo was in terrible trouble.

Iona closed her eyes. New images entered—the angel cruiser's control panel and, above that, a view through the windshield. The hum of the engines blended in as the craft flew over a forest, apparently a rural area.

The scene shifted. Leo now stood in front of the control panel, smirking. "Ha! Maybe your potion isn't as potent as you think. Spiking my drink failed."

"Do you think I would be fool enough to risk detection by your talented nose?" The new voice was her own, much closer and clearer. "I didn't spike your drink."

Leo's mouth dropped open, and he toppled to the floor next to her. Again the scene shifted, and Leo's face filled the view. A hand patted his cheek. "My timing was a bit off. It seems that Leo's body is more resilient than I expected."

Iona gasped. Was she seeing through the eyes of her body—a body possessed by Alex?

Like walking in a dream, she entered the luxury cruiser's cockpit, sat in the pilot's seat, and manipulated the controls. The engines revved as she spoke again. "I know you can still hear me. The paralysis affects only your gross motor skills, not your ability to see or hear. Also, you should be able to speak, though with difficulty."

Her hands appeared, one pressing a button and the other steering a yoke. As they moved, her own hands felt like they were trying to move. Was her soul connected somehow to her body? Could she try to move one of the hands?

"Now we can discuss the next step, Bartholomew. The point on the map is a general area, not the precise location of my body. If you cooperate, I will give you an antidote to the paralysis. If not, I will kill you. The choice is yours."

Iona concentrated on the yoke hand and shifted it to the right. The yoke turned clockwise, and the cruiser bent that way. The hand quickly corrected, and the fingers flexed, breaking Iona's hold. It seemed that Alex was fighting off the influence, but did she know that the movement came from a soul trapped in hell? Maybe. Maybe not.

Either way, the situation seemed hopeless. Alex, disguised as one of the good guys, was on a mission of evil, and she had already neutralized the only person who knew her real identity.

Iona heaved a sigh and whispered, "It's useless."

"What?" Charlie asked, her voice muffled in the fibers. "What's useless?"

Iona gave her a summary of what she'd experienced. When she finished, she added, "No one can stop Alex. She's in complete control."

Charlie's response came in breathless surges as she ran on. "I see your point … but you're wrong."

"Wrong? How?"

"Her arrogance is blinding. She thinks she's in control, that no one can stop her, but you are able to see what she's doing. Keep watching and listening. Remember every detail. Maybe she'll give away something that will help us defeat her."

"Okay. I can do that."

"And pray. Pray more fervently than you ever have before."

"That won't be hard. I haven't prayed much at all lately. Ever since my parents died, I kind of got out of touch with God. I guess I didn't think he paid much attention to me."

"I can sympathize. When I have more time, I'll tell you my story. But hear this. God has been with me, even in hell. I have witnessed God's hand in my life more times than I can count. So I say, pray all the more. He has not abandoned us. He can crush Alex like a cockroach, but for some reason he has allowed her to succeed to this point, and he has chosen us to orchestrate her downfall. No matter what the reason for all the mysteries, we should ask God for help. Otherwise the credit for the victory will not be his."

"Okay. I'm all for getting help from above, but that 'credit for victory' stuff sounds like a scripted sermon, like a preacher."

Charlie huffed. "Don't criticize my words simply because they sound rehearsed. I have spent most of my years in hell alone, thinking about what I would say if I ever had a chance to do something worthwhile. Now I finally have that chance, and I'm making the most of it, including reciting a few scripted words now and then. Our song was also scripted. You seemed to enjoy that."

"All right. Fair enough. I'll shut up and pray."

"Good. But let me know if Alex does anything worth mentioning."

"Will do." Iona closed her eyes. Charlie was right. The time to pray had come. Maybe God really kept his eye on her, even in hell. If so, she had to keep spying on Alex and relaying the information. The only other option was to hunker down in a corner of this cloak and pout. And that would be a coward's cop-out. She had to fight in any way she could, and, for now, that meant talking to God about how to be the spy that he had called her to be.

# Chapter Seven

Ben followed Winella through the lush forest to a waterfall. When she reached the edge of the stream, far enough from the cascade to speak in a normal tone, she stopped. "This is strange. Caligar's whistle said to meet him at the falls, but he is not here."

Something rustled in the undergrowth, and an odd growl followed. Winella whipped an arrow from her quiver and nocked it to the bowstring. "Savages. I can protect us against one, maybe two. If there are more, prepare to run."

Ben instinctively grabbed at his belt for a weapon, but none were there, not even a knife.

One of the male giants staggered toward them, his legs stiff and his mouth foaming. He took a final step and splashed face first into the stream. A female giant followed. She fell to her knees and stared at Ben, her mouth agape. A second later, she toppled to the side and lay motionless.

A third giant, another male, appeared from the forest, clutching his throat, his tongue protruding. When he saw Ben, he lunged but tripped and lumbered past him toward a tree. He smacked his face against a limb and crumpled to the ground.

Winella lowered her bow. "How odd that they perished as they arrived."

"Right," Ben said, scanning the trio. "Like it was scripted."

Laughter emanated from the forest in the direction the giants had come. A moment later, a human male carrying an automatic rifle emerged from between two bushes. Wearing military fatigues and a broad smile, he gestured with the rifle toward the dead female. "She was the funniest. Wolfed down the meat so fast she nearly choked."

Winella aimed her arrow at him. "Dr. Harrid, where are Caligar and Bazrah?"

Harrid gave her a head bow. "Is that how you greet me, Winella? After all I've done for you?"

She drew the bowstring back, ready to shoot. "You threatened my son."

"Wait. Wait." He set the rifle on the ground and lifted a hand. "You're right, but I did it to restore your world to you. It was all part of my plan to rid both Viridi and Earth of the scourge, the foul beasts who murdered and consumed my wife and also threatened you and your family for years."

"Why should I believe a man who threatened a child?"

"Because of the results." He lowered his hand and nudged one of the dead giants with his foot. "Here is the evidence of my purge, and there are many more corpses behind me. I told them a living human would show up at the waterfall, and these three made it this far before succumbing to the poison I injected into some of the dead humans I brought from Earth. I also fed the poisoned humans to the giants there. Now they're all dead."

Heat surged through Ben's ears. "You murdered them?"

Harrid looked at one of the corpses, avoiding eye contact. "I executed them for their crimes."

"Who appointed you their judge, jury, and executioner?"

Harrid jabbed a finger at Ben. "I rescued you, so don't get uppity with me. You fell into an area where the giants would have found you. I hoisted you into the SUV and carried you to a safe place. Then I led Winella to find you, making her think she was following game." He waved a hand toward Winella. "Kindly lower your weapon. I am not your enemy. I have done you a service."

She kept her bow and arrow in place. "I ask again. Where are Caligar and Bazrah?"

"In the hunting grounds beyond the giants' cooking cauldron. They are safe, still hunting, unaware of what I have done. That was my whistle that summoned you to the waterfall, not Caligar's."

Winella lowered her bow and returned the arrow to its quiver. "I must go and find them to ... verify?"

"Yes, Winella," Harrid said with a condescending tone. "Verify my words. You will see."

Winella looked at Ben. "I will stay if you need me."

He gave her a nod. "Go. If Harrid wanted to kill me, he could've done it long ago."

"Very well."

Winella picked up the rifle and took off at a run through the forest. When her heavy footfalls faded into the forest, Harrid crossed his arms over his chest. "Now that we're alone, we can talk."

Ben copied his pose. "About what?"

"First, your acting prowess is as exceptional as you described. Especially the part about me murdering the giants and being judge and executioner. Well done. Second, why are you here so soon? I thought you'd try to restore your soul to your body before coming. I was surprised to see you at the tower, and I guessed that you wanted to use it to come to Viridi, so I had to hurry to kill the giants here as quickly as possible."

Ben forced a straight face. This man's words were too bizarre to figure out. Careful probing was in order. "Before I explain my early arrival, tell me everything I need to know."

Harrid smiled in a schoolboy fashion. "As I mentioned, I killed the savage giants here. And I did the same on Earth. I wanted revenge, of course, for the death of my wife, but I also hoped to make this planet a suitable refuge for you. Now you can live here safely."

Ben nodded. Harrid seemed ready to talk, like he was trying to impress someone important. Maybe he would spill more with another prompt. "Ah. Good work. But there is still the issue with restoring my soul to my body."

Harrid's smile wilted. "Couldn't you find it? You said you would bring Bartholomew because he knew where it was being preserved."

Again Ben kept his expression blank. The truth was coming together. Alex told Harrid she would possess a body to resurrect from hell, but he was wrong about which body. Now Ben needed to mimic Alex. "Trust me, I don't want to be within this inferior body any longer than I have to, but I decided to come here first because the Alaska tower is close to collapse."

Harrid spread his hands. "What difference does that make? I thought you wanted to build a more powerful system of towers. I left the schematics on a computer drive exactly where I told you. Couldn't you find it?"

Ben again stayed calm. He had to think fast. "The computer drive was corrupt. I had to hurry to use the tower to come here to search for you. If it had collapsed too soon, I would have had no recourse."

"Corrupt?" Harrid cursed under his breath. "Then I should go back to Earth with you. Make another copy of the schematics."

"Exactly what I was thinking. We should use the transport device you have here."

"Agreed." Harrid strode downstream toward the precipice. "This way, please."

As they walked side by side, Harrid kept glancing at Ben, half smiling at times as if awed by the person he thought he was with. "It feels odd to call you Alexandria, but I guess I should, even if you do look like Ben Garrison."

Ben nodded. "Alexandria is my name. I prefer that you use it."

"Okay. That's fine, but, just curious, what happened to Ben's soul? Is he trapped in hell?"

"What does it matter to you? Are you worried about him?"

"Not at all. I want to know that he's suffering. He and his crew nearly ruined my plans." Harrid's smile returned. "It's an excellent twist of fate that you're here in his body. A delicious irony."

"My, aren't you the vindictive one?"

"Vindictive?" Anger flashed in Harrid's expression, but he maintained his sycophantic tone. "I like to think that I'm an avenger

Bryan Davis

of wrongs. Anyone who stands in my way of avenging my wife's murder gets what he deserves."

"I understand. Your anger toward the murderous giants is warranted."

"Thank you." Harrid raised a finger. "I hope you don't mind, but I have a personal question."

Ben nodded. "As long as it's pertinent, you may ask it."

"It's definitely pertinent." Harrid cleared his throat nervously. "Should I assume you were never able to find my wife's soul in hell?"

Ben stared straight ahead. "You are correct. My minions searched everywhere. She is not in hell."

"I'm glad to hear that." Harrid stopped at the precipice and straddled the ladder that led down to Caligar's cave entrance. "Then when we return, you can search for Quinn here. I mean, that is your theory, that souls don't go to hell from Viridi."

Ben motioned for him to descend. "I will answer soon."

Harrid climbed down to the landing, and Ben joined him. When they began descending the switchback trail, Harrid leading the way, Ben stayed quiet. Fortunately, since Harrid thought he needed Alex, he could play the queenly role and speak whenever it suited him. That would give him time to figure out how to get more information. The idea that Alex planned to come here to escape going back to hell needed more probing. Maybe that would be a good place to start. "Why are you convinced that Quinn's soul did not go to heaven?"

Harrid slid a hand into his pocket, still facing forward. "I didn't give you details before. Quinn was not only an atheist, but also a liar, a thief, and a bully to nearly everyone. I was the only exception, but probably because I never dared cross her." He shrugged. "What can I say? I loved her, and I want to make sure her soul's in a comfortable place."

"Interesting." Ben passed a collapsed edge in the path and stepped to the other side to avoid it. That was the spot where he, Leo, and Iona rescued Caligar from his spill. The terrible storm had blinded him. Ben nodded. That might be a good segue. "Blindness is one of the many pitfalls of love, but when I return to Viridi permanently, I will do what I can to find Quinn's soul. Yet, since she could be anywhere on the planet, the task could take a long time."

"I have more confidence in you than that. I apologize for snooping into your affairs, but I studied your era's history. Apparently you were well known for your ability to find wandering souls, far more capable than other Reapers."

Ben kept his stare straight ahead. Reapers were the stuff of legends—real history blended with myths to the point that discerning between truth and fairy tale was difficult. He had to steer clear of the topic to avoid revealing his ignorance. "I have no comment about my past or my abilities. I will do what I can to find Quinn. That is the best you can hope for."

"Of course. Of course. I'm not rushing you. But, if I may, I would like to give you more incentive to return to Viridi. Killing the giants on both Earth and here allowed me to verify my cell degeneration research. There is no longer any doubt. When you settle here, you will be in an Eden-like paradise that will slow your cell degeneration. You will survive for at least two hundred years."

"Excellent. With the hope of long life and the absence of the savage giants, Viridi will be an ideal place to live."

When they reached the end of the switchback trail, Harrid accelerated to a quick march over the flatter terrain. "I'm glad you approve. If you can't find Quinn now, when you return in your real body, I'm sure your soul-locating power will be enhanced."

"True. There is very little I can do in this inferior vessel, and I am anxious to leave it. Let's hope we have no trouble with the transporter device."

"We shouldn't. I designed it. No matter what condition it's in, I can get it working."

Soon, they crossed the stream, no longer swollen by rain. Then, after a few miles, they arrived at the mesa and climbed the stairway to the top. Ben looked out over the mirror at the bottom of the ravine while Harrid examined the control panel atop a rocky shelf.

The reflective disc looked like it did before. Maybe Caligar hadn't taken many steps to dismantle it yet.

"Power grid is intact," Harrid said, "but the conduit generator's core isn't functioning. Caligar probably either untethered it or removed it completely. I'll have to check the innards embedded underneath the disc to find out."

Ben turned toward him. "Do you have a time estimate for the inspection?"

"Only a few minutes, but I won't know how long any repairs might take until I—"

Something thudded. The point of an arrow jutted out of Harrid's chest. His eyes rolled upward, and he dropped to his knees, then slammed face first to the ground.

Behind him, Caligar lowered his bow as he spoke through clenched teeth, flashes of light in his eyes. "If you have questions about my judicial actions, Benjamin, you are free to ask them."

A knot swelled in Ben's throat as he stared at Harrid's body, twitching in death strokes, a pool of blood spreading underneath him. "No questions. He's a murderer."

"And a kidnapper. On Viridi, both crimes are punishable by death. I was Supreme Judge here before the others turned to barbarism, and I exercised my judgment."

"I understand." Ben looked at the control panel on the rocky table. It seemed callous to move on so quickly, but too much was at stake to pay any respects to a scoundrel like Harrid. "Is your transporter operational?"

"Not at the moment. I dismantled a few parts, but I can get the system back online quickly. From what Winella told me, it seems that you came to Viridi by accident."

Ben nodded. "And now I need to return to Earth."

"I will begin the repairs at the mirror immediately."

When Caligar flexed to turn, Ben raised a hand. "What about communications? Can I call through the Oculus Gate with a ham radio signal?"

"That function is intact." Caligar strode to the control panel, pulled a set of headphones from a cubbyhole in the side, and put them on. He manipulated the controls on the panel for nearly a minute before taking the headphones off and handing them to Ben. "The Alaska tower is no longer responding. I contacted the Russia tower. It will relay your transmission from there." Caligar hurried to the mesa's stairway and quickly climbed down.

Ben knelt next to Harrid and checked for a pulse at his neck—nothing. With a firm grip, he pulled the arrow out, tossed it to the side, and heaved a sigh. So much death, much of it caused by Harrid bringing the angels to Earth. And now was his soul in hell? If what he said was true about souls not going there from Viridi, maybe not. He could be standing right here, invisible to the naked eye. Either way, Harrid's fate was up to God.

Ben rose to his feet, slid the headphones on, and adjusted the attached microphone stem. After finding the dial that altered the frequency, he set it to the proper shortwave channel and spoke loudly, hoping his voice would cut through any static. "Kat. Jack. Trudy. This is Ben. Can anyone hear me?" The expected static responded for a few seconds, then a voice blended in.

"Ben! It's Jack! Where are you, Bro? Are you all right?"

"I'm on Viridi. And, yeah, I'm all right. A little bruised from a rough landing, but nothing's broken. I'm calling from Caligar's transport station. It's mostly intact."

"Glad to hear. Listen, Trudy and I are at the Alaska tower. I mean, what's left of it. The top half crashed, and some of it burned. Kat went home with Leo and Iona to pick up supplies to rebuild the tower. Kat's thought was to go to Viridi to look for you, but if Caligar's contraption can send you back to Earth, we can shut down our efforts on this side."

"Caligar's putting it back together as we speak."

"Are you sure you can trust him? I know you two kissed and made up, but he tossed you into hell. Hard to forget that."

"I can trust him. Long story, but Harrid killed the other giants on Earth, then he came here in the SUV. Killed them all here, too. Fed them poisoned human meat. Only Caligar and his family are alive."

"Yuck. Harrid's a monster. I feel sorry for the humans who were driven mad by the vaccine, but I'm not shedding any tears over those giants."

"Agreed. Anyway, Caligar executed Harrid for his crimes. Arrow through the heart. And now he's helping me fire up the transporter so I can come back to Earth."

"Before you make that leap, let me give you an update. Leo and Iona have both been acting off kilter, so I gave Iona a test to see if she's on the up and up. She failed. This might sound insane, but Kat and I are thinking, and Trudy agrees, that Iona is really Alex. I mean, Alex's soul is in Iona's body."

Ben ran a hand through his hair. This was all just too crazy. "Yeah, it sounds insane, but it has to be true. Harrid thought I was Alex when I showed up here, and he said something about Bart telling Alex where her body is being preserved. That means Leo is probably possessed by Bart."

"Yep. It's all coming together. The transfer happened in the healing pool. The stabbings were orchestrated to make it all work."

"Then where are Leo's and Iona's souls?" Ben asked. "Stuck in hell?"

"I guess so. They're disembodied, so the portal wouldn't have worked for them."

"That's the theory." Ben looked over the edge of the mesa at the mirror. Caligar crouched at the rim, but his huge body blocked what he was doing. Maybe he could restore the mirror's ability to create a portal to hell. "I guess I don't have much of a choice."

"Let me guess. Don't save a plate for your supper here. You're thinking about going to hell to save Leo's and Iona's souls."

"If I can. Caligar's down at the mirror working on it now. I'll have to ask him if it's still possible to go there."

"Listen," Jack said, "we're sure that Leo and Iona aren't themselves, but without proof that their souls are in hell, going there is way too crazy, especially without an exit strategy."

Ben blew out a sigh. It felt good to have Jack around pulling his reins, keeping him in check. "Agreed. We need proof first. Any idea how to get it?"

"Maybe. It wasn't hard to trick Alex into making a mistake, but now she'll probably double her guard. It'll be a lot harder to get her to spill about where Iona's soul is. I'll call her first to see if I can trip her up and figure out who is who, then I'll call Kat to get her up to speed."

"I'll wait here and brainstorm with Caligar to come up with an exit strategy."

"Good luck with that. Hell probably doesn't have many exits. Back at you soon."

Something clicked, and static again flooded the channel. Ben walked to the edge of the mesa and gazed at the mirror again. His previous visit to hell was worse than any nightmare, but if Iona's soul was really still there, he wouldn't hesitate to charge back in. Yes, she was tough and independent, but what if Bart's soul didn't go with Leo's body and Leo's soul left hell instead? That would mean Iona's soul would have to endure the terrors of hell alone. With Leo at her side, she could face anything, at least short term. But this was far from a short-term ordeal. This was eternity. She needed help, and nothing could stop him from giving it.

# Chapter Eight

Now seated in the copilot's seat, his limbs barely moveable, Bartholomew looked out the front windshield while Alexandria guided the cruiser over a rural area that was once the Chicago suburbs. With impish eyes darting and freckled brow furrowing, it seemed impossible that this girl could be housing the queen of hell, but her occasional barking commands spiced with hate-filled invectives proved the presence of a monster again and again.

"I see the cemetery," she said, pointing forward as the cruiser hovered a hundred feet or so above the ground. "Now tell me which mausoleum."

Bartholomew inhaled slowly, then forced the words out through barely moving lips. "It has been … many years."

She kicked his shin. "Don't be a fool. It's made of stone. It hasn't changed."

Bartholomew grunted, though the pain in his nearly numb leg wasn't severe. "Not sure of location … but I remember … a phoenix bird."

"Ah. A phoenix statue. How appropriate." Alexandria guided the cruiser over an area dotted by many mausolea. "Anything else unusual about my body's abode?"

"Generator station … small separate structure."

"I see a candidate." She turned the cruiser to the right. "And there is the phoenix next to the entry door. Perfect." After a few more moments, she landed in a grassy area near the mausoleum and opened the side door. "I'm sure I can trust you to stay out of trouble. Keeping that fine specimen of a body intact is a lot more appealing than going back to hell." Flashing a wicked smile, she exited and strode toward the mausoleum door, a strut in her gait that looked awkward on her girlish frame.

Bartholomew scanned the controls. Might it be possible to fly away and leave that witch behind? Probably not without an improvement in his numbed condition. Maybe he could close the door and—

"This is Jack calling." The voice came from the dashboard speaker. "Leo? Iona? Can you hear me?"

Bartholomew eyed the radio. The microphone toggle had been switched off. Summoning all of his strength, he lifted an arm, slung his body toward the toggle, and flipped the microphone on as he flopped to the floor. Gasping for breath, he spoke toward the dashboard. "This is Leo."

"Leo. Great. Are you alone?"

"For the moment."

"Not a problem. Listen, I have a question. When you were in hell looking for Iona—"

"Stop."

"Stop? Stop what?"

"Your question. I need ... your help."

"Uh ... sure. What's up?"

"Iona is really ... Alexandria. Possessed."

Jack's voice spiked. "Iona is possessed by Alexandria?"

"Yes. And I am not Leo. I am Bartholomew, possessing Leo's body. The souls of Leo and Iona are still in hell. We have to stop Alexandria. I tried, but she drugged me, and I am paralyzed on the floor in the cruiser's cockpit."

"Okay. Listen, Bartholomew. We already suspected the truth about you two. Glad you're willing to help. Where are you? How can we stop Alex?"

Bartholomew took a deep breath and focused on his diaphragm and lips, allowing him to speak more easily. "We landed the cruiser at a mausoleum near where Chicago used to be. Her body is stored here, preserved for many years. The mausoleum entry's access control is on the back of a phoenix statue next to the door. Near its neck. Right now, Alexandria is planning to go inside to transfer her soul from Iona's body to her own. If she succeeds, she will become much more powerful. During her life, she was one of the Reapers. Have you heard of them?"

"Yeah. I read about them."

"Good. She is a special kind of Reaper, what we called an Owl. With the ability to read minds to an extent, she will be extremely dangerous."

"What do you think she'll do with Iona once she's out of her body?"

"She didn't say. She is unpredictable. She could kill Iona out of spite. She might simply leave her in the mausoleum, knowing she can't cause any trouble. She might also bring her along to use as leverage if the opportunity arises."

"I'm guessing number three."

Bartholomew managed a nod. "I agree. She often uses leverage to great advantage."

"Okay, so we'll assume Iona's body is not in immediate danger. Here's what we're going to do. Kat can control that cruiser with her voice. I'm going to get her to call you and tell it to take off, maybe hover where Alex can't reach. That'll buy us some time."

"Good. That should help."

"You hang in there while I get in touch with Kat. We'll try to save you both."

"Do not underestimate Alexandria. She is far more cunning than anyone I have ever known. She always stays multiple steps ahead of her adversaries."

"Understood. Before I go, I have a question. Suppose one of us goes to hell to try to rescue Leo and Iona. Any thoughts on how to do that?"

"Based on the lore, it is impossible for a disembodied soul to leave hell. You have to find a vessel the soul can reside in."

Jack hummed as if in thought for a moment before responding. "We know a living human can be a host for someone else's soul, but can a person host more than one soul, his own and the souls he's rescuing?"

"No. Alexandria was certain of that." Bartholomew inhaled deeply, battling the pain from speaking so much. "If you go to hell to try to rescue them, look for a Reaper named Charlotte. She is a living human who patrols the area looking for wayward souls. She's highly skilled and is drawn to souls who aren't in the right place, so if you can't find her, maybe she'll find you. If anyone can help you get out of hell with other souls, she can."

"Charlotte. A Reaper. Got it."

"But beware. Charlotte is unpredictable. Living in hell can have strange effects on a person."

"Understood. You should hear from Kat in a couple of minutes. Let's hope she can commandeer the cruiser."

Bartholomew raised a finger. "One more issue. Alexandria is sending laborers to rebuild the Alaska tower and reengineer the other three. I assume once she is restored, she wants to travel to Viridi."

"To do what?"

"I'm not sure, but knowing her, I have a guess. She wants to rule that world. With its depleted population and its superior living conditions, it is a much easier and valuable target."

"Good news for us, then. She'll be gone."

"Not likely good news. She is a vindictive monster. If she chooses to leave Earth, count on her to try to destroy it. I have no idea how, but she has a team of one hundred talented people she calls influencers. Watch for a plot to manufacture a worldwide cataclysm, one that those influencers can escape."

"Maybe she would let them die in their own cataclysm."

"I expect not. She would try to have them join her on Viridi. She wouldn't want to be there alone."

"Power mad," Jack said. "She needs someone she can control."

"Exactly."

"Got it. Now I'd better go. I have a lot of intel to pass along."

"I understand." Bartholomew let out a long sigh. Jack's plan to have Kat commandeer the cruiser was a reasonable one, but Alexandria had likely already plotted a counter move, which would probably mean death to Leo's body and a return for himself to damnation in hell. Even if she didn't have a counter, what would happen? There was no exit plan for his soul. Either way, he was doomed.

While waiting for Jack's next update, Kat shifted to priority number two—finding Damien. Since the Refectors succeeded in their mission to deliver souls to Alex, he would soon begin plans for their next step, whatever that might be.

She touched the remote controller in her front pocket, then glanced at the handheld vacuum unit on the desktop and touched the handcuffs in her back pocket. Everything would be easy to reach at the proper time. Setting a trap for Damien with some of the weapons and electronics in the cache hadn't taken long, but whether or not it would work remained to be seen. Failing might mean getting shot again. He would likely come with a weapon.

As if responding to the thought, Kat's arm twinged at the spot where Damien shot her, the source of the blood he had taken. Since she was once possessed by the angel queen, he probably needed her DNA to access something the angels had secured. Not only that, she hadn't yet figured out the reason for the second key in the bank's safety deposit box. It might be related to the DNA theft.

On the wall display, dozens of camera outputs created an array of city views—factories, apartments, warehouses, and the like. Not a soul stirred. Since most of the inhabitants had fled the contagion to procure the vaccine in Alaska, and since the others were hunkered down in fear, the city looked like a post-apocalyptic war zone. And it was. After the fake angels purged all dissenters with violent force, the people remaining were angel advocates, whether real or pretend, as well as the few rebels who hid themselves as they fought against the alien monsters.

After initiating a facial-recognition search for Damien on all the cameras, Kat focused on her desktop display and brought up the bank's security feed. She selected a camera that showed the safety deposit boxes. Since Jack thought the key might open one of the boxes, Damien might show up there to access them, though sitting and watching didn't seem like a good use of time. It was possible that he had already been there and departed. Maybe it would be a good idea to see what was left in the weapons room.

Just as she rose from her seat, Jack's voice broke the silence. "Kat, you got ears on?"

She sat again. "Yeah, but I feel like I'm wasting time. I can't—"

"Hush and listen. First, Ben's alive. He's on Viridi. I talked to him."

Kat sucked in a breath. "Thank God!"

"Yeah. For sure. And now the bad news. We got confirmation that Alex is possessing Iona's body, and Bart is inside Leo. Their souls are still in hell."

"Oh, no! So we were right. Something was going on with those two."

"True, but there's good news—well, bad news, too. I talked to Leo ... I mean, Bart. He's in the cruiser at a mausoleum where Alex is going to revive her body and somehow transfer her soul from Iona to it. Bart's turning coat and wants to keep Alex from succeeding, but she drugged him, and he's paralyzed in the cruiser. This is happening right now."

"I can call the cruiser and tell it to leave Alex where she is."

"Exactly what I was thinking. Iona will probably be okay because Alex will want to keep her alive as leverage."

Kat nodded. "Yeah, that sounds like her."

"And there's more. Alex sent laborers to rebuild the tower. I assume they're on their way, but there's another storm brewing here in Alaska, so it might take them a while to get here. Anyway, Bart thinks Alex is planning to set up her tyrant shop on Viridi and destroy Earth out of spite."

Kat slammed a fist on the computer table. "Demonic witch!"

"Yeah. She's a scourge from hell. But with this intel, maybe we can do something about it. Remember those one hundred people who got the vaccine first?"

"Sure. I still have the list on the computer here."

"Then try to put some recon on them. Since they're scattered all over the world, they might be the key to figuring out how Alex plans to destroy Earth."

"Got it. Back to you in a minute. First step is to call the cruiser to take control."

"Sounds good," Jack said, his voice filling with static. "I'll call Ben with an update."

"I hope you can. It sounds like the signal's getting weaker."

"Could be. Wind's kicking up. Anyway, Bart had an idea about a possible exit strategy, a Reaper who patrols hell. It sounds shaky, but it's all we've got."

"Copy that. Keep me posted." She typed in a code that switched the computer's transmitter to the cruiser's frequency. "Bart, this is Kat Garrison. I'm calling to take control of the cruiser."

# Chapter Nine

Alexandria walked across the mausoleum's threshold, kicking aside leaves and other debris that had gathered over the years. She grasped a ring attached to a lion's mouth on the door and pulled. The huge metal door wouldn't budge. Although Iona's smallish body wasn't as strong as her own, she was still big enough to heave an unlocked door open, even one this size. Since there was no keyhole, the locking mechanism had to be located elsewhere, maybe a hidden trigger in the stone structure.

She looked at the statue of a phoenix standing on a concrete pedestal to the right of the door. With its fire-orange wings spread and its red beak pointing toward the sky, it looked like an escapee from the crypt, a likely place to hide the mechanism.

Running her hands along the pedestal and the bird's legs, she searched for a loose section that might hide a switch, but the surface proved to be intact—smooth and even. She stood on tiptoes and reached for a wing, but Iona's petite frame made the effort hopeless.

She backed up a few steps, ran toward the phoenix, and leaped onto its pedestal. Once she steadied herself, she searched the bird. On its back between its wings, a small metal door the same orange color as the smooth plaster feathers came into view, though some of the paint had peeled off. She pried the door open, revealing a toggle.

Alexandria switched the toggle's position and looked at the mausoleum's entry. The door swung slowly outward, its bottom edge scraping the concrete entry pad and sweeping aside more leaves.

She leaped down, snatched a flashlight from her belt, and flicked it on. As she walked to the threshold, she focused on a rectangular sarcophagus inside at the center, then halted at the doorway. She shifted the beam from place to place, scanning the walls, floor, and ceiling for any sign of a trigger for a snare. Suspended two feet or so off the floor, two flexible tubes about the width of a finger ran from the sarcophagus to a cubical machine sitting on a supply cart that abutted the right-hand wall. A hum emanated from the machine, probably her body's preservation system.

With no apparent traps around, Alexandria walked to the side of the sarcophagus, a sealed box that served as her safety capsule. Its glass top allowed a view of her body. Wearing her signature black leather pants and jacket along with a V-neck white T-shirt, she lay on a bed of purple satin, her hair, as blonde as ever, splayed under her head, somewhat oily near the scalp. As Bartholomew had mentioned, the caretaker was gone, dead. He had extorted the remaining funds for fueling and maintaining the system, now running in automatic mode. It wouldn't last much longer.

She stepped over to the machine and read the various meters. As a ruling council member during the radiation years, she had seen such devices before, a last resort to save a Reaper, though it always took another Reaper to retrieve a soul and return it to its body after doctors performed whatever surgeries were necessary to put the body back into a survivable state. Since the body was dead, they could perform more radical procedures if needed.

Being a high-level Reaper in those days, she was a candidate for this pseudo-hibernation status, and Bartholomew, one of her obedient lackeys at the time, did his duty to see to the repair of the eye rupture and fatal brain damage inflicted by a rival Reaper. Now she had to bring her own soul back to its body, a process that might or might not work since Iona had no Reaper powers of her own, only the remembered skills of the soul that now dwelled within her.

An alarm beeped on the machine. Alexandria scanned the meters. A fuel cell had died, and the other two had less than twenty-four hours remaining. Other meters indicated that the system had already decreased preservation components because of the lower power, and only moments remained before her body would begin degrading.

She pressed the device's resurrection button. The hum grew louder as the machine began extracting synthetic fluids and replacing it with her blood. When the process finished, it would try to restart her heart, but that wouldn't work until she had transferred her soul from Iona to her body.

The timing had to be perfect. Transfer before the restarting of her heart, and her soul wouldn't be able to attach to her brain. It needed active blood flow for that. Transfer too late, and her heart would stop beating, not having a soul within to keep her body alive. In either case, her body would expel her soul, and it would return to hell.

At the side of the capsule, she turned a lever that unsealed the hinged lid. She opened it, lifted one of her body's arms, and set its hand over Iona's eyes, the windows to the soul. Soon, if the resurrection procedure worked correctly, it would restart the corpse's heart and start an energy flow through the arm and into Iona. Then her soul could ride the energy flow into her body. Although this self-transfer had never been tried before, the theory behind it was sound, but only because she was so experienced in soul migration.

The machine's hum altered, a sign that the synthetic fluid extraction and blood restoration had completed. In seconds, it would restart her heart, and she would be back inside her body. Yes, little Iona might die, maybe after existing in a zombie state for a short while. Without a soul, she wouldn't be able to last for long. But sacrifices had to be made, and the bad-tempered twerp was no big loss, though it would have been amusing to see her face if she were to realize that she had a hand in the resurrection process, a useful tool that could be tossed away after finishing its task.

Alexandria's eyes tingled. Energy flowed in. She mentally detached her soul from Iona's brain and let it ride with the energy stream into her own body's hand. Now blinded visually, she followed her sense of position and crawled up her arm and into her head. Now to find the brain stem.

Her body jerked. The heart-starting process had begun. She had to hurry. Fortunately, the revived stem would now draw her the rest of the way. She followed the pull, reaching with her stretching appendages. Seconds later, a gasp sounded. Light poured in. The stem was within reach.

She grasped the stem and wrapped herself around it. Vision flowed, the ceiling of the mausoleum now in view. A mirror had been installed in the stonework, showing a reflection of herself as she stared straight up. Tubes penetrated her body, one plugged into a valve embedded in her sternum and another into a socket in her abdomen next to her navel.

Concentrating on her newly awakened muscles, she lowered her hand from Iona's eyes, peeled her other arm away from the stimulation electrodes in the capsule's bed, and grasped the tube running into her sternum. She disconnected it from the valve and laid it to the side. That was the easy one, though the valve itself had to stay, one of the unfortunate drawbacks of this resurrection process.

With her other hand, she pulled the tube from her stomach and closed the valve's cap, creating an artificial seal that would allow the incision wound to heal. Then, clutching the sides of the coffin-like capsule, she pulled herself to a sitting position and looked toward the exit. Iona stood next to the capsule with a blank stare.

Alexandria hummed a laugh. "Thank you for the use of your body."

A gleam sparkled in Iona's eyes. A reaction? Alexandria looked more deeply with her Owl-endowed vision, though her repaired eye couldn't quite focus. Iona's soul couldn't possibly be in there, but maybe it was still connected somehow.

Alexandria spoke softly. "Can you hear me, Iona? If so, blink once."

After a brief pause, Iona blinked.

"Very interesting. And unexpected." Alexandria climbed out of the capsule and walked on unsteady legs to the preservation machine.

After turning the machine off, she opened a door on the supply cart, withdrew a weapons belt complete with a knife, handgun, miniature camera, and spool line, and began strapping the belt around her waist. "I'm sure you want to see Leo, don't you, Iona?"

Iona blinked again.

"Good." Alexandria pulled her cloak from the cart and looked it over. Most of the material retained its color, lighter than the cloaks of most other Reapers because of the blonde hair intermixed with flax and other fibers. The hood also seemed to be in good shape in spite of the many years in storage. She slid her arms through the roomy sleeves and raised the hood over her head. When she retired from Reaper work to join the world-governing council, it felt good to finally shed this cloak along with its laborious duties, but now it felt empowering, renewing.

She plugged the cloak's clasp into her sternum valve. The energy the capsule had infused sent a flow of vigor through the clasp and into the fibers, making the entire cloak shimmer for a moment before settling back to normal.

Alexandria took Iona's hand. "Come with me. Leo is waiting."

From within Charlie's cloak, Iona cringed. Holding this witch's hand felt disgusting, humiliating. Not only was she evil, she also reeked of superiority, arrogance, and condescension—the ultimate in self-perceived invincibility.

This connection to her body might prove to be the most important task possible, at least while trapped in the cloak. What else could she do?

Iona left her hand in place. She had to keep the goal in focus— find Leo, both his body and his soul. Feigning cooperation with this slimy eel would be worth it. At this point, there was no other option available.

# Chapter Ten

Now able to force his arms and legs into stiff, painful movements, Bartholomew struggled back to the pilot's chair. Apparently the drug was wearing off, but how long would it take before he could do anything more than crawl?

A voice came from the control panel's speaker. "Bart, this is Kat Garrison. I'm calling to take over control of the cruiser."

"Go ahead. And hurry. Alexandria's not here, but she could return at any moment."

"Okay." Kat cleared her throat. "Queen Laramel is now the pilot."

The panel responded with a robotic, "Voice authenticated. Proceed."

"Ascend to fifty feet and hover in place."

"Cruiser is moored."

Kat growled. "The mooring cap. Alex must have taken it off."

"No surprise," Bartholomew said. "Obviously she planned ahead for this possibility."

"I assume she'll put the cap back on when she returns. The moment she does, I'll tell the cruiser to lift off before she can board."

"That would work if we were dealing with a typical enemy, but rest assured that she has already planned a counter move."

"How could she possibly have a counter move? She has to put the cap on before she can fly the cruiser, and she has to do it from the outside."

Bartholomew sighed. "Yes, your logic is sound, but you don't know her like I know her."

"Okay. I'll grant you that. While we're waiting for her to come back, maybe you can help me with our plan. Ben is on Viridi, and he's thinking about going back to hell to rescue Leo's and Iona's souls. But he's waiting for Caligar to repair the portal, and I don't know how long that will take. Based on your knowledge of hell, do you have any hints for Ben on how to find them?"

"Jack asked me a similar question, and I have put more thought into the situation." Bartholomew extended an arm, but it quickly flopped to his lap. Not good, but better than the previous attempt. "Leo and Iona won't be able to stay in the castle. In Alexandria's unlimited vindictiveness, she broke a spell on the area. The castle is in ruins by now, and a warding that protected her forest from beasts is gone. Leo and Iona will be vulnerable, and they will quickly learn that they can't stay there."

"Where might they go?"

"Hard to predict, but with the warding gone, Charlotte will likely go to the forest to find Alexandria. Charlotte is a soul Reaper who has been trying to take us back to the abyss for years. I already mentioned her to Jack."

"A soul Reaper. I've heard of them. They haven't been around for more than a century."

Bartholomew glanced out the cruiser's window. Still no sign of Alexandria amidst the broken and tilted mausolea. The war-torn cemetery raised images from times long ago after the massive nuclear blast covered Earth with radiation, the days when Reapers guided every soul to his or her final destination, carrying the souls in their cloaks for protection and easier conveyance. "Because Reapers were no longer needed on Earth after the radioactive period."

"Will Charlotte try to take Leo and Iona to the abyss?"

"Not likely. She'll know they don't belong in hell. Reapers are experienced that way, and Charlotte is highly skilled."

"If she finds them, where will she take them?"

"She will find them. Reapers are perceptive and extremely stealthy. Where she will take them, however, is beyond my—"

A new voice pierced the engine's hum. "Bartholomew, I find your conversation quite interesting."

Bartholomew turned toward the sound. Alexandria stood in the passenger compartment, fully restored. Wearing her usual leather outfit as well as her Reaper's cloak, she stood next to Iona, who stared with wide eyes. The side door still open, a cool breeze batted Iona's red locks across her face, but she seemed oblivious to the motion.

Alexandria smirked. "I especially enjoyed the part about a Reaper's stealth. It seems that my own stealth kept you from noticing my approach." She then glared at the control panel. "Obviously your treachery has continued, but I expected that."

"Alexandria is here," Bartholomew whispered toward the dashboard. "Restored to her body."

"Cruiser," Kat said, "switch off manual controls. Voice control only."

The robotic voice replied, "Manual controls deactivated."

"Very clever." Alexandria whipped out her knife, strode to Bartholomew, and set the blade against his throat. "Katherine, it seems that my ally has betrayed me. Now, I know you have no reason to value Bartholomew's soul, but it is housed in Leo's body. When I slit his throat, you will have no hope of restoring Leo's soul to its proper place, assuming you can resurrect it from hell."

"Is resurrection possible?" Kat asked.

"There is always hope. I learned only moments ago that Iona's body still has an attachment to her soul, and her body continues to function. In fact, she is standing in the passenger compartment at this moment. Although she is little more than a lifelike mannequin, she is breathing."

"It's true," Bartholomew said. "I'm looking at Iona right now. Her eyes are glazed, but otherwise she seems normal."

Alexandria focused on the dashboard. "I assume that since Iona never died and her soul is not supposed to be in hell, her soul is drawn to her body. I think the attachment will eventually weaken and perhaps break completely, but if she can somehow escape hell soon enough, she can be restored. The same is true for Leo."

"But Bartholomew's soul is in Leo's body," Kat said.

Alexandria pressed the blade a hair deeper, raising a painful sting. "In my previous life, I was a Reaper. I can remove Bartholomew's soul from Leo's body at the proper time. There is also a Reaper in hell who can help you with Leo's and Iona's souls, which should provide you with assurance that resurrection is possible. Simply cooperate with me, and all will be well."

Kat sighed. "All right. What do you want me to do?"

"Return the cruiser's control to me. No more voice commands. Do it now."

"Cruiser," Kat said, "restore manual controls. Disable voice input."

The ship's robotic voice again responded. "Manual control restored. Voice commands cannot be deactivated."

"Interesting." Alexandria returned her knife to its belt sheath and flipped a switch on the control panel. The passenger door closed with a swoosh. "Katherine, I am going to end our conversation and turn the radio off. You will not be able to call back and take over the cruiser. If you want the bodies of Leo and Iona to survive, I suggest that you don't try to reestablish the link."

"I understand," Kat said.

"Good." Alexandria terminated the call. "Now to take off." She flipped another switch and pushed a lever, but the engine's idling hum stayed the same.

The computer responded with, "Cruiser is moored."

She patted the sides of her pants. "The cap is in Iona's pocket."

Bartholomew looked toward the passenger section, but Iona was no longer there.

"She's gone!" Alexandria rushed to the side door and slapped the control button. When the door opened, she leaned out and called, "Iona! Where are you?"

After a few seconds, she spun and stalked back to the cockpit. She snatched the ship's portable radio, clipped it to her belt, and grabbed Bartholomew by the collar, hoisting him out of his seat. Not waiting for him to get his balance, she half dragged him to the door and shoved him out. He tumbled to the ground and looked up at her as she leaped out of the cruiser and withdrew her knife.

He struggled to his knees and scrabbled on the cold grass to try to get away. She pounced on him like a lioness, flattened him on his stomach, and pricked his back with the knife. He tried to steel his body, but it trembled all the same.

"Iona!" Alexandria shouted from atop his back. "If you don't bring the mooring cap to me, I will stab Leo's body. If he dies, his soul will never be able to return to it."

Bartholomew glanced around, moving only his eyes. With mausolea all around, Iona could be hiding anywhere. Would she come out to save him? In her half-alive stupor, she might be too confused to figure out what to do.

"You have five seconds." Alexandria began a slow count. "One … two … three …"

Iona appeared from around an angel statue at a nearby mausoleum. She padded toward them, the mooring cap cradled in her palms.

When she arrived, Alexandria rose from Bartholomew and snatched the cap. "Good choice." She pushed the cap into her cloak pocket and the knife into its sheath. "I am a woman of my word, so I won't stab him, but I'm wondering what to do with you. I don't know what you heard or saw while I was hatching this part of my plan, and maybe you were able to read my thoughts since some are still present in your brain."

She detached the portable radio from her belt and turned a dial on its front. "Either way, you might know too much. My safest option is to kill you, but keeping you hostage is also valuable. Still, dragging you along with me could cause more trouble than you're worth."

Iona slowly backed away, her eyes wide, probably torn between trying to escape and hoping to rescue Leo's body. Yet, Alex didn't seem to pay attention to Iona's retreat. She pressed a button and held the radio unit close to her mouth. "Damien, it's time to mobilize. Your next assignment is Katherine Garrison. I can't have her calling the cruiser on the sly and controlling it by voice, so we'll have to change our schedule. Neutralize her as soon as possible."

Someone responded, but the words were unintelligible.

"And now to take care of another sly vixen." Alexandria reclipped the radio, strode to Iona, and grasped her wrist. "Cooperate fully, and both your body and Leo's body will stay alive." She knelt at Bartholomew's side and pulled Iona down with her. "First, we have to turn him over."

Still riding in Charlie's cloak, Iona focused on the foggy input. Alex rolled Bartholomew over to his back, grabbed his arms, and pulled him to a sitting position. "Both of you are physically compromised," Alex said to Iona, "so I will help you go to the mausoleum. We'll put him in the preservation machine to keep his body intact." Alex clutched his arm. "Go to the other side and help me get him up."

Iona concentrated once again and forced her body to obey. Although helping this witch stung like acid, it might be Leo's only hope. She half walked and half stumbled to the other arm and grabbed hold. Together, she and Alex hoisted him to his feet and balanced him on his stiff legs.

"Now we'll walk him to the mausoleum. No more than a dozen steps."

Iona braced his body with her arm around his waist while her shoulder pushed up against his ribs, but she was too short to give much support. With each step, he sagged further, his own support of his body weakening. By the time they reached the entry, they had to drag him across the threshold as his feet made twin trails through the scattered dirt and leaves.

Still holding him with one hand, Alex lifted a glass lid on a coffin-like box lying within a crypt. "Now we have to put him into this capsule. It preserved me for two centuries."

Iona nodded.

Alex gripped his arm firmly. "Now, Bartholomew, give us all you've got. We can't do this without your help."

He set his hands on the side of the capsule, gasping. "I'll do my best."

"On three. One … two … three." Alex and Iona hoisted while Bartholomew pushed with his arms and swung his legs up. He rolled with a thud into the capsule's bed, facing up.

"Although he is not a Reaper," Alex said as she positioned his limbs, "the system should keep his body from deteriorating for a while even if he dies. He doesn't have valves for fluid circulation, which means his maximum time after a possible demise is about twenty-four hours. If he does die, we'll have to hurry to get Leo's soul here."

Bartholomew breathed in rapid pulses. "How will anyone … know to come here?"

"I will contact Katherine and give her the location—assuming, of course, she cooperates with me." Alex withdrew a small camera from a belt sheath and took a picture of Iona standing next to the capsule. "I'm sure this photo will convince her to comply."

"Most likely." Bartholomew coughed and wheezed. "I feel cold, like a chill is crawling into my heart."

Alex gasped in mock surprise. "Really? That must be because I applied more paralysis ointment to your skin, and it's taking effect." She reattached the camera to her belt, moved a pair of tubes from the capsule, and reached up to grasp the lid. As she paused for a moment, a sneer dressed her face in pure hatred. "Go to hell, traitor."

His eyes widened. "Iona! I'm coming. I'll try to find you. Watch for me."

"Good luck with that." Alex closed the lid.

Iona tried to suck in a breath, but she couldn't draw in more than usual. This sicko witch had sealed Bart's fate. His soul would soon be ejected from Leo's body, and he would return to hell.

Alex walked to a machine sitting on a nearby cart and turned it on. A hiss emanated from the capsule. She looked at a meter on the front of the machine. "The battery has about nineteen hours remaining. Let's hope Katherine acquiesces to my demands quickly." She flipped a switch that turned on a bulb embedded in the machine. "You'll need this light."

Without another word, Alex walked out. Seconds later, the mausoleum's door swung closed with a dull thud, shutting them in and darkening the room, though the lamp on the machine provided enough light to see the capsule.

Iona walked to the door and pushed on it, then pulled on a metal handle. The door wouldn't budge. She was locked inside, unable to escape. She returned to the capsule and stared through the glass lid. Leo's body had already stopped breathing. It was too late to help him, but maybe somehow Bart would help her and Leo, even from hell.

Facing the door, Iona sat with her back against the capsule and folded her hands in her lap. There was nothing more to do here. It was time to get some help.

She pulled her senses away from her body and refocused on the surrounding cloak. "Charlie, how close are we to the Lake of Fire?"

"Not far." She gasped for breath, obviously tired. "Five minutes."

Iona whispered, "Five minutes. I can do this."

"Is something wrong?"

"Lots of things are wrong, but listen. Watch for Bartholomew's soul. I'll explain how I know later, but I think he wants to help us."

"Really? That's hard to believe. He's always been a self-serving viper."

"Yeah, well, maybe he's trying to change. I know what that's like. Don't you?"

Charlie sighed. "I do know. Good point and well struck."

"Just let me know if you see him, and we'll see what he's up to."

"Understood."

Iona rode on quietly, bouncing with Charlie's strides. It felt so strange to be sequestered with a keyhole view into the real world, able to operate her body like a marionette with several broken strings—helpful but frustrating. Yet, being stuck within these rough fibers was worse—helpless to do anything at all. "How close are we now?"

Charlie's respirations slowed a bit. "I can see the Lake of Fire. Two minutes. Prepare yourself for a terrifying experience."

Kat switched the temple computer's radio to the ham frequency, trying to slow her breathing as she called, "Jack, it's Kat. Are you there?"

"No, it's Trudy." The response crackled with static. "Jack's at the relay. We're getting a nasty storm. What's up?"

"Yeah, Jack said a storm was coming. Did you call Ben with an update yet?"

"No. We went dark until a couple of minutes ago. Jack must've got the antenna up again. Probably on his way back."

"I had a conversation with Alex and got another confirmation that Leo and Iona are in hell, like Jack told me. Alex resurrected her body, and her soul's inside it now. I don't know what she has in mind for Iona's body, but she has the cruiser, and she's using Iona for leverage to keep me from calling it to take control."

"Conniving witch."

"Yeah. I had different words a while ago. But, yeah."

"All right. We'll try to call Ben again. But once he gets confirmation and even an inkling of an exit strategy, you know what he'll do."

Kat bit her lip hard, tears brimming. "He'll charge straight into hell."

"Right. Without hesitation. Just wanted to make sure you're on board with that."

"No choice. I have to be on board. It's going to happen." Kat brushed a tear away. "I'm his wife. I believe in him."

"I'll let him know you said that." Trudy sighed. "Listen, Kat. We've been to hell and back before. We know it can be done. And Ben's a warrior. He'll be all right."

Kat concealed a sniffle. "I know. We can trust Ben."

"After we contact him and as soon as this storm blows over, Jack and I are going to try to bug out of here. With Alex's laborers coming, no use waiting around."

"You'll travel on foot? It's more than twenty miles to the nearest road. And it's dark. No daylight for weeks or months. No one will be driving by to give you a ride."

"Yeah, that's what *I* said, but you know Jack. Getting him to hole up and wait when there's a job to do will make him a ticking time bomb. I'd rather face the cold and dark than watch him explode."

"I get that. Jack's going to be pacing day and night if he's stuck there. Anyway, try to keep in touch the best you can. On my end, I'll see if I can call for a vehicle to come out and pick you up."

"Great. If you can do that in the next hour, give us a heads up. Otherwise, we're hoofing it."

"You got it." Kat began typing on her keyboard to search for a military outpost in northern Alaska that might be able to send a vehicle. "I've been listening to the spy bug I planted on the cruiser. Since Alex turned the cruiser's radio off, there's no interference. Nothing coming through so far, but if I get any actionable intel, I'll let you know."

"Hello, Katherine," a man said behind her.

Kat spun in her chair toward the voice. Damien stood a mere five steps away, a rifle at his shoulder. "Damien!" she called, loudly enough for Trudy to hear. "How did you get in? The vault door is triple locked, and I sealed the vent."

"There are access channels you don't know about." He aimed the rifle at her face. "Turn the radio off. Now."

Kat pivoted and tapped the proper command on the keyboard. "It's off."

"Yes, I can tell." He lowered the rifle to his hip, keeping it aimed at her, his finger on the trigger. "Alexandria ordered me to kill you, but maybe you and I can come to an agreement that will keep you alive."

"Ben," Trudy called through the mesa radio's headphones. "It's me. Trudy."

Ben adjusted the microphone stem. "I'm here. What's up?"

"It's all confirmed. Leo's and Iona's souls are in hell. And get this. Alex's soul is possessing her own body now. Some kind of zombie-rising-from-the-dead thing, I guess. And she's holding Iona's body hostage to keep us at bay. Apparently Iona's somehow staying alive without a soul. We've seen that before when the vaccine purged souls. Good thing she doesn't have that violence-inducing payload in her."

"Okay. That settles it. I'm going after them."

"Hold your horses, cowboy. We got some intel for a possible exit strategy. A Reaper named Charlotte patrols hell. Bart thinks she might know how you can get out of there. Hell's a big place, so finding her isn't a sure thing at all, but Bart thinks she might find you. Some kind of soul-locator skill. It's not much, but it's something."

Ben nodded. "It's enough to go on."

"Figured that, but before you leave, think you can send the SUV back here? We're kind of marooned in Alaska, and we have to get home to help Kat. I was talking to her and got interrupted. Lots of static in the transmission. In fact, Jack's out at the relay station right now holding wires together so we can talk. It's super windy outside.

Anyway, I think Damien showed up at the vault. We need to get back to the temple and try to help her."

Ben clenched his teeth, his ears burning. Kat might be in trouble. Diving into hell while she had to deal with an alien and Alex at the same time felt like abandonment.

"Ben. You still there?"

"Yeah. Just thinking about our options."

"Well, stop thinking so much. No one else can go get Iona and Leo. Trust us to handle the rest. We trained for this. Well, not exactly this. No drills can prepare you for battling the queen of hell, but you know what I mean."

Ben heaved a deep sigh. "You're right. You guys can handle it. I'll make sure the SUV is on the way before I go."

"Got it. Be careful. And, by the way, Kat says she believes in you. Thought you'd want to know."

Ben's cheeks flushed hot. "Yeah. That helps. A lot."

"Ciao, Brother Ben. We'll pray for you."

"Thanks. I'll need it. Talk to you later." Ben removed the headphones and looked down at the mirror. Caligar was nowhere in sight. Ben pivoted toward the mesa's stairway just as Caligar ascended to the top.

As he approached, he steered clear of Harrid's corpse. "The portal is now operational."

"Great. Thank you." Ben gave Caligar a summary of what he had recently learned. When he finished, he added, "So I have to go to hell, and I need you to send the SUV back to Earth. Are both possible?"

"My device's pullback capability is able to make the SUV fall slowly enough, but I'm not sure how close to the Alaska tower the SUV will land. If it is too far away, it might not be able to drive that far through the snow."

"Yes, I can see why that might be a problem."

"I have an idea for a solution that involves some castoff parts of an all-terrain vehicle I was constructing and never finished. I will see what I can do."

Ben clasped Caligar's arm. "Thank you again, my friend. If you see my family, tell them that I love them."

"I will. And I am grateful that you consider me a friend."

Ben glanced back toward the distant forest. Winella probably still had Harrid's rifle. "Do you have any weapons I can borrow besides the bow and arrow? I'm not much of an archer."

Caligar slid a knife sheath from his belt and handed it to Ben. "I have this."

"It'll help." Ben added the sheath to his belt. "Thanks."

"You are welcome, Benjamin. I hope you have a successful journey." Caligar stepped to the controls and made a few adjustments. "The portal to hell is now open."

"Thanks again." Ben refocused on the mirror. The last time he made this entry, he had no choice. Caligar threw him in. Now he had to leap into hell of his own accord. Maybe it would be best to just shut off his brain for a second and go for it. Thinking about it might make him freeze up.

After grabbing a pair of gloves from his belt and putting them on, he ran to the edge of the mesa and threw himself as far out as he could. As he sailed through the air, he whispered, "God, help us all."

# Chapter Eleven

As the cloak's undulating movements slowed, Iona steeled herself. Charlie's words seemed so ominous—*a terrifying experience*. The abyss was gut-wrenching enough. How much worse would the Lake of Fire be?

"We are here," Charlie said, her breathless voice filtering through the fibers. "Brace yourself for the extraction process. It is not as painful as the absorption, but it will be uncomfortable."

Iona clenched her eyes shut. "Go ahead."

As before, her body stretched in all directions, as if someone were pulling her arms and legs at the same time. After a few seconds, the sensation of weight on her feet gave evidence that she now stood on her own. Then heat coursed along her skin, if a soul's exterior could be called skin. It stung, but not badly.

"We're done, Iona."

She opened her eyes. Charlie stood at her side, one of the headphones propped an inch above her ear. She stared at a huge expanse of darkness, like an ocean of ink had been spilled with no end in sight ahead or to either side. The air immediately above the expanse shimmered like heat waves, and above that the air turned to rising vapor that shot upward and dispersed high in the slate gray sky. High-pitched screams emanated from the vapor, as if they carried the voices within the mist, probably the reason for Charlie's headphones. "The Lake of Fire, I assume?"

Charlie nodded, her mouth and nose covered with a camo mask, muffling her voice. "Black fire. Pure darkness. The river Leo fell into feeds this lake, and it flows at a fast rate. By now, he is out there. Somewhere."

Iona inhaled through her nose. A sulfur stench permeated the air—noxious and nauseating. If the odor really was worse for the living, as Charlie had said, it was no wonder she needed a mask. "The lake's so big. How can we find him?"

"I am drawn to displaced souls. The other souls in the lake belong there, the most despicable humans of all. But at the end of days, all who are in the abyss will join them in everlasting torment."

Iona shuddered. Although the idea of everlasting torment seemed harsh, this might not be the best time to question the justice of the situation. "So that's your job? To find out-of-place souls and put them in the right places?"

"That is somewhat accurate, though it is not the entire story."

"If they're all coming to this lake eventually, why does it matter if they're here now or in the abyss or in Alex's castle?"

"Because some souls, like yours, don't belong in hell at all. But enough of that. We have to venture into the Lake of Fire."

Iona drew a step back. "You mean wade in it like we're going for a swim?"

Charlie laughed under her breath. "No. That would be impossible. Far too painful for you, and I would be burned to a crisp in seconds. I have summoned a boat."

"Summoned? I didn't hear you say anything."

"My presence summoned it. The keeper of the exit gate has extraordinary eyesight and has surely seen me by now. The boat will arrive soon."

Iona scanned the blackness—completely empty. "But there isn't a boat as far as the eye can see."

"Ah!" Charlie pointed. "There it is."

Squinting, Iona looked again. A shadowy, canoe-shaped craft floated toward them, large enough for two people, maybe three, though it had only two benches—one near the front and one near the back. "I see it."

When the canoe arrived, its shimmering black bow slid over the shoreline and stopped with a short hiss. Iona touched the hull. The material felt like some sort of metal, radiating warmth. "I assume it's ultra-resistant to heat."

"Without a doubt." Charlie climbed in, sat on the rear bench, and picked up a pair of paddles that appeared to be made of the same material. Iona joined her and sat on the front bench.

Charlie gave her a paddle and raised her voice to be heard over the surrounding screams. "Let's push off."

Working together, they pressed their paddles against the ground and shoved the canoe into the lake. With each stroke, Iona lifted her paddle. White vapor rose from the blade, and thick black goo dripped back into the lake like molten rock.

Iona also raised her voice. "Obviously capsizing is the worst possible option."

Charlie grimaced. "It would be excruciatingly painful for both of us, fatal to me but not to you. If you could endure the pain, you could swim back and wade to shore. Unlike the others here, the lake cannot hold you. You are of the light, not the darkness."

"Did you extract me from your cloak so I could help you haul Leo into the boat?"

"That's one reason. I won't know if I'll need your help until we find him. I'll explain more later." She dug her paddle into the fire and made the boat accelerate. "I sense Leo now. Let's hurry."

Iona paddled harder. The heat rising from the lake grew more and more intense, making her wince, and the odor worsened. When she tried to push even harder, her paddle slipped from her hand. Before she could catch it, the blade slapped the surface and sent a spray of black fire that struck her leg and sizzled. She yelped, then bit her lip.

Charlie used a cloak sleeve to brush the goopy stuff away, but some of it remained adhered. Pain roared up into Iona's back, sending rippling shockwaves along her spine and into her brain. Her entire body quaked. A scream begged to erupt, but she bit her lip again to stifle it. If the fire hurt this much from a mere splash, how bad was the pain for the souls in its depths? How could they tolerate being submerged, coated with blistering torture for all eternity?

Charlie spoke through her mask in a smooth, even tone. "Try to put the pain out of your mind. Remember that Leo is out here somewhere. Think about how bad the pain must be for him. Let your passion for his safety drive you."

Nodding, her lip still locked between her teeth, Iona picked up her paddle and continued laboring through the strokes, harder than ever now. Charlie did the same, propelling the canoe faster and faster across the black expanse.

Charlie slowed her strokes and gazed farther ahead. "We're getting closer. Much closer." She turned the canoe a few degrees to the right and paddled on, still at a slower pace. Iona did the same, gritting her teeth as the pain from her wound assaulted her senses. Like Charlie had said, she had to put it out of her mind ... for Leo.

Soon, a moan entered her mind, then words ran along the lake's surface and drifted into her ears. "Help me. It hurts so much."

Iona looked at Charlie as she paddled on. Would it be all right to talk to one of these souls? Charlie hadn't warned her not to. She scanned the surface but couldn't find anyone—no heads bobbing, not even a ripple other than the ones their paddles traced in the inky goo.

Loosening her tense jaw, Iona whispered, "How could I possibly help you?"

The voice returned, closer now. "Ask your Reaper to take me out of here. She has the power."

"But why? Don't you deserve to be here?"

"I did many terrible things during my life, and I am so, so sorry. The torment here has opened my eyes to my mistakes. I am begging for another chance."

Iona swallowed hard. Another chance? A plea to change? Others had given her another chance, allowing her to change, though she changed without dying first. "But isn't it too late for that?"

"No. There is one chance remaining. Ask your Reaper. She knows."

"Why don't you ask her yourself?"

"Iona!" Charlie banged her paddle against the side of the canoe. "Don't talk to the souls. They prey on your pity."

Iona winced at her harsh rebuke, then replied in a lamenting tone. "I feel so sorry for them. I know how much that stuff hurts. And he asked a good question."

"I heard it. I'm keeping one headphone off my ear so I can listen to you." Charlie blew an annoyed sigh. "He asked you instead of me about another chance because I know his repentance is a sham. These souls will say anything to get out of here. They are masters of the art of deception."

Iona let her shoulders sag. "Okay. But I can't blame them for wanting to get out of here."

"I see that he already planted a seed of doubt in your mind." Charlie leaned closer and grasped Iona's wrist. "Concentrate on finding Leo. Nothing else matters."

A small object bobbed in the lake ahead of the boat. "I see something." Iona pointed. "There."

Charlie turned toward the front. "Yes. It's Leo. He's struggling to stay above the surface."

They both paddled with all their might. A few seconds later, the object clarified—a man's head rising above the surface and then submerging again, gasping for air with each repetition.

Charlie raised a hand. "Put your paddle down. We'll glide from here." She withdrew a pair of gloves from her cloak pocket and put them on. "Make room. I will try to pull him in myself. If I can't, you'll have to help me."

Iona nodded and shifted as far back in the canoe as she could.

When they drifted to the man's side, Charlie leaned over, grabbed Leo under his shoulders with both hands, and hoisted him up. His chest hit the side of the canoe and snagged there, fiery goo dripping from his clothes.

Iona lunged, wrapped her arms around his waist, and heaved him the rest of the way in. The canoe rocked for a moment before settling as Leo lay on the canoe's floor, writhing and moaning, no longer wearing his cloak.

Iona's sleeves sizzled. Material burned away. She stripped the torn parts off and slung them into the lake. Just as she turned to check on Leo, Charlie knelt and covered him with her cloak. "Stay back, Iona. He is in agony. Only I can help him now."

Iona shifted away, trembling as she watched. Charlie closed her eyes and concentrated while Leo's moans continued. Second by second, he grew quieter, and the lump under the cloak shrank. After what seemed like a full minute, Charlie settled back on her bench and heaved a sigh, vapor rising from her cloak. "Leo is comfortable now."

Iona blew a sigh of her own. "Good. Thank you."

"Yes, be thankful, but we can't rest." Charlie picked up her paddle. "If we stay in one place, the condemned souls will soon attack the boat. Since their appeals for mercy failed, they will turn to violence. It's in their nature."

Iona settled to her seat and dipped her paddle into the black fire. As the canoe continued skimming across the lake, the sky grew darker. She looked back at the shore they had left, now barely in sight. Light in the sky cast a clarifying sheen across the black expanse, revealing more objects bobbing on the surface. Some appeared to be moving in their direction with each reappearance of their goo-coated heads, but they were too slow to catch up.

"It's so sad," Iona said. "If it's in their nature to be violent, how could they help but be violent? I mean, they had no choice, right?"

Charlie continued paddling without looking back. "They had a choice. They became violent by nature because they corrupted themselves through their own violent actions. They have nobody to blame but themselves. But don't focus on them. Like I said before, they will use your pity against you."

"Okay. Then on to new stuff. We both promised to explain things later. I'll go first. While I was in your cloak, I somehow got connected to my body on Earth. I could see what my body saw and hear what it heard. Everything was warped and twisted, but I could make it out. And I could move my body, but it was super hard to do."

As they paddled on, Iona gave Charlie a rundown of what happened at the cemetery. During the story, Charlie glanced at her from time to time, flinching at the mention of Alex's soul getting restored to her body. When Iona finished, she added, "And that's why we need to watch for Bart. I think he's coming back to hell to help us stop Alex."

Charlie nodded. "That could be. He wouldn't be the first condemned soul who appeared to be altruistic."

Iona narrowed her eyes. "*Appeared to be?* How can it be wrong to want to help us?"

"The action wouldn't be wrong, but it's likely that he is driven by hate and thoughts of revenge. Or maybe he's seeking a reward."

Iona drew her head back. "That's a dark outlook. Do you doubt everyone's motivations?"

"Did I say that I do?"

"You're dodging the question."

"Because it's a foolish question. I was talking about condemned souls, and you expanded the topic to everyone."

"Okay, you're right. You caught me. Can you answer the question anyway?"

Charlie gave Iona a brief glare, then focused on her never-ending paddle strokes. "I doubt the motivations of most people, but I don't doubt yours. I can see that you are a child of the light, and I know for a fact that Bart is a child of darkness. Regarding Leo, I'm not sure, but I am concerned."

Iona gave her a reluctant nod. Her own doubts about Leo rose from somewhere deep inside, doubts she had suppressed ever since he suddenly became her ally. He said Charlie jilted him, but was that the whole story? Maybe he did something that made Charlie want to leave him. "Why are you concerned about Leo?"

"I told you I would explain something about him later. Now is a good time." Charlie pulled her paddle through another deep stroke.

"I was concerned about being able to draw him out of the Lake of Fire because the lake keeps its own. That is, it won't allow those who belong here to escape except under extraordinary circumstances. Darkness embraces darkness, while it expels the light. This lake could no more hold you than a dark room could prevent a light from dispelling its influence.

"Yet, I'm not as sure about Leo. It took both of us to drag him out of the lake. Darkness recognized itself in his heart and tried to embrace him. I suspect that both light and darkness dwell within him. Otherwise we would not have been able to pull him out at all. The two forces are at war in his heart, and my guess is that he has allied himself with the light of late. Otherwise, you and he would not have such a close friendship."

"Yeah. We're close. Real close. But does the darkness in him mean he won't be able to escape hell?"

"I don't think so. If Alex could leave, then surely Leo can, though I don't know how to accomplish that feat yet. I have no experience in that area. To this point, my role here has been to find wayward souls and return them to where they belong. Sometimes they escape from the abyss, and I take them back there. Alex is one of the few I couldn't capture. If I had, I would have thrown her directly into the Lake of Fire. She was too dangerous to leave in the abyss."

"Why is that important? I mean, what does it matter if they're in the abyss or wandering around? They're still in hell."

"Because outside the abyss, the craftier souls can cause mischief, or they can create a comfortable situation for themselves. Alex did both. And now she is planning to terrorize Earth. She couldn't have launched her plan from the abyss."

Iona firmed her lips and nodded. "Fair point. Now back to Leo. Are you saying you've never dealt with someone like him before?"

"Exactly. During my stay here, no disembodied soul has ever escaped hell, because they can't leave without being housed in a living human. Yet, there is a possible way around that, and I'm sure it will work for you because you are filled with light, but maybe not for Leo. The darkness within him might make it impossible."

Iona watched Charlie's relentless paddle strokes. She was so strong, so determined, and she wasn't doing any of this for herself. She was the model of loving sacrifice. "How long have you been here?"

"It's hard to track time in hell, but I think it's been about fifteen years. I was identified as a Reaper during my teen years, and the powers-that-be assigned me to come here to do this job. As you can probably imagine, being a soul shepherd in hell wasn't exactly appealing to a teenager. I rebelled and ran off to do as I pleased."

"And what was that?"

She glanced at Iona for a moment, her eyes giving away a hidden smile as she spoke through her mask. "I became an intellectual. Highly educated. I earned degrees with honors from esteemed institutions, and the adulations filled me with pride and arrogance. In short, I was a selfish pig. I was also considered beautiful in appearance, and I used my looks and intellect to get what I pleased, especially from men with lonely hearts or wandering eyes. I used those men for my pleasure and promotion."

"So you had a dark heart."

"The darkest. And I inflicted a lot of pain and suffering on people who didn't deserve it. When I hit bottom, I begged God to forgive me through the blood sacrifice of Jesus the Messiah." Now looking directly at Iona, Charlie blinked her misting eyes. "Are you familiar with him? We sang about his sacrifice, but did you understand the words?"

Iona nodded. "I believe in Jesus and what he did, if that's what you mean. My parents taught me."

Charlie faced the front again, still paddling. "Good. Sacrificial death is the key to your deliverance. Anyway, back to my story. God sent an angel to bring me here, to the place I was supposed to serve when he first called me to be a Reaper."

"So now you inflict pain and suffering on souls who *do* deserve it."

Charlie chuckled. "Trust me. That ironic twist has crossed my mind many times. But now, with you and Leo, I might be able to finally bring relief instead of pain. If I can get you out of hell, I will feel like my purpose has been fulfilled."

"Do you think you'll ever get to leave hell yourself?"

Charlie's shoulders drooped. "Probably not until I die. Only then will the angel search for a younger Reaper to take my place. But since my heart is filled with light now, my soul will not stay here."

Tears crept into Iona's eyes. "Do you *want* to leave before you die? Maybe you can pray for the angel to—"

"Hush, Iona. I want only what God wants. He is with me, even here. I will be content."

"More rehearsed words?"

"Yes, but I make no apologies. I keep quoting truths to myself until they are ingrained in me, and they naturally come out when needed. It's the only way to keep my sanity."

One of the tears trickled down Iona's cheek. She brushed it away. "Fair enough. I've done that myself."

Charlie stopped paddling and stared ahead. "I see the other side. From here to the shore the danger will grow. The souls who are thrown directly into the Lake of Fire come from that direction, and they usually stay in the area, hoping that the angel who put them here will respond to their cries."

Iona looked that way. As Charlie had said, a shoreline was now in view, though still a long way off. "But not a chance that'll happen, right?"

Charlie shook her head sadly. "The angel is never mistaken."

"And now we have to paddle with all our might to get past the desperate souls, right?"

"Right." Charlie again dug her paddle into the fiery goo. "Let's go."

Kat rose from her seat, crossed her arms, and glared at Damien. "Do you think I would be stupid enough to come here without a way to counter an attack from you?"

He kept the rifle aimed at her. "I admit that I was surprised to find you unguarded, but I assume that's because you're short on allies. They're occupied elsewhere."

"True. They are. But I'm not without a way to defend myself."

Damien glanced all around before focusing again on Kat. "I'm sure you could attack me and relieve me of my weapon if I let you come close, which is why I'm keeping my distance. If you move even an inch in my direction, I will shoot you. You know I will. I've shot you before."

Kat cast a stealthy glance at the vacuum, still on the desk. No problem reaching it when the time came. She shifted her stance into a cocky pose. "But you need something from me. I'm guessing the blood you collected wasn't helpful."

"It was helpful. It allowed me to get past the first level of security." Damien held out his hand. "Now I need a key. It wasn't at the bank, so I assume that you have it. If you give it to me, I will let you live."

Kat lifted her brow in mock surprise. "Oh? A key? Well, supposing I have this key and give it to you, how do I know that you won't shoot me anyway?"

"You don't." He lowered his hand. "But rest assured that I will certainly shoot you if you don't give me the key. I must have it because it unlocks the only way to stop the queen of hell from executing her plans. I oppose her, not you. Perhaps that will be enough for you to choose to help me."

"If you want me to believe you, tell me her plans."

Damien frowned. "She wouldn't confide in me. She merely said that she would be the queen of the world. But she is perfectly confident that I won't oppose her because the Refectors, as they are sometimes called, are little more than worker drones. They will obey their queen without question." He patted his upper arm at the typical injection site. "Alexandria put a coding sequence into one batch of the vaccine that invades the victim's brain cells to recognize her voice as that of their queen. We included that formula with one hundred of the leading influencers in the world. The rest of the vaccine was used to purge souls so that they could provide energy for her escape from hell."

Kat gave him a derisive laugh. "Then I suppose you're one of her obedient worker drones."

"So she thinks. I faked my vaccination but still took on a Refector so that I could have the powers it gives. My human soul still has control of my brain. The Refector is livid, of course, but it has no power to change the situation."

Kat uncrossed her arms. "Let's say I help you, what's your end game? Your motivations?"

Damien rolled his eyes. "My motivations are not your concern. What is your answer? Will you help me, or not?"

Kat pushed her hands into her pockets. "Let me put it this way—"

Damien fired the rifle. The bullet zipped past Kat's ear and slammed into the wall display behind her. The screen cracked, and a wisp of smoke seeped from the bullet hole as the entire display flickered, then turned black. He fired again, smashing the monitor on the desktop. His voice calm, he spoke slowly. "What is in your pockets, Katherine? Pull whatever it is out slowly or the next bullet will drill a hole between your eyes."

"Okay. Okay. Cool your jets." Kat slid the remote from her pocket. "It controls the wall display."

"Prove it."

"I can't, you moron. You shot out both monitors." She extended the remote in her palm. "It's not a weapon, if that's what you're scared of. See for yourself."

"Slide it on the floor to me."

"Not a problem." Kat set the remote on the floor and gave it a shove. It slid to a stop near Damien's shoes.

Keeping the rifle's aim on Kat, he picked up the remote and looked it over. "It seems harmless."

"Of course it is. If it was a weapon, I wouldn't've given it to you."

"True." He pressed a button on the remote.

Pops echoed from a side wall. Prongs with trailing wires shot out and struck Damien's side and leg. As the prongs sizzled, he stiffened, dropped the rifle, and fell to his back, his eyes wide.

Kat grabbed the vacuum and ran to Damien as he writhed in jerking twitches. Seconds later, gray mist flowed from his ear. Kat turned the vacuum on and sucked the smoke into the unit. After nearly a minute, the emissions ceased.

She turned the vacuum off, set it on the floor, and knelt next to Damien. The surge of electricity had stopped, and he appeared to be unconscious. From her back pocket, she withdrew the handcuffs, turned Damien to his side, and fastened his wrists behind his back.

Still on her knees, she scooped up the vacuum, opened the access panel, and removed the debris collection bag. After dropping the bag on the floor, she pulled a matchbook from her pocket, struck a match, and lit the bag. It burst into flames. The blaze emitted a high-pitched squeal, as if the Refector were screaming in agony.

When the flames died down, Kat turned toward Damien and patted his cheek. "Time to wake up, creep."

He blinked his eyes open, his face ashen. "What happened?"

"A change of plans." She pulled the prongs out and slung them away. "I have the key you want. Let's discuss how we can stop the queen of hell."

# Chapter Twelve

Ben landed softly in the now-familiar forest, if it could be called a forest with its twisted trees that looked as if they hadn't sprouted a leaf in centuries. Without a guide this time, he ran straight toward the thorny hedge that led to Alex's domain. From there, maybe he could track Iona or find Charlotte.

When he arrived at the narrow gap in the hedge, he withdrew the knife from his belt and whacked at the protruding thorns as he inched his way through, his clothes snagging and tearing. After a few minutes, he broke free and jogged toward the castle, the knife still in his grip.

Soon, the castle came into view, but it now lay in ruins—gutted and broken down, as if it had been the target of a wrecking ball.

A man dressed in jeans and T-shirt stood on the drawbridge, a hand at his brow as if searching for something in the distance. When he saw Ben, he waved both arms. "Ben Garrison! Over here."

Ben slowed to a stop a few steps away from the end of the drawbridge next to a pile of dead beasts—Alex's pets. "Bart? Is that you?"

"Bartholomew, but you can call me Bart if you wish." He walked to Ben's end of the drawbridge and faced him. "You were in a drug-induced stupor when you saw me last, so your lack of recognition is understandable."

Ben tightened his grip on the knife. "I was awake enough to know that you're in league with Alex."

"A pretense, I assure you. I exited hell in Leo's body, and when I tried to stop Alexandria's plans to resurrect her body, she killed me, and now I'm back in hell."

Ben felt his mouth drop open. "Killed you? Does that mean Leo's dead?"

"Well … in a way. His body is in a preservation capsule, which will keep his corpse viable, but it won't last long. Iona is with him—that is, her body is with his. It's a long story that I will be happy to tell, but I should do so while we're traveling."

Ben slid the knife back to its sheath. "To find Leo's and Iona's souls."

"Of course. I suspect that Leo's soul has an item that you'll need to stop Alex. I searched the castle but couldn't find it."

"What item?"

"I will explain the details when we find it. If we cannot find it, there is no reason to explain." Bart walked toward the pile of corpses. "Come. I'll show you our first clue."

Ben followed him to a tree where one of the dead beasts sat with its back against the trunk. Bart pointed at the beast's forehead. "It says, 'Seeking shelter. Look for signs. I and L.' I assume it means Iona and Leo."

"Without a doubt." Ben stooped next to the corpse and picked up a twig, one end covered with goo, likely Leo's makeshift pen. "Leo is a huntsman. He knows the value of a trail. That's why he wrote to look for signs."

"Such as?"

"Something less obvious than this one." Ben rose and tossed the twig to the ground. "It was designed to get our attention. The next one will be harder to find so only an ally can track them. He wouldn't want to leave an obvious trail for an enemy."

Bart nodded. "I hope you're right. My concern is that a Reaper named Charlotte might have found them. She patrols the area and has long desired to capture Alexandria and me, especially Alexandria. If Charlotte collects them, Leo won't be able to give further tracking signs. Although she might be able to help them, we won't be able to follow as easily."

"I heard about Charlotte. I hope she'll help us leave hell."

116

"Don't get your hopes up. Although she is highly skilled and knowledgeable, she has to stay in hell until her term as a Reaper expires. Still, if anyone can help you, she can."

Ben gestured toward the castle with a gloved hand. "Speaking of leaving, how did you get to Alex's forest? I thought condemned souls went to the abyss."

"I went to the abyss, but after learning how to escape the first time I arrived there many years ago, it was a simple matter to replicate the feat, though I had to wait until the other souls weren't paying attention. Fortunately, they are all drawn to the mirror Leo and Iona restored to the abyss. I didn't have to wait long. If you want to know how I climbed out—"

"I don't. I'm heading for the abyss to look for Leo's signs. If you want to help, stay with me."

"Gladly." Bart extended a hand toward the abyss. "Lead the way at whatever speed suits you."

Ben took off at a trot. Bart caught up and jogged at his side, keeping up without a problem. His disembodied state probably made him lighter, enabling him to move with ease.

As they ran, Bart told Ben about how he took possession of Leo's body in the healing pool, ascended through the portal with Alex, who was in the guise of Iona, and returned to Earth where Alex took over the angel cruiser and resurrected her body. He also included how Alex paralyzed him and put Leo's body in a preservation capsule. As he spoke, his anger and venom proved that he hated Alex with a passion. Along the way, evenly spaced holes in the ground provided hope that Leo had continued leaving signs.

Seconds after he finished, they broke out of the woods and stopped near the abyss where they had leaped into the portal's upward pull. Ben studied the ground in every direction. So far, no new signs from Leo.

"You won't find footprints," Bart said. "It never rains here, so no mud to leave a track in." He walked to the right, plucked something from the ground, and showed it to Ben. "A physical hair, not from a soul. Does it belong to anyone in your crew?"

Ben pinched the strand of red hair and studied it. "Iona's hair is this color, but she's not physical anymore."

"Then it's probably Charlotte's. She's a redhead. We should assume she found them."

Ben dropped the hair. "Where would she take them?"

"From my few encounters with her, I found her to be diligent, patient, not quick to judge, which is why she didn't collect me the moment we met. Since Leo's and Iona's souls are so unusual, seeing that they don't belong here in hell at all, she might have led them to her refuge to investigate them further."

"Do you know where her refuge is?"

Bart shook his head. "She mentioned it once, a place to protect herself from the hellcats at night. As you might expect, she would want to keep her refuge's location a secret from Alexandria. Charlotte hoped to capture her and throw her into the abyss or perhaps the Lake of Fire, which is another reason she didn't grab me right away. She thought I might provide a means to get to Alexandria."

"Understood." Ben drew a mental path from where they exited the forest to where Bart found the hair, then extended the line beyond that point, curving it around the edge of the abyss. A small, dark object lay on the ground a hundred feet or so away, barely in view.

Ben jogged to the spot and picked up a marble-sized smoke bomb. When Bart joined him, Ben displayed the bomb in his palm. "Leo carries these."

"And only an ally would know that, as you said." Bart eyed the smoke bomb. "It's not a physical object. It is a soulish copy of what he carried on Earth, and it will soon vanish as would any such object that separates from his soulish body. The same would be true of his clothing or a strand of his hair. Since Charlotte is alive and physical, she doesn't have the same limitations."

"Which means any other smoke bombs he left behind won't be there long."

"Correct. Also, his supply will be limited. He'll need a clever way to continue leaving signs."

"Maybe. From this point on, only an ally would be on his trail. The next sign doesn't have to be so personal."

Bart gave Ben an affirming nod. "You would have made a good huntsman yourself."

"I don't have the nose for it." Ben turned toward a forest in the distance. "Time to go. Faster now."

"Again, set the pace, and I will match it."

Ben ran toward the forest while scanning the ground. Every few steps, he came across a hole punched in the hard-packed dirt—more of Leo's work. Bart again ran alongside until they entered the woods. Ben decelerated to dodge trees while still looking for signs.

Here, broken twigs proved easy to spot, some probably stepped on while others might have been intentionally broken off low branches and left on the trail. After a few minutes, they came to a tree with an egg-shaped structure built within its woody network. Made with intertwining branches and vines, it looked big enough to hold at least two people. "Charlotte's refuge?" Ben asked.

Bart looked up at the structure. "Could be. It's high enough to keep the hellcats out. Low enough to climb in and out of, perhaps with a ladder. I can't tell if anyone's inside. The gaps are too small."

Ben peered through a hole in the structure's bottom. A coil of ladder rungs lay in view. "I think it's vacant." He scanned the ground. Several long white fibers lay here and there. He picked one up and looked it over.

"More hair?" Bart asked.

Ben nodded. "But too thick to be from a human. I'm guessing horsehair from a mane or tail."

"Hmmm. It's physical, not soulish." Bart plucked another hair from the ground and eyed it closely. "It's violin bow hair. Alexandria owned a violin, and I'm certain it had some kind of power, though

I don't know what it could do. Maybe Leo and Iona discovered its abilities and brought it along with them."

"Then how did it lose the hairs? There must be more than twenty on the ground."

Bart strode to the shelter's tree and ran a hand along the trunk. "Scratches. Deep ones." He pried something small and dark from one of the marks and showed it to Ben. "A hellcat claw."

Ben eyed the long, sharp claw. It could easily slice a victim into shreds. "Maybe the hellcats trampled the bow while clawing to get up to the shelter."

"Quite likely." Bart tossed the claw away. "Then the cats left when they decided their quest was futile, or maybe when dawn arrived. They are normally nocturnal beasts, though they are also opportunistic and will attack during daylight hours if prey is easily available."

"Interesting." Ben scanned the forest floor. Knobby roots protruded everywhere. No sign of Leo's holes. Maybe the roots made penetration impossible.

About twenty paces away, another bow hair lay on a root. Ben hurried to it and picked it up. "Okay. A new sign. Let's look for more hairs."

With Bart following, Ben ran in the direction the latest hair indicated and found more, spaced at increasing intervals. After nearly a mile, a chasm appeared. As he drew near, he slowed, looking in each direction for a way to cross, maybe a log bridge or a hanging vine, but he found nothing.

At the edge of the chasm, a dark cloak lay spread across the ground. Ben crouched next to it and lifted a sleeve. "This is Leo's."

When Bart arrived, he knelt and touched the cloak's back. "Not a good sign. It's badly scratched. But one good sign is that the cloak hasn't disappeared yet. Leo left it here fairly recently."

Ben looked over the edge of the chasm. Far below, an orange river ran at a quick pace. "Is that lava?"

"Yes. Falling in would mean certain death for a living human like you. For me, it would only mean intense pain. It flows into the Lake of Fire where it turns into superheated blackness."

Ben lifted his brow. "The Lake of Fire? The one mentioned in the Bible?"

"The same. Where all condemned souls will eventually be deposited." Bart tapped a finger on his chin. "The only destination beyond this chasm is the lake, at least as far as I know. I wonder why Charlotte would take them there."

As Ben imagined the terror of the lake—eternal burning in molten rock and scalding sulfur—he shuddered. "She wouldn't throw them in the lake, would she?"

"Not likely. Charlotte is fastidious. Never departs from her principles, much like another Reaper I knew in my day, but that's another story. In any case, I think we should go to the lake to see what we can learn."

"Can we follow the river of lava to get there?"

Bart waved a hand. "No, no. We would have to cross a deep swamp that's infested with fire snakes. And there are bats in that direction as well. In fact, we're already close to their habitat. I wouldn't be surprised to see one. They are curious, and we are making enough noise to draw them out."

"Are they dangerous?"

Bart shuddered. "Extremely poisonous. Fangs and claws. Excruciating pain for me. Death for you."

Ben scanned the empty sky. "I guess I shouldn't be surprised that hell is loaded with dangers."

"No, you shouldn't be." Bart pointed toward the chasm. "If we decide to go to the lake, our safest option is to cross here and continue on a straight line."

"Cross the chasm?" Ben eyed the craggy depths. "Easier said than done."

"Much easier. I don't know of any bridge, but Charlotte apparently knows how to cross. Maybe we can figure it out."

"Back to Leo." Ben ran a hand along the cloak's dry material. "I guess the absence of blood doesn't mean anything. I assume souls don't bleed."

"No, we don't, but it looks like the claws didn't penetrate the material deeply. Maybe one of the cats caught hold of it, and Leo shook the cloak off to escape."

"But escape where?" Ben scanned the ground once more. The forest floor seemed undisturbed. "No signs of a struggle or any dragging."

"Then they likely did escape, but the hellcats might still be close. Since Leo was here recently, and since they probably lost their prey, they might be prowling, watching, waiting for the right moment to pounce."

Ben held his breath and listened. A few twigs cracked, and a low growl rode the air, then several more. He withdrew the knife from the sheath. "Do you hear the growls?"

"I heard." Bart trembled as he scanned the forest. "Hellcats. They formed an arc to trap us against the chasm. There's no escape."

"Do they have any weaknesses beside losing their claws?"

"None that I know of."

"Almost anything has a weakness to getting whacked in the head." Ben picked up a fallen branch and used the knife to hack away its twigs, making it into a baseball-bat-sized weapon. He tossed it to Bart. "Catch."

Bart caught the branch and held it clumsily with both hands, his feet set in an awkward stance. "Thank you, but I'm not sure how much good this will do against several of the beasts."

"Better than nothing." Ben grabbed another branch. As he stripped off its twigs, he scanned the forest.

A panther-sized cat appeared from around a tree. Dark gray, it prowled closer, its hackles raised. Another skulked around a tree about twenty paces from the first. For some reason, both cats walked as if wounded. Maybe they were still suffering from losing claws while trying to get into Charlotte's refuge. That weakness might be helpful after all. "Aim for their paws."

Bart gulped. "To get to their paws, we have to dodge their teeth."

"That would be advisable."

Soon, three more cats joined the first two, and they edged closer as Ben backed toward the chasm's edge. "Stay with me, Bart. If we can get them to charge, maybe we can use their momentum to fling them into the chasm."

Bart joined Ben and backed up at his side, the branch shaking in his hands as he licked his lips. "Okay. Okay. You can do this. Bash its paws. Use its momentum."

When the first cat drew within a few paces, it leaped toward Ben, its teeth bared and its forepaws extended. Ben swung the branch and smacked the paws, then dodged. The cat flew past, yowling. It landed on all fours only inches from the chasm's edge, yelping as it lifted one of its forepaws.

Ben lunged at the cat and shoved it into the chasm. As it squealed, he pivoted back. Bart swung his branch at a second cat but missed. The cat's forepaws slammed against his chest, flattening him.

Ben slung his knife at the cat. The blade plunged into its neck, sending a spray of dark blood into the air. The cat shrieked and toppled off.

A third cat pounced at Ben. He dropped to his back, planted his feet against the cat's underbelly, and launched it toward the chasm. It sailed through the air and disappeared into the depths.

His heart thumping, he hustled to his feet, ran to the second cat, and retrieved his knife from the dead beast. Bart sat next to it, shaking his head as if casting off a fog. "Are you all right?" Ben asked.

"I think so." Bart blinked at the forest. "The other cats are gone."

"I guess we scared them away." Ben cleaned the knife's blade on the cat's coat and slid it back to its sheath, then extended a hand. "Ready to move on?"

"Definitely. Before the remaining hellcats come back with reinforcements." Bart grasped Ben's wrist and let him haul him to his feet. "Now that I think about it, I have a question. Why did those hellcats leave? Normally they would have continued the attack, especially with me down. I was the proverbial sitting duck."

"Do you have a theory?"

"Perhaps." Bart crouched at the cloak. Next to one of the sleeves sat a metal box the size of a tin of mints, its lid open. "Ah. I was right." He picked the box up and set it in his palm for Ben to see. "This is what scared the cats away."

Ben looked the box over—no label, just dull gray metal. Inside lay a reflective square of glass, about three inches in length and width, no thicker than a coin. "What is it?"

"Part of the mirror that resides in the abyss. Alexandria once told me that the mirror repels all dangerous beasts in hell. During our scuffle with the hellcats, the box must have come out of the cloak's pocket, and the lid popped open. I mentioned earlier that Leo might have something that could be of benefit to us. The hellcats' retreat prompted me to look for it."

"Then we have protection from here on out."

"More than that. This mirror is also the key to Alexandria's downfall." Bart touched the edge of the square. "It has abilities that are quite interesting. One is that it always reflects the truth. If you say something that isn't true, it will react with flashes and sizzles."

"Interesting. A reflective lie detector. "

"Exactly. A great benefit when dealing with Alexandria. Lies are frequent weapons in her arsenal. She is a skilled deceiver." Bart took the square out of the box and hid it in his fist. "If you conceal the mirror in your hand, she won't know that you have the lie detector to counter her deceit. You can feel it react to a lie." He opened his hand again. "It tingles when someone lies."

"That definitely could help." Ben took the mirror, put it in the box, and closed the lid. "Can it do anything else?"

"Actually, it has an even greater benefit, but I know only a little about it. The mirror can see realities from far-off places, even other worlds, and ..." Bart moved the cloak to the side, revealing a black violin and bow on the ground. "Excellent. A few bow hairs are loose, as expected, but it should work well."

He picked the items up. "As I was about to say, Alexandria's violin is able to conjure the images. She did that while Iona was in the abyss. I wasn't around to see what appeared on the mirror, but it has the ability to show the past or the present. The key aspect for us is that if it's showing something that exists in the present time, a person can be transported to that location, though there are limits. For example, it couldn't transport Alexandria out of hell. It is impossible for a disembodied soul to leave hell without some sort of transport vehicle."

Ben nodded. "Like being within a human body."

"Correct. But it can transport someone, whether physical or soulish, *into* hell."

"I see. If we can show hell in the mirror, it's possible to send Alex here."

"Exactly."

"But how do you make it show hell and then send Alex through it?"

"Regarding how to make hell appear, I will keep that to myself for the sake of leverage. Regarding sending Alexandria through it, she needs only to touch the mirror's surface once the portal is open."

"Touch the mirror? That sounds like a fairy tale. A fantasy story."

Bart chuckled. "Indeed it does. In fact, at one time, its powers were even more fantastical. Once open, the mirror portal could absorb someone standing nearby if a bright light flashed."

"How did it lose that ability?"

"I don't know for certain that it has. Since the mirror works by touching it now, I suppose no one has bothered to test the light flash." Bart shrugged. "How close does the light have to be? How bright? How close does a person have to be to transport? It's far from an exact science. Touching is simpler."

"True. We'll focus on that." Ben tapped a finger on the box. "I suppose that'll be the hardest part. Getting her to touch the mirror once it's activated."

"True. Playing the violin would alert her to the deception. In order for it to work, she would have to be asleep or perhaps unconscious. Since she is always wary, achieving that would be quite a task."

"Definitely, but we'll use it if we can."

"And maybe the mirror can help us now." Bart set the violin and bow down and gestured toward the mirror. "May I try something?"

Ben gave him the box. "Go ahead."

Bart removed the mirror square and pointed the reflective surface toward the chasm. "It also reveals what is invisible to the naked eye."

Ben stepped in front of Bart to see what the mirror showed. In the reflection, the chasm remained the same, but now a vine dangled from a limb high above. He swiveled his head and looked at the chasm. No vine hung anywhere in sight.

Bart peeked at the mirror. "A vine. I suspected as much. They couldn't have flown across the chasm."

"How did they know the vine is there?"

"Charlotte knows. She likely hung it there herself. How it seems invisible to the naked eye, I don't know. Some kind of transparent material, I suppose."

Ben studied the vine and gauged the distance. "It's too far to reach. I'll have to take a running leap and grab it."

"Grab something you can't see?" Bart smirked. "That's a literal leap of faith."

"I'm not sure I have enough faith to leap without a guide." Ben looked up at the canopy and scanned the network of branches down to the trees on each side. If Charlotte hung the vine, she likely climbed a tree on the other side of the chasm. None of the branches from this side reached that far over the gap.

After searching and failing to find a fallen branch long enough to catch the vine, he chose a small branch, stood close to the chasm's edge, and faced away from the vine. "Hold the mirror in front of me."

"As you wish."

When Bart complied, Ben tossed the branch over his shoulder while watching the reflection. One end of the branch struck the vine, making it sway from side to side. He spun toward the chasm. The vine shifted in and out of visibility as it moved. When it slowed, it disappeared. "Okay, I know exactly where it is now."

"And you're going to take the leap?"

"I have to."

"Again, as you wish." Bart nodded toward the violin, still resting on the cloak. "How will you get the violin and mirror across?"

"Good question." Ben picked up Leo's cloak, put it on, and slid the violin and bow into one of its roomy outer pockets, then extended his hand. "The mirror."

"Of course." Bart put the square in the box and gave it to Ben. "Do you want me to follow?"

Ben lifted an eyebrow. "Do you *want* to follow me to the Lake of Fire?"

"I think it's my duty to be helpful. I know you don't fully trust me, but you can trust me when it comes to exacting revenge against Alexandria."

"Okay. When I get to the other side, I'll swing the vine back to you. Since it'll be moving, you should be able to see it. And I can tie something to it to make it even more visible."

"Good. I have a lot less faith than you do."

Ben backed away from the chasm, keeping his eye on the point where he had last seen the vine. He had only one chance to grab it. A miss meant certain death. He inhaled deeply and glanced at Bart, who stood a few paces from the chasm, nervously biting a fingernail.

Ben sprinted to the edge. Planting a foot, he leaped toward the invisible vine, both gloved hands outstretched. One hand struck something. He held on and grabbed hold with the other hand. The vine pulled against the limb above and sent him in an upward arc that nearly spanned the gulf, but not enough to let go and sail the rest of the way.

As he swung back, he shifted his body to aid the swing. He sailed over Bart's head at the launch point and zoomed back, again shifting to add momentum.

When he neared the far side, he extended his legs and planted his feet. The vine jerked back, but he held on. He picked up a fallen branch and walked with it back to the edge.

At the other side, Bart looked skyward and pointed. "Bats!"

Ben tied the branch to the vine and swung it toward Bart. "Catch!"

Bart leaned over the chasm, teetering as he reached. When the vine drew near, a hawk-sized bat swooped low. He swatted it away and missed his chance to catch the vine. As it arced back toward Ben, another bat attacked Bart. He swatted again and again. The bat snapped its jaws and clawed, dodging the flailing arms as it beat its wings furiously.

Ben shed the cloak and leaped for the vine. He caught it and swung toward Bart. "Grab me!"

The moment Ben drew close, Bart spun toward him but lost his balance and toppled. Ben slid lower on the vine and stretched his legs, straining with all his might. As Bart fell, he caught Ben's foot with both hands and held on.

The vine again swung toward the far side of the chasm. Above, a limb creaked, sending both men lower. They slammed into the wall on the other side, Ben's hands several inches below the ledge, and bounced back. As they swung, they dropped lower and lower, the limb ready to snap at any second.

Ben clenched his jaw. The only way to make it to safety would be to force the vine into a bigger swing, but any extra force generated by his own shifting weight might make the limb break.

Bart shouted from below, "What are we going to do?"

"I'm thinking!"

The vine dropped another inch or two in spastic jerks. "Think faster!"

"I'm trying."

"Since you didn't throw the mirror box to me to fend off the bats, I'm not sure I trust your thinking abilities."

The slender vine tightened around Ben's fingers. "No apologies. Using a mirror against a bat wasn't the first option that came to mind."

"Well, you'd better come up with a good option in the next few seconds, or we're both going to plunge into a literal hellfire."

"Okay, okay. I'm going to try to climb hand over hand and then swing you to the ledge. You're light enough. I think I can do it."

"I'm light but not weightless. The vine held firm when I wasn't hanging on."

"Maybe. But I'm giving it a try." Ben released with one hand and grabbed the vine higher up. The limb creaked once more, and they dropped another notch.

"It's not going to work," Bart called.

"We don't have a choice!"

"*I* have a choice." Bart let go with one hand and dangled by the other. "Thank you for trying to save me."

"Bart! No! I'll come up with another option."

"There are no other options. I hope you'll remember me as a hero." He slipped away and plunged into the chasm's depths.

The sudden change in weight sent Ben higher, but he dropped again and bobbed like a yoyo. Looking down, he searched for any sign of Bart, but only darkness and a ribbon of fiery light lay in view far below.

Ben sighed. Bart was probably right. There were no other options. And he sacrificed himself for someone he barely knew. That was truly heroic.

With no more time to ponder, Ben climbed hand over hand until he ascended to the top of the chasm. He again shifted his weight to make the vine swing. With each increasing arc, he drew closer to the far edge, and the limb above creaked louder. It couldn't last more than another few seconds.

He swung into what he hoped would be his final arc. Just as he reached the high point at the far side, the limb broke, and he dropped. He threw his arms out, slammed them and his chin against the ledge, and held on.

His head and body throbbing, he muscled up, rolled to safe ground, and lay face up at the edge of the precipice. A bat swooped toward him. He whipped out his knife and slashed at it, cutting off part of its wing. With a squeal, it fluttered wildly as it dropped into the chasm.

Ben searched the sky. No other bats flew in sight. He slid the knife away, climbed to his feet, and looked into the depths once more. Somewhere down there, Bart flowed with the lava toward the Lake of Fire, a torture-filled nightmare that would never, ever end.

As heat coursed across Ben's skin, he whispered, "Thank you, Bart. I know you conspired with Alex to hurt billions of people, but at least for one moment, you proved yourself to be a hero. I'll try to remember that. May God have mercy on your soul."

Ben turned his head. There was no more time to think about his doomed helper. Now without a guide, he had to find Leo and Iona, or Charlotte.

His head pounding, he picked up the cloak and put it on. He checked the pockets for the violin, bow, and mirror box. Everything seemed to be intact. But for how long? If Bart was right about soulish clothes disappearing, the cloak might not last much longer.

Ben strode away from the chasm and out of the forest. Ahead lay miles and miles of barren, rocky terrain with ridges and furrows that would make for laborious travel. The land sloped downward, maybe leading to the Lake of Fire. Since, according to Bart, the chasm's lava spilled into the lake, the destination had to sit at a much lower elevation.

As he walked, he searched for Leo's signs, but the rocks were impossible to penetrate, and Leo no longer had the violin's bow. Since he obviously had trouble at the chasm, he might not have been able to continue marking his trail at all.

Ahead, an odd cloud interrupted the otherwise clear sky near the horizon. Smoke, maybe? That could be a sign of the Lake of Fire. With no clues from Leo, the smoke and lower elevation would have to be his new guides. And if Leo was hurt or missing, that meant Iona might be alone to face the terrors of hell by herself.

Putting his aches aside, Ben accelerated into a quick jog. He had no time to lose.

# Chapter Thirteen

Jack knelt at the radio relay station as wind-blown snow pelted his face. Although the precipitation had stopped and the clouds had given way to a starry sky, howling gusts lifted layers of flakes from drifts and flung them at him, trying to rip off his coat and hat. But he had to fix this connection yet again, this time more permanently.

Holding a small flashlight in his mouth, he wrapped wire around two pieces of the antenna to splice them together, then pushed his numb fingers back into his gloves, dropped the flashlight into his palm, and picked up the radio's handset. "Trudy, can you hear me?"

"Speak up. The logs in Caligar's fireplace are crackling too loudly."

"Don't be a twerp. Next time it breaks, it's your turn to fix it."

"If you fix it right, it won't break again."

"Easy to say when you're sitting in a soft chair, roasting marshmallows over a fire."

"Yeah, I gotta admit, it was pretty easy to say. But don't worry, I'll save you a marshmallow."

"You do that. I'm heading in again. If I'm not there in a few minutes, send a search team." Jack set the microphone in its cradle, rose, and stamped his feet to pound out the numbness in his toes. When he turned toward Caligar's underground refuge, a bright streak dropped through the sky, slowing as it neared the ground, far too slow to be a meteor. He snatched the microphone again and pressed the button. "Trudy, I'm heading north. I think something landed in the launch zone."

"Not by yourself, you're not. I'll meet you at the tower ruins."

"Copy that." Jack set the microphone in place again. His flashlight beam leading the way, he trudged to the tower site and waited, bouncing on his toes to keep warm. Within seconds, Trudy arrived on a pair of snowshoes, another pair under an arm.

She set the extra snowshoes next to him. "Better than plowing with our legs. Even these'll be tough in all that powder."

"True." Jack began putting the snowshoes on. "We'll have to be careful. If something besides the SUV came through the Oculus Gate, no telling what it could be."

"I'm not worried." Trudy patted a holster on her belt. "I brought a sidearm."

"Great." Jack straightened and lifted the snowshoes in turn. "Ready. Let's make tracks."

They tromped northward single file. As always, cold wind and ice particles assaulted their chapped skin, forcing them to take turns as the trailblazer. Soon, the roar of an engine reached their ears, and headlights came into view, drawing closer at a rapid clip.

"Sounds like the SUV," Jack said, puffing.

"Yeah. I'm wondering how it's managing to plow through this snow so easily. And who could be driving? Caligar's too big to fit in the driver's seat."

"I think we're about to find out."

When the headlights came close and swept across them, the vehicle slowed to a stop. Jack shone the flashlight on it. It was the SUV, but instead of tires, it ran on tank treads. He shifted the light to the driver—Caligar hunched way over in the seat with an elbow protruding through the open window. Only the sleeve from his usual frontier-style leather tunic covered his arm.

Jack waved his light and shouted, "Want me to drive while you curl up in the back?"

Caligar nodded. "That would be a far more comfortable option." The door opened. He squeezed out, unfolding his huge body, his joints popping as he straightened and pulled his long braid from a tangle with the seatbelt. He nudged one of the tank treads with a foot. "It seems that my modifications are working well."

Jack smiled, vapor from his breaths puffing through the flashlight beam. "Good thing. We're going to need them."

"Do you have a plan?"

"Yep." Jack waved a hand in the direction of Caligar's Alaska home. "Let's get back to your cave. We'll pick up what we need and head to the nearest airport. With all the turmoil from the angel exodus, we're bound to find an abandoned plane we can borrow."

Trudy huffed a stream of white vapor. "It has to be one you can fly, Ace. You've never flown anything bigger than a two-seater or one of those SkyNet drones. We'll need something with more room than one of those to fit Caligar inside."

Jack shrugged. "We'll find a cargo plane. How hard can it be to fly?"

"To fly? Not a problem. To land? That's a different story." Trudy grasped Caligar's arm. "If you don't want to endure another tight squeeze, I have an idea. Are you game for something even more dangerous than flying with Jack as pilot?"

Iona plunged her paddle into the black fire and pulled it through furious strokes that matched Charlie's, one after another in rapid pulses. The canoe shot forward, zipping past flailing souls in the churning fire. Hands reached for them with desperate lunges. Faces appeared on bobbing heads, their skin covered with sizzling welts as their gaping mouths shrieked with pain.

A fist punched through the lake's surface. The hand uncurled and grabbed the side of the canoe, then another hand joined it. They pulled, tilting the boat until Charlie bashed the fingers with her paddle. Breathless, she shouted, her mask now pulled down to her chin. "Keep going! We're almost there."

They paddled on, smacking heads, arms, and hands as the metallic craft hurtled through the black fire. After another torturous minute, the churning ceased, and the canoe ran aground in silence.

Iona looked ahead for the first time in what seemed like an hour. A closed iron gate spanned a twenty-foot gap in an enormous cliff that rose out of sight—thousands of feet straight up, obviously too steep to climb. Dense mist veiled everything beyond the gate.

A man stood at the middle of the gate. His military camo, visible between the plackets of his open cloak, matched Charlie's, appropriate garb for living humans to conceal themselves from hell's beasts.

Charlie set her paddle down, stepped out of the canoe, and pulled off her headphones, still wearing a patrol cap with red hair spilling out at all sides. "Come. We must hurry."

"Yeah. I'm definitely ready to get out of this boat." Iona dropped her paddle and climbed out onto the dark, sandy shore.

Charlie clipped the headphones to her belt, curled her arm through Iona's, and walked with her toward the gate. At their feet, the ground soon became white rock with sparkling crystals embedded within, making the ground glitter. "Let me begin the conversation with my fellow Reaper. The idea that you are not condemned will seem odd to him."

"I'll keep my mouth shut. I have no idea what's going on."

Charlie stripped her mask off and stuffed into a pocket. "You'll figure it out soon."

As they neared the gate, the man stared at them, cocking his head but otherwise staying motionless. Now that they were closer, the man's features clarified—about five-foot-ten with a peach-fuzz beard that made him appear to be in his late teens, though his dark, piercing eyes and gaunt face made him look at least twenty, and his ragged, over-the-ears light brown hair looked like he cut it himself with a knife without using a mirror.

When they drew within a few paces, Charlie bowed her head. "Greetings, Austin."

Austin lowered his hood, revealing an unruly mop. "Why so formal, Charlotte?"

Charlie lowered her hood as well. "Because this isn't a social call. I'm here on official business."

"Well, that sounds ominous." He nodded toward Iona. "Who is this?"

"Iona. She is my official business."

"Is that so?" Austin leaned forward and studied Iona. "She is of the light. How can that be?"

A hint of a smile broke Charlie's stoic expression. "I knew you would notice right away."

"Of course. Light is easy to spot when we're surrounded by darkness. But how did she get here? And why is she dressed in camo? It's almost identical to ours."

"It's a long story, and I'm carrying another soul in my cloak who is also not condemned."

A smile broke through on Austin's face as well. "Now I'm getting the picture. You brought them here because you want to help them escape from hell."

Charlie squared her shoulders. "Isn't it a Reaper's responsibility to shepherd a soul to its proper place? These souls don't belong here."

"I agree, one hundred percent." He grasped one of the gate's iron bars. "But how do you propose to get them past the gate?"

Charlie folded her hands at her waist. "I hope to ask Azrael, which is why I hurried to arrive here. I assume that since you're here as well, you expect him soon. It's often difficult to track time, but I think he's due."

"He is. But even an archangel like Azrael can't take a disembodied soul past the gate. The warding prevents it."

A slight tic at the edge of Charlie's eye revealed her disappointment. "Maybe there's a way to break the warding."

Austin shook his head. "Not that I know of. God put it in place. Azrael merely maintains it. But I don't think it would hurt to ask him when he comes. He's always been open to respectful questions."

Charlie smiled fully. "I agree. After all, this is a special case. I mean, how often do we see uncondemned souls here?"

"Iona is the first I've seen."

"Proving my point." Charlie looked at Iona. "Austin patrols a different part of hell, and we take turns reporting to Azrael, the archangel, once each week. As you heard, the angel's expected arrival is why I hurried to get us here."

Iona nodded, staying quiet. This conversation between Reapers in hell was way beyond her understanding. Better just to watch and listen.

Charlie set a fist on her hip and eyed the gate. "I have a theory about the warding."

"Let's hear it," Austin said.

She narrowed an eye. "You remember me mentioning Alexandria and the warding on her forest, right?"

"I remember." Austin chuckled. "That ancient witch has been a thorn in your side for a long time."

"It's not funny. The warding's gone, and so is she."

Austin's brow shot upward. "She's gone? Where?"

"That's part of the long story I mentioned, but we—Iona and I—believe Alexandria went to the living world in Iona's body."

"What? Impossible!"

"Not for Alexandria. She knows the wardings better than anyone. She knew that a soul cannot leave hell without a physical host, and she also knew she couldn't pass through this gate, because it is impossible for a condemned soul to pass, even if within a host. So she obtained a host and left another way, through a portal that apparently no longer exists."

While Austin stared, his mouth slightly ajar, Charlie continued. "I think Alexandria came to the gate and studied the warding, then returned to her forest and created her own warding there based on what she learned."

Austin nodded. "Very interesting theory."

"Do you think it's true?"

He shrugged. "You're the veteran here, not me."

"I thought maybe since you're an Owl you might have some insight that I don't."

"Now that you mention it …" Austin stared at the gate as if trying to bore a hole through the iron bars. "If Alexandria was able to replicate the warding, that means it might have an evil source instead of a holy one."

"Ah!" Charlie waved a hand toward the Lake of Fire. "So the presence of evil is part of the warding formula—betrayal, malice, greed, hate."

"Exactly. And I'm sure Alexandria could supply plenty of those ingredients."

Charlie tapped her chin with a finger. "I learned that a living human's blood broke her warding, so I'm wondering if that would work here. The shedding of human blood is the unlocking key."

Austin scrunched his brow. "That doesn't sound right. Too easy to break the warding. One of us could prick a finger and open the gates of hell for souls to escape."

"Think again, Austin. Do you remember hearing what happened the last time the warding was broken to set souls free from this place? Think back. Way back."

Austin stared at her, then at the gate, obviously deep in thought.

Iona glanced between him and Charlie. Apparently they were tuned to the same mental radio station, communicating a secret thought between the two of them, something they didn't want a certain disembodied soul to know about.

After a few more excruciatingly tense moments, Austin nodded. "Okay. It's not so easy to break the gate's warding."

"But it's possible. The shedding of human blood might be the answer. Maybe I could—"

"No!" Austin shook his head hard. "Charlotte, seriously? Do you honestly think you're on that level? That's just … well … it's far from humble."

Charlie crossed her arms tightly. "I'm not on that level, Austin, but we're all called to act in kind, even if not in magnitude. We do what we can to sacrifice for others."

"Sacrifice, yes. You serving here in hell is a huge sacrifice. But you're talking about—"

"Don't lecture me, Austin." She glowered at him. "You are not my superior. You have no power to stop me."

"No, but I am your friend." He pointed at the canoe. "I think you should go back to your duties. Be sacrificial out there."

"You mean hunting down wayward souls and throwing them back into the abyss? Dashing their hopes? Making them suffer more? Those duties?"

Austin raised his voice a notch. "Yes, those duties. If you're right about Alexandria, she's now wreaking havoc on Earth. It was your duty to capture her and throw her into the Lake of Fire, and you couldn't do it. You needed to dash her hopes, because all she hopes for is evil."

Charlotte lowered her head. "I know. I know I failed to catch her." After a moment of silence, she took a deep breath and refocused on Austin, fire in her eyes. "But now I can redeem myself. For the first time, I have a chance to really help a soul. Two of them. And they can go back to Earth to stop Alexandria."

Austin shook his head again. "No, no, no, Charlotte. You haven't thought this through. Even if you can get them past the gate, what happens then? They have no bodies."

She touched Austin's cloak sleeve. "If their bodies are dead, their souls will go to heaven. If their bodies are alive, their souls can be restored to those bodies."

"Who will restore them? You and I are the only Reapers remaining."

"I know. I thought maybe you could—"

"Me?" Austin laughed under his breath. "Charlotte, you know better. We have our assignments. Azrael wouldn't allow it. Besides, I've never restored a soul to a body. Have you?"

Her head drooped. "No."

"Then neither of us can do it. It's a lost cause."

"Maybe." Charlie refolded her hands at her waist. "We'll wait here for Azrael and ask him about my idea. He might have a suggestion."

Iona took a step closer to the two Reapers. "Charlie, I know you said for me to stay quiet, but this is my soul we're talking about. And Leo's. What's this idea you have cooking that's got Austin so worked up?"

Charlie sighed. "I'd rather not say until we hear from Azrael. If he says no, there's no use discussing it."

Iona turned toward Austin, but he quickly waved a hand. "Don't look at me. I'm just guessing at what Charlotte has in mind. Well, a little more than guessing. After all, I am an Owl. But I'm not saying. Like she said, we should wait for Azrael."

"Then at least tell me what an Owl is. A special kind of Reaper, right?"

"Right. Owls, like both Alexandria and myself, are gifted with extraordinary vision." He blinked, then squinted toward the lake. "And speaking of that, someone is approaching the lake's far shore. A man. A living man. He'll get there in a few minutes."

Charlotte gasped. "A living man? How is that possible?"

"I don't know. It seems that we're having quite an influx of unusual visitors."

Iona looked that way, but only the faintest outline of the far shore lay in view. "What does he look like?"

Austin's eyes narrowed further. "Crew cut. Firm jaw. A cloak opened in front. Camo clothes underneath. His determined expression looks like he's ready to destroy anything that stands in his way."

Iona breathed, "Ben." But why was he wearing a cloak? Could it be Leo's cloak?

"He's come to rescue Iona." Not bothering to put the headphones and mask back on, Charlie jogged to the shore, climbed into the canoe, and launched it. Paddling furiously, she shot out into

140

the lake. Within seconds, the condemned souls attacked, but she swatted them away and continued on.

Austin stared at Iona. "What's so special about you that a man would come to hell to rescue you?"

"Well ..." Iona imagined Ben bashing hellcats with tree branches, swinging across the chasm with bats clinging to his back, and marching toward the lake with his shoes on fire. Yes, those were exaggerated illusions, but there was no doubt about Ben's passion. "It's not me who's special. It's him. His name is Ben Garrison, and he would definitely storm the gates of hell to rescue someone, even someone like me who doesn't deserve it."

Austin nodded slowly. "I could see that in his eyes. Love-driven obsession. It is both rare and wonderful. Unfortunately, some who bear that quality don't live long. Since they are willing to die for great causes, they often do. Die, I mean."

Iona eyed his serious expression. He really did have a lot of insight. "Since you and Alex are both Owls, maybe you can help me in case I ever have to face her. Do Owls have any special weaknesses?"

"Not so much a weakness, but keep in mind that her power lies in her vision. She's able to stay a step ahead of her enemies by figuring out what they're likely to do. When she sees someone, she takes a mental photograph and studies it long after the meeting. She relies on this skill without reserve. If you can disable it somehow, she'll be crippled, probably even more so than most people because losing it would rattle her. At least that's my experience."

"Maybe get her into a dark room?"

Austin shook his head. "Owls can see in the dark. In fact, that's how the name came about. Owls are night predators. She would be even more formidable. To expose the weakness, you would have to physically attack her eyes."

"Like with acid?"

"That might work. But there are other ways. I once had a concussion that took my eyesight away for a couple of days. I was worthless. Confused. In near panic mode. My guess is that it would be the same for Alexandria."

"Good to know." Iona smiled. "Thank you."

"You're welcome." He smiled in return, looking younger again, maybe eighteen or nineteen. "It's a pleasure talking to you, a soul who's filled with light instead of darkness. I truly hope you can get out of here, and I'll do whatever I can to help you."

"Thanks. I've enjoyed talking to you, too." As they looked at each other, Iona's cheeks warmed, but how could that be if she had no blood flow? Still, this young man's Owl eyes definitely penetrated, as if he were probing her mind. She pivoted and looked at the lake. "So now we wait?"

"Now we wait."

"Then while we're waiting …" Iona sat cross-legged on the ground, avoiding eye contact. "Can you tell me more about what you do?"

"Sure." He sat next to her in the same pose. "Like I said, I don't get to talk to souls like you. The ones in the lake don't listen, and they're all liars. They'd say anything to escape."

"Yeah. I guess I would, too." Iona imagined herself in the lake, begging Austin to let her out. As the pain from being splattered by the fire returned to mind, she shuddered. "It seems so cruel. Making souls suffer for eternity, I mean."

"I know. I struggled with it myself for years. But I was comforted by something Azrael said."

She glanced at him. He was staring at the lake, maybe watching Charlie's progress. "What did he say?"

Austin looked at her, but his eyes no longer probed. "God is a perfect judge. If he weren't, he wouldn't be God."

"Then any soul in the Lake of Fire deserves to be there."

"Exactly right. It's tragic, but they made their choices. They knew what they were doing."

"What about the souls in hell who aren't in the lake yet? Do they have a chance to avoid it?"

Austin smiled. "You like to ask tough questions, don't you?"

"Yeah, I'm kind of a pest that way sometimes."

"You're not a pest at all." Austin continued gazing at the lake. "Long ago, this place used to be the destination of every soul. Think of it as a big waiting area with two sections, one for people who are wicked and faithless, and the other for the righteous, and souls couldn't cross from one section to the other." He gestured with his thumb toward the gate. "Then when the Messiah died, he came through those very gates and took every faithful soul to heaven. After that, the comfort section vanished, and the righteous went straight to heaven when they died. Only wicked souls reside here now."

Iona let his words seep in. The story about the death of Jesus was one of the few she knew well, but the part about the souls coming here added a fascinating component she had never heard before. She gazed again at the lake and imagined the torment those within suffered. If only someone could rescue them. "Can souls that are here now change? Is it too late for them?"

"As far as I know it's too late, but I don't claim to be an expert. I just keep going back to what Azrael said."

"God is a perfect judge."

"Right. I have to rely on that. Otherwise the wails and laments would break my heart."

"I know what you mean." A tear trickled. Iona brushed it away and looked at Austin again. "Let's change the subject."

"Gladly." His intense eyes pierced again. "Anything in particular you'd like to talk about?"

"Um …" She averted her eyes, though she kept him in the periphery of her sight. "How about the history of the Reapers? I don't know much about them."

He lifted a finger. "Now that's a subject I know a lot about."

"Good." Iona folded her hands in her lap. "Let's hear it."

"Sure." He slid closer. The urge to ease away from him was nearly overwhelming, but she stayed put. So far he seemed to be true to his word, that he really wanted to help.

As he gestured with his hands, his voice took on an animated, storyteller's cadence. "More than two hundred years ago, a massive explosion at a nuclear power reactor created a radioactive shield that surrounded Earth. Because of the shield, the souls of the dead were trapped. They couldn't escape to the afterlife."

# Chapter Fourteen

Kat grabbed Damien and hauled him to his feet, keeping a grip on his wrist. "What does the key unlock, and what is Alexandria planning to do?"

When Damien gained his balance, he gasped. "It's gone!"

"What's gone?"

His eyes darted, as if searching for something. "The Refector. It's no longer inside me."

Kat released him and drew a gun from a belt holster as she spoke in a sarcastic tone. "Odd. Do you think the electric shocks might have driven it out?"

"You fool!" He jabbed a finger at her. "You did that on purpose, didn't you? I needed its power. I can't stop Alexandria without it."

"Stop her? But you're in league with her."

Damien clenched his hand into a fist. "She merely thinks I am. I agreed to participate in her plan, but, like I mentioned before, I faked my vaccination by taking a dose of my own design. Pretending to be on her side was the only way to stop her."

Kat shook her head. "Nope. Don't buy it. You tried to kill me several times."

"No, I was trying to capture you. If I had wanted to kill you, I would have shot you through the heart, not the arm. And when I riddled that door with bullets, I could have marched in and finished you off. As I told you before, I need you to help me get through a series of security checks. A vault holds items that Alexandria desperately wants me to destroy."

"Destroy?" Kat looked him in the eye. He seemed so sincere. Maybe it wouldn't hurt to hear him out. "Tell me what the items are, and I'll think about it."

"All right, but this will sound strange." Damien inhaled deeply. "A violin and a mirror."

Kat again checked for any sign of deception. The items he mentioned were too odd to be a lie. "What can the violin and mirror do that would hurt her?"

"According to her arrogant ramblings, the mirror is a lie detector. It reacts to a spoken lie in a way that is quite noticeable. Regarding the violin, she said very little. I think it is a transportation device of some sort if combined with the mirror. I don't know how transportation can hurt her, but clearly it can. Otherwise, she wouldn't want them destroyed."

"Where is the vault?"

Damien shook a finger. "No, no, no. If I tell you, you won't need me anymore. You would either imprison me or kill me."

Kat eyed his finger. His dramatic pose gave him a comical aspect, but laughing at him might send him into a fury. "I can see why you'd think that. You're probably right."

"The solution to our impasse is rather simple." Damien extended a hand. "Give me the key. Release me, and I will find the violin and mirror. Then I will bring them to you and combine our considerable brainpower to figure out how to use them to neutralize Alexandria."

"That's reasonable, but Alex is already a step ahead of you. She anticipated your lack of loyalty."

Damien blinked. "What? Impossible. I have practically kissed her foul feet."

"Maybe so, but she told me how to purge a Refector, knowing I would use it against you. You've outlived your usefulness to her."

"But I haven't finished my mission. I concocted the vaccine based on her formula, but that was a mere first step. I was commissioned to find her greatest obstacles, the violin and mirror, and give them to her."

"Maybe she's using you to reveal the location of the items she wants you to destroy, then she'll ambush you to take them. That way you can't betray her with them."

Damien nodded slowly. "I must admit that assuming treachery on her part is reasonable."

"Then you should plan accordingly."

"Since you ruined my plans, perhaps you can offer a suggestion."

Kat tapped a finger on her chin. "Are you able to send her a photo of you with the items?"

"Yes. She told me she would have control of the angel cruiser and its onboard computer. I can send a photo to her there."

"Here's my suggestion." Kat slid the gun back to its holster, withdrew the key from her pocket, and laid it in Damien's palm. "Go to the vault, get the violin and mirror, and send her a photo of them. Then bring them back here to me. I'll be watching the security cameras so I can let you in."

Damien stared at the key. "Why would you trust me to do that?"

"Since you won't tell me where the vault is, I don't have any choice but to trust you."

"That's true." Damien, still cuffed, dropped the key into his pants pocket. "But I'm not sure I trust you yet. I shot you, and you tased me. I betrayed my own kind, and you were once the queen of the angels. We have no reason to trust each other."

"This is a business arrangement. We have a common enemy. We can trust each other as long as we both benefit."

Damien's brow scrunched for a moment. "Agreed. We are both driven by a desire to stop Alex. That makes us allies."

"For the time being." Kat withdrew the handcuffs key from her pants pocket, unlocked Damien, and tossed the cuffs to the computer desk. "Don't cross me." She unfastened the computer pad from her belt and unlocked the main entry. When the mechanism within the thick door thudded, she set the pad on the desk and strode to the door. Using both hands, she spun the wheel and pushed the door open. "Go. I hope to see you back here soon with the violin and mirror."

Damien massaged one of his wrists. "I'm having a difficult time believing that you trust me to simply walk out of here and return to you with the coveted items." He looked at the wall display as it continued smoking. "You won't even be able to track me with the city's camera system."

"You're right, but I do trust self-preservation instincts. Now that you know Alex wants you dead, I'm your only refuge. Come back here, and I'll protect you from her."

"You make a compelling argument. I will do as you asked." Damien hustled out and jogged down the hallway, calling back, "It shouldn't take long."

Kat heaved the door closed and locked it with the computer pad. When the mechanism clunked, she leaned back against the door and muttered, "Gullible freak."

The computer pad on the desk chimed, and a voice emanated from the speaker. "Kat, this is Trudy."

Kat hustled to the pad, grabbed it, and spoke into the microphone. "I'm here. What's up?"

"Got an update. Jack and I borrowed an old military jet that got mothballed. It's rickety, but it flies even faster than that angel cruiser. By the way, Caligar showed up with the SUV, modified to get through the snow better. We left him in Alaska to see what Alex's goons will do when they show up."

"Caligar? How did he come—"

"Long story. Tell you when we get there. Maybe two hours."

"Wow! That's super fast, but where will you land?"

"This bird has pivoting jets, so it'll land almost anywhere. We'll pick out a vacant street as close as possible to the temple."

"Good." Kat brought up a tracking program on the pad's screen. The city map showed a flashing dot that represented Damien's location, an apartment district in an older section of town. "I'm going to give you info for a tracker I implanted in Damien."

"A tracker? How'd you plant it without him knowing?"

Kat magnified the area around Damien and watched his progress as he hurried along a sidewalk. "It was on a taser prong. He knew he got zapped, but he didn't know the prong inserted the bug."

"Pretty sly, Kat. You've got your mojo back."

"Yep. I'm on a roll, but I can't get cocky. Too much in my brain is hazy. I know the area Damien went, and I need to start chasing him, but I'm not sure what kind of mess I'll be walking into. I have a hunch that an Alex ambush is waiting around the corner, so I have to be on the alert."

"Send us the coordinates, and we'll back you up."

"That's my plan. Anyway, short version of the story, Damien says he's going after something Alex wants to destroy, but he might be lying through his teeth. When I send you the tracking data, you can get a fix on him and give me an updated ETA. Call me on the earbud frequency."

"Sounds good. And we'll show up close by. Jack's learned how to land this bird on a dime. As long as it's a honking big dime. You know, the size of a sports stadium. Fuel stops have been an adventure."

"Hey," Jack said, "the last stop wasn't so bad."

"If you don't mind your stomach taking up residence in your throat."

"I don't see you volunteering to land."

"Yeah, but I'm not Captain I-Can-Fly-Anything-With-Wings."

"Stuff it, Sis."

"Nice comeback. I'm hurt. Psychologically damaged. I'll never recover."

"Hey, you two," Kat said, trying not to laugh. "Focus. Lives are at stake."

Trudy sighed. "You're right. Ready to receive the tracking info. You can send text to me through this channel."

Kat typed on the pad. "Coming right up."

# Chapter Fifteen

Ben swung his paddle and whacked a hand clawing the canoe, then whipped the blade around and bashed the head of a man who had climbed nearly halfway in. Screaming in pain, the man toppled back into the lake with a splash of black liquid and a plume of smoke.

Charlotte lifted her paddle to hit yet another attacker. Ben lunged and smacked the clawing hand. Choking on the horrific stench, he shouted, "You paddle. I'll fight."

"Sounds good. Hang on." She plunged her paddle in and pulled through a powerful stroke, then another while Ben continued warding off attackers with kicks, punches, and swings of the paddle. Steaming black fire spattered, some droplets hitting his sleeves and pant legs and burning holes in the material.

Ahead, the shore drew closer and closer, maybe three minutes to go. A cloaked man sat in front of a gate with a camo-clothed redhead sitting next to him, a helmet at her side. She had to be Iona.

By the time the canoe drew within a hundred feet of shore, the attackers ceased. Ben settled to his bench and blew out a long breath. "Does that happen every time you cross the lake?"

Charlotte pulled her paddle through the dark liquid, more slowly now. "They always attack the boat, but usually not so fiercely. And I have never seen them rise so far above the surface before. Maybe they made an extra effort because they thought you would be an easy target, not a strong fighter." She smiled. "You proved them wrong."

Ben gazed at the lovely woman. For some reason, her smile reminded him of someone, but he couldn't place it. "Bartholomew gave me a mirror that he said would ward off the beasts of hell, but it didn't work against the souls in the lake."

Her eyes widened. "You spoke to Bartholomew?"

"Yes. Before he fell into a chasm."

"Oh. He fell into the chasm, did he?"

"Yes. He made a huge sacrifice to save me from falling into it."

"Interesting. And highly unusual. But it does explain a lot."

"What do you mean?" Ben asked.

"I will try to explain soon."

Ben dipped his paddle into the lake and helped Charlotte propel the canoe the rest of the way. When it slid aground, Charlotte disembarked. "Go on ahead. I'll check the boat for damage."

"All right." Ben set his paddle down and stepped out. Ahead, the cloaked man rose and pointed. Iona leaped to her feet and ran, her arms outstretched.

Ben sprinted to her. She leaped into his arms and hugged him tightly, her voice muffled in his shirt. "Oh, Ben! It's so good to see you."

He pivoted slowly, holding her close. Her embrace felt heavenly. "Same to you." He kissed her forehead and lowered her to the ground. "I can't believe I found you."

"Yeah. It's all pretty crazy." Beaming at him, she held his hand. "Did Charlie tell you what happened to Leo and me?"

"She told me a lot. Not sure if I digested everything. It all seems so impossible. She actually has Leo's soul in her cloak. And now we're supposed to wait for an archangel to come to tell us what to do next."

"Yeah. Leo's hurt. That's why he's in her cloak. But Charlotte says he'll be okay. Souls heal quickly." Iona touched Ben's cloak. "And you're wearing Leo's cloak."

Ben nodded. "I found it next to a chasm. Charlotte said that Leo fell into it."

"Hellcats attacked us. Long story."

"Yeah, I had a scrap with them myself."

Iona turned toward the gate. "Austin told me Azrael should be here soon. He's an angel, and I want to be there when he shows up."

As they walked hand in hand, Iona narrowed her eyes at him. "Did Charlie tell you what she's planning? About getting us all out of hell, I mean."

"No. Only that she has a plan."

"Yeah. A secret one." Iona stopped near the gate, picked up her helmet, and looked back at Charlie. "I don't like secret plans, especially when they're cooked up by someone I barely know."

Ben looked as well. Charlie stood facing the lake with her cloak fanned, as if blocking their view of what she was doing. "Agreed. Too mysterious. She must know we won't like her plan."

"But she's been great so far—smart, brave, willing to do anything to help me. I like her a lot." Iona pulled Ben toward the man at the gate. "This is Austin, a Reaper who guards the gate."

Ben and Austin shook hands. "Why does it need guarding?" Ben asked.

Austin offered a courteous nod. "I'm not really a guard. When Azrael, the angel of death, comes, I open the gate and close it behind him because his hands are always full, carrying condemned souls into hell. I think he could open and close it with his mind, so my job here is really just ceremonial. Anyway, that's only one of my duties. The rest of the time, I'm a Reaper like Charlotte. We split hell into two sections. She patrols one, and I patrol the other."

Ben scrunched his brow. "Two Reapers for all of hell? Is it small enough for just you two?"

"Hell is vast, but I don't have to travel more than a few miles. I haven't even seen all of it. And it's rare for souls to escape the abyss. The few who have escaped don't stray far for fear of the wild beasts, and we Reapers are drawn to any wayward soul."

"So you're able to find them quickly."

Austin nodded. "The job's not hard. Kind of boring, actually, except for the hellcats. I've had a few run-ins with them." He waved a hand toward Charlotte, now heading their way. "Her territory has more cats than mine does. I offered to trade with her, but I think she likes the thrill. It breaks up the monotony."

"Don't tell tales, Austin," Charlotte said as she joined them. "You know the real reason I always wanted to keep my territory."

Austin smirked. "To capture your nemesis, Alexandria."

"And to learn more about her warding." Charlotte looked at Ben. "I think the warding she put on her forest is similar to the warding we have here at the gate."

"Yes," Ben said. "You mentioned the gate's warding. Anyone who tries to pass through gets zapped."

Charlotte pressed her lips together. "Zapped is a good word. I am told that humans would be fried by an electric shock and they would die instantly, though I haven't seen that actually happen. I have seen what happens to souls. They are repelled and bounce back. Only Azrael can pass without harm."

"And the souls he's carrying?" Iona asked.

Charlotte waved a hand as if ushering someone through the gate. "They enter hell without a problem. It's a one-way warding."

Iona forked her fingers at the two Reapers. "What about you two? If the warding is so dangerous, can you ever leave?"

Austin nodded. "I can leave when my Reaper tour is over in twelve years, but Charlotte is here for however many years God chooses. Long story. Anyway, when it's time to go, Azrael will weaken the warding temporarily to allow us to pass. Then he'll replace us, assuming he can find candidates. But even when the warding is weak, souls can't pass. Azrael doesn't have the power to remove it completely."

Charlotte touched her chest with a thumb. "But now I think I do."

"How?" Ben and Iona asked at the same time.

"Too soon to explain." Charlotte set a hand on Ben's shoulder and looked into his eyes. "If my plan works, I will not be able to take Leo and Iona through the gate when the warding breaks. They will need a shepherd. If they were to return to Earth without one, they would be swept from the world immediately with no chance to search for or be reunited with their bodies." Her gaze seemed to burn into Ben's eyes. "Can you be that shepherd for them?"

Ben let her words soak in for a moment. Of course he would do anything he could, but the question didn't make much sense. "How can I be a shepherd? And why can't you take them through the gate?"

"To answer your first question, when Leo and Iona are both in my cloak, you can wear it through the gate. Within its fibers, they will be protected as you shepherd them out of danger. They won't be swept away when their souls return to Earth."

"Then I should take Leo's cloak off." Ben withdrew the violin, bow, and mirror square and laid them on the ground, then shed the cloak. The moment he set it next to the other items, it crumbled to sparkling dust and vanished.

He stepped back. "I heard that might happen." He looked at Charlotte. "Because it was soulish, right?"

She nodded. "Soulish items separated from their owners soon dissolve. If you had left hell with the cloak on, it would have disappeared immediately."

"Okay, back to my other question. Why can't you take Iona and Leo through the gateway? I mean, I'm glad to do it, but what's your part?"

Charlotte shook her head. "I won't answer that question at this time, but you will soon understand." She turned and walked toward the lake. "I will be back in a moment."

Iona slid her hand into Ben's. "I don't like the sound of all of this. Too many secrets."

He compressed her hand. "Agreed. But we're in a new world. We can't demand to be informed."

"True, but that doesn't change the eerie feeling. Something's wrong. Sick-to-my-stomach wrong."

Ben sighed. "I know. Let's just keep our eyes and ears open. We might have to make quick decisions."

At the lake, Charlotte helped a man get out of the canoe. Standing tall and brushing thick hair away from his eyes, his identity was obvious.

"Leo!" Iona ran to him and jumped into his embrace. As they walked back hand in hand, Ben's cheeks warmed. She had done the same with him only moments ago. Feeling like Leo was a competitor for a fatherly role was wrong, so very wrong, but shaking it off seemed impossible.

Behind Leo and Iona, Charlotte helped another man out of the canoe. Bearing lesions on his face and scorch marks on his clothes, he looked like he had suffered greatly. Supporting him by an elbow, she helped him stagger toward the gate.

As they drew closer, the man's identify became clear—Bart, Alex's henchman.

When Leo and Iona arrived, Ben hugged Leo. "Good to see you again, my friend."

Leo smiled as he drew back, wincing. "And the same to you, Farmer Jones. It's been a rough ride—falling into a chasm, swimming in lava that sent me into that lake, and sizzling like bacon in a frying pan until our ever-ready Reaper pulled me out. Hell is the worst carnival ride I've ever been on."

"Glad you survived." Ben looked Leo over. Although a few small blisters marred his face, and burns pockmarked his pants and shirt, he seemed relatively unhurt by the lake, especially compared to Bart. "I found your cloak and brought it with me, but it disappeared."

Leo looked at the violin and mirror on the ground. "I see the other items survived relatively unscathed."

"They did." Ben picked up the mirror square's box and slid it into his pants pocket. "I don't understand how all of this works."

"Nor do I. And I don't want to become an expert on the topic, if you understand my meaning."

Charlotte arrived with Bart and faced the others. "This is Bartholomew, an associate of Alex. While I was crossing the Lake of Fire to pick up Ben, I sensed Bartholomew's presence because he doesn't belong in the lake yet, so I rescued him and absorbed him into my cloak to give him some time to heal."

Bart nodded, grimacing and breathless. "And I appreciate your kindness."

"It wasn't kindness. It was duty. You are the first condemned soul I have ever retrieved from the lake, so I wasn't sure I could do it. The lake tends to keep its own. It embraces dark hearts."

"Azrael's coming!" Austin ran to the gate and swung one side open. As he hurried to the other side, bright light burst from beyond the gate, growing brighter and brighter as it streamed from a tall humanoid figure walking out of the mist.

When Austin finished opening the other side, the figure clarified—a huge, winged man, every bit as tall as Caligar, carrying a flailing person under each arm. As he passed through, he glanced at Ben and company, then continued walking toward the lake without a word. When he arrived at the shore, he began chanting something in an odd language. With meter and rhyme, it sounded like a poem, maybe a lament for the souls who were about to be thrown into the Lake of Fire.

Charlotte glanced at the shining angel. "We have a few minutes, but we should hurry. Once he leaves, Austin will have to close the gate, and our chance will be lost. Azrael's presence disengages the gate's locking mechanism." She spread her arms, fanning her cloak. "I will draw Leo and Iona into my cloak so they can be transported to Earth."

"What about me?" Bart asked.

Charlotte turned toward him. "I will not take you with me. You are a condemned soul. Hell is your final destination."

"But I can help you fight Alexandria. I know her secrets, her methods, her vulnerabilities." He pointed toward the violin. "And I know how to use music as a weapon against her."

"I'm sure your skills are valuable, but God condemned you to hell, which means you are a foul beast who cannot be trusted. You will stay here."

Bart looked at Ben, his eyes wide as he heaved quick breaths. "Ben, tell her. I helped you find this place, and I sacrificed myself to keep you from falling into the chasm. You wouldn't have made it without me."

Ben gave Charlotte an affirming nod. "He's telling the truth. His efforts were heroic."

"Did you hear that? Did you hear that?" Bart grabbed the front of Charlotte's cloak and pulled her nearly nose to nose, his voice anguished. "I'm not the man I used to be. I can be trusted. I should be allowed to go."

Charlotte whipped a knife from a belt sheath and flashed the blade between her eyes and Bart's, growling. "The breaking of the warding will be *my* doing. *I* will be the one deciding who will leave hell, and my decision is to trust God's judgment, not yours. God decided to send you here, and here you will stay. Do you understand?"

Bart released her cloak and retreated several steps. "I ... I understand. And I think I've figured out what you plan to do. I know what breaks the warding."

"Perhaps you have figured it out, but keep quiet." Charlotte shoved the knife back into its sheath. She took a breath and exhaled, a trembling smile emerging as she gazed at Ben, Leo, and Iona. "I have so much to tell you but so little time. Azrael will return in mere moments, which means if we're going to act, we must act now."

Bart lunged at her, grabbed the knife from its sheath, and stabbed her in the chest. He jerked the knife out and ran toward the open gate, gasping as he raced on his burned legs.

Charlotte toppled into Ben's arms. As he laid her down gently, he shouted, "Someone stop him!"

"I got this." Iona dashed after Bart, her oversized helmet falling off as she pumped her arms and legs into a full sprint.

Charlotte coughed and gurgled. Blood oozed between her lips. "Ben …"

"Shhh." He pressed a hand over the wound. "Don't try to talk."

Iona dove and tackled Bart by the legs a few steps in front of the gate. He dropped and skidded, grinding his face into the ground.

Austin ran over and planted a foot on Bart's back. "I have him."

"Thanks." Iona scrambled to her feet, raced back to Charlotte, and knelt across from Ben. Tears streamed as Iona spoke through gasping breaths. "How bad … is she hurt?"

"Bad." Ben lifted his hand. Blood had already soaked Charlotte's shirt. "Real bad."

Leo knelt next to Iona and pushed a strand of hair from Charlotte's eyes. His lips trembled as if he were trying to speak, but no words came out.

Iona shouted toward Azrael. "Charlie's been stabbed! Can you do something to help her?"

Azrael, no longer carrying souls, turned toward them. "I am coming." He flapped his wings and flew low to the ground until he settled next to Charlotte's head. He looked her over for a moment before speaking. "I could heal her, but she does not wish to be healed. She planned her demise."

"Planned her demise?" Ben swallowed hard. "Why?"

Charlotte spoke with halting breaths, her lips shifting between a smile and a grimace. "I … I'm walking … in the footsteps … of the Messiah."

"Then you *want* to die?" Iona asked.

"Yes. This is the critical part of my plan to help Iona and Leo leave hell."

"No!" Pain streaked Iona's shout. "Charlie, don't do this! Let the angel heal you. We'll figure out some other way to escape." She looked at Azrael. "It has to be possible. Alex got out. So we can get out, right?"

Azrael, his expression shining but stoic, turned his blazing eyes upon her. "Alexandria used the terror of thousands of newly arriving souls to energize a portal. That method could theoretically be repeated, but it would require the deaths of a similar number of people on Earth. God does not sanction such murders."

Iona's tone spiked with anger. "But couldn't God have stopped Alex from doing it?"

The angel's glow continued unabated. "The Almighty One surely could have stopped her, but he often chooses to allow evil events to happen for various reasons that are beyond even the understanding of angels. Yet, trusting in those decisions is always wise, and Charlotte's way of providing for your escape is now the only way. And I will not heal her because, again, she does not want to be healed. She will die in mere moments."

Iona broke into a sob and said no more.

Ben's entire body shook as he kept pressure on the wound. Of course he wanted to save Charlotte, but after the angel turned aside every possible reason to save her, how could he? "What …" His voice breaking, he cleared his throat and tried again. "What do you want me to do? Lift my hand and let you bleed out?"

"Wait." She grasped his forearm. "I … I need to say something to … to Leo and Iona before I die." Blinking hard, she reached her free hand toward Leo. "Leo?"

He enveloped her hand in both of his. "I'm …" His voice cracked worse than Ben's. "I'm here."

Tears streamed down Charlotte's cheeks. "Please forgive me. I treated you … so badly. I broke your heart … and I did it … with malice. I was arrogant… thoughtless … cruel."

Leo brushed a tear from his own eye. "I forgive you. Completely."

"Thank you." She smiled, her voice quivering. "I don't deserve it."

Leo sniffed hard. "And I don't deserve anything good. I've done so many wrong things in my life."

"As have I. … But I'm glad … we've given one precious gift … to the world. Maybe she'll make up … for some of our wrongs."

"A gift?" Leo's brow lifted. "She?"

Charlotte's gaze drifted toward Iona. "Our daughter."

Iona gasped. "What? You're my mother? And Leo's my ..." Her voice quaked. "My father?"

Ben's ears heated. The news felt like a sledgehammer, and again, his thoughts felt so wrong. He had to shake them off.

Charlotte nodded, more blood trickling from her lips as she spoke, though her voice steadied. "Leo never knew about you. I secretly gave you up for adoption ... because I was ... too self-absorbed to be a mother. Then I went through a ... a dark valley. Drugs. Alcohol. Self-abuse. As low as I could go. When I reached bottom, I cried out to God ... to forgive me for the damage I had done." She took a deep, gurgling breath. "And he answered. He lifted me ... out of my pit and called me to return ... to being a Reaper, a calling I rejected as a teenager." She released Ben's arm and caressed Iona's cheek. "And now, all these years later ... I've finally seen the wonderful young woman you've become. I am content with my life. I blessed the world ... with you."

Iona laid her head on Charlotte's shoulder and wept. "Oh, Mother. Don't die. Ask the angel to heal you. Please. We can find another way out of hell. I know we can."

Charlotte combed her fingers through Iona's fiery hair. "There is no other way to break the warding. As it was for Jesus, a betrayer spilled my blood, and hell's gates will soon open because of my willing sacrifice. God has set your deliverance in motion. Now you must receive it."

Iona drew back and clutched Charlotte's hand. As she looked at Leo, new tears dripped. "Father?"

Leo gulped, his face ashen. "I didn't know. I swear."

"I know you didn't." She reached her arms around his neck and hugged him close. "I love you, Leo. I mean, Father."

When she drew back, Leo's tears flowed freely as he gazed at her. "I love you, too, Iona, my dear daughter."

Charlotte sucked in another gurgling breath and let it out slowly. "I'm ... I'm fading. Leo and Iona, come close and pull my cloak around you. Quickly. No questions."

Iona lay at Charlotte's side while Leo crawled around to the other side and did the same. Ben pulled the cloak over both of them.

Charlotte spoke with renewed energy. "I now absorb you into these fibers to keep you safe on Earth until your bodies can be found. Once you do find them, a Reaper must restore your souls to your bodies." She looked past Ben and focused on Austin. "Can you?"

Austin's cheeks reddened. "I ... I don't know. Maybe."

"You must. You're their only hope."

Azrael's voice boomed. "Be at peace, Charlotte. Austin is wise to have doubts. Such a task is beyond the abilities of most Reapers. Yet, there is one Reaper on Earth who is able to do what you ask."

Charlotte smiled weakly. "Good. Thank you. I can go in peace." Seconds later, the lumps under her cloak flattened. She unfasted a set of headphones from her belt and put them on over her cap, then stretched a mask over her nose and mouth. "I choose to pass away without the sounds or smells of hell invading my senses." She closed her eyes and whispered in halting phrases. "Now I lay me ... down to sleep. I pray the Lord ... my soul to keep. If I should die ... before I wake ... I pray the Lord ... my soul to take." She took in a final breath and exhaled for the last time.

Ben's throat clamped shut. Iona's mother lay dead, and Iona grieved somewhere within the cloak fibers, likely devastated by the loss. And now he had to find this other Reaper and restore Iona and Leo to their bodies. At the same time, Alex still lurked. Who could guess what trouble she had caused by now?

Austin's voice broke the silence, his foot still planted on Bart. "Azrael, what should I do with the murderer?"

"Leave him to me. I will throw him into the Lake of Fire, and this time, he will not return."

Swallowing to loosen his throat, Ben looked at the angel. "Has the warding been broken?"

"Yes, but it will soon be rebuilt by the evils it is designed to keep in this place. Take her body, and be on your way." Azrael walked toward Austin, his glow brightening the area around him. "And you, having served me well here, will go with him. I am terminating all Reaper duties in hell for the time being. As for Charlotte, her soul will remain in her body long enough for Austin to safely reap her into a cloak when you return to Earth. Then transport her body to her family and explain her heroic sacrifice."

Austin bowed his head reverently, his own tears evident. "Of course, Azrael. It will be my honor."

Azrael turned toward Ben. "And you may take Charlotte's cloak and rescue the souls of your friends from hell. It is clear that you are longing to do so."

Ben also bowed his head. "I am. Thank you."

Leaning over, Azrael grabbed Bart around the neck, pulled him out from under Austin's foot, and held him above the ground. He dangled, loose and motionless, his mouth tightly shut and his eyes wide. "Benjamin. Austin. I will return in a moment. Wait for me at the gate, prepared to leave." He strode toward the Lake of Fire, dragging Bart behind him.

While Austin collected the violin and bow, Ben put Iona's helmet on, then gently slid the cloak's sleeves off Charlotte's arms, rolled her to the side, and pulled the cloak free. Iona's cross necklace tumbled out of the folds and dropped to the ground.

"That's odd." Ben picked it up, slid it into his pocket, and rose. Time would tell if the necklace was real or soulish. "Austin, I plan to carry Charlotte on my back. Can you fold her cloak over my shoulders to make it easy to take with me?"

"Of course." Austin reverently folded the cloak and laid it in place, then helped Ben hoist Charlotte over his shoulders. He straightened and balanced her weight. She felt lighter than expected, maybe underfed in this barren world. Yet, she weighed him down. This courageous woman, this loving mother, battled the fiends in the Lake of Fire with one purpose in mind—to hurry back to her daughter. Though practically a stranger, Iona was beloved. Nothing would stop Charlotte from doing what she must to save her precious girl.

A sob tried to break through, but Ben quickly squelched it, though his body still quaked and tears trickled down his cheeks. Like Charlotte, he had to embrace a single purpose. Nothing could stop him from destroying the witch who caused all this heartache.

Austin set the violin and bow down. "I can carry her. Azrael told me to take her to her family."

Ben sniffed, trying to chase away the tears. "I know, but I'd like to carry her for now, if you don't mind."

"Not at all." Austin picked up the violin and bow once more. "You have a Reaper's heart. You came to take souls where they belong."

Charlotte's final words returned to mind. She had prayed "my soul to take," and now he had been charged with answering that prayer. "Yeah. Something like that."

Ben and Austin walked side by side to the gate and waited. When Azrael returned, Ben focused on his expressionless face. "Where can I find the Reaper who can put Leo and Iona back into their bodies?"

Azrael's eyes glittered like twinkling stars. "The one who fashioned herself as the queen of hell, Alexandria, is the only remaining Reaper on Earth. She has the power to restore them."

A shout of *What?* nearly exploded from Ben's gut, but he swallowed it down and kept his voice under control. "She's a villain. Our enemy. She would never agree to help us."

"I know of her evil character. It will be a difficult task to convince her to do a good deed while you are seeking to vanquish her. My understanding from Zachariel, however, is that you are a master planner. I am confident that you will find a way."

Ben whispered, "I hope so." Although the angel's words provided a boost, they were just words. "I'll do my best, but first I have to find her. There's no telling where she might hide while she's plotting something horrifically evil."

"You are correct. Your plan will need to be extraordinary. And it should begin with a decision regarding your reappearance on Earth. Where do you wish to go? I can send you there."

"Since I don't know what's been happening while I've been gone, I guess the best place to go would be wherever my wife is."

Azrael looked upward for a moment before refocusing on Ben. "I have located her. I will send you there. Walk forward through the gateway. Once past the barrier, you will come to a wall with an arched opening, lit by embedded lanterns on the opposite side. When you pass that, you will be safely out of hell, and you will be automatically transported to Earth."

"Thank you." Ben turned toward the gate boundary, thick mist only a few paces ahead. Refusing the urge to look back, he took a deep breath. "Ready, Austin?"

Still carrying the violin and bow, the young Reaper nodded, a smile emerging. "I'm ready, but you're not. The area between this gate and the wall Azrael mentioned is loaded with sulfur gas. You'll need a mask if you don't want to choke." He withdrew a camo handkerchief from his cloak pocket. "I have a spare. Washed it yesterday."

"Thanks. I'll take it." After they put their masks on, Ben strode across the boundary and into the mist of a swampy area. As Austin had warned, noxious sulfur fumes assaulted his nose, even through the mask, stinging his nostrils and burning his eyes. Soon, a ten-foot-high wall appeared, stretching out of sight into the mist to the left and right. Light shone from within an arched opening straight ahead.

As bats flew here and there, Austin broke into a jog and led the way. "Almost there."

"I'm right behind you." Seconds later, Ben passed through the opening into fresher air. He stripped the mask off and stuffed it into a pocket. Hell and all of its darkness lay behind, including souls who would stay there forever, eternally lost and suffering. His Reaper's heart, as Austin had put it, longed to rescue them all. But it was too late for them. He had to move forward, take these soul-laden steps— for Iona, Leo, and all of Earth.

Blinding radiance lay ahead. The two men walked directly into the light and rocketed into the sky.

# Chapter Sixteen

Kat stood in an alley next to an apartment building, her rifle leaning against an industrial dumpster. A mattress protruded through its partially open lid like a diseased tongue—covered with ripped fabric, rusted coils, and moldy padding. A putrid odor wafted out, evidence of spoiled food or maybe a dead rat.

She checked her earbuds to make sure they were firmly in place. The bud in the left ear, its microphone off, monitored the spy bug's channel, while the one in the right ear stayed connected to Jack and Trudy in their jet. So far, Alex hadn't said anything, though the hum of the cruiser's engines came through, as did an occasional cough from Alex and the clearing of her throat. Since she had recently entered her long-preserved body, it was possible that congestion had collected in her lungs. It would take some time to clear it out.

Kat shed a heavy backpack and peeked around the building's corner, her cheek against the coarse red bricks. Across the narrow, two-lane city road, the door to the bomb shelter stood less than a hundred feet away. Little more than a one-room, unlabeled shack, the entrance was probably the proverbial tip of the iceberg. Much more of the facility likely resided underground.

She whispered, "Trudy, still got a bead on Damien?"

Trudy's voice blended with the roar of the jet. "Not anymore. He was at the bomb shelter, but the signal disappeared."

"Yeah. Same reading here. He must've gone inside. No telling how deep the shelter goes."

"Right. To be bombproof, it probably goes way down."

"Okay. Remember how we play mousetrap?"

"Yep. One of my favorite maneuvers."

"Good. I'm going to use myself as bait. You know what to do."

"All right," Trudy said. "Dangerous, though. We don't have schematics for the bomb shelter."

"Just be there to nab the mouse when it tries to escape."

"You bet. We're going to land as close as possible. Maybe ten minutes. Then we'll have to walk. I assume you brought some weapons for us."

"Definitely. When you get here, look for a dark green backpack in a dumpster across the street from the shelter and around the corner of a brick apartment building. Meet you inside the shelter."

"On our way."

Kat unzipped the backpack and withdrew two high-capacity magazines. After attaching them to her belt, she rezipped the pack and set it in the dumpster under the mattress, then grabbed the rifle and jogged to the shelter's entrance.

The gray metal door stood ajar, an obvious breach of security. Ever since Chantal destroyed the angels, many of the government and corporate protection devices had fallen prey to bandits. Apparently the lock on this door was one of the victims.

She pulled the door the rest of the way open, revealing a concrete stairway that descended to a landing where it switched back to a second set of stairs. She snatched a flashlight from her belt and aimed the beam downward between the two flights. The switchbacks continued beyond the beam's reach, at least five more levels.

Aiming the beam and her rifle straight ahead, she descended the first set of stairs, then turned a one-eighty and descended the next, repeating the process six times before reaching a pair of metal doors. A rectangular box the size of an electrical outlet hung next to the righthand door. A finger-sized hole at the box's center had no label.

Kat eyed the hole. Since Damien said he was able to get past the first security check with her blood, this was probably the place where he used it. She leaned the rifle against the wall and pushed her finger through the hole. Something stung her fingertip. She jerked it out. A bead of blood leaked from a tiny puncture wound on the pad.

The door opened inward in perfect silence. Beyond it, a few widely spaced fluorescent ceiling fixtures flashed to life, illuminating a dim corridor that led to a partially open door at the end. Damien was likely in there somewhere, though the fact that the lights had been off indicated that he probably hadn't arrived in the last few minutes, depending on how long it took for the motion sensor to deactivate the lights.

Leaving the door open, Kat walked in, glancing at the walls and ceiling for hidden cameras, though with the angels long gone, the chances of anyone monitoring this hall from a security station seemed low. In any case, it was too late to worry about that now.

When she reached the next door, she nudged it with the rifle barrel and looked inside. Light shone from a glass ceiling fixture as well as from a lamp on a table next to a double bed. The scene looked like a motel suite, complete with a kitchenette and a computer-monitor combo on a desk.

A closed metal door dominated one of the walls—the vault Damien mentioned earlier. Like other vault doors in the angels' facilities, a ship's-helm wheel protruded from the center, almost close enough to the bed for someone to turn it while sitting on the mattress. A smaller door about six steps to the left of the vault stood closed, likely the entry to the bathroom or another bedroom. Maybe that was where Damien had gone. Yet, if he had the key to the vault, why would he go there?

Kat scanned the main room. If she could get into the vault quietly, grab the violin and mirror, and escape unnoticed, she wouldn't have to worry about Damien at all. Then she could find him later with the tracker.

She tiptoed to the vault and touched a key protruding from a locking mechanism at the center of the wheel. This was the key she had given Damien. Obviously he had been here, but why did he leave the key behind?

She laid her rifle on the bed, grasped the wheel, and tried to turn it, but it wouldn't budge. A red light flashed at eye level from a nearly imperceptible retina scanner embedded in the door. This hidden security check had to be the reason he hadn't opened the vault yet.

As she shifted her body to set her eye in front of the scanner, Alex's voice entered her ear. "Has Katherine arrived?"

"Yes," Damien whispered, also through the earbud. "The vault will be open in a moment."

"Good. I spotted her backup team. I will make sure they don't give you any trouble. When they are neutralized, you can use the alternate exit to escape."

"Understood."

"Remember. Do not show pity on the violin. It is a magnificent instrument, and I know you will be tempted to play it, but you must destroy it immediately, then kill Katherine at your first opportunity."

"I will."

Trudy pulled the backpack out of the dumpster, opened the main flap, and withdrew four semiautomatic handguns, four loaded magazines, and two tactical vests. As she and Jack put the vests on and attached the guns and magazines to their belts, the buzz of propellers drew near.

Trudy nudged Jack with an elbow. "I hear a drone."

"Yeah." He slapped a magazine into a handgun and chambered a round. "It's the angel cruiser. I'd know that sound anywhere."

"With Alex as pilot, I assume." Trudy loaded a gun and scanned the sky, searching the low clouds for a glimpse of the cruiser. "She could be anywhere."

"And we could be sitting ducks. That cruiser's got bomb bay doors between its landing runners. If she picked up a weapons payload, she could deploy it."

Trudy fastened her tactical vest. "Then let's hustle. Kat's had plenty of time to set the bait."

They ran toward the bomb shelter entrance. When they drew within a hundred feet, the angel cruiser swooped out of the clouds, its bay doors open. Three missile-like bombs dropped out and hurtled toward the shelter.

Trudy and Jack pivoted and dove back toward the alley. The moment Trudy hit the pavement and rolled, Jack at her side, a loud boom thundered. Hot wind whooshed over her, along with wood splinters and hunks of bricks. The debris jabbed at her body, mostly protected by her vest, though some penetrated her pant legs and long sleeves.

When the noise and wind ceased, they climbed to their feet and looked around. The cruiser no longer flew anywhere in sight, and its telltale propeller noise had silenced. Bruised and aching from head to toe, Trudy jogged with Jack to the shelter, the entrance building now in ruins. Jack lifted a section of the shattered door, revealing the stairwell—collapsed and hopelessly blocked.

Trudy kicked a broken board. "Now what?"

Jack dropped the door. "We have to call Kat. Let her know we're looking for another way in."

"If there is one." Trudy touched her earbud. "Kat, it's Trudy."

---

Kat stepped away from the scanner, grabbed her rifle from the bed, and stood in front of the door to the adjacent room. Aiming straight ahead, she pushed the door open with her foot. Damien stood in a bathroom, a finger pressed against his lips and another pointing at his ear. With no weapon, he appeared to be feigning cooperation with Alex through an earbud.

She waved the rifle, gesturing for Damien to come out and stand near the exit door. When he obeyed, she set her eye close to the retina scanner. After the quick scan, something clicked inside. She turned the vault wheel, oddly slick for some reason, and heaved the huge metal door open several inches, revealing a shallow alcove that housed a small table. A violin and bow rested on top, along with a head-high, floor-standing mirror in a gilded gold frame.

"I heard the vault open," Damien said, apparently to Alex.

Kat stepped into the vault and blocked Damien's view with the door. She stood in front of the mirror and looked at her reflection, undisturbed by his true statement. Yet, if it really was a lie detector, only a lie would let her know.

"Are you still in the adjacent room?" Alex asked.

"Yes, I want to make sure she removes the items so she can't close the vault to keep me from getting them. I will sneak out of the room in mere seconds."

Kat's reflection warped. The mirror emitted yellow sparks along with a sizzling sound, a reaction to Damien's lie, likely too quiet for Alex or even Damien to hear. After a couple of seconds, it settled to normal.

"Good," Alex said. "I want no mistakes. This is the most fragile part of my plan."

"Your plan is working perfectly," Damien replied. "She has fallen for your trap."

Kat stared at the mirror, waiting for it to react, but the reflection stayed normal. Damien had told the truth. This really was supposed to be Alex's trap. Was he playing a double agent's role to see who would win this battle of wits?

She backed away from the mirror far enough to see him. He stood at the exit doorway, still with no apparent weapon. If Alex had planned a trap, how could Damien pull it off without a way to neutralize an opponent?

Dizziness washed in. Damien seemed to split into two men, both images swaying as if standing on the deck of a storm-tossed ship. Trying to keep her balance, she grabbed the vault door. "Did you drug me?"

Damien smirked. "It's an Alex specialty, an ointment that I applied to the vault's wheel."

Kat fired the rifle multiple times, sweeping her aim to try to hit both images of Damien. He dove to the floor. The bullets drilled into the wall behind him. More dizziness swamped her mind. Numbness crawled along her stiffening limbs. She fell flat on her back, her fingers locked around the rifle. Begging her legs to move, she tried to kick the vault door closed, but they wouldn't respond.

Something boomed above, muted by the distance. The room shook but held firm. Kat looked at the ceiling. What could have happened up there?

"Katherine is now paralyzed," Damien said as he snatched the rifle from her stiff fingers.

Trudy's voice entered Kat's ear. "Kat, it's Trudy. Alex dropped bombs on the entrance. We're looking for another way to get in."

Kat gnashed her teeth. No use trying to reply. Damien and Alex would hear it, and nothing she could say would make Trudy and Jack work any faster.

Damien stepped past Kat, entered the vault, and retrieved the violin, bow, and mirror. After setting the mirror upright next to the bed, barely visible in Kat's point of view, he gazed at the violin, his trembling fingers caressing the polished wood. His eyes darted, as if nervously looking for someone who might stop him.

He set the bow on the strings and played a long note, adjusting a tuning peg as the sound resonated in the room. The mirror reflected his playing form. With each alteration of the note, the image bent and twisted. As soon as the string played the note properly, he switched to another string and tuned it, then the third and fourth.

When he finished, he closed his eyes and played a lovely melody that sounded classical. The reflection warped from Damien playing the violin to the bunker vault at the temple, the wall display in full view, including the new cracks Damien's gunshot had added.

Kat studied the image. Could this be a live view?

Damien stopped playing. Within seconds, the mirror returned to normal. "Alexandria, the violin and mirror work exactly as you described. There is no need for me to search for an alternate exit. I can use the mirror to leave."

"Don't you dare!" Alex shouted. "Destroy both immediately."

Damien smiled. "Why should I? I have the ultimate weapon in my hands, the only way to stop you from carrying out your evil schemes."

"You must obey. Your programming won't allow you to do otherwise."

He chuckled. "So you think."

"How did you overcome the vaccine's payload?"

"Wouldn't you like to know?" He lowered the violin. "Now let's discuss terms. I will be glad to destroy the violin and mirror if you will do me one small favor."

"And that is?"

"When you go to Viridi, instead of destroying Earth, you will leave it intact. I will restart the vaccine program with a payload that will force people to obey me. Earth will be mine, and Viridi will be yours."

Kat bent her brow. So Bart's suspicions were true. Alex did plan to destroy Earth.

A humming laugh emanated from Kat's earbud. "You are such a fool. There will be no negotiations. You will either destroy the violin and mirror immediately, or you will die."

Damien let out a derisive huff. "Is that so? How do you propose to kill me? You are flying in the sky, and I am buried deep in a bomb shelter."

"I'm sure you remember meeting Camilla, one of my hundred influencers."

"Yes, of course. She is a brilliant medical research scientist. A lovely woman."

"Indeed she is, and unknown to you, she planted what you might call a ticking time bomb in you, using technology similar to what the angels used to implant themselves in humans. Yet, the nearly microscopic chip required no incision, just a prick with an instrument she hid in her hand at the back of your neck when she kissed you."

Damien's face reddened. "What will this chip do?"

174

Alex hummed a laugh again. "As I said, it's a ticking time bomb. In less than four hours, it will release a toxin that induces insanity. One hour later, if you haven't already committed suicide, you will die from the toxin."

Damien touched the back of his neck. "I feel where it went in. Maybe Camilla numbed the skin when she injected the chip."

"Which proves that I am not lying, but you have hope. If you report to me with proof that you have destroyed the violin and mirror as well as Katherine Garrison, I will send a signal to the chip that will disable it."

Damien's respiration grew rapid. "How can I be sure that you will keep your word?"

"Simply put, you can't. But you should realize that I don't readily kill highly capable allies. You are free to believe what you wish."

"Vile witch!" He swung the violin and bashed it against the vault door. Splinters flew, some raining on Kat's face. He tossed the violin's broken neck to the bed and punched the mirror with a fist. It shattered, a hole at the center with crooked streaks radiating to the sides.

His face a twisted mask of pure rage, he shook the frame over Kat. Shards drizzled across her body until every piece of the mirror had fallen. "You women are all the same—you, Alexandria, Camilla. You use men. Deceive them. Then throw them away when you're finished with them."

Kat stared at his maniacal eyes. Although she could speak, anything she might say would probably make him even more furious. Considering the fact that he was letting Alex hear his unhinged rant, he probably was half out of his mind already.

Damien withdrew a camera phone from his pocket, took photos of the debris, and typed into the phone with his thumbs as he spoke. "Alexandria, I am sending you proof that the violin and mirror have been destroyed. In one of the photos, you will also see Katherine paralyzed on the floor. I have fulfilled your demands." He pressed a final button. "The photos should be there in a few seconds."

"Good," Alex said. "I will tell Camilla to arrange for your extraction from the bomb shelter. It might take quite some time, but I'm sure you have a water supply down there somewhere." After a brief pause, she added, "Ah, yes. I see your photos. Please tell Katherine that her position is appropriate. No one can help her. She has no hope."

"I'll tell her." Damien looked at Kat. "Alexandria said—"

"Don't bother." Kat grimaced at the pain. "I know your kind. You talk about women deceiving and using you, but you grovel at a wicked woman's feet like a tuck-tailed lapdog. You can't think for yourself."

"Easy for you to say. You don't have a deadly chip in your neck." Damien grabbed the rifle from the bed, set the butt against his shoulder, and took aim at Kat's face. "Alexandria, I am ready to shoot Katherine in the head at point-blank range. I will send a photo of the result."

"Good. Kill her. Kill her now."

# Chapter Seventeen

Kat stared at Damien. His evil smile grew as he slid his finger around the trigger. She tried to jerk her body into a roll but managed only a twitch.

Just as he squeezed the trigger, something crashed into him from the side. The rifle fired. The bullet thumped into the floor next to her head. A man wearing a military helmet knelt nearby, punching downward again and again, his gloved fist making contact with something out of view. With each blow, Damien cried out, "Stop! Please, stop!"

The man rose. Clutching Damien by the front of his shirt, he threw him onto the bed. As Damien gasped for breath, the man tossed the helmet to the floor and looked at Kat, his face finally clear. *Ben!*

"Kat," Ben said, his face red, "are you all right?"

Again she tried to move, but her limbs wouldn't obey. "No. Damien used some kind of paralysis ointment on me. I can breathe and talk, but not much else. And he's got an earbud. Alex is listening."

Ben spun toward Damien, plucked the earbud out, and turned the microphone off. "Is there a cure for the ointment?"

Lying on his back and trembling, Damien nodded as he sputtered through his words. "Time. She will be able to move in a few more minutes, maybe ten or so. If you help her try to walk, probably faster."

"Put him in the vault," Kat said. "He can't get into any trouble in there, but keep your gloves on if you touch the wheel. It has the paralysis stuff on it."

Ben grabbed Damien's arm, shoved him into the vault, and pushed it closed before kneeling next to Kat. "Want to try to get up?"

"Not yet. My arms are getting better, but I don't have any feeling in my legs."

Ben took his gloves off and slid them into a pocket. "Then we'll give it some time while we trade stories."

"First let me update Jack and Trudy." Kat touched her earbud. "Jack. Trudy. It's me. How are things topside?"

"Frustrating," Trudy said. "We haven't been able to find another door."

"Yeah. No surprise. Listen. Ben's here."

"Ben? How in the name of—"

"Don't ask. I haven't gotten the scoop yet. Just keep looking for another door, and I'll get back to you with the story."

"Copy that. But make it quick. That's one story I gotta hear."

With new tingles running down her legs, Kat lifted an arm toward Ben. "I'm ready to try now."

He grasped her wrist, hoisted her to her feet, and embraced her, holding her in place. A new wave of dizziness sloshed through her brain, and her vision glazed over. Someone else stood in the room, a person too fuzzy to identify.

"Can you stand on your own?" Ben asked.

"Give me a second." She blinked several times, clearing her vision. A young man wearing a hooded cloak and holding a violin and bow stood near the door, and a red-haired woman lay on the floor in front of him, both dressed in military camo. A dark splotch of blood covered most of the woman's chest, and a cap and headphones lay near her head. "Who are they?" Kat asked. "And is that woman dead?"

"Yes, Charlotte is dead." Ben helped Kat walk toward them. Her legs felt like rubber, but they began to accept more weight with each step, though if Ben let go, they might buckle. "Austin, here, is a Reaper. So was Charlotte. Bart killed her, but her sacrificial death opened the gates of hell for us to leave. The souls of Leo and Iona are in the fibers of a cloak I brought. We rescued them from hell."

Kat sucked in a deep breath. "Thank God! Oh, Ben, that's wonderful." Then the shadow of death made her smile wilt. "I mean, wonderful for them. Tragic for Charlotte."

Ben sighed. "You're right, and there's more to the tragedy. You see, Charlotte is—"

"Benjamin." Austin raised a hand. "Before you tell the story, there is something I must do immediately. Azrael's orders."

"Right. You need to reap Charlotte." Ben lifted a reddish cloak from the floor. "Can you put her in his one?"

"Her own cloak?" Austin smiled. "A reunion?"

"That was my thought."

After Austin shed his cloak and set it on the floor, Ben gave him the reddish one. When Austin put it on, he let out a gentle shushing sound. "If I may have quiet during the process, the procedure will be much easier."

Kat intertwined her fingers with Ben's and kissed his cheek, warmth racing along her awakening arms and legs. Excitement and sadness blended together, the saving of souls and the loss of life. So many questions flooded her brain, but for now she needed to be patient and wait for the answers to come at the right time.

Austin pulled a cloak sleeve over his hand and laid his palm over Charlotte's eyes. "Charlotte, since I am wearing your cloak instead of my own, I will need your help to complete the procedure. I am using the older method to reap your soul. I will extend my disembodied hand into your brain to draw you out through the windows to your soul, but since your DNA is in this cloak, you will have to exert your will to be absorbed into it."

Closing his eyes, he inhaled deeply. After a few seconds, he smiled. "Ah. There you are, my friend. I have you in my hand. As a shepherd of souls, I am walking in the footsteps of Jesus. I will take good care of you."

Kat shivered. A good shiver. This felt like a holy moment.

Sparkles of light ran along the cloak's sleeve and up to the shoulder. Another splash of sparkles raced up the back, as if drawn to the first one. They combined in an explosion of glitter. Austin laughed, a tear trickling down his cheek. "They are so happy. A mom reunited with her daughter."

"Mom?" Kat whispered. Then she covered her mouth. "Sorry."

"No. It's fine. The reaping's finished." Austin brushed the tear away. "Charlotte is Iona's birth mother. I never knew that before today."

"That's huge news." Kat drew away from Ben and set a fist on her hip, unable to suppress a grin. "What else did you discover during your latest adventure in hell?"

"I'll tell you all about it soon." He glanced around the room. "No windows. I get the impression that we're underground, maybe a basement."

Kat lowered her fist. "Bomb shelter. And we're trapped, unless there's an alternate exit. Trudy's up top. She said the main one's collapsed, and she can't find another access door. She'll contact us if she does."

"Then we'll wait a few minutes." Ben cleared a space on the bed. "Let's sit and get each other up to date."

After they exchanged stories, Ben rose from the bed and looked at the debris from the shattered violin and mirror. "So what you're saying is that Alex believed these could take her down. She had to destroy them."

Kat nodded. "I don't know how they could be used against her, but it's obvious that she believes they can."

"Bart told me his theory, but I'll save that info for after we get out of here. Escaping is priority number one, then we can hatch a plan to go after Alex. And I was warned by the angel that it'd better be a great plan."

"Then we'll put our heads together and pull out all the stops. But, like you said, escaping comes first, and the violin might be the key. I think Damien knew a way to use them to transport himself out of here, but Alex threatened him. A chip embedded in his neck will poison him in four hours unless someone removes it."

Ben pointed at her. "That's the ticket. Let's offer him a deal. Tell us how to use the violin and mirror to escape. In exchange, Trudy will extract the chip."

Kat lifted the violin's broken neck from the bed. "I'm afraid its playing days are over."

"Not a problem. We brought Alex's violin from hell." Ben turned toward Austin. "Where is it?"

"I'll get it, but first ..." He shed his cloak and extended it toward Ben. "Careful. Precious cargo in there."

"You bet there is." Ben took the cloak. The moment he put it on, a woman's voice entered his ear, as if whispered from far away.

"Raise the hood." A slight tremor in his hand, Ben pulled the hood over his head. A shimmer ran along his shoulder, then out of sight, apparently into the hood. "Now I can speak to you more easily. Directly into your ear."

Ben blinked. "Charlotte?"

"Yes. Even though I am now a disembodied soul, I am still a Reaper, and I have the power to talk to you. Leo and Iona can't speak to you directly, but I can relay their messages."

"Are they all right?"

"They're as well as can be expected. Iona is a trooper and refuses to complain about the stuffy conditions. Leo says he feels like a squashed sardine, and he mentioned that the odor suddenly worsened, but he'll get used to it."

Ben smiled. "No apologies. It's hard-earned sweat."

"Ben?" Kat squinted. "Are you talking to Charlotte's soul?"

"Yeah. Pretty amazing, isn't it?" He ran a finger along a sleeve. "She and Leo and Iona are in these fibers, and they're doing fine.

But we can talk more about them later." He turned toward Austin. "The violin?"

Austin lifted his cloak from the floor, revealing the violin and bow. Ben picked them up and withdrew the mirror square from his pocket. "Let's make our offer to Damien."

Covering her hands with her sleeves, Kat grasped the vault's wheel and opened the door. Damien sat inside with his back against the vault's rear wall. He blinked at the light, dark bruises on both cheeks. "I heard your conversation." He grimaced as he spoke. "I accept the parameters of the deal."

Ben extended the violin. "If you break this one's neck, I'll break yours."

"No need for threats. I am motivated by self-preservation and revenge." Damien climbed to his feet and took the violin and bow. "We are allies now. I will take us to the temple's vault room."

"Can you go somewhere besides that room?"

"Anywhere I've been before. I visualize that place and play the tune that comes to mind."

"Then the first place we go should be to the shelter entrance at street level. That's where Trudy is. She'll do the surgery to save your life."

Damien nodded. "Understood."

Kat cocked her head. "Is your ability something you learned, or is it an inborn talent?"

"Both. Only a few people have the natural ability, and the talent must also be developed." Damien played a long note on a string. "Give me a moment to tune this violin. It won't work otherwise."

While Damien tuned the strings, Ben eyed his nimble fingers. Since he was a chemist intimately involved with the vaccine production, maybe Alex called on him for other scientific projects. Using his ability to travel to the towers might come in handy. "Have you been to any of the Arctic Circle towers that create a conduit to the Oculus Gate?"

A proud smile stretched Damien's bruised cheeks. "Of course. I formulated the coating for the antennas so they could withstand the extreme cold in that environment as well as the extreme heat that accompanies their use."

"Which towers did you visit?"

"All four. I personally supervised the application of the coating in order to ensure consistency. Why do you ask?"

Ben stroked his chin. Better to keep the reason a secret. "It helps to know the depth of your involvement. I might ask more questions later."

"As you wish."

While Damien continued tuning, Ben drew Kat and Austin closer, whispering, "It's time to brainstorm. Can we get Jack and Trudy on board?"

Kat took one of her earbuds out, used a fingernail to adjust the frequency, and gave it to Ben. "Here."

He pushed the bud under his hood and inserted it. "Jack? Trudy? You two listening?"

"Yep," Jack said. "We found another entry two blocks from the main one, but the stairwell's collapsed there, too. Looks like it's been that way a long time. Probably happened during the angel takeover. Trudy's heading back to the main entry, and I'm hustling to our transport jet to get a first-aid kit. Trudy said it sounds like she's going to be doing some minor surgery soon."

"You're right. Good to think ahead. Now let's do a bit of brainstorming." Ben guided Kat and Austin to the corridor, though still in sight of Damien. "It's clear that Alex wants to go to Viridi and destroy Earth, probably out of spite. How could she do that?"

"Nuclear arsenal's gone around the world," Kat said. "At least the most recent intel says it is."

Ben nodded. "That's probably true, but we shouldn't rule it out. We'll keep it in mind."

"It's pretty obvious," Jack said. "They'll use the Arctic Circle network to send the wicked witch of the far south to Viridi, then the one hundred influencers will follow without bothering to turn the towers off when they leave. Massive quakes could wipe out nearly everyone."

Ben looked at Kat. "Your thoughts on that theory?"

"Since Alex sent laborers to rebuild the towers, my guess is that they'll make all four more powerful than before, probably with failsafe measures to protect them from saboteurs like us."

"And the result?"

She looked upward in thought as she spoke. "Worst case, the conduit creation could cause massive plate shifts throughout the world. We would have enormous tsunamis, continental collisions resulting in the folding and faulting of strata, which, in turn, could set off severe tectonic uplift and orogeny."

Jack whistled. "I didn't understand all of that, but it sounds like Earth's surface would buckle like wadded aluminum foil."

"Yeah, pretty much. And with no escape. Going underground wouldn't help. You'd get fried by upwelling magma, crushed by collapsing walls, or thrown into a chasm by the Earth bucking like a bronco. And flying wouldn't help either. Volcano eruptions would spew so much gas and ash, you would die from toxic fumes."

"Then no survivors," Ben said. "Alex would achieve her goal."

"Most likely."

Charlotte spoke from the hood. "Iona would like to add something."

"Charlotte's speaking." Ben touched his hood. "This will be my signal that she's talking to me."

When the others nodded, Ben focused on the voice. "What does Iona want to say, Charlotte?"

"She said if the plan to destroy the world is obvious, it's probably not Alex's plan. Count on her to use the towers as a distraction. She'll have something else up her sleeve."

"In other words, an alternate way to destroy Earth." After Ben repeated Iona's theory to the others, he sighed. "Okay, we have our work cut out for us. Distraction or not, we have to stop the towers from creating earthquakes, and we have to watch for an alternate plan at the same time."

"I have more information about the violin's ability," Charlotte said.

Ben touched the hood again. "Tell me."

"If I have understood the situation correctly, the violinist you have there … Damien, I believe."

"Yes. That's his name."

"He said he can create a tune to make a place appear in the mirror so you can travel there. This is true. During my years as a professor of Middle Eastern antiquities, I learned about this mirror and music phenomenon, but there are other ways to conjure the images. Another option is to know the correct melody to match the place you want to go, which requires a spiritual connection. The violinist must compose the melody based on the notes that come to mind when he establishes the connection through prayer and meditation. A final option is to play an already composed melody that is specifically coordinated with the place."

Ben glanced at Kat. She fidgeted, her eyes locked on him, obviously eager to hear the conversation. It would be best to prompt Charlotte for answers quickly.

"Do you know of melodies like that?" Ben asked.

"The great master Antonio Vivaldi composed a piece in his day that opened a critical portal. He called it *Il Salmo dell'Eternità*, that is, *The Eternity Psalm*. If the piece is played, the mirror opens the gateway to eternity."

Ben blinked. "Eternity? As in heaven or hell?"

"A passage that leads to one or the other. A person who touches the mirror would be transported to the eternity that God judges appropriate for that person."

Ben squinted at Kat, a sign that Charlotte said something hard to believe. "That sounds like a myth. How could anyone possibly prove where it goes?"

"According to Vivaldi's journal, he knew that the piece was powerful because he saw his own mirror change when he played it. A fellow priest touched the mirror and disappeared into it. Terrified, Vivaldi prayed for understanding. An angel appeared to him and explained the music's power."

Something squeaked in the other room. Ben stepped toward the door and peered inside. Damien sat on the bed, shifting on the squeaky springs while staring at the broken violin.

Ben retreated to the corridor. "Why would Vivaldi compose a piece like that? What motivated him? How did he know what notes to write?"

"No one knows for sure. Only theories."

"What about the mirror? Was it somehow special?"

"Indeed it was. Made up of many identical squares, it covered a wall, and it eventually came into the possession of an American a couple of centuries ago, but that's another story. Our quest must be to obtain the music."

Ben lowered one hand and touched the hood with the other. "How can we do that?"

"As you might imagine, Vivaldi considered the music too dangerous to allow anyone access to it. So, because he dedicated it to King David of Israel, he secretly sent it to Jerusalem where it was hidden in a museum archive. During my studies, I learned about the secret and sneaked into the archive in a deep cellar where I found the original piece preserved under glass. It is quite short. No more than twenty seconds of playing time. But before I could take a photo, a guard chased me out. Fortunately, I avoided being arrested."

Ben whispered, "We could use it to send Alex back to hell."

"Exactly. Straight into the Lake of Fire, I hope."

"Okay. I have a plan coming together. Let's get it rolling." Ben turned toward Damien. He stood within the main room, the violin and bow no longer in playing position. "Did you finish tuning it yet?"

"A few moments ago, but you seemed busy with your comrades, so I waited." Damien lifted the violin and played a long, crisp note. "This violin is not as exquisite as the one I destroyed, but it is adequate."

Ben led the others back into the room and displayed the mirror square in his palm. "Let's hope this is adequate."

"We'll soon find out." Damien closed his eyes. "Pardon me while I visualize the entry to this bomb shelter."

"You do that." Ben sidled to Kat and whispered, "Record anything he plays."

"On it." She activated a recording app on her computer pad.

Damien took a deep breath and began playing a melody that shifted from a slow dirge to a more upbeat modern tune. After a few seconds, he whispered while still playing, "The mirror?"

Ben, Kat, and Austin looked at the mirror in Ben's hand. The image showed a city street with scattered construction debris.

Kat pointed. "The entrance used to be right there. And there's Jack with Trudy behind him. Jack has the first aid kit, so this is current." She touched the surface near the corner. "See? They're—" Her voice warped, unintelligible. Her body stretched, thinning to transparency. As if caught in a suction, she streamed into the mirror. Seconds later, she appeared in the image, sitting among the debris.

While Damien played on, in the mirror, Jack and Trudy ran to Kat and helped her rise. She brushed dust off her pants and spoke to Jack and Trudy as they held her upright.

"Austin," Ben said. "Can you carry Charlotte's body? You're next."

"Sure." Austin scooped her into his arms and sidled up to Ben. "Now just touch the mirror?"

"It seems so." Ben moved the mirror, still in his palm, close to Austin's finger. "Ready?"

"Ready." Austin touched the image. Like Kat, he and Charlotte elongated and disappeared into the mirror, then appeared on the street.

Damien stopped playing. "According to the lore, because I played the tune three times, the image will remain for about sixty seconds, which means that we both have plenty of time to touch it, but I doubt that it can send itself through its own portal."

"True. So either one of us has to stay here, or we have to leave the mirror behind."

"And since we made a deal, I shouldn't be the one to stay."

"True again." Ben looked around for any sign of a secret way out, but nothing came into view. Yet, something moved in the broken mirror shards scattered on the floor—images of Kat, Jack, Trudy, and Austin. Damien's playing had created a portal in every piece. "I need something to carry the broken pieces in."

Damien pointed at the bed. "A pillowcase."

"Perfect." Ben set the mirror square on the bed, grabbed the pillow, stripped off the case, and, touching only the edges of the mirror shards, placed more than a dozen of the biggest pieces in the case. He saved one and set it next to the square, then grabbed Iona's helmet and put it on. "I'll take the square with me, and we'll touch the other one."

"You go first," Damien said. "If the image disappears, I can bring it back."

Ben looked him in the eye, studying him for any sign of deception. Trusting him felt shaky. He could easily transport himself somewhere else, but then who would remove his deadly chip?

Damien huffed in a derisive way. "Okay, we'll touch it at the same time."

"Good. No apologies for not trusting you." Ben slid his hand under the square and set it in his cloak pocket, then, clutching the pillowcase, he gave Damien a nod. "Now."

They each set a finger on the shard's image.

# Chapter Eighteen

Ben felt himself stretching, though no pain accompanied the sensation. Like plunging headfirst with a toboggan on a steep slope, he zoomed into the mirror at what seemed like lightning speed. Seconds later, he stood upright with his hands in the same position, one holding the pillowcase and the other ready to touch the mirror shard.

Less than a second later, Damien appeared next to him, the violin and bow in hand. He looked himself over. "Well, that was an interesting experience."

Trudy pointed at a clear spot on the pavement. "Sit. I'll have a look." When Damien complied, she crouched behind him and ran a finger along the back of his neck. "Yeah, something's here. Tiny, though." She reached toward Jack. "I need the kit."

He set it on the ground and opened the lid. Trudy plucked a scalpel and cleaned it and Damien's neck with an alcohol pad. "It's shallow, so I won't have to cut deep. I can inject some lidocaine. It's up to you."

Damien shook his head. "Just get the chip out. If Alexandria can send a signal to disable it, she might be able to tell it to activate early."

"Okay. Here goes." Trudy cut into his neck and caught the seeping blood with a gauze pad. As she worked, Damien squeezed his eyes shut, wincing. "I see it." She grabbed tweezers from the kit and pulled the chip out. "Got it." She wrapped the chip in the gauze pad and passed it to Jack. "Now to clean him up."

Ben shifted close to Jack. "What do you make of it?"

Jack dabbed at the chip with a clean part of the pad. "Too small to study with the naked eye, but if it can receive a signal, it can be tracked."

"And that means we can be tracked if we take it with us."

"Exactly."

"But if we can figure out how to track it ourselves, we could find any influencer who has a chip."

"True." Jack peered at the chip. "I could encase it in lead to make it untraceable. I saw a box at the temple bunker that might work. Probably has some tools in it to study the chip with."

Ben took the helmet off, tucked it under his arm, and raised the cloak's hood over his head. "Then let's go. We'll work out our plans there."

"Wait," Charlotte said. "Iona has an urgent point to make."

Ben touched the cloak's hood. "Go ahead, Charlotte."

"Remember that Leo's in a preservation capsule, and it's running out of energy. We need to find it and restore him before we do anything else."

"Good point." Ben waved for everyone to come close. "Let's brainstorm again."

"One second." Trudy applied an adhesive bandage to Damien's surgical wound. "Ready."

When they gathered together, Ben guided Damien out of earshot, huddled with the others, and told them what he knew about the situation at the mausoleum. Iona, speaking through Charlotte, interjected a few details at times. "So the number one priority is to save Leo's body. Any ideas?"

Jack raised a hand. "Bart told me the mausoleum is near where Chicago used to be. That narrows it down some."

Charlotte spoke up. "Iona says it's a small building with a generator and a statue of a phoenix bird."

When Ben relayed Iona's words, he added, "That narrows it down even more. Is there any way to get a heat-signature reading from cemeteries in that area? Since only dead bodies are there, any heat reading would be something to check on."

Kat tapped on her computer pad. "I'm sending a SkySweep drone in that direction right now. It'll scan for a heat reading. The temple computer can give us a satellite look at the area. When we find the cemeteries, we can pinpoint the locations for the drone."

"How long till the drone gets there?" Jack asked.

Kat squinted at her pad. "Three hours."

"And how long does Leo have left?"

Ben looked at the time on the computer pad. "Based on what Iona told me, I think about six hours. We can get there before the deadline with the right transport."

"Okay," Jack said. "We'll need something with a higher passenger capacity than that jet we borrowed. On the way here, I saw a helicopter close by that should hold everything we need and get us to the area in plenty of time."

"And you'll *borrow* the chopper?" Ben asked.

Jack smiled. "Yeah. We'll give it back. I promise. But once we're at the cemetery, how do we restore their souls to their bodies?"

"Alex has to do it, and that's the trickiest part, but I'm working on a plan. The priority for now is to keep Leo's capsule running. We can take fuel and our own generator to power it until we figure out the rest." Ben patted Jack's shoulder. "You and Trudy procure the chopper and fly it to the temple to pick up our supplies. Think about what you and Trudy will need to fly that jet to Jerusalem."

Jack blinked hard. "Jerusalem? Why there?"

"Spy mission. Underground archive in a museum. I'll tell you more later."

Trudy grinned. "Mysterious. I like it."

"We don't speak Hebrew," Jack said as he tapped out a message on his phone. "I know a guy there who'll help. That is, if he's still alive. He was the angel-resistance commander in Israel, and most of them got smoked out. I haven't heard from him in months."

Trudy cringed. "Do you mean Daniel the Destroyer? We don't want to go in guns blazing, or Alex will hear about it. Stealth is better."

"Daniel can do stealth, but we'll need bribe money. Greasing palms is one of his specialties." Jack made a final tap on his phone. "Done. Let's hope we hear from him soon."

"Money's no problem," Kat said. "You have the access code to Queen Laramel's account. Take what you need."

Jack grinned. "Unlimited funding from heaven. Gotta love it."

"Time's wasting." Ben waved a hand. "Get your butts moving."

Jack and Trudy took off at a fast trot down the street.

Kat's computer pad chimed. She tapped on her screen and frowned. "Message from Alex." She turned the screen toward Ben. "It's a photo of Iona at the mausoleum. The text says to halt our activities or Iona will, and I quote, 'be torn from limb to limb.' Alex said she would've told us exactly where Iona is if we had cooperated with her, but it's too late for that."

Ben squinted at the image. Iona stood within an open mausoleum. She appeared to be fine, though a bit glassy-eyed. "Run the background against all mausoleum photographs in the Chicago area to see if we can get a match."

"On it." Kat began tapping on the computer pad. "Shouldn't take too long."

"Good." Ben grasped her arm and drew her close. "Keep working on it. I still have Charlotte's body to take care of and Damien to deal with."

"I understand." Kat kissed him. "But don't trust Damien. He's a termite."

"True. He's the reason I didn't tell you everything I learned in hell. I'll explain more later when we're alone."

"Got it." Kat looked again at the pad and continued tapping.

Ben retrieved Damien and joined Austin. Damien inhaled, swelling his chest. "Benjamin, seeing you collaborating with your kin is quite inspiring." He touched the bandage on the back of his neck. "And I appreciate your help with the chip."

"Then maybe you can help me plot against Alex."

"If I can."

Ben gestured with a hand toward Austin. "This Reaper doesn't have any experience transferring souls from a cloak into a body. But we heard from an angel that Alex is able to do it."

"Ah!" Damien nodded. "That is quite a dilemma. We need the queen of hell to interfere with her own cause."

"True, but since she probably doesn't see Leo and Iona as big risks, I think she would be willing to do it if we can negotiate a trade."

Damien's lips thinned. "She does enjoy bargaining. But she always wants an unbalanced deal, one that heavily favors herself."

"Okay, then we have to offer her something that's valuable to her and not necessarily valuable to us."

"Yes, that would be equitable, since Leo and Iona are valuable to you but not to her."

"What if we offer her Viridi?"

Damien blinked. "How can you do that?"

"We are in close contact with the head of the only remaining family from that planet. If he stands down, Alex won't have to worry about battling him for control. Caligar is not only physically formidable—he knows the secrets of his world. He would be difficult to conquer."

"But would Caligar agree to give up his home?"

"With the right incentive." Ben stroked his chin. Now that a seed had been planted in Damien, it was time to plant another in Alex. Whether or not something would sprout from the seeds remained to be seen. The plan would have to be adjusted according to Alex's response to the offer. Of course, he and Caligar would never hand Viridi over to her, but with the right kind of persuasion, maybe she could be convinced that they would make the trade.

Yet, that plan would have to wait for another priority to be taken care of. Ben looked at Austin and bowed his head. "I'm sorry about the loss of your friend. Is there anything special we should do with her body?"

Austin crouched next to Charlotte and ran a hand across her hair. "In the past, Reapers have been buried or cremated, but after the radioactive era, most chose a ceremonial rite that includes cremation and the spreading of the ashes at whichever site the Reaper chose before dying. She never told me of her preferences, but you can ask her. I will be glad to take care of the arrangements."

Ben touched his hood. "Charlotte? Did you hear?"

"Cremated," she said. "Then send my ashes to my family in an urn."

"Suppose we can find the preservation capsule soon. Is it possible to get your body into it in time?"

"I don't have any experience in that area, Ben, but I doubt it. My physical brain is probably already deteriorating, and rigor mortis is setting in. Besides, I gave my life willingly, and I am not taking it back."

Austin lifted Charlotte's corpse into his arms again. "Since I am a Reaper, I was able to hear what she said. I will do as she asked." He glanced around. "I don't know this city. Could you tell me where to find a local crematorium?"

"I will." Damien set a hand on Austin's elbow.

While the two talked, Ben returned to making his plans for his battle of wits with the queen of hell. The photo of Iona served not only as a warning, but as emotional bait. Alex provided the background scene to lure her enemies to the mausoleum, a way to find the right place, probably to set a trap. Then again, she might have set everything up so she could offer her services to restore Iona and Leo in exchange for Viridi. In other words, she was already multiple steps ahead. She wouldn't mind at all trading her hostages for an entire planet.

Ben tightened his jaw. Outsmarting her would be a monumental task. The pieces of a strategy were coming together in his mind, but to make it work, every person on the team would have to be able to adjust on the fly. Fortunately, he had just the team to pull it off.

Now it was time to set his own bait.

Ben pointed at Damien. "Can you take us to the temple vault room?"

He lifted his brow as if surprised. "I assume so. I have been there."

"Then get ready. We need to move fast, and transporting is faster than walking. We'll use one of the mirror shards."

Kat set a finger on her computer pad, a signal that she was ready to record Damien's next tune.

After stepping away from Damien and Austin, Ben withdrew Damien's earbud from his pocket, turned its microphone on, and inserted it. "Alex, this is Ben Garrison. Are you listening?"

"Benjamin, how good to hear from you." As usual, her cocky tone dripped with pretension. "To what do I owe this pleasure?"

Ben rolled his eyes A wisecrack would feel good, but angering Alex when he needed her help wasn't a good idea. "I have a proposal for you."

"Oh, really? A proposal? How intriguing. Do tell."

# Chapter Nineteen

Ben, still wearing Charlotte's cloak, sat in the helicopter's pilot seat as he flew at the bird's maximum speed. According to Iona's guess, communicated to him by Charlotte through the cloak's fibers, they had less than an hour before the preservation capsule would run out of juice. Getting everything ready had taken far too much time, but all the preparation would be worth it.

The urgency kept everyone quiet for most of the trip, though they did go over the plan a few times, at least the parts that Ben wanted everyone to know. He had to keep a few critical details between himself and Kat, having written those portions for her eyes only. Speaking them would have alerted Charlotte, and she likely would have passed them along to Leo and Iona.

Sitting in the copilot's seat, Kat scanned the controls. With Damien stowed in the cargo hold and the rotor noise shredding their words, they could speak through their earbuds without concern that he could listen in. She pointed at the GPS map. "The coordinates Alex gave us lead to a cemetery, four minutes away. Let's hope it's the right one."

"The heat signature says so. Someone's alive down there."

"The satellite scan wasn't all that clear. And Alex could've easily fooled the scanner by tying a dog or some other animal there."

"It's the right place. Alex wants to do this deal. She wants Viridi."

Kat sighed. "True, but trusting her at any step along the way feels like bad strategy."

"Which is why we put so many failsafe measures in the plan. We trust her when her words match her self-interests. Otherwise, we consider her to be Satan's housecat."

"And the first failsafe is what you'll give to Iona if Alex does what you're predicting she'll do."

"Exactly." Ben pulled two miniature tracking transmitters from his pocket and set them on his palm. The size and shape of thick coat buttons, they would be easy to conceal. "If Alex balks, I'll secretly give Iona the mirror and the transmitters. We're all on board with that."

"The plan was already balancing on a razor's edge." Kat reached over and used a fingernail to flip a tiny switch on each transmitter, turning them on. "Don't get me wrong. It's an amazing plan, but it's super complex, and we all have to adjust on the fly in a split second, depending on how Alex responds. It'll be nerve wracking."

"True. But I have confidence in everyone." Ben pushed the transmitters back into his pocket. "Our team will get the job done."

"Speaking of the team …" Kat touched her earbud. "Jack. Trudy. Got an update?"

Her voice emanated from Ben's earbud, followed by Trudy's. "We're going Mach two over the Atlantic. This eagle's got some serious kick. We'll get to Jerusalem ahead of schedule."

"Good," Kat said. "Let us know when you find the museum. We're almost to the mausoleum, so we're going silent for a while."

"Oh. Wait. We've got a bogey on our tail. Out of sight distance, but Jack spotted it on radar. Someone's definitely following us."

"One of Alex's hounds is my guess," Ben said. "She wants to know what you're up to."

"Let's hope it's just recon. This buggy's got no air-to-air weapons to fend them off. When we land, we can take care of ourselves with the sidearms we brought. Until then, we're sitting ducks if they decide to try to take us out."

"You'll be fine. Alex's curiosity will get the best of her. Just watch your back when you're on foot. Maybe you can lose them in the city."

"Copy that. Update you when we can."

197

"We'll do the same." Ben began a slow descent. Below, the cemetery drew closer, a group of mausolea in the midst of hundreds of gray, mildew-covered tombstones. Close to the center, a generator shack stood nearby. A parking lot lay about a hundred yards from the site, much of the pavement pockmarked with holes. "I see the burial vault. I'll put us down in the parking lot. Short walk from there."

"All right," Kat said. "Keep your earbud turned on. Let's hope she won't have any communication jammers."

"Hard to guess what tricks she'll pull, but I'll have the flare gun. I'll fire it if I get in trouble."

Kat scanned the sky. "No sign of the angel cruiser yet. Maybe she sent us to the wrong place after all."

"No. I expected her to be late. She'll want to pinch the deadline to the max. Good thing we brought a power supply." Ben set the chopper down between two shallow craters on the lot's pavement and cut the engine as he scanned the lot. At least five other craters marred the pavement, and the rusted remains of military vehicles lay scattered about. Grass and weeds grew through hundreds of cracks throughout the lot. "This place is literally a warzone. During Apocalypse One, this area housed a major military outpost. They probably parked tanks or missile launchers here. Big target for the enemy to hit."

"No worries about targeting the graves," Kat said. "Waste of ammo. That's why the mausoleum was preserved."

"Right. Though from the air it looked like a few of them took some damage. I saw a crater where a grave used to be." Ben picked up a pen and a pad of paper from the console and wrote: *That's where to gather the bones, but it's out of sight of the chopper.*

Kat read the note and wrote her own note in response: *I saw it from the air, but no worries. Damien's secure. He won't go anywhere.*

Ben gave her a thumbs-up sign.

"I'll get your gear." Kat rose and, lowering her head, shuffled to the passenger seat. She lifted a wheeled metal box from the seat and rolled it toward the cockpit. "Flare gun's in there with the battery pack. It has a universal power adapter, so you should be able to figure out how to plug in Leo's capsule. Also water bottles, snack bars, and a change of clothes for both Iona and Leo. Her helmet's in there, too."

"Let's see if we'll need those right away." Ben raised the cloak's hood. "Charlotte, does Iona have a read on her body's hunger and thirst?"

Charlotte spoke through the hood's fibers. "She's famished. Iona is unable to tell if she needs anything else. Hunger and thirst are overwhelming her senses."

"We'll be ready to deal with anything." Ben touched the hood. "Charlotte, just a reminder of the plan. I'm counting on you to give me Reaper coaching while I talk to Alex, maybe clue me in on her behavior. I don't want her pulling the wool over my eyes."

"I remember, but one thing I forgot to mention earlier. Since Alex is a Reaper, she will be able to hear me if I speak at a normal volume. You will have to train your ears for my whispers. Also, remember that she is an Owl. Avoid eye contact if you can. Owls aren't true mind readers, but their perception skills are extraordinary. I learned that from my years with Austin."

"Understood."

"Do you have the extra earbud?" Kat asked.

Ben patted his pants pocket. "Right here." He opened the cockpit door, picked up the box, and hauled it out as he stepped down from the chopper. After zipping his jacket, he extended the box's handle. As he walked toward the mausoleum with the box in tow, he looked at the sky from one horizon to the other. On this clear but cold day, Alex had no clouds to hide the cruiser behind. It would be easy to hear her coming from far away. "Winter finally hit here," he said into the earbud. "Any rain or snow in the forecast?"

"Clear for now," Kat replied. "Snow coming in three hours. If we finish this fast enough, we can buzz out of here and stay ahead of the storm on the way home."

"Let's hope so." Ben stepped off the parking lot pavement onto a narrow gravel path that led toward the mausolea section. Wading through browning, knee-high weeds, he weaved around broken or toppled tombstones, damaged by lack of maintenance over the many years, or debris slung by the nearby bombings.

When the mausoleum came into view, he spoke in a low tone. "Two minutes away. No sign of Alex."

"Copy that," Kat said. "I got a transmission from Caligar on the ham relay. Patching him in on the earbud channel."

"Good. Did you prep him with the plan?"

"Yep. He's on board. Not sure how good he is at the art of deception, but we'll soon find out."

Caligar's voice came through, blended with static. "Katherine is right to be concerned about my ability to deceive, but I will do what I can to help."

"We can work with that," Ben said as he continued pulling the box through the rugged terrain. "Where are you right now?"

"I am at the shack where you met the Radiant. At least fifty laborers are here reconstructing the tower. It is dark, and they are busy, so they haven't noticed me. They have light standards that illuminate their work quite well, which makes it easy for me to stay out of sight in the shadows."

"How's their progress?"

"The work is going quickly. The new tower is an all-metal design, and based on the width of the foundation, it will likely be much taller than the original. Also, they dug a deep shaft under it, and they are installing machinery below, most likely a protected place for the devices that control the antennas at the top."

"Is there a way to get to the underground machinery without being seen?"

"Yes. The shack now has a trapdoor inside. It leads to a tunnel that connects the shack to the shaft below the tower. I have not investigated that route myself, but I have seen workers enter the shack with electronic devices and exit from under the tower with the devices no longer in hand. That exit is a mere hole with a cap, like a manhole cover."

"Interesting. If you get a chance to see what's under the tower, let me know. It would be great intel."

"Now is a good time. A shift is ending, and the workers will be eating a meal in a barracks they constructed for shelter. The shack now merely houses the alternate route to the base of the tower."

Ben halted at a rut and lifted the box over it before continuing. "Which means that the capped hole they use to exit the base at the tower probably won't be available while the tower is in operation mode. Otherwise, there would be no need for the trapdoor in the shack."

"That is logical. In about five minutes, I will have access to the underground portion for approximately half an hour."

"Okay. Go for it. Let me know what you find." Ben halted in front of the mausoleum. As Iona had described, an eight-foot-tall statue of an orange phoenix, much of the height coming from a pedestal, stood like a flaming sentinel next to the door, its beak aimed skyward. Now to find the door's control embedded high on the bird's back.

Leaving the wheeled box at the door, Ben leaped, grabbed a wing, and climbed up to the back. Between the wings, a metal panel the size of a phone had been embedded. He opened the door and flipped a switch inside.

The mausoleum door began swinging outward with a grinding growl. He leaped off the statue and hurried to the opening. Iona sat with her back against a sarcophagus with a glass top. Leo's body lay on its back inside.

Iona blinked at Ben. Her lips moved, but she said nothing.

Ben touched his hood. "Charlotte, I'm with Iona's body."

"She sees you. She's trying to speak, but she's never been able to get any words to come out."

Ben crouched in front of her and looked her over. "Okay. I smell body odor but nothing else. I brought a change of clothes in case she hadn't controlled her bladder, but that doesn't seem to be an issue. She's probably dehydrated."

Iona nodded, her eyes focused on him.

He pivoted to the box and retrieved a bottle of water. After twisting the cap off, he set the bottle in her hands. "Can you drink on your own?"

She lifted the bottle to her lips, missing at first and splashing some water on her face. Then she managed to drink. Within a few seconds, she drained the bottle.

"That'll do for now." Ben took the bottle, set it to the side, and gave her a nutrition bar from the box. "I'll get another bottle of water for you after I see about Leo." He rose and looked through the coffin's glass top. Leo seemed pale but otherwise unchanged, still dressed in his usual huntsman's clothes and cloak. A tube ran from the coffin to a machine sitting on a nearby table. A digital meter read 00:18, which probably meant that eighteen minutes remained before the power to the preservation capsule would run out.

Ben fetched the battery pack from the box, pulled the plug leading from the coffin, and inserted it into the battery. A readout on the battery indicated that it was checking the rate of power consumption. A few seconds later, a meter read 02:57—a little less than three hours of power remaining.

He unplugged the cord and inserted it into the original power supply. It read 00:16. Now they could buy Leo more time if needed.

"Benjamin," Caligar said through the earbud, "I am in position. The machinery is more than fifty feet underground, surrounded by a concrete silo that goes up to the base of the tower. A ladder is in place to climb out. As you suspected, it appears to be a temporary exit."

Ben set the new power supply back in the box, uncapped another bottle of water, and gave it to Iona. "Can you tell what the machinery does?"

"It is similar to my mirror," Caligar said. "Based on the various control displays, I think it has more capabilities. I am sure that it could lift a much larger object from Earth and set it on Viridi with a light touch."

"Harrid gave Alex the technology, and her influencers had the brainpower to make the advances."

"True, and I'm concerned that the new system's power would generate a massive earthquake, much more devastating than the quakes the previous tower network caused. The result could be catastrophic."

"Right. We've been talking about that. We're sure she wants to destroy Earth once she gets herself and her troops to Viridi. She wouldn't bat an eye. And I haven't told you this yet, but I offered your services to her. She doesn't know yet that the savage giants on Viridi are dead, and I said you would help her settle safely there and abdicate authority over the planet in exchange for her cooperation in restoring both Leo and Iona."

Silence ensued, then Caligar's voice returned with a hint of agitation. "That was a presumptuous offer."

"I realize that, but your abdication won't really happen. I'll tell you more when we're together, but here's the bottom line. Alex probably won't restore Iona unless she's certain of success, and our plan has multiple contingencies to get her to that place of comfort."

Caligar's tone softened. "I trust you, Benjamin. After my treachery toward you, I am willing to do whatever is necessary, within reason. Giving my planet to that devil, however, is not within reason."

"Understood. Just remember that she thinks she needs you, so we can use that to our advantage. She wants to live in a place where she won't go back to hell when she dies." Ben glanced at the power meter. Thirteen minutes remaining. "Speaking of hell, can you tell if the new system there can create a portal to hell like your mirror can?"

"Without a doubt. It is nearly identical to my system. I have four nodes equally spaced under the edge of my mirror. This is like one of those nodes, and there are three other towers around the Arctic

Circle. I am confident that they have duplicated that ability, again, with more power."

"Do you think it can create only a one-way portal, like yours, or might it be set up as a two-way path?"

"I cannot determine that yet," Caligar said, "but, unlike mine, the power can be focused in multiple directions, which indicates that the possibility exists, or at least they were hoping to try it."

"If it can make a two-way portal, could she draw souls out of hell with it? Maybe Bart or someone else who could help her?"

"I have no experience with that beyond what I witnessed when my portal drew your team out of hell. My understanding is that disembodied souls cannot leave, and I don't know if that rule can ever change."

"Good point. Give me a minute to think about it." Ben sat next to Iona. She slid her hand into his and looked at him, trying to focus. After a few seconds, her eyes locked on him, and her lips moved.

He compressed her hand. "Are you trying to tell me something?"

"I will relay," Charlotte said through the cloak. She pitched her tone higher, as if trying to imitate Iona. "Ben, I've been listening to your side of the conversation. Can you tell me what Caligar saw?"

Ben gave her a quick summary of the machinery and access paths under the tower.

"I see," Charlotte said, still speaking for Iona. "I doubt that Alex wants to pull souls out of hell. It's not like she'd be compassionate or have any pity in her evil heart. And she couldn't control them. Way too many, and they'd be unpredictable."

"Unless she wants them to swarm here after she leaves," Ben said. "Cause hell on Earth while she's in comfort on Viridi. You know, out of spite."

"Maybe." Iona's lips were now moving only slightly ahead of Charlotte's relayed words. "But I don't think she'd go through all that trouble just out of spite. There has to be something in it for her. Something positive."

"I agree. Maybe there's an energy source in hell that she wants to tap, like the lamenting souls. If that was powerful enough to reverse Caligar's portal, she might know a way to use it for her benefit again."

"If our plan works out the way you expect, I'll try to probe Alex for intel. Get her to spill what her real goals are."

"That's our hope. A spy behind enemy lines. We're counting on you."

Iona gave him a weak smile. "I'm glad you trust me."

"I do. Completely. You're a warrior."

Kat's voice knifed in. "Company coming, Ben. I hear the angel cruiser."

"Figures she'd show up at the last minute." After compressing Iona's hand again, Ben climbed to his feet. "Did you hear my conversations with Caligar and Iona?"

"Yes. Some of the speculation is pretty wild, but it makes sense. And I've been listening to the spy bug I planted on the cruiser. I heard a conversation between Alex and someone else, a woman who sounded desperate. I got the impression she's a prisoner."

Ben rolled his eyes. "Insurance."

"Right. Negotiation tactics one-oh-one. And Alex knows the prisoner doesn't have to be someone we know. A random innocent person will do."

"Playing on our sympathies. Typical. And effective."

"I have eyes on the cruiser," Kat said. "It's about to land close to your location."

"All right. Let's see if we can neutralize her insurance. Do you want to go to the cruiser on a rescue op? Free the prisoner before Alex has a chance to use her as leverage?"

"Sure. I just finished the other op." The slamming of the helicopter's door came through Ben's earbud. "I'm on my way. I'll stay out of sight until I hear that Alex is there with you."

"Okay. Go silent until you've secured her prisoner."

"Copy that."

Iona rose and tugged on Ben's sleeve while Charlotte spoke for her again. "Alex has a prisoner?"

"We think she does. Kat heard a conversation through a bug she planted on the cruiser."

"I wouldn't be so sure. Alex is good at mimicking—"

"Benjamin."

Ben turned toward the voice. Alex stood outside, a step or two beyond the mausoleum doorway, hands on the hips of her black leather pants as leaf debris swirled around her legs. Wearing a matching black leather jacket, open to expose a form-fitting white T-shirt, she looked far more menacing than she did in hell. "Hello, Benjamin." She pulled a band from her pocket and fastened her blonde locks behind her head. "I am ready to restore lost souls."

# Chapter Twenty

"They're not lost." Ben crossed his arms over his chest, hoping to show a confident posture. "They were stolen."

"Semantics." Alex ran a hand along one of the phoenix statue's wings. "This is actually a tribute to a Reaper from long ago, an opponent of mine named Phoenix. I assume it was Bartholomew's attempt at irony—my killer standing guard over my body, making sure I never rose again, like a phoenix rising from the ashes."

Ben glanced once more at the power meter. Only three minutes left. Alex had probably seen the meter, and she planned to milk that time to gain an advantage. He took the cloak off and laid it over an arm. "Leo and Iona are in the fibers. Can you restore them?"

"Of course." Alex took the cloak. "But what of your proposal? How can I be sure that Caligar won't turn on me after I grant your request?"

Ben slid his free hand into his pocket and clutched the mirror square. "Caligar is my friend. He will do as I ask. I give you my word."

"I trust your word, Benjamin, but how can I trust Caligar's? His daughter died in hell, not by my hand, of course, but if I had not captured her, she would be alive today. He would be insane not to blame me for her death. What would motivate him to help me, especially since I plan to rule his world?"

The mirror stung Ben's hand. Something that Alex said wasn't true. Maybe she had killed Caligar's daughter herself. He checked the power meter. Two minutes left. "I have no way to prove that Caligar will help you, but he told me he would. That's the only assurance I can give you other than this." He shifted his hand to the extra earbud in his pocket, withdrew it, and gave it to Alex. "Listen."

"He's here on Earth?"

Ben nodded.

"Interesting." Alex inserted the bud and spoke with an even cadence. "Caligar, I assume you have listened to the conversation."

"I have." His tone sounded sharp, angry.

Alex adjusted the earbud. "If I restore Ben's allies, how can I be sure that you will help me get to Viridi safely and take it for my own?"

"I am already at the Alaska tower and ready to escort you to my planet. It is my hope to send you to a place where you will never harm anyone again."

"Such a good heart you have, Caligar, but I find your expression of kindness far from believable." She set a fist on her hip. "Do you have proof of your whereabouts?"

"Two minutes ago, I was standing in the subterranean chamber under the Alaska tower next to the portal engine your workers are putting together. The label on the largest magneto says that it was manufactured by G-Star Electronics, and the pressure reading on the thermal—"

"Enough. You have proven your point. I believe you are there."

"Good. You also need to know that I planted a bomb, and I am exiting the tunnel. I have a remote detonator that will destroy the chamber and cause your new tower to collapse. If you restore Leo and Iona, I will not press the button, thereby proving my promise to allow you to go to Viridi without encumbrance."

A smile crept along Alex's face. "Interesting. Using blackmail to verify a promise of fidelity. Not exactly a sign of good faith." Her smile transformed into a sinister smirk. "I can play this game as well. I have a prisoner aboard my cruiser, a person I am sure you would like to keep safe."

"We already knew about your prisoner. That's being taken care of."

Alex's smile widened. "So you think."

Ben touched his earbud. "Kat, what's your status?"

Only light static answered.

"I found your surveillance device," Alex said. "I fed you information to make you think I had a hostage. Now I really do."

Heat burned in Ben's ears. The hellish witch had turned the leverage tables. With Kat as a hostage, Alex could demand anything she wanted. And now he had forgotten to check the mirror to see if she was lying about having a hostage. Probably too late for that.

Alex glanced at the timer. "You have fifteen seconds left. Not enough time to rescue your wife and return to restore your friends."

"To quote the queen of hell, so you think." Ben hustled to the box, retrieved the battery pack, and swapped it in again. When it powered up, the meter showed more than two hours remaining. He slid a hand into his pocket and enclosed the mirror. "That should be enough time for a rescue."

"Very clever." Alex crossed her arms in front, the cloak still draped over one arm. "Benjamin, let's avoid an impasse and settle the matter here and now. I will take Iona with me to Alaska, both her soul within the cloak and her body. Once I determine that my tower system is still intact and I safely arrive on Viridi, I will give Iona back to you, fully restored. I'm sure Caligar will help me send her back to Earth."

Ben kept his face slack. "And Leo?"

"I will restore him immediately. That should give you confidence that I can do the same for Iona."

Ben stared at Alex. Her steely eyes glinted, piercing, probing. Since the mirror didn't respond, she had to be telling the truth. He broke the stare and looked at the cloak. He couldn't let this witch read his mind and figure out his plan. That would ruin everything.

Keeping his voice calm, he laid an arm around Iona's shoulders and pulled her close. "I can't let you have Iona. Restore both of them, and take me as a hostage. You have my word that I will go with you, bound hand and foot if needed."

Iona pulled away. "No!"

Ben looked at her. The voice had come from her body's lips, not the hood. "Iona?"

She swallowed, her eyes imploring. She whispered, barely audible, "Ben. Let me. Please."

He caressed her cheek. "Listen, I know I said you're a warrior, not a child, but I can't let you—"

She took a hard step back, her eyes aflame. She mouthed, "I'm going," apparently no longer able to speak.

Ben let out a deep sigh. Iona's acting skills were superb. He had to match them with his own. "All right. You can go."

She smiled weakly but said nothing more.

Alex hummed through a laugh. "How touching. A competition between sacrificial heroes. But I wouldn't have accepted you as a hostage anyway. You are far too dangerous. Keeping the redheaded firebreather in this state until we arrive in Alaska will be much easier. A walking vegetable instead of a trained soldier. I prefer having you stay here and stew in your juices, pining for the safe return of a daughter you could never have." Her eyes glinted again. "Don't think that I can't see right through you, Benjamin Garrison, the man who longed to be a father but never could."

"Shut up, witch." Ben pointed at Charlotte's cloak. "Restore Leo. When I get Kat back, you can head for Alaska. Like you said, we'll be right behind you."

Alex kept her arms crossed. "And Caligar?"

Ben touched his earbud. "Caligar, I assume you've been listening."

"I have. I am back in my underground home, but the remote will work from here."

"Thank you, but you have to stand down. I repeat, stand down. Do not detonate the bomb."

"I will comply."

"Your tower is safe." Ben extended his hand. "The earbud."

"Good." Alex removed the earbud and placed it on Ben's palm, then began sliding her arms through the sleeves of Charlotte's cloak.

When she raised the hood, she smiled. "Hello, Iona. Hello, Leo. I sense your presence and ..." She cocked her head. "And a third presence. A woman. Who are you?"

Ben looked at Iona, avoiding Alex's eyes. Charlotte had warned that Alex would be able to detect her presence. This was no surprise.

"Oh, Charlotte." Alex smiled. "When Benjamin first offered a proposal, he told me a Reaper had put Leo and Iona in a cloak. I suspected that Reaper was you, but I didn't know you would be in the cloak as well. How did you die?" Alex frowned. "Very well. It is none of my business, but I assume Austin will be quite busy patrolling hell by himself. Is a replacement being planned?"

"Stop the chatter." Ben set a hand on Leo's capsule. "Get on with it."

"As you wish. Unplug the capsule from the power supply to start the resurrection cycle."

Not really trusting her, Ben complied. What choice did he have? The moment he unplugged the cord, an alarm squealed.

"Now we must hurry." Using both hands, Alex lifted the capsule's lid. Air whooshed. When the sound subsided, she pulled a sleeve over her hand and laid her palm on Leo's eyes. "Come, Leo. Let's not make this difficult. Though I don't know the specifics, I learned that you are related to Iona, and you're reluctant to leave her behind in the cloak. Realize that this restoration is what she wants, and ..."

Alex blinked. "Is that so?" She looked at Ben, her eyes again glinting with a metallic sheen. "Interesting."

"What?" Ben asked as the alarm assaulted his nerves.

"In his present state, I can read Leo's frontal thoughts. Now that I have said this, of course, he will likely guard them more carefully, but he has revealed something I didn't know before." Alex focused on Leo's body. "Fear not. This knowledge will not affect my efforts or our deal."

A stream of sparkles ran down the cloak's sleeve and vanished. After a few seconds, Alex closed her eyes tightly. "Leo's soul is now in his brain. I am helping him attach. This is the most delicate step.

Go over to the preservation device and be ready to push the green button. It's connected to a device under his back that should restart his heart."

Ben stepped over to the machine, found the button, and poised his finger near it. "Ready."

Alex's brow furrowed. "The attachment points are tender. When his soul touches one, it causes a jolt of pain. Attachment needs to be quick. Otherwise, we'll lose his soul, and it will be transported from Earth. To heaven, I assume."

The alarm continued its relentless squeal. "How much time does he have?" Ben asked.

"Seconds, not minutes. I will give him an extra dose of incentive." Alex clenched her teeth. The reddish fibers in the cloak brightened. Iona's eyes widened, and her mouth dropped open. She let out a low moan.

"Iona!" Ben called. "What's wrong?"

"I am torturing her soul," Alex said. "The moment Leo attaches, I will stop."

"Augh!" Iona dropped to her knees, her face bright red.

"Leo!" Alex shouted. "For Iona's sake, you must attach."

"What's wrong with him?" Ben stepped toward them, then retreated. He had to stay put at the machine. "Of course he would do it for her."

"It's not that he won't. He can't. He is trying, and I am incentivizing him to try harder."

The alarm pounded in Ben's brain. Iona's moans felt like stabs from a dagger. If Leo failed, he would soon be dead forever, and there was nothing Ben could do about it.

Alex nodded vigorously. "Yes, Charlotte, that might help. Go ahead."

Another stream of sparks ran along the sleeve and vanished, apparently into Leo's head. Alex lifted her hand. "We have attachment. Hit it."

Ben pushed the button. Leo's body jerked, but his eyes stayed closed. Alex pressed a palm against Leo's chest. "Hit it again!"

Ben pushed it once more. A new spasm rocked Leo's body. Alex set two fingers against his neck. "No pulse." She reached into the capsule and, with incredible strength, hauled Leo out and laid him on the floor. She straddled him, sat on his stomach, and pressed both hands, one over the other, on his chest. Using all her weight, she pushed and released with a fast rhythm, her eyes seeming to flicker with fire. "Come on. Come on. I need you to live."

Ben walked closer. "Should I try?"

"No!" Her blonde locks shook loose and fell over her face as she grunted her words in time with her frantic pushes. "Do … you … think … my … efforts … inadequate?"

"I don't know. Maybe I'm more motivated to—"

Leo heaved in a breath, though his eyes stayed closed. Alex sat upright and felt his neck again. "His heart is beating." She pushed her hair out of her eyes and rose to her feet. "We won't know if he suffered any brain damage until he wakes up."

Ben found the machine's main power switch and shut it off, killing the alarm. Iona, still on her knees, looked at Ben, tears streaming. He rushed to her and helped her rise. "Is she still in pain?"

Alex shook her head. "I am no longer hurting her. She will recover in a few moments. I am not so certain about Leo."

Relief washed in along with fury, blending into a confusing rush. This evil sorceress had tortured Iona but did it to help Leo. Supposedly. And now Leo's status remained shaky. Had she somehow disabled him on purpose to get more leverage? Ben clenched a fist, not knowing whether he should shake this witch's hand or punch her in the nose. "What happened?"

Alex, her face ashen, inhaled deeply. "Leo's brain suffered two soul detachments—once in the healing waters and once when Bartholomew left. With the first separation, Bartholomew attached immediately to Leo's brain. The attachment points were still receptive, such as when a soul leaves a body for mere moments during a near-death experience. When Bartholomew left, the points had time to heal somewhat, similar to a scarring over, making it much more difficult for Leo's soul to attach."

Ben relaxed his hand. "How did you solve the problem?"

She gathered her hair and refastened the band around it as she looked at him. "Charlotte suggested that she could tear away the scars while I attached Leo's soul. The process was excruciating for him, but it worked. And the trauma is why he is now unconscious. When I restored myself to my own body, the attachment points had healed long ago, so they accepted my soul with no trouble."

"Will the same problem crop up when you restore Iona?"

Alex crossed her arms and gazed at her for a moment before answering. "Not likely. She's younger than Leo, so she'll heal more quickly, and when I left her body, being far more skilled than Bartholomew, I did so without damage. There will be no scarring. No need for Charlotte's help."

"Where is Charlotte now?"

"Gone. Since I was busy saving Leo's life, I didn't see her leave, but I know she's no longer in this cloak." Alex shrugged. "It's to be expected. The cloak kept her on Earth, just as it is doing for Iona."

"I understand." Ben studied Iona's expression—blank, as usual. Yet, she gave him the slightest of nods. That had to mean something. He turned away and knelt next to Leo. The huntsman breathed easily, his expression relaxed, apparently reflecting a lack of pain. "When do you expect to leave for Alaska?"

"Right away, if possible." Alex nodded toward Ben's box. "I see that you have clothes for Iona. If I may take them, I need not delay at all. The sooner I can verify the safety of my tower, the sooner I can go to Viridi where I will restore Iona's soul and send her back to you."

When he opened his mouth to reply, Kat's voice came through the earbud. "Ben, can you hear me?"

"Yes."

"Finally."

Ben kept an eye on Alex as she combed a hand through Iona's hair and whispered to her as if being motherly—a nauseating gesture. He stepped away and whispered, "What's going on? Alex said she set a trap for you."

"Yeah. I heard that, but I couldn't answer. Alex installed a signal jammer. I had to get out of its range to call you."

"So there was no prisoner?"

"Nope. I searched everywhere. And the mooring cap is missing. I couldn't hijack the cruiser."

Ben glared at Alex. It wouldn't matter if she heard his thoughts. "It was a ruse to get extra leverage. Throw me off balance. The vile shrew will do anything to get her way."

Alex cast her own glare at him but only for a moment before walking with Iona toward the box.

"I'm not buying it," Kat said. "I'm worried that she might have sent someone to compromise our musical asset, if you know what I mean."

Ben nodded. Someone might have gone to the chopper to free Damien. Or to kill him. "I do know what you mean."

"What's up at the mausoleum?" Kat asked.

"Some good. Some bad. Fly the chopper as close as you can. I'll fill you in when you get here."

"Copy that."

Alex lifted the clothes from the box, set them in Iona's arms, and walked toward Ben. "I have one more issue to discuss with you."

"And that is?"

She leaped into a flying leg sweep and smashed Ben in the mouth with her foot. He staggered back and smacked his head against a wall. As he blinked, his vision dazed, she set a fist on her hip. "That's for calling me a vile shrew. You will treat me with respect or suffer more injury. It's up to you."

Ben pushed away from the wall, rubbing his throbbing chin. "I apologize. Really. To the shrews, I mean. I shouldn't have insulted their species that way."

Alex lunged at him and threw a punch. He blocked it with an arm and kneed her in the gut. When she doubled over, he drove his fists down on her back. She collapsed to her stomach and writhed.

Ben planted a foot on her neck, pressing her cheek against the floor. After a moment, she stopped twitching and glared at him, one eye visible. "What is the point of this dominant posturing? A foot on a woman's neck is classic masculine bravado, too cliché for a man of your chivalrous stature."

"And attacking me like a wildcat is too random for a calculating strategist like you. You had a purpose behind it. And it wasn't to show me how rusty your reflexes are." He lifted his foot and extended a hand to her. "Shall we call a truce?"

"I will accept a truce." Alex interlocked thumbs with him and let him pull her to her feet. She brushed off her clothes and looked him in the eye. "I am a bit rusty, and you won our brief scrap handily. But, as you suspected, my attack was a test. I wanted to learn more about the kind of man I'm dealing with. I already knew how intelligent you are. Now I see that you're a formidable fighter." She drew closer until they stood nearly nose to nose. Her stale breath warmed his skin as she spoke with slow, deliberate words. "You won't take me by surprise next time."

Ben held his ground, not moving an inch. "Will there be a next time?"

Her eyes once again glinted with a metallic sheen. "I guarantee it." She pivoted, strode with a swagger to Iona, and, setting a hand on her back, guided her out of the mausoleum.

Ben eyed her cocky gait. Her attack had to be more than a way to expose his skill set. Might she have been trying to steal something? The mirror he had found in Leo's cloak? He slid a hand into each pocket and palmed the mirror square in one and the two miniature transmitters in the other, along with Iona's cross necklace.

He stifled a gasp. The plan called for Iona to have the devices if Alex took her, but the scuffle jarred him enough to make it slip his mind. How could he recover from this mistake without alerting Alex?

"Wait." He pulled the necklace, mirror, and transmitters from his pocket, the cross dangling in one hand as he palmed the devices in the other. "She had this cross in hell. I assume it's her real one. I'm sure she'll want it."

Alex rolled her eyes. "What do I care if Iona wants that silly—"

Iona spun away from Alex and hurried back to Ben. She wrapped her arms around him and laid her head against his chest. As he draped the necklace over her head, she slid her hand into his and allowed him to push the devices into her grasp. She stealthily dropped them into her pants pockets and mouthed as she drew away, "Don't worry. I got this." She then pivoted and returned to Alex.

Alex held out her hand. "What else did he give you?"

Iona shrugged and showed Alex her empty hands.

"Liar!" Alex slapped Iona's face. "I'm no fool. I know he gave you something besides the necklace."

Ben winced. His muscles flexed hard. Resisting the urge to deck Alex again was probably the hardest thing he'd ever done.

Iona pushed her hand into a pocket, withdrew one of the transmitter devices, and displayed it on her palm. Alex snatched it up and looked it over. "Something to spy on me with." She turned to Ben and glared at him as she dropped the transmitter and smashed it with a stomp of her foot. "Benjamin, you are far too predictable."

Ben bit his lip. The words that flew to mind deserved to be shouted, but they wouldn't do a bit of good. He had to stick with the plan.

Without another word, Alex and Iona strode into the midst of the tombstones.

Ben walked to the doorway. His stomach tossed. Bile burned in his throat. Watching Iona leave with that monster felt helpless, like being stuck in hell yet again, this time with no way out and no angel

217

to open the gate. Yes, this was all part of the plan, but the plan never felt more fragile than it did right now.

When they walked out of sight, Ben reached over to close the box's lid, but the helmet inside made him pause. He drew it out and caressed the surface. He had meant to give it to Iona, but the frenzied events drove it from his mind. And somehow it seemed appropriate. He had let her go with Alex, unprotected and unaware of the entirety of the plan. Keeping her out of the loop for certain details was also part of the plan, a way to keep Alex from squeezing information from her. Now that decision felt like the worst one yet. Iona was on her own.

Trying not to tremble, he whispered, "God, I need your help. Iona needs your help. I can't go with her, so I need you to watch over her. Protect her. Make her whole."

The sound of whipping blades drew close. The helicopter landed nearby. Moments later, Kat helped Ben carry Leo onboard, and they laid him on the back passenger seat. "Damien still in the cargo hold?" Ben asked.

"Yep. Still tied, but his gag came loose. Mad as a hornet. I re-gagged him to get him to shut up."

"So I'm still wondering why Alex sent you on that prisoner hunt. She used it as leverage to get me to do something, but I think there was more to it than that."

"I have an idea, but let's talk about it later." She leaned close and whispered into his ear, "Security sweep for bugs."

Ben nodded. The prisoner ploy could have given one of Alex's minions a chance to plant a listening bug in the chopper. They checked the entire cabin with a signal detecting app on Kat's computer pad but found nothing.

Ben settled in the pilot's seat. "She's a cunning one. For some reason she kicked me in the face out of the blue. I haven't figured out why. She made an excuse, some rubbish about wanting to know what kind of man I am. There has to be another reason."

"True." Kat took the copilot's seat and strapped in. "Maybe it was an excuse to make physical contact. Could she have planted one of those chips in you, like they did to Damien?"

"I didn't feel an extra sting." Ben rubbed the back of his neck. "She didn't touch me here, but I guess she might've put it anywhere while the pain from her kick distracted me."

Kat rolled her eyes. "Okay, I'll fly this bird while you look for a chip. When we get to the vault, I'll check the places you can't see."

Ben buckled his seatbelt and unbuttoned his shirt while Kat flew the chopper toward home. As he checked his chest and stomach for a chip insertion, he glanced toward the cargo hold. Maybe Damien was meant to be a listening bug for Alex. If one of her minions had come while Kat was away, what did Damien share with him or her? Anything he knew about the mission might now be compromised. Fortunately, what he thought he knew was untrue, corrupted intel fed to him in case he was compromised. He had no idea that they had planned for Iona to be a spy, and he thought they had set their sights on the Russian tower as a target for destruction. If he had spilled that to Alex's minion, all the better.

After checking every viewable inch of his body, Ben spoke at a low volume, his earbud transmitting to Kat's. "I couldn't find anything."

"It's tiny, so it's no surprise. Jack has the chip Trudy removed from Damien. When we get back, we'll ask him if it's traceable. If so, we'll check your body with a scanner." Kat turned the chopper slightly, then accelerated. "In the meantime, give me the scoop. What happened at the mausoleum?"

"Here's a summary. The plan worked. Alex restored Leo to prove she could do it but kept Iona for leverage. Now Alex and Iona are on their way to Alaska."

"With Charlotte in the cloak?" Kat asked.

"Not so sure about that. Alex said she couldn't sense Charlotte in the fibers, so either she's hiding herself well, or she got taken to heaven."

Kat pressed her lips together. "Charlotte's one of our contingencies. Everything has to go perfectly if we don't have her."

"True, but Iona gave me a hint that the plan's on course. A slight nod."

Kat half closed an eye. "A nod? Is that enough?"

"Enough for me." Ben exhaled heavily and looked out the front windshield. "Listen, I know you haven't been the biggest fan of Iona, and we're trusting her to take on the most dangerous part or our plan, but I'm confident—"

"Stop."

He turned toward her. She reached across and slid her hand into his. "I was wrong about Iona. I trust her completely to get this done. She's a superstar spy."

He compressed her hand. "What changed your mind?"

"*She* changed my mind. Her courage. Her intelligence. Her quick thinking. And ..." Kat's voice cracked. "And her love for you."

Ben's cheeks warmed. "Um ... yeah. It's mutual. But Leo's her father. I have to put anything else out of my mind."

"Good luck with that." She patted his hand and drew back. "You fly while I see if the transmitter's working." When Ben took the controls, she tapped on her computer pad and zoomed in on a map. "Yep. Alex and Iona are heading northwest."

"Going to Alaska. No surprise. Let's hope Alex doesn't get wind of the tracker. She confiscated one of them, just like we predicted."

"The tracker's muted," Kat said. "No static. Not that it matters, though. Alex knows we'll come after her."

"But the tracker will store signals that you send even while it's muted, right? We can send messages Iona can listen to when she's alone."

"Right. And stop worrying. I told you I'd take care of that part." Kat fastened the pad to her belt. "Now tell me more about what happened. Every detail."

During the flight, he told Kat the entire story. As he had said, not everything went perfectly according to plan, but the results turned out as they had hoped. Their scarlet-headed spy was on board the cruiser, but whether or not Charlotte rode along in the cloak was uncertain.

When he finished, he looked at Kat. "Any questions?"

Kat shook her head. "Nope. Now to launch the rest of our plan. I have the bones, the accelerant, and the flash powder. It's the timing I'm worried about. Pulling this stunt off will take more than a simple sleight-of-hand move."

"True, but it's critical. Alex needs to let her guard down. I can't think of any other way to make that happen. She's too cunning."

"Yeah, but are we skilled enough? This won't be anything we've trained for."

"We'll practice a couple of times. We can do it." Ben lifted a chain around his neck and dangled a dog tag. "Do you have yours?"

"Yep." Kat showed him her tag. "I've worn it since the beginning."

"Thought so." Ben faced forward again. "Let's get ready to go to Russia."

# Chapter Twenty-one

Riding in Charlotte's cloak, Iona looked out through her body's eyes. She sat in the angel cruiser's co-pilot seat, facing the front windshield. They flew a couple hundred feet above the ground, close enough to see details below. Prairie fields dominated the landscape, likely the farms of the Northfields, dimming as evening approached. The short days of winter, especially in the more northern latitudes, wouldn't allow this view much longer.

As Alex piloted the ship while wearing the cloak, she chattered about how this area was once called Canada before the radioactive years, relatively unscathed by the nuclear blast that scorched the areas to the south. Whether she wanted to show off her knowledge of geography and history or she was just trying to pass the time was unclear. Either way, her monologue was interesting, a departure from the history in the official school textbooks.

Iona stayed quiet, though questions abounded. Would it be a bad idea to ask, try to learn more, maybe get a read on Alex's mood or intent? Since Alex could hear her speak within the fibers, communication wasn't a problem, but now that Iona had conquered her inability to speak through her body, at least somewhat, maybe it would be a good idea to practice.

She forced words through her lips, slow but steady. "Where … are … we … going?"

Alex swiveled toward her, smiling. "Ah. Very good. Your soul's connection with your body is strong. Perhaps because you're so close."

"You …" Iona swallowed. "Didn't answer … my question."

Alex smirked. "Still combative, I see." She pointed toward a navigation system on the dashboard console. "First, we are going to the tower in Alaska. I assume you're familiar with it."

Iona nodded. "Why so slow?"

"The tower's systems aren't finished yet. Soon, though. I've been in contact with my workers, and they assure me that everything will be finished by nightfall. Since it's so cold there and already dark, I prefer to stay away until the proper time. After that, we will go to Viridi. Once there, I will restore you to your body."

"If Caligar ... does what ... you want."

Alex lifted her brow. "Are you saying that your friends might have lied about their intent?"

Iona bent her face's features into a frown. Alex's question was bait, designed to lead to a no-win scenario. Admitting that they might lie would incite Alex to refuse to restore her hostage, a tactic to maintain her leverage until after years of living on Viridi to prove that the planet did, indeed, belong to her. And she would scoff at any claim that they wouldn't lie—a reasonable scoff. Ben would definitely lie to save an innocent life. Countering Alex would be difficult. "You're ... afraid of them."

"What?" Alex laughed. "Nonsense. As long as I have you, they won't dare take action against me."

"That's ... my point. You have to ... keep me because ... you're afraid of them. They're stronger ... than you are... mentally and physically."

"What game are you playing?" Alex stared at Iona, her metallic eyes shimmering. After a few seconds, she focused on the view ahead. "Without your soul inside, I can't get a read on you."

"And now ... you're afraid of me."

"A little girl? A disembodied sprite?" Alex scoffed. "Don't be ridiculous. You are merely a means to an end, a tiny cog in my enormous machine."

"We'll see ... about that."

Alex smiled. "Stay cocky, Iona. I like that about you. A young woman after my own heart. But you have no idea whom you're dealing with. I have sparred with greater warrior princesses than you, and I conquered them all."

When Iona opened her mouth to reply, something touched her hand—not her physical hand, but the spot on her soul where it felt like her hand should be. A tapping sensation followed. Could it be Morse code? She deciphered the dots and dashes, spelling out, "Stay quiet. Understand?"

Iona grasped the tapping appendage and relayed her own message. "Charlie?"

Charlie replied with a coded, "Yes. Hiding from Alex."

The taps passed back and forth, feeling excruciatingly slow during the longer messages.

"Why?" Iona asked in code.

"I learned how Alex restores a soul. I can restore you."

"How?"

"Get the cloak. Cover yourself."

"Okay. Then what?"

"Cover eyes with hood. I will guide you into your brain. Attachment hurt Leo. Will hurt you. Avoid reacting."

"Can do."

"If we succeed, she has no leverage. But keep pretending."

"Got it." Iona focused on the connection with her body, hugged herself, and forced a shiver.

"Are you cold?" Alex asked.

Iona nodded.

"It's warm enough. Your body's circulation is probably not functioning properly."

Iona pointed at Alex. "Cloak?"

Alex rolled her eyes. "Iona, speak to me through the cloak instead of spitting out a single word with your crippled lips."

She complied, speaking through the fibers. "My body is cold, Alex. I need something to wrap up in."

"Your parka is in the back. Go get it."

"I was thinking if I could wear Charlotte's cloak, I could get a better connection with my body, and maybe my lips would be less crippled."

Alex stared at Iona's physical face. "I'm trying to detect a ruse in your eyes, but once again I can't perceive any intentions at all. It's like trying to probe a rag doll."

"Then maybe it's better if I don't wear the cloak. Getting a stronger connection might make me more transparent to your probing."

Alex hummed a laugh. "That is either a clever reverse-psychology ploy or an honest avoidance of my talents. Yet, either way, I don't see a drawback. You're not a Reaper, so you can't do anything with the cloak." She rose from her seat, took off the cloak, and handed it to Iona. "Put it on and look at me. I want to see if I can probe you."

"Um … sure." As she guided her body through the steps, Charlie tapped out a new message.

"Fool her by thinking about someone you love. She will have trouble understanding. Love always conquers evil."

When Iona finished putting the cloak on, she raised the hood and looked directly at Alex. As expected, the connection with her body was stronger, much stronger.

Alex stared, her pupils pulsing like a throbbing heart and her steely irises gleaming. They pierced deeply, probing, searching. Iona turned her thoughts to Leo the moment he showed up in the abyss, ignoring the danger in hell's festering cavity, his one thought to rescue her no matter the cost to himself. That was love. Pure love. A father's love for his daughter, though he didn't realize it yet.

Alex cocked her head, narrowing her eyes, as if puzzled. Then her gaze drilled even deeper. Iona again escaped, this time by recalling Ben as he searched for her in hell. He had already been to that horrible place once before, not by choice that time, but he went again, the second time voluntarily, to hunt for both her and Leo. Such love! For a daughter? Not in reality, but in heart.

Tears trickled unbidden, coursing down her chilled cheeks. She was blessed, so incredibly blessed to have two men who loved her so much, who would give their lives for her, expecting nothing in return.

Alex averted her gaze. "I've seen enough. I can't penetrate those moribund eyes."

Charlie tapped a new message. "Cover your eyes. When I take you to the light, try to hold it."

Iona set her feet on the chair, pulled the hood over her eyes, and drew her knees up to her forehead.

"What are you doing?" Alex asked.

She spoke slowly, though her enhanced connection made the tedious cadence unnecessary. "Getting ... warm."

"Suit yourself."

Something pulled Iona's soul through the fibers. The sensation felt like a hairbrush running along bare skin, irritating but not painful. Far worse pain likely lay ahead.

Soon, darkness flowed in—cold, empty blackness that pervaded everything, even her mind. She shivered, both in body and soul. If Alex noticed, the reaction might help with the deception.

Seconds later, a light pulsed far ahead, like a strobe at the exit to a long tunnel. As the pulling sensation strengthened, she accelerated, like zooming down a mine shaft. The light ahead swelled and pulsed brighter and brighter. Sound entered, similar to a heartbeat through a stethoscope, the whoosh of air blending in.

She slammed into a sphere of pure radiance and slid around it. Pain roared into her brain, but she refused to flinch, not wanting to alert Alex.

Iona pawed at the sphere, trying to get a grip. With each attempt, new pain knifed in, but her fingers slipped away again and again. Could the light be her brain? Her soul's attachment points? If so, holding to it was her only hope of being restored.

Something grabbed her wrist and held her in place. It forced her hand to again paw at the sphere, but to no avail. If only she could dig her nails in, maybe she could hold on, but did her soul even have fingernails? She seemed to have a hand and fingers, so maybe she did.

She flexed her fingers and tried to dig in. This time when she pawed, her fingers penetrated, making claw marks. New pain stabbed through her physical skull. Forcing her body to take a deep silent breath, she held on. Pain sent shooting spasms into her arms and legs, locking her muscles in torturous knots.

As she steeled herself to keep from quaking, the sphere's light absorbed her soul. A new kind of light entered her mind—muted and tinted reddish brown. She was now seeing through her physical eyes, her head buried in Charlie's cloak. It worked. Charlie had restored her.

Her muscles still cramping, she slowly lowered her feet to the cockpit floor and stretched her tight calf muscles. They loosened, and the pain ebbed, both there and in her arms.

Warmth enfolded her mind. A soft whisper passed by like a gentle breeze. "You did it, my dear daughter. My beloved. My champion. I knew you could."

Iona cast a thought, hoping her mother could hear. *Can we still communicate?*

Silence ensued. Had she departed, somehow spirited away to heaven? Or had she now settled back into the cloak, unable to speak but able to deliver that message because she was still near Iona's brain at the time? If she remained in the cloak, could she signal her presence? Sometimes the fibers sparkled to indicate a soul's presence, but maybe she wanted to avoid that telltale sign. Alex would probably know the difference between a Reaper's sparkles and someone else's.

Iona bit her lip. Not knowing whether her mother was still around seemed intolerable, but she would have to press on. They had managed to complete the restoration without Alex's help, a huge benefit. The next step, to send Alex to hell, could be done solo, but only if she could keep her emotions in check. Stay steady. Be a robot-like spy.

As she tried to steel herself, a headache throbbed, probably because of the recent soul attachment. Heat coursed through her

227

body, then tears flowed. She balled a fist. *No! Don't let Alex see your grief.*

She stealthily dabbed at the tears with the cloak then at a trickle of mucus from her nose. After taking a deep breath, she lowered the hood and stared straight ahead, peeking at Alex from the corner of her eye.

Alex glanced at her. "Is something wrong?"

Iona nodded. Using her hesitating voice, she spoke softly. "I tried ... to restore myself."

"And you failed. It's impossible to do it on your own unless you're a Reaper. And most Reapers would be unable. I could do it to myself because of my experience. Even then, it was extremely difficult."

Iona nodded again. "I had to try."

"Of course you had to. You're a warrior. I don't blame you for that." Alex smiled. "That's why you wanted the cloak, isn't it? You weren't really cold. It was a ruse."

"I was cold. That gave me the idea."

"I detected that you were in pain while you were covered. I guessed what you were trying, but since I knew a solo restoration was impossible, I let you continue so you would learn the truth on your own."

"I learned."

Alex looked straight ahead, her eyes narrowing. "Why are you being so truthful now?"

Iona continued the slow cadence. "I want ... to help you ... go to Viridi. It will be ... better for everyone."

Alex nodded. "I see. A temporary alliance. You will endure what you despise in order to gain a long-term benefit."

"But I can't ... let you ... destroy Earth."

Alex chuckled. "How could I possibly benefit from destroying Earth?"

"So no one ... could go to Viridi ... to conquer you."

Alex raised a finger. "Ah, now that's a valid point, but I have installed devices under the towers that will destroy them, disabling any ability to use them to go to Viridi."

"Someone could ... rebuild the towers."

"To no avail." Alex gripped the steering yoke with both hands and looked at Iona. "As you might have heard, the new towers are far more powerful and advanced than any before them. After I leave with my one hundred servants, the towers will close the Oculus Gate and then self-destruct. Building new towers won't do any good, because there will be no gate to pass through. And that will convince Caligar to do my bidding, to take you and his family to Earth before I close the Oculus Gate. As you said, that will be better for everyone."

Iona firmed her jaw. The witch had to be lying. According to Caligar's description, the underground devices appeared to be designed for Earth's destruction, not the Oculus Gate's, but without proof, it made no sense to argue the point. She nodded. "That's good."

"Now that you understand, perhaps you would like to help me achieve our mutually beneficial goal."

Iona gave her what she hoped was a cooperative expression. "How?"

"Benjamin doesn't trust me, and I don't trust him, which is why I could never tell him the truth about everything. Since I have you as a hostage and you need to stay in my favor to be set free, I will tell you what Benjamin clearly doesn't realize."

Iona resisted the urge to roll her eyes. Once again, Alex was playing her dramatic pause game. "And that is?"

"The Oculus Gate is unstable. It was created out of one man's desperation to find his missing wife, and conduits have connected planets to the Gate multiple times. With each connection and breaking of the connection, the Gate has been made more volatile, especially when one of your agents destroyed the temporary hell I created and smashed the conduit leading to Earth."

"Temporary hell? ... Do you mean ... the Never-ending Highway ... Jack went to? ... The place where ... he saw his wife and daughter?"

"The same. It was a test, an experiment. I wanted to create an environment that simulated hell along with the torment of suffering souls agonizing in a tedious existence. When the Oculus Gate appeared, a rift in space, I saw that I had an opportunity to manufacture that laboratory, of sorts."

"Why would God ... let you make ... souls suffer like that?"

Alex laughed softly. "Your question should be why *does* God allow souls to suffer? It happens all the time, on Earth, in hell, and on the Never-ending Highway during our experiment."

"But why the experiment?"

"To see if hell could be destroyed. My ultimate goal is to destroy hell, not Earth. And the experiment worked brilliantly. I now know how to destroy the real hell."

"Wouldn't God ... just make hell again? He has to ... have a place ... to put ... condemned souls. Right?"

"That question proves your lack of understanding. God created hell for a different purpose, not as a place to punish souls. That was secondary. Once I am finished with my plan, God's primary purpose will be gone. But I prefer not to explain that. It is way above your understanding."

"Try me."

"No. I have already told you more than you deserve to know. The Never-ending Highway laboratory, for example."

"How did you ..." Iona took a deep breath. She had to keep her speech cadence slow in spite of the urge to spew her questions rapid fire. "Have the power ... to make the laboratory?"

"Oh, trust me. I didn't have the power. I knew I needed help. I am not the only one who hopes to avoid eternity in the Lake of Fire. Someone far more powerful than I longs to end God's sadistic torture chamber."

"Do you mean ... Satan?"

"Lucifer. The morning star. The archangel cast out of heaven for daring to question God's authority." Alex smiled. "Yes, he is Satan, but that name carries too much baggage. Most people think of a horned, red-suited man wielding a pitchfork, torturing souls in hell. But that is a vacuous lie. Lucifer has never been to hell, and he doesn't want to go, which is why he called on me to help him."

Iona's heart thumped, but she kept her composure. "Satan asked … for your help?"

Alex beamed, obviously proud of her status. "I have personal experience in hell while he does not. With his power and my knowledge, we created the Never-ending Highway. And knowing about the angel-killing missile Katherine Garrison was creating, we wanted to learn if her weapon would destroy our laboratory. And it succeeded, just as we had hoped."

"You wanted … the weapon to work?"

"Yes. We built the highway to be destroyed. Of course, we had to hope events transpired as they eventually did. We had no control over that, though we did what we could to influence the events."

"For example?"

"Let me think …" Alex tapped her chin with a finger. "Oh, yes. You might remember the SkySweep drones that chased you and your allies while you were searching for the missile's whereabouts."

Iona nodded. "I remember."

"It would have taken an extraordinarily stupid drone controller to miss locating you, but Lucifer led them away so you could be free to launch the angel-killing missile."

Iona's cheeks warmed. Hearing that Satan was involved in their success felt like being stabbed in the gut. Maybe it was a lie. It had to be a lie. But for now, she had to calm down. Fortunately Alex wasn't looking at the moment. It was a good time to check for lies by using the mirror. She slid a hand into her pocket and clutched the mirror. "Are you saying … Satan helped us succeed?"

"That's exactly what I am saying."

Iona flattened her palm on the mirror's reflective surface. It felt normal. No lie so far. "How could you know that? ... Does Satan talk to you?"

"On occasion, through the portal I had in hell. I have not been in contact with him since that time, but we have arranged a meeting."

The mirror again indicated that Alex was telling the truth. Iona's cheeks flamed. She covered her head and face with the hood and shivered.

"Cold again?" Alex asked. "It's no wonder. Thinking about being in Lucifer's presence can chill the heartiest of souls."

Iona spoke through the fibers, muffling her voice. "I don't want to meet Satan."

"It would be the most wondrous adventure of your life, one that I eagerly look forward to. In any case, with the data we gathered from the destruction of our copy of hell, we were able to design a device that will destroy the real hell, and it is nearing completion as we speak."

Yet again, Alex told the truth. Iona shivered hard, a quaking shudder. This was all far too terrifying. It seemed that Alex had no desire to hide anything, which felt even scarier than when she lied. And meeting Satan himself? The worst idea possible, the stuff of too many childhood nightmares.

Iona took a deep breath. She had to keep control of herself, the only way to be a competent spy. Yet, maybe this sign of weakness could work to her advantage—let Alex underestimate her. Still, if she couldn't overcome the terror, Alex's low estimate might be accurate.

Alex let out a tsking sound. "Dear Iona, you saw how horrific the conditions in hell are—the torment, the grief, the wailing lamentations. And the souls will suffer for eternity. Everlasting agony. And why? Offending a lofty deity by not loving him enough? Is that fair? Is that justice? Lucifer thinks not, and he and I will destroy that awful place. We will end God's retribution against souls who refuse to worship a vindictive tyrant."

"Stop." Iona buried herself deeper within the cloak. "Just …
stop."

"I know how hearing this might be damaging to your faith. You
have been indoctrinated into a belief system that says God can do
no wrong, and now you are learning that he's the cruelest being in
the universe. Such a drastic shift is hard to bear. It's a cataclysmic
upheaval, and it will take time for you to adjust. But I assure you
that once you meet Lucifer, you will understand. He is powerful.
Beautiful. Magnificent. And I saw him only in the mists of my portal.
In person, he must be a thousand times more amazing. Meeting him
will be wondrous, a dream come true."

Iona stayed quiet. Although retorts begged to be shouted, she
couldn't let herself slide back to her old ways, a brat who couldn't
control her verbal eruptions. She had to peacefully and quietly
sort through the turmoil. First, how could Alex inflict suffering
on innocent people and then accuse God of the same crime?
Hypocritical to the max. Second, criticizing God for people's
suffering, when in reality people like Alex caused it, was simply
blaming the wrong person. Yet, God forcing people to suffer forever
in hell didn't sit right either, and no answer to Alex's criticisms came
to mind.

"Obviously you're shaken," Alex said. "I will not mention that
topic again. What should comfort you now is that as long as I keep
you alive and healthy, you will be all the leverage I need to get to
Viridi safely. Then, and only then, will I restore your soul to your
body."

# Chapter Twenty-two

Ben sat at the desk in the temple computer room, cutting and gluing some of the mirror shards into squares more practical for travel while Kat ran a hand along his scalp, the only place she hadn't yet searched. Damien stood nearby, tuning the violin, and Leo lay in the vault's sleeping quarters, apparently on his way to recovery from his soul's reattachment. Unfortunately, a splitting headache had forced him to go to bed, but not before hearing the outline of the plan to stop Alex and how he could play a part if he were to recover enough. He promised to rouse himself soon, for Iona's sake.

"Nothing." Kat drew back and sighed. "If Alex planted a chip, I can't find it. And Jack said he hasn't had time to reverse engineer the one we got from Damien."

"Then we'll proceed as if we were wrong about our guess." Ben stacked a makeshift three-inch square on top of two others. "That's three mirrors, but I'd feel better if we had a fourth to leave with Leo. We can use that one to leave from here and take the others with us."

"Fine with me. More is better. No telling where the zigzags in our plan will take us."

"Exactly my thinking." Ben began assembling another square, cutting pieces with a diamond blade and attaching them with a specialized glue. "One mirror for hopping from here to Russia, another for Russia to Alaska, but after that depends on Alex. I just want to make sure we have enough." He almost added that Iona had the little square mirror he had gotten from Leo's cloak, but with Damien listening, it was better not to air that detail. Kat already knew.

Damien played a final note. "The violin is tuned. I am ready to imagine my presence at the Russian tower."

"Go ahead," Ben said as he attached two mirror pieces together. "I'll have this done in a few more seconds."

"But ..." Kat pulled a handgun from her belt holster. "It'd better be the Russian tower. If you send us to the Alaska tower or anywhere else we don't want to go, it'll be lights out for you."

Damien scowled. "When will you learn that I am not Alex's ally?"

"You're not ours, either." She pulled the slider back, chambering a round. "I'm not taking any chances."

"I can see that, but your intimidation tactics won't alter my actions." Damien set the bow to the strings and closed his eyes. "The Russian tower was incomplete when I visited the site, and I arrived on a relatively warm autumn day." He played a series of quick notes that sounded like a warbler's song. "An angel scientist showed me the transmission equipment that needed the protective coating I invented, and I went right to work." He played longer, deeper notes, then shifted back and forth between them and the earlier ones, fashioning a tune that lacked an identifiable melody.

As before, Kat recorded the tune, though this time she transmitted the stream to the vault computer, making a copy to keep here, as planned.

Ben finished the final mirror square and laid it on his palm. The reflection warped for a moment, then clarified, showing a tower in the midst of darkness, visible because of lights blinking from the base of the tower's frame to the top. He set the mirror on the desk and packed the others in a padded box, careful to avoid touching the tower reflections that now appeared on all of them. "Keep playing while we get our gear."

Damien complied, continuing the shifting sequences. Ben and Kat each slung on a backpack, strapped a rifle over a shoulder, and checked the weapons and ammo attached to their belts. Ben slid the mirror box into Kat's backpack, avoiding the bag of bones and ashes within, the part of their baggage Damien didn't know about. The bones and ashes in his own backpack also had to stay hidden, though Damien did know about the bombs they each carried in their packs.

Ben motioned toward Damien. "Let's go."

He lowered the violin. "Without a coat?"

"Too bulky. We have to move fast. And we won't be in Russia long. Caligar will have coats for us in Alaska."

"If you say so, but if my fingers are too cold, I won't be able to play the Alaska tower tune. If I had gloves, I could keep my fingers warm until it's time to play."

Kat threw a pair of gloves that slapped Damien in the chest and dropped to the floor. "You're taking the plunge into Russia first."

Grumbling under his breath, he zipped the violin and bow into a case, retrieved the gloves, and marched to the desk. With a petulant toss of his head, he touched the mirror's surface. As before, he elongated, lifted from the floor, and streamed into the mirror.

"Our turn." Ben touched the mirror and felt himself stretch as he plunged into shimmering darkness. Although pain seemed minimal, lack of control felt like falling from an airplane without a parachute. With no way to change direction or gauge his speed, he was at the mercy of whatever science—or magic—controlled this device.

After several tense moments, bitter cold pressed from all around, and frigid air swirled, carrying a fetid odor. He grabbed a flashlight from his belt and flicked it on. The beam shone on Damien a few yards away, shivering as he put his gloves on.

Damien wrinkled his nose. "What is that stench?"

"Not sure." Ben climbed to his feet and swept the flashlight around. The blinking tower loomed about a hundred yards away across an icy field where several dead giants lay, likely Harrid's victims. Smaller bodies peppered the white landscape with bloody remains, maybe humans the giants had started eating before succumbing to the poison. "The odor could be a lot worse. It's too cold for them to rot quickly, but with no vultures to strip the carcasses, they'll be around a long time."

Kat appeared in the glow, tumbling to the ground as if tossed through an open doorway. Groaning, she rose to a sitting position and massaged her hip. "How many more times do we have to do this?"

"Are you saying you never trained for five-thousand-mile jumps through a magic mirror?" Ben grasped her wrist and hauled her to her feet. "Hold your nose and let's get moving. As quietly as possible."

After Ben doused the flashlight, he and Kat slid their rifles from their shoulders and trudged across the field, careful to soften their footfalls on the snow-covered ice, while Damien brought up the rear. With every step, Ben watched for movement but saw nothing. A barracks-like building stood about fifty yards to the left, barely visible as the blinking tower cast intermittent light on the structure.

A guard leaned back against the door, embers at the end of a lit cigarette adding to the profile. Wearing a heavy parka and ski mask that hid his or her gender, the guard probably had no motivation to walk a patrol route. After all, who could show up in the middle of this wasteland without some kind of engine noise sounding an alarm?

When they arrived at the base of the tower, they found nothing at ground level but four concrete pads that anchored the tower's feet. No surprise. With the new technology, all of the controls were probably housed safely underneath. They just needed to find the access point.

Ben flicked on the beam and ran it across the ground until it came upon a five-foot-wide circular metal plate, probably a duplicate of the manhole-like cover at the Alaska tower. After reattaching his rifle and light, he slid his fingers into a gap around the plate and heaved it to the side. Light rose from below, along with a humming sound. Only a bare tiled floor lay in view about thirty feet down. Metal ladder rungs protruded from the side of the access cylinder, an easy climb.

He turned toward Kat. "I'll go first. If it's clear, then Damien, and then you."

She nodded. "Copy."

Ben set a foot on the top rung and crept down with his backpack in place, listening for any sign of an alert. When he reached the bottom, he set his feet quietly on the floor and looked around the room, lit by dim fluorescent panels in the ceiling, most of which had been turned off. He stood at the edge of a room that spanned about fifty feet by fifty feet, roughly the area of the tower's base. A massive metal shaft dominated the center from ceiling to floor, maybe a conduit carrying wires from the tower equipment above to another chamber below.

A console with knobs and sliders abutted an adjacent wall—a control panel. It made sense to provide a room like this, safe from cold outside and from heat produced by any equipment running below. He glanced at his wristwatch—10:14 p.m. in this time zone. The workers were likely either asleep in the barracks or getting ready for bed. As hoped, the timing was perfect.

He looked up into the access cylinder and waved. Carrying the violin case with one hand and holding ladder rungs with the other, Damien descended clumsily. Halfway down, his foot slipped. The case dropped, and he tumbled, slapping at rungs to slow his fall and banging his chin against them several times.

Ben caught the case and threw an arm around Damien to keep him from slamming against the floor. When he balanced Damien on his feet, he handed over the violin case. Damien offered a thankful nod and exhaled, saying nothing.

Seconds later, Kat arrived, landing nimbly as she slid her rifle into position.

Ben whispered, "We need an access to the next level below." He walked around the central shaft and found another manhole cover embedded in the floor, smaller than the one at ground level.

He removed the cover, revealing a dark hole, not wide enough for a person wearing a backpack to squeeze through. A louder hum emanated from below, as well as warm air.

"I'll check it out." He slid his backpack off and set it on the floor. "When I leave, get a mirror and be ready to play whatever will send us to Alaska. Planting the devices might set off an alarm."

"Caligar mentioned another access at the Alaska tower. The one that leads to the shack. They might have one here as well." Kat pulled a computer pad from her backpack. "If all else fails, maybe we can escape that way."

"I'll look for one." Ben unzipped his backpack and withdrew ten stick-on spherical bombs about the size of a baseball. A toggle switch protruded on the surface of each. He flipped the switch on one of the bombs.

Kat tapped on her computer pad and studied the screen. "The bomb's now connected to the angel satellite. I'll be able to control it from anywhere."

"Being the angel queen continues to reap benefits." Ben eyed the bomb. In the dimness, it looked like a professionally constructed device, not something Kat had slapped together from materials in the vault's weapons room. It could probably do some serious damage, but setting them off wasn't their real purpose, and they couldn't let anyone else know that.

He flicked on his flashlight, took the bomb, and began descending the ladder. "Drop them down to me one by one when I call for them."

"Will do."

The flashlight beam leading the way, Ben lowered himself slowly. With each step, the air grew warmer and the hum louder. Whatever these machines were, the workers must have built them quickly. No surprise. The one hundred influencers were hand chosen. They could probably move mountains if need be.

When he reached the bottom, he swept the beam across a bank of light switches. Flipping them on would help, but no use risking setting off an alarm too early. As he continued his sweep, he spotted several cylindrical head-high machines that looked important, including one that emanated the loudest hum. He attached the bomb behind that unit, well out of sight of a casual observer, then called for another bomb from Kat.

After a few minutes, he had installed the ten bombs and checked with Kat to make sure all were communicating with the satellite. When she confirmed the connections, he began looking around again. "Now to find an escape tunnel."

When he aimed the light at a bare wall, something sparkled at chest level. He walked to the spot and found a metallic sign with printed words written in Russian. Too rusty with the language to try to translate, he withdrew his phone, took a photo, and sent it to a translation program. A text message provided the English words. *Tower self-destruct. Authorized access only.*

Ben whispered, "Okay, but where is it?" He touched the sign. It depressed, then popped open like a small door, revealing a two-foot-deep recess. A lever protruded upward from the floor of the recess, like a big joystick. A cage of vertical laser light beams surrounded it, each a different color, obviously an alarm trigger.

Ben eyed the lever. Would grabbing it and manipulating it somehow destroy the tower? And if so, what would happen to the person holding the lever? Regardless of the answers, they didn't need the lever. The bombs would do. But the alarm might be a perfect way to set this plan into motion.

Shifting the light beam again, Ben found an open access door with another sign written in Russian. He repeated the translation process and learned that it said *Barracks tunnel.* Perfect. The stage would soon be set.

Footsteps sounded from beyond the doorway. A little early, but they could improvise. Ben hurried back to the hole and climbed, hissing, "Someone's coming."

A man shouted in Russian, probably a command to halt.

A shot rang out from below. Ben scrambled the rest of the way up, shoved the cover over the hole, and stood on it. "Damien. Quick. Play the piece that'll get us to Alaska."

Damien began pulling his gloves off one finger at a time. "The cold air has certainly thrown the instrument out of tune."

Kat grabbed a glove and jerked it off his hand. "No time to be so dainty."

"Right." Ben looked at the hole leading to the outside. "It won't take him long to run back to the barracks and sound the alarm."

"Fine. Fine. But I cannot hurry the transport-tune-finding process." He retrieved the violin and bow from the case, set them in playing position, and began tuning it.

Ben removed the box of mirrors from Kat's pack as he whispered to her, "He's stalling. I'm sure he set us up. You know what to do."

Kat tapped on her computer pad, turned her back to Damien, and walked to the other side of the room. Ben opened the box, withdrew the top mirror, and held it on his palm.

Damien played a final note. "It was not as out of tune as I expected. I will now mentally put myself at the Alaska tower site." He closed his eyes for a moment before beginning a new tune, clearly not the same as the one that brought them to Russia.

Ben put the mirror box into his backpack as he watched the mirror. The reflection warped. Within seconds, the image showed another tower, again highlighted by blinking lights. Although the tower was bigger than the one he had seen and climbed while in Alaska, the familiar shack stood nearby.

"Mirror's ready, Kat. Are you?"

"Yep." She walked back to them and fastened her pad onto her belt. "Time to travel."

"Perhaps," Damien said, "but—"

Shouts in Russian volleyed from above. Ben looked at the hole in the ceiling. No one descended yet, likely worried about getting shot. Teargas might be their next step.

Damien smirked. "I think your game is over." He nodded toward the mirror. "The Alaska scene is already gone, I think because I played the notes only once instead of several times, and I won't play the tune again. I'm sure I will be treated better by Alexandria's allies than by you."

Ben scowled. "You ratted us out, didn't you?"

"Of course. You think you have a chance at winning, but you don't know Alexandria like I do."

Clanging footsteps sounded from above. Ben set the mirror on the floor, drew his handgun, and aimed it at the hole. He fired three rounds. When their echoes subsided, silence ensued.

A teargas canister clanked on the floor and spewed white fumes. Ben kicked it to the far side of the room, but the vapor had already penetrated his nostrils. His throat tightened, and his chest burned. "Let's do it, Kat."

Coughing, she tapped on the computer pad, still attached to her belt. A tune played by a violin emanated. On the floor, the mirror's reflection showed the computer room at the temple vault. Ben snatched it up by its edges and pushed the reflective side against Damien's face.

The mirror square seemed to slurp him in and swallow him whole. Within seconds, he was gone.

"Try to hold your breath," Ben shouted through his own coughing. "Let's get below!"

Leo sat at the computer room's desk chair, a hand on the back of his head. Getting his soul restored felt great, of course, and suffering the worst headache in the history of the world was a price worth paying. But getting assigned guard duty in the temple vault seemed intolerable, especially with Iona out there taking on the most dangerous role possible.

He touched the rifle he had put on the computer desk next to a square mirror lying in the midst of scattered reflective shards.

It seemed odd that Ben would insist on having the weapon ready, considering that the vault was locked down with triple-level security. Ben explained why, but this blasted headache must have throttled his words. The reason didn't make any sense. Using music and a mirror to travel through a portal? Crazy. But was it crazier than walking through hell as a disembodied soul and getting restored by a quixotic queen who escaped from hell to rule the world? Maybe not.

Leo rose from the chair and checked his cloak's deep pockets. Only one smoke bomb remained. Apparently Bart had removed everything else, even the flask of angel tea, which might have helped battle the headache.

Something popped. Midway between the desk and the vault door, a man appeared out of nowhere and tumbled to the floor. Cradling a violin and bow, he rolled to a stop and moaned.

Leo grabbed the rifle from the desk. This intruder had to be Damien. Now Ben's bizarre explanation made sense. Damien did turn out to be a traitor as they had feared, and Ben sent him back to the temple to be put into custody.

Aiming the rifle at Damien, Leo called, "What did you do to the Garrisons?"

Damien rose to a sitting position and glared at Leo, the violin in his lap. "Your allies misinterpreted my actions. I wanted us to be captured so we could learn more about what Alex's plans are." He touched the violin. "With this, we could escape anytime we wished. I didn't tell Ben my strategy because he would never have agreed."

"Because he's no fool." Leo took a step closer and aimed the rifle at Damien's head. "Are Ben and Kat in danger?"

"Since they don't have me or the violin, most certainly. We were trapped under the base of the Russia tower, and the guards were closing in."

"Take me to them." Leo rushed to the desk and grabbed the mirror. "Now."

Holding his breath, Ben set the rifle down, lifted the floor hole's cover, and helped Kat to the ladder. When she reached the bottom, he lowered the backpacks, the rifle, and the mirror to her, then, sliding the cover overtop, climbed down.

Kat had already turned a flashlight on, illuminating her tablet. The residual glow washed over her face as she sniffed and coughed. "I can see now."

Heavy footsteps thudded beyond the door leading to the barracks. Battling a wheeze, Ben coughed through his words. "Start the music." He set the mirror square on the floor, aimed the rifle at the door, and fired three rounds. The footsteps halted. "That should give us time."

While music flowed from the computer, Kat unzipped the backpacks. Ben pulled out the bags of bones and ashes along with the accelerant and flash powder. They each poured a bag of bones out on the floor in front of them, then saturated both piles with the accelerant.

"Dog tags." Ben stripped off his tag and set it on top of his pile, and Kat did the same with hers. They added a belt buckle, a handgun with a loaded magazine, and Kat's wristwatch.

When they rose, Kat set the flashlight beam on the mirror. Ripples of light ran across the reflection until it changed to the view of the Alaska tower.

The footsteps returned, slower now.

They faced the door, Ben holding the flash bomb in one palm, the mirror in the other. Kat turned on a translation app on the computer pad and set it to Russian, then slung her backpack on and looked at Ben. "Ready?"

Ben put his backpack on and tightened the straps. "Let's do it."

She spoke into the pad. "One of you come out alone. We will negotiate the terms of our surrender." She played the Russian translation at full volume.

From the tunnel, someone called, "I speak … a little English."

244

Ben shouted, "We want you to assure us that we won't be harmed."

"Lay guns down."

"Already done."

A rifle barrel protruded from around a corner within the tunnel. A clean-shaven young man peeked at them, his bushy brow low. Wearing sweatpants and a sweatshirt, probably his pajamas, he padded out in sock-covered feet and stopped several paces away, his rifle aimed at Ben's head. "What is it you hold in hands?"

Ben extended the bomb. "This is an explosive device. We planted several more in your machinery, and we will tell you where they are if you let us leave peacefully."

The man narrowed his eyes, obviously not understanding.

Kat played the translation on the pad. When it finished, the man's eyes widened, and he jabbered in Russian.

Kat played the English version. "You fool! Do you think you can plant bombs here and expect to leave without consequences? We will torture you to learn the bomb locations."

"That's what I was afraid of." Ben set the flash bomb's activation switch. "We would rather die than be tortured."

The moment the translation finished playing, Ben threw the bomb down at the piles of ashes. It erupted in a blinding flash and billows of smoke.

Kat touched the mirror. She elongated and flowed into the reflection. Ben let out a fake moan and shouted, "It burns! It burns!"

A barrage of gunfire burst from the barracks tunnel. Bullets ricocheted, zipped out from the doorway, and thunked into the surrounding walls. A bullet struck Ben's foot. With a stifled yelp, he fell to his stomach. The mirror dropped and cracked in half, both sections sliding out of reach.

With a thrusting stretch, he slapped at the surface of one of the pieces, but did he hit his target? Light flashed again, more fireworks from their bomb. The usual stretching sensation took over as he dove into the dark Alaska scene.

# Chapter Twenty-three

Jack and Trudy ducked under the museum's arching entrance, taking shelter from the cool, drizzly late evening in Jerusalem. Both dressed in stereotypical tourist garb—jeans, baseball jerseys and caps, sunglasses, and sneakers—they scanned the quiet street. Only a few people passed by, most wearing topcoats with collars pulled high and hats with brims pulled low. The recent departure of the angels and the loss of their rod-of-iron justice system had left the citizenry on edge. Yet, crime stayed low, most likely because so many people had lost their souls to the vaccine, and they had hunkered down, probably waiting for marching orders from Alex.

Jack eyed a tall woman he had seen at the nearby shop where they bought the clothes. When she saw him looking, she pulled her coat collar higher and hustled on. He whispered, "People are antsy."

Trudy's eyes darted. "I noticed. Either zombified if they're angel vaccinated or terrified if they're not. "

"Exactly what I was thinking a second ago."

"I know. You're as transparent as glass. Foggy glass, sometimes, but still easy enough to read, like smeared letters on a page, like skywriting with a breeze blowing the—"

"Just shut up and let me know if you spot Daniel." Jack glanced at his wristwatch. "He's already five minutes late."

Trudy crossed her arms and cast her gaze from side to side. "He's always been paranoid. Probably watching us right now. Wouldn't doubt it a bit if he planted a listening device somewhere close, and he's heard every word we've said."

"I have been listening."

Jack and Trudy spun toward the voice. A tall, bearded man wearing blue coveralls stood between them and the museum's entry door, his gray beard so long and thick, he looked like a lanky Santa Claus dressed for street sweeping.

"Daniel?" Jack asked.

He smiled. "Didn't recognize me, did you?"

"No, but I recognize your voice."

"And that's only because I'm not disguising it. I heard enough of your conversation with Trudy to know you're not angel robots." He bowed his head toward Trudy. "My, my. The rumors were true. You've become a true soldier. You have the eyes of a warrior."

Trudy smiled. "Thank you, Daniel." She winked at Jack. "I'm glad someone thinks so."

"Yeah, yeah," Jack said. "Time to get down to business. How do we get into the museum without setting off alarms?"

Daniel gave each of them a photo ID card. "Here are your identities. You have only a couple of minutes to memorize them. Good news, though. You're married now. Mazel tov."

As Trudy studied her card, she smirked. "Prepare to be a hen-pecked husband."

"Better be careful," Jack said. "This rooster has sharp spurs."

"Everyone's a comedian." Daniel tapped on his phone. "Jack, I'm sending you the museum's bank account number so you can set up the donation transfer. He agreed to the amount we discussed, but if you can make it higher, I think he would be far more helpful."

Jack's phone chimed. He read the number on the screen, copied it to his bank app, and prepared the transfer. "Done."

"It's time." Daniel turned toward the entry. "It should be unlocked. Go through the metal detector I told you about earlier and tell the security guard that you have an appointment with the curator. The rest is up to you."

"We'll make it work."

"You'd better. You'll have no backup." Without another word, Daniel hustled down the steps and strode into the shadows.

"Okay. Let's do this." Jack opened the phone's translator app and chose the English-to-Hebrew option, then spoke into the microphone. "We're here to see your Antonio Vivaldi display." When he tapped the translate button, the phone replied with a Hebrew sentence that sounded like gibberish. He glanced at Trudy. "Any clue how good the translation is?"

She shrugged. "Why don't we just ask to see Levi Jakobson? The security guard will recognize the name."

"Good thought." Jack slid the phone back into his pocket and led the way into the museum's spacious, marble-tiled lobby, passing through a metal detector immediately after the door without setting off an alarm. At an adjacent desk, a young, dark-haired female attendant wearing a beige security guard uniform smiled and spoke in Hebrew, her brown eyes studying the newcomers. "Erev tov."

"Um ..." Jack glanced at Trudy. "Shalom?"

"Shalom!" The woman laughed. "I speak English," she said with a thick accent.

"Good." Jack cleared his throat. "We are here to speak to the curator, Levi Jakobson. We have an appointment to see the Vivaldi display."

The woman's smile thinned. "I will contact Mr. Jakobson for you, but we do not have a public Vivaldi display." She picked up a desk phone and punched in a number as she lifted the handset to her ear. "We do have some artifacts that are being restored, but they will not be ready for at least a few more days."

"Oh? What kind of artifacts?"

The woman shook her head. "I do not know." Her brow lifted, and she spoke in Hebrew. After a few seconds of silence, she nodded and hung up the phone. "Mr. Jakobson will be here in a moment."

Trudy stepped closer. "Where are the artifacts stored?"

The woman glanced toward a corridor. "I ... I do not know if I should—"

Jack took a stealthy peek that way. A balding man wearing an expensive-looking gray suit walked toward them, his eyes wary as he glanced in all directions. When he drew within earshot, Trudy snapped her fingers as she looked at Jack with a frown. "Can you believe it, honey? We came all this way for nothing. Now what are we going to do with all that money we were planning to give?"

"I'm not sure. I guess we'll have to delay the donation until the artifacts are restored."

"Mr. Spitzer?" the man said as he closed in.

"Yes." Jack squinted at him. "Are you Levi?"

"Levi Jakobson. This museum's curator." Levi extended a hand. When Jack shook it, Levi smiled. "I am glad to meet you, Mr. Spitzer."

"Oswald Spitzer. My friends call me Oz or Spitz. Your choice." He gestured toward Trudy. "And this is my wife, Aster."

Levi nodded. "I am pleased to meet you both. And I am certain that we can accommodate a benefactor, but I am sure you understand that we can't let just anyone into areas that are sensitive to traffic. We don't want to damage the artifacts."

Jack gave him an exaggerated nod. "Oh. I see. You want proof that we have the cash." He withdrew his phone again, switched to the banking app, and doubled the agreed-upon amount. "I have the wire transfer all set up." He showed the screen to Levi. "Will that be enough to get a tour?"

Levi's eyes widened for a moment, then he blinked and cleared his throat. "Yes. Quite enough. I will be happy to let you see the Vivaldi artifacts."

"Great." Jack pulled the phone back and tapped on the screen. "Half of the donation is on its way. I'll send the other half after we see what we came for."

"That will be fine. The artifacts are housed in the laboratory on the lowest level." Levi pivoted on his heels and strode toward a side door while he tapped on his own phone. "This way, please."

Jack and Trudy followed, staying far enough behind to converse in whispers. "Did you really transfer the money?" Trudy asked.

"Yep. Couldn't risk a fake. He's probably checking the museum's account now. It should be there."

Levi slid his phone into his pocket and continued walking without a word, his shoes clopping on the tile. Since the museum was closed, the vacant lobby allowed the cavernous room to cast an echo.

When they reached a door with an illuminated *Exit* sign above it, Levi pulled the door open. "Proceed downstairs to the lowest level where you will come to a freight elevator. Pull the cage up, step into the car, and lower the cage again. I will send you to the archive room from a control panel on this level. When you arrive, exit into the corridor and proceed to a metal access door with a security pad embedded in the wall. The entry code is nine, seven, nine, three."

Jack nodded. "Nine, seven, nine, three. Got it."

Levi gestured with his hands. "The Vivaldi artifacts are being restored on a table that abuts the far wall. A specialist named Hannah is working late. We're hoping to have the restoration complete as soon as possible. Be sure to tell her that I gave you permission to view anything you wish to see. When you are finished, return to the elevator and press the Up button. The car will return to the level where you first entered. When you return, I will escort you to the exit."

Trudy nudged Jack's ribs. "Aren't you going to ask him why he's not going down to that spooky place with us? I mean, seriously, a basement in a centuries-old museum? By ourselves?"

"Yeah, I was just about to—"

"I assure you," Levi said with his hands folded at his waist, "the building is secure. I am not going with you because I am working on the display room for the artifacts on this floor. We are all doing our share to get everything ready."

"Thank you. We won't be long." Jack walked down the concrete stairs with Trudy close behind. Above, Levi closed the door with a loud click.

"I didn't buy his excuse," Trudy said. "About not coming with us, I mean."

They reversed direction on a landing and continued down a second stairway with fewer lights on the walls. Jack slowed his pace. "Are you thinking this might be a trap?"

"Or an ambush. I don't trust Levi's beady eyes."

"Yeah, he might be a weasel, but he wants the second payment." They pivoted on a second landing and headed down a third stairway, even darker. "I'm guessing he'll look into our backgrounds to see if we're legit. Daniel created our backstops, and you saw how careful he is. Levi's beady eyes won't be able to find out who we really are."

"Unless whoever was following us shows up. Then all bets are off."

"True. We have to be ready for anything."

"How?" Trudy asked. "We don't have any weapons. I feel like I'm naked."

"We'll improvise, the way we always have before. But not naked, I mean. It's getting cold down here."

She swatted his arm. "You're so funny."

"I like to think so."

They turned back to yet another stairway, the darkest one yet. Made of wood this time instead of concrete, it appeared older, maybe a sign that they were finally near the bottom. After padding down to the landing, they arrived in front of an elevator car, the interior visible through a metal cage door.

Jack stared at the crisscrossing lattice. "When we get to the final door, I should go in without you." He lifted the cage door and rolled it to the top. "While you hide somewhere to watch for an ambush from behind, maybe I can get some intel from Hannah and make an excuse to get her to leave."

"Why should I be the one to hide?"

"Because I'm such a charmer. Hannah will be putty in my hands."

"Don't make me barf." Trudy inserted an earbud and stepped into the elevator car. "I'll find a restroom to hide in. This deep down, there's got to be one. No one wants to haul herself that far upstairs just to use the toilet."

Jack joined her, inserted his own earbud, and lowered the cage door. The moment it clicked into place, a motor hummed. The car jerked and began a slow descent into darkness. After about twenty seconds, light returned, revealing a corridor as the car thudded to a halt.

When Jack lifted the door, he and Trudy walked out into a musty hallway lit with flickering fluorescent ceiling lights. She pointed at a door marked "Toilet" and hustled inside. Her whispered voice filtered through his earbud. "Keep me up to date. And make it quick. This room smells like a wet dog. A dead one."

"Will do." Jack strode past the restroom to the end of the corridor where a metal door blocked further progress. He found the security pad in the wall to the right and punched in the code, each button making a low beep.

When a buzz emanated from the door, he pulled the handle. With a whoosh of cool, dry air, the door opened. Inside, dim light revealed tables covered with glass cases. At the far wall, a woman in a lab coat, likely Hannah, stood working over a table. A huge mirror covered most of the wall and reflected her lowered head, while a nearby lamp sent a bright beam over her worktable.

As Jack eased closer, he studied the mirror. It wasn't a single big mirror but rather a collection of mirror squares pieced together to form a much larger whole.

Hannah called out a short phrase, apparently in Hebrew. Jack recognized only Levi's name.

Jack whipped out his phone and looked at the screen. Fortunately, he had left the translator app running. The screen reported her words. *Is that you, Levi?*

"I'm in," Jack whispered. "A woman's here. She must be Hannah."

The woman, a graying brunette, turned and gasped. She spoke again in Hebrew, and Jack read the screen. *Who are you?*

He touched his chest. "Oswald Spitzer. Levi sent me. Do you speak English?"

"A little." She offered a nervous smile. "Why are you here?"

"I asked Levi if I could look at the Vivaldi artifacts. Are you Hannah?"

"Yes." She gestured with a latex-gloved hand. "Come."

As Jack walked toward her, he whispered, "Grandma type. Should be a pushover."

"Don't get cocky, Mr. Charm," Trudy said. "Remember Grandma Bea? She could kick your butt."

"I remember, and duly noted." Jack halted at the table. A browned parchment lay on the surface, with words and notes written with care on a musical staff. An eyedropper bottle sat next to the parchment, maybe containing a cleaning solution or a protective liquid. "What is this parchment?"

Hannah touched a corner of the tawny paper. "A composition by Antonio Vivaldi. In English it is called *The Eternity Psalm.*"

"Composed for a violin?"

"Oh, no, no. It is a …" She glanced upward for a moment. "A choral piece. To sing." She pointed at a line of words. "See?"

"Ah. Lyrics." Jack leaned close, but the words were indecipherable. "Italian?"

Hannah nodded. "His greatest work."

"Oh. Then you have heard it sung."

She touched her chest. "I sing it myself. At home in the shower."

"Not here?"

"Oh, no, no, no. I do not want his … his spirit to hear me."

"Do you really think his spirit is here?"

A blush colored her cheeks. "No. I know it's a … a super …"

"Superstition."

She nodded. "I still feel like it's wrong."

"You were right, Jack," Trudy said. "She's putty in your hands. Remember to record the song when you talk her into singing it."

Jack resisted the urge to roll his eyes. Of course he would remember. "Would you sing it for me, Hannah? I love Vivaldi, and it would mean the world to me to hear his masterpiece. Please?"

Hannah's blush deepened. "But I am not ... skilled."

"I'm sure you'll do fine. In fact, I'll bet Vivaldi's spirit has seen you working so meticulously on his masterpiece, and he would be delighted to have you sing it." Jack withdrew his phone and began the recording, then shifted to the translation app and switched it from Hebrew to Italian.

"No camera," Hannah said, waving a hand. "Not allowed."

"I'm running a translation program so I can understand the lyrics. I don't know Italian."

"Okay. But no camera." She reverently lifted the page with both hands. After taking a deep breath, she began singing with a lovely alto. As the Italian lyrics flowed through the air, Jack read the English translation.

*When the tempest blows my ship at sea ...*

The mirror on the wall flashed. Jack stepped closer. The reflection warped, altering from the contents of the room to a dark expanse. A doorway stood in the midst, a familiar sight. With brilliant light emanating from within, it looked exactly like the door he saw before he was drawn to the Never-ending Highway. Could it be the door to heaven?

Hannah, facing the opposite direction, didn't seem to notice the change as she continued. Since she sang the piece at home and not here in the laboratory, maybe she had never witnessed the mirror's change.

*I call to my rock from my soul.*

The image in the mirror deepened, so real it seemed that he could walk right into the expanse. A feeling of perfect peace washed through, just as it had when he saw the door as a disembodied soul. In his mind, he saw an old ship being driven by crashing waves and brutal winds. A sailor dressed in ancient garb held to the mast as torn sails whipped at his body. He seemed to be shouting, but no voice came through.

*Hear my cry and protect.*

"Jack," Trudy said. "I heard the elevator. Trouble might be on the way."

He whispered, "The song's not finished."

"How much longer?"

"Not much, I think. It's just one page."

"Whoever it is, I'm going to let them go by without confronting them. Keep playing your role and let me know if you're in trouble. I've got your back."

"Copy that."

*My life from the snares they set. Give me an escape for my soul.*

When Hannah finished, she let out a deep sigh, set the parchment on the table, and looked at Jack with an expectant smile, still unaware of the mirror's change. "You like?"

"It was truly heavenly." Jack shut off the recording app and nodded toward the mirror, hoping to get Hannah's take on the change. "Is that also a Vivaldi artifact?"

"Yes. He kept it in his study. It is said that he thought it helped him compose." She looked at the reflection and gasped. "What ... what is happening?"

The metal door flew open. A man and woman burst in, each armed with an automatic rifle. The man aimed at Jack. "Hands up!"

Jack raised his hands. "Whoa, whoa! What's this all about?"

"That is Alexandria's question for you, Jack Garrison. Why did you come here?"

"I'll be glad to tell you." Jack nodded toward Hannah. "Just let her go. She's got nothing to do with this."

"She's a local, Kato," the woman said. "I saw her photo on the museum's website."

Kato looked at Hannah and gestured with his head toward the door. "Leave. Now."

She rushed out and disappeared into the corridor.

"Jenn," Kato said. "Search him for a weapon."

While Kato kept his rifle aimed, Jenn frisked Jack from shoulders to shoes. "He's clean."

Jack glanced from Kato to Jenn and back to Kato. No way could he disarm both of them without getting shot. Of course, Trudy was listening in. What move might she make?

Kato lowered the barrel but kept his finger on the trigger. "Like I said before, our mutual friend, Alexandria, wants to know why you've come here."

"Strange question. Is she always poking her nose into other people's business?"

Kato aimed his rifle at Jack's chest. "Care to change your answer, smart guy?"

"Cool it, Kato. I'll come clean." Jack lowered a hand and nodded at the parchment on the table. "I came to look at this." The mirror flickered, catching his attention. The reflection changed to a dark body of liquid, maybe a lake, with a shining gate on the far shore. Smoke curled up from the lake's surface.

Kato blinked at the mirror. "Is that being projected from somewhere? Like a movie?" His eyes darted, though the rifle stayed aimed at Jack. "I don't see where it's coming from."

Jack peeked out of the corner of his eye. Trudy skulked through the open door while Kato and Jenn stared at the mirror. Keeping his focus on the reflection, Jack pointed, faking a gasp. "What's that thing in the middle of the lake?"

"What thing?" Kato edged closer. "I don't see it."

Jack pushed the table out of the way and set his finger closer. "Right there. See? It looks like a human head."

"A human head?" Kato squinted. "I don't see a head."

Jack lifted his hands again. "I'm just trying to figure out what's going on. Same as you are."

"Wrong answer. I think you're stalling." Kato fired at Jack's leg. The bullet slammed into his knee, making him crumple to the floor in a sitting position. Blood seeped down his leg. Pain roared.

Everything in the room seemed to rock back and forth, like the ship on the sea. Someone grunted. Kato flew into the reflection and zoomed toward the lake, his arms and legs flailing. Trudy, now holding Kato's rifle, swung the butt at Jenn and bashed her in the head. Jenn tottered toward the mirror and extended a hand to brace herself, but she toppled into the reflection and hurtled toward the lake.

Two splashes erupted on the surface, one a few seconds after the other. Smoke billowed at the spots, then quickly settled.

Trudy rushed to Jack's side and touched his pants. "How bad is it?"

Jack grimaced. "On a scale of one to ten? It's terrible."

"Probably shattered your kneecap. You'll need surgery." Trudy helped him lie on his back. "How're we going to get out of here? The elevator's controlled from above. Hannah probably signals the curator when she's ready to leave."

Jack grunted between phrases. "Even if we ... could use the elevator ... no way I could ... climb those stairs."

"Wait." Trudy stared at the mirror. "Let's contact Kat. She can send us the recording of Damien playing the tune that sent them to the temple vault."

Jack took in a strained breath. "And we can use this mirror to go there."

"Exactly."

"First ..." Jack tapped on his phone, brought up the recording of Hannah singing *The Eternity Psalm*, and sent it to Iona's transmitter, then to Kat's computer. "Okay. That's done."

"Don't talk. Save your strength." Trudy took his phone, punched in Kat's number, and set the phone to her ear. "Kat. It's Trudy.

We're in a world of hurt. Jack's been shot in the knee. But we have a transport mirror. We need the recording that'll catapult us to the temple vault. I can do surgery there." When she terminated the call, she watched the screen. "Okay. The temple audio file's coming in. Hang in there, Jack."

The room continued to rock, now nearly spinning. Jack touched Trudy's arm. "Can you tell if Iona's device received the Vivaldi file?"

"Yep. I don't know if she's accessed it yet or not, but she has the file."

"Good. Mission accomplished." Jack clenched his eyes shut. "When you're ready, let's splint my leg and go through that mirror."

# Chapter Twenty-four

Still on her knees, Trudy patted Jack's cheek. "Hey, macho man. I know you have a super high pain tolerance, but splinting a leg with a broken kneecap and putting weight on it? No way!"

Jack licked his lips. "The other option is to carry me through the mirror. You up for that?"

"I carried you in training. I can do it again."

"Okay, but let's brace my leg first." His began unbuttoning his shirt. "Use this."

Trudy helped him pull the sleeves off his arms, revealing a sleeveless undershirt, then wrapped the shirt around his knee. "This is going to hurt a lot."

"Can't hurt any more than it already does."

"Actually, it can." She pulled the sleeves together and fastened them in a knot.

Jack groaned, then gasped for breath. "Okay. Okay. You were right. But do whatever you have to. I'll bite the bullet."

"If the bullet went all the way through, maybe I can find it for you. I hear a nine-millimeter has a nice texture."

"Very funny."

"I thought so." She closed his eyelids with her fingers. "Try to relax until it's time to go. I don't see much blood, so I don't think there's any danger. Just trust me to get you home."

"I do trust you." He smiled with trembling lips. "Next time I'll cower in the restroom and you can be the charmer."

"Cower? I single-handedly threw those two goons into hell, thank you very much." Trudy looked at the phone. The file transfer from Kat was so slow, only halfway finished.

"Yeah, well, I was about to—"

Trudy set a finger on his lips. "Stop talking and rest before I break your other kneecap." She rose and turned toward the mirror. The reflection had reverted to normal, probably because it had been so long since Hannah sang Vivaldi's composition. Jack had said, "Mission accomplished," but would the recording work for Iona? Maybe a test was in order.

She pulled the file up on the phone and aimed the screen at the mirror. Hannah's voice came through the speaker, quiet and tinny. The mirror's reflection stayed constant, still showing the laboratory.

Trudy turned the volume up to maximum and walked closer. Still no change. She set the phone within an inch of the mirror, restarted the recording, and played it all the way through. Again, the reflection remained unmoved.

She stamped a foot, nearly shouting, "It doesn't work."

"Because your phone cannot perfectly reproduce a human voice."

Trudy spun toward the speaker. Levi Jakobson stood only a few paces away, his hands folded at his waist. She looked him over. He seemed to be unarmed. "Um ... hi."

Levi stepped closer, almost within reach. "I found my security guard bound and gagged, and Hannah reported a violent attack by two intruders. I came to check on the artifacts."

"Yeah, but the intruders are gone. They ... well ... kind of—"

"Went through the mirror?"

Trudy cocked her head. "Yeah. How'd you guess?"

"Aster, I am well aware of the mirror's power. Hannah told me she sang *The Eternity Psalm* and opened the portal, and I saw you trying to duplicate her feat. I surmised the rest, though I'm not sure why you would want to reopen a portal to the afterlife, unless you're planning to go to heaven prematurely."

Trudy showed him the phone. "Ja—I mean, Spitz recorded Hannah's song, and I was testing it to see if the song made the mirror change. I definitely don't want to go where the intruders went."

"Then you saw the Lake of Fire." Levi looked at Jack. "Your husband seems badly injured. Should I call for an ambulance?"

"No. I want to take him home. I'm a doctor. I can care for him there."

"How will you carry him up the stairs?"

Trudy looked at the phone. Kat's file had finished transmitting. "I have an audio file that's supposed to alter the mirror and show my workplace. I hoped to go through the reflection and take my husband with me."

"Ah, so you already knew more about Vivaldi's composition than you were letting on. No wonder you were willing to donate so much money to see it."

"Right, but since a recording doesn't work, I guess we'll have to call an ambulance."

Levi shook his head. "No, no. A recording of other pieces will likely work without a problem. *The Eternity Psalm* is a special case. It is a song for the human voice, not an instrumental piece. Since it opens eternity's doors, it must come from the singer's heart with a passion that cannot be reproduced after the fact. In short, the passion must be present in real time."

"Does it have to be sung in Italian?"

"Not at all. If the singer is unfamiliar with the lyrics, then singing in Italian is worthless. Passion is ignited by the heart. If the words have no meaning to the singer, then passion is dead. It has no power without meaning."

"Then an English speaker would have to sing it in English."

"Correct. And a rote performance would also be futile. The words would have to resonate in the singer's heart, and they need not be a perfect translation as long as the meaning is similar and the tune is replicated. The perfection of the translation comes from the heart and soul."

"Okay. Great. Good information."

Levi nodded toward the phone. "Play the piece that will send you home. I expect that it will work."

Trudy tapped the screen. Damien's violin played the odd tune at the phone's full volume. Instantly, the mirror's reflection warped and morphed into a view of the temple vault room. Mirror pieces lay on the desk with a few shards on the floor.

"Perfect." She pushed the phone back into her pocket, hurried to Jack, and grasped his arm. "I'll bear his weight on one side. Can you get the other?"

"Of course, but I have a question that I am sure will make me sound like a greedy merchant."

"Oh. You want the other half of the donation." She reached toward her pocket.

Levi waved a hand. "Not now. I will help you first. I trust you to keep your word about the donation. The angels looted our budget, and we have a long way to go to recover."

"I'll send it. I promise." Trudy and Levi each pulled one of Jack's arms and hauled him up until he balanced on his good leg. "Good and steady, hon?"

He draped an arm over her shoulders, then another over Levi's. "Yeah," he grunted. "I'm good."

Trudy and Levi helped him hop toward the mirror. When they reached it, she imagined an uncontrolled flight into the vault and smacking the floor with their faces. "Let's turn. It'd be better if we land on our butts."

Once they had pivoted and faced the lab, Trudy gave Levi a nod. "Thanks. I've got it from here."

Levi drew away and watched while he put on sterile gloves from a box near the Vivaldi parchment. "I wish you well."

"Thanks." Trudy leaned back against the mirror, and they passed right through. Light flashed, and the laboratory zoomed away, Levi standing within while holding the parchment. "Thanks again!" she shouted, though she had no idea if he could hear her.

After a few seconds, she and Jack dropped to the vault room's floor and slid backwards until their momentum stopped. Grimacing, he blinked at her. "Thanks for the fun ride, Sis."

"Wait'll you see what I have in store for you next." She helped him rise to his good leg again, hobble to a cot in the vault's sleeping area, and lie on his back. With every motion, Jack winced but stayed quiet.

Once she had him settled, she pulled out her phone and called Kat.

"Hello, Trudy," Kat said. "How's Jack?"

"Awake and cracking jokes, but you know Jack."

"Yep. Super soldier. No crying allowed."

"Right. Why let a bullet to the kneecap slow you down?" Pressing the phone between her ear and shoulder, Trudy hustled to the supply room and grabbed a first-aid kit. "Listen. Quick update. I'm at the temple, prepping Jack for surgery." She jogged back to the cot, knelt at Jack's side, and flipped the kit open. "Here's an important bit of intel. *The Eternity Psalm* has to be sung live. A recording won't work. Iona has the file with the words sung in Italian, but she can't simply sing what she hears." Trudy grabbed a pair of scissors from the kit and, after untying the shirt, began cutting Jack's bloody pant leg out of the way. "She has to sing it in a language she knows and mean it from the heart. I can send the lyrics in English, but I have to run them through a translator app first. They're in Italian right now."

"Let me do that. You have your hands full with Jack."

"You got that right." Trudy tore open an alcohol prep pad and began wiping blood off Jack's knee. With each touch, he grimaced more tightly than ever. "Literally full." When she exposed the bullet hole, she swabbed around. Fortunately, the wound merely seeped blood. As long as he lay motionless, he wouldn't bleed much more until it was time to repair the damage. She snatched a syringe vial and read the label—morphine. "All I've got is a first-aid kit, but I can stabilize him and knock him out until I can find the surgical supplies I need to patch him up."

"Sounds good. You take care of Jack. We'll take care of the rest. But if you can look into that chip you took out of Damien, we'd appreciate it."

"Copy that. I'll give you an update as soon as I have one."

"We'll do the same."

"By the way, where are you now?"

"Alaska. Already did our gig in Russia. More later."

"Gotcha." Trudy terminated the call, plucked a syringe from the kit, and filled it to the proper level from the morphine vial. "Time to ease your pain, Brother."

Jack swallowed. "All right. Shoot me up. But I claim no responsibility for what I might say while under the influence."

"No problem. Nothing's being recorded, and I'll forget every word." She jabbed the needle into his arm and injected the morphine. "When you're comfortable, I'll call a supplier to have the surgical supplies delivered here."

"Thanks." After taking a few deep breaths, he gazed at her with unblinking eyes. "I love you, Sis. You know that, right?"

Trudy smiled. "Yeah. I know."

"I'm not under the influence yet, so you don't need to forget those words."

"Never." She brushed hair out of his eyes and kissed his sweaty forehead. "I love you, too, Jack." She closed his eyelids again and held his hand. "And I'll be here when you wake up."

Carrying his rifle, Leo dodged the bodies of the fallen guards and burst into a dark room—hot, humming, and smelling of petroleum lubricants. After feeling the wall next to the door for a moment, he found a panel of switches and turned the lights on. In a room filled with machinery, a pile of blackened bones lay on the floor, smoke rising from surrounding ashes. A broken mirror lay nearby, as did bent metal fragments.

He rushed to the mirror and looked down at the reflection. It showed a blinking tower that quickly faded. Within seconds, his own face looked back at him. Had Ben and Kat escaped to Alaska?

He gazed at the pile of ashes. Something glimmered near the top. With a gloved hand, he lifted a chain with an attached dog tag and read the imprinted name—Benjamin Garrison. He ran his hand through the other pile, found another tag, and read the name—Katherine Garrison.

His hand trembling, he picked up one of the metal fragments and sniffed it—explosive powder, recently detonated. He draped both chains around his neck and let the tags dangle in front of his chest.

Heat surged across his cheeks. Tears welled. Ben and Kat were dead, killed in some kind of superheated explosion. Of course, this was no time to grieve, but what should he do now? With the master planners gone, what would become of the plan? Since Iona was with Alex, he couldn't simply abort. She had to continue with no way of knowing that Ben and Kat were dead, but how could he take over for them when he didn't even know what role they were supposed to take in the next step of the plan?

With a quick lunge, he snatched up one of the mirror pieces and pivoted toward the door. "Damien! Are you coming?"

"I am on my way. You left quite a mess in your wake."

Leo kept his stare on the doorway. A guard lay dead just beyond it, one of five who kept watch on the tower. All of the others in the barracks appeared to be laborers who quickly scattered when Leo showed up, guns blazing at anyone who aimed a weapon in his direction.

A moment later, Damien appeared. He grimaced as he sidestepped the corpse. Now wearing a heavy coat he had purloined from the barracks, he carried the violin and bow in a gloved hand. "I was surprised at your ferocity. How did a huntsman become so emotionally attached to his conspiratorial allies?"

New heat coursing through his body, Leo yelled at the top of his lungs, "My allies are dead! These piles of bones and ashes are all that's left!"

Damien's shoulders drooped. "Oh, my. I'm so sorry. Really I am."

"You should be. I'm sure it was your fault. Otherwise they wouldn't have sent you back to the vault."

"I assure you, I wasn't—"

"Shut up!" Leo inhaled deeply, then exhaled slowly as he lowered his voice. "Just shut up."

"I will, but first I must tell you something I know about Iona."

Leo lifted his brow. "What?"

"First, let me say that I'm telling you this in order to prove that I am not on Alex's side. I am still your ally."

Leo growled, "Spit it out, you sniveling snake, or you'll be my dead ally."

"Yes. Of course." Damien straightened and spoke in a fast, nervous cadence. "Alex told me that she needs Iona's help to do something that she would never do without being persuaded to violate her principles, and only one being in the universe is crafty enough to be that persuasive."

Leo nodded. "Who?"

Damien trembled. "Satan. Lucifer. The devil."

"What?" Leo roared. "Alex is taking Iona to meet with Satan?"

"That's what she told me, and I am confident that it's true. Alex seemed quite excited about the prospect."

Leo set the mirror on the floor. "Send us to Alaska. Now. One of the guards got away, and he's sure to contact his cohorts to be on the alert."

Damien sighed. "I assume I have no choice."

"No. You don't." Leo aimed the rifle at him. "Do it."

Damien set the bow on the strings and began playing while Leo watched the mirror. The reflection twisted, morphing his facial features. Seconds later, a tower came into view. "Okay. It's here. Now let's—"

A shot rang out. A bullet burst through Damien's forehead in a splash of blood. He crumbled in place, and the violin clattered to the floor next to Leo. A guard stood behind him, a rifle aimed at Leo. He shouted something in Russian.

Leo grabbed the violin and bow, dropped to his knees, and touched the reflection. A flash of light blinded him. Another shot rang out, but no pain followed. Glass shattered, the sound echoing from far away. He flew through a tubular tunnel of blazing light while jagged cracks zigzagged along the walls.

He looked back. Not far to the rear, pieces of the surrounding conduit broke away and flew into oblivion, and the destruction sped toward him, accelerating. If it caught up, would he join the pieces and catapult into the unknown?

A second later, he thumped into something cold, protecting the violin as he rolled. When he stopped, he sat up and scanned the area. In the midst of darkness, the blinking tower stood far off, maybe several miles in the distance. Apparently a bullet had shattered the mirror, and the degrading conduit couldn't carry him all of the way to the tower.

Obviously, Damien was dead. The plan had been blown to smithereens. Now no one could play *The Eternity Psalm*. They had no hope of using it to create a mirror portal and send Alex back to hell. Only two choices remained. One was to find another violin player and have him or her play the psalm. The other was to simply rescue Iona from Alex's clutches and let Earth and Viridi fend for themselves. In either case, a meeting between Iona and the devil would be the worst possible scenario.

Leo rose, strapped the rifle to his shoulder, and brushed snow from his cloak, the violin and bow still in hand. He would prevent that meeting from happening at all costs. Not even the devil himself could stop him.

# Chapter Twenty-five

Ben stood with Kat behind the Alaska tower's shack and peered around the corner. The tower's blinking lights illuminated the snow-covered area. No guards stood anywhere in sight. Apparently, the Russian crew had tipped everyone off. No need to worry about guarding the tower. They believed that Ben and Kat Garrison were dead.

He pulled back and whispered to Kat as she looked at her computer pad. "Got a lock on the bombs in Russia?"

"Five of them. Looks like someone found the others."

"Perfect. Now they have our supposed motivation for going to Russia. Our mission there and supposed deaths will be more convincing than ever."

"Yep. Now there are four bombs active. Someone's still searching."

"How about Iona? Got her pinpointed?"

"She's closing in on our location. Maybe twenty minutes away. And before you ask, Trudy's doing surgery right now. I'll let you know Jack's condition when she's finished."

"What about Leo and Damien at the vault?"

Kat shook her head. "No word, but the vault's locked tight. Damien's not going anywhere. He can't spill any information to Alex."

"No worries, then. We don't need Damien anymore." Ben hiked up his light backpack. Since he had moved the remaining bombs to Kat's pack, the only valuable that remained in his was one mirror, still worth keeping, just in case. "Let's carry on."

They hustled toward Caligar's lair, Ben ignoring the pain in his foot and trying not to shiver in the frigid air. When they reached the entry, a cave in the side of a hill, Caligar gestured for them to enter. "Come. I have coats ready for you."

All three turned flashlights on and navigated the short downward slope. Caligar opened a wooden door, and they walked into the underground lair. He flipped a switch on a wall, firing up a generator, ceiling lights, and a control console embedded in the wall.

While Caligar studied the console's monitor, Ben and Kat shrugged off their backpacks as they looked on. Caligar pointed at the screen. "I installed miniature cameras in the shack next to the tower and in the underground machinery room. According to these views, there are no guards watching the access path to the tower's equipment, at least from the viewable angles." He touched the screen. "I have an older camera that provides a view of the platform. I see five people standing there. They appear to be waiting for something to happen."

Kat kept her stare on her computer pad, her fingers tapping on the screen. "They're a bunch of sycophants. They're expecting the queen of hell to arrive soon. Everyone wants to lick her boots when she makes her grand entrance on the platform stage."

"And they think Kat and I are piles of bones and ashes," Ben said as he put on a coat and gloves, "and Jack and Trudy were neutralized in Jerusalem. They're not worried about sabotage."

"Supposedly, she has a hundred influencers." Kat put on a coat of her own and turned toward Caligar. "Any sign of them showing up?"

Caligar shook his head. "I see no lights that would indicate an approach."

Kat again tapped on the computer pad. "It shouldn't be long."

Ben gestured toward the pad. "Are you working on the psalm's translation?"

"No. Watching Iona's signal. I finished the translation a while ago, but I still have to speak it, or maybe sing it. Her device is audio only. Too small for a screen."

"Are you going to include instructions that explain why you're sending the translation?"

Kat looked up from the screen. "I will, but if she listens to the file Jack and Trudy sent, that is, the audio of the woman singing in Italian, she might not realize that my translation file follows. She might just play the Italian one for her mirror, not realizing she's supposed to sing it herself in English."

Ben began pacing as he tapped his chin. "Then we have to get the message to her in a way that's clear but also hidden from Alex. That won't be easy."

"Let me have another look." Kat refocused on her pad, her eyes narrowed. "One issue we haven't thought about is Iona's ability to sing. It's a simple tune. Minor key. Doesn't span more than an octave and a half. But she probably has to sing the notes accurately. It'll take a fair amount of talent."

"Good point. I've never heard her sing. That might be another problem she'll have to overcome." Ben halted and turned toward Caligar. "I need to add to your role in the plan."

Caligar looked at him. "I assume you want me to inform Iona about the translation when I join them on Viridi."

Ben nodded. "Let's go over the steps to make sure we're all straight." He raised a finger. "Our first priority is to restore Iona's soul to her body, but Alex won't do that unless she actually is on Viridi and feels like she's succeeded, so we let Alex and Iona go there in the cruiser, then send you behind them in stealth, and we'll destroy the tower network to keep her influencers from following. Then, when Alex restores Iona and Iona sends Alex to hell, you'll send Iona back to Earth. The only addition is that you'll have to get word to Iona about the translation without cluing Alex in."

"I will think of a way," Caligar said, "but how do you know Alex will keep her word to restore Iona?"

"If she refuses, you'll offer to abdicate and give her Viridi in exchange for the restoration. Tell her that you and your family will go to Earth with Iona once she's restored."

"Yes, you mentioned that part of the plan and that it would never have to happen, but I am concerned about deceiving someone who is highly skilled in detecting lies. As I understand it, she has a supernatural ability that resembles mind reading."

"Then don't consider it a deception. You will fully intend to do exactly what you say, and if Alex reads your mind, she'll believe you. Once she's convinced and restores Iona, Iona will use the psalm to send Alex to hell through the mirror. Then you won't have to abdicate."

Caligar stroked his chin. "The plan is being played out on a fragile stage. The weakest plank is Iona's role, that is, opening the portal to hell and tricking Alex into going through it."

Ben let out a long sigh. "True. It's fragile. But Iona has proven herself capable. I have faith in her."

"You are correct that Iona has proven herself thus far, but if Alex has received word that you and Katherine are dead, she will use that against Iona to try to make her feel alone and abandoned. And even more worrisome, will Alex read Iona's mind and learn that you're really alive?"

Ben bit his lip. That was the question he hoped not to hear. Caligar probably wouldn't like the answer. "I'm sure Alex will try that, but she won't be able to learn anything by mind reading. We never told Iona about our ruse for that very reason. You, Kat, and I were the only ones who knew we were going to fake our deaths."

Caligar's huge eyes widened. "Then Iona is truly vulnerable to an emotional attack. Once Alex tells her that you're dead, she will be devastated."

Ben glanced at Kat. Her furrowed brow raised a reminder that she had warned him about this exact possibility. "Kat and I talked about that. We agreed that she can handle it."

"We did agree," Kat said. "Like I said once before, she's a superstar. But I did mention her emotions. She's really still a kid. And you can bet Alex will find any vulnerability and stab her in the heart with it."

A tear trickled from Caligar's eye, and he quickly brushed it away. "Benjamin, if you will allow me to be straightforward, I would like to offer an unguarded opinion."

A slight tremor invaded Ben's voice. "Speak freely, my friend."

Caligar took a deep breath. "It is not difficult to see that you wish to honor Iona as a warrior while at the same time feeling like a father to her. As you know, I had a daughter, Lacinda, and I felt the same way about her. To allow her to be a warrior, I let her go out on hunting expeditions without me, trusting her skills to avoid the savage giants. Time and time again, she returned home safely with fresh game, and my confidence in her swelled. Then one fateful day, Lacinda failed to return. I searched nearly half of Viridi and would have searched the other half, but I discovered that Alex had used my own portal to kidnap my daughter. As you know, she died in hell."

Caligar and Ben stared at each other for a long moment. Tears crept into Ben's eyes, but he let them come. This story was tragic, too important to interrupt with the slightest movement.

Caligar took another deep breath. "This is what I am trying to say, Benjamin. My pride in my daughter's warrior abilities blinded me to the fact that she was still vulnerable to attacks she had never faced. I wish with all my heart that I could go back and alter my approach. Instead of being a proud teacher of warrior tactics and sending her on journeys without limits, I needed to decide her boundaries for her, make the difficult decisions to limit her forays, even if it meant facing her wrath. In short, I needed to be her father, and I rue my foolish pride with every fiber of my being."

Tears trickled down Ben's cheeks. Caligar's words plunged like a spear to the heart. He was right. Oh, so right. And now his own pride in Iona had put her in a similar situation, trapped in Alex's clutches, in danger of dying. How could he possibly have thought this was a good idea?

Ben stepped forward and embraced the gentle giant. They both wept. Kat joined the hug, and all three cried together.

Soon, Caligar backed away and turned again toward his monitor while Ben and Kat looked on, holding hands. The camera view showed the tower's top platform. Five people in heavy parkas bustled around, as if preparing for something.

"Maybe they see the cruiser." Ben brushed away a tear. "The subjects are getting ready for their queen."

"I see something odd." Caligar squinted. "I will zoom in on it." He swiped a finger across the screen.

A human figure skulked across the snow-covered terrain, barely visible in the tower's blinking lights, obviously trying not to be seen as he trudged on a path that would take him around the tower in a wide circle. The man's long hair blew in the breeze, making his identity obvious.

"Leo's here," Ben said.

Kat began tapping her computer pad. "He doesn't know we're in Caligar's lair. We need to signal him."

"Have you tried his earbud lately?"

"Just static last time. I'll try again." She turned on her bud's microphone. "Leo. It's Kat. Can you hear me?"

Ben listened to his own earbud, but only light static emanated.

Kat shook her head. "Nothing."

"And Damien's not with him. That could mean trouble."

"He wouldn't leave Damien unguarded," Kat said. "Is it possible Leo never saw him when we sent him back to the temple?"

Ben shook his head. "No way. Leo couldn't get to Alaska so fast without Damien playing the violin."

"Good point. So where's Damien and the violin?"

Caligar pointed at the screen. "The details are difficult to see in the darkness, but I am confident that Leo is carrying a violin and bow."

273

"Okay. Let's think about this." Ben began pacing again. "Leo knows Iona needs to play *The Eternity Psalm*, but he doesn't know it has to be sung. He probably thinks we were following our original plan to have Damien fake a surrender to Alex and to play the psalm on the violin. That means he's trying to get the violin to Iona, maybe guessing that someone else could play it."

"Damien must be disabled," Kat said. "Maybe killed."

Ben pointed at her. "Exactly where I was heading."

"Leo stopped." Caligar leaned closer to the screen. "He's looking at a medallion attached to a chain."

"A medallion?" Ben rushed over to the monitor. As light from the tower flashed, brief glimpses of Leo appeared. A silvery rectangle on a chain around his neck reflected one of the flashes. "That's a dog tag."

Leo clutched the tag with a tight fist, tucked it under his shirt, and broke into a jog toward the tower.

"He went to Russia first," Kat said as she looked on. "He found the bones. He thinks we're dead."

Ben swallowed hard. "He'll think he's alone now, the only one who's left to rescue Iona. Knowing him, he'll get to Iona come hell or high water."

"Or a death hangover," Kat added. "Nothing will stop him."

"Then we have to intercept him."

In the camera view, Leo spun and looked at the sky. A bright light shone all around, making him much easier to see.

"The angel cruiser," Kat said. "I wonder if Alex saw him."

On the screen, Leo resumed his jog, now heading straight toward the tower.

Ben spun toward the exit. "We have to go."

Caligar grabbed a parachute pack. "I will make my way to the launch zone."

Ben and Kat threw their backpacks on over their coats, flung the door open, and ran with Caligar into the dim cave. As they hustled, Ben spoke with halting breaths, again trying to ignore the pain in his foot. "Kat, you get in position to disable the tower. I'll try to intercept Leo and join you down there as soon as I can."

Caligar puffed as he ran. "When I reach my transport mirror on Viridi, I will send an update on your ham radio channel, assuming the weather allows a transmission. The season of storms has begun on Viridi, and the early ones are often the most violent."

"Understood." Ben burst through the cave exit and sprinted side by side with Kat. They exchanged glances. Nothing needed to be said. They both knew what they had to do. Ignore the guilt. Swallow the pride. Rescue Iona. Nothing else mattered.

# Chapter Twenty-six

Still wearing Charlie's cloak while sitting in the angel cruiser's co-pilot seat, Iona looked out the windshield. Although darkness veiled nearly everything, the blinking tower stood in clear view as they approached at a slow speed. Alex turned the mooring lights on, illuminating the tower's platform and the surrounding area.

Iona peered at the ground. Leo looked up at the ship, then lowered his head and ran toward the tower. She stifled a gasp. Keeping a straight face, she gave Alex a furtive glance. She didn't seem to notice Leo at all.

As they drew closer to the tower, several people on the top platform scurried about, apparently preparing for the cruiser to dock somehow.

The transmitter device in Iona's pocket vibrated, indicating an incoming transmission. It vibrated a couple of hours earlier. At the time, she thought it might be *The Eternity Psalm*. But what was transmitting now? She couldn't risk checking until she could get some privacy.

Alex stopped the cruiser a few feet above the people who waited on the platform. She turned to Iona and heaved a deep sigh. "Before we depart for Viridi, I have some bad news to share with you. It's about your allies."

Iona kept her stare on Alex while stealthily sliding her hand into her pants pocket. She grasped the mirror square and spoke in her halting manner. "What ... news?"

"Benjamin and Katherine were at the Russia tower, and they planted bombs in the underground machinery. Our guards confronted them, and a fierce gun battle ensued. Several guards died in the hail of bullets, and other guards who checked the scene later examined the aftermath. Apparently an explosion occurred, and a superheated fire followed. All that remained where your friends stood were two piles of bones and ashes. Dog tags were found in the remains with the names Benjamin and Katherine Garrison. Also, Damien, my former helper who turned out to be a traitor, was killed."

Iona trembled. Tears flowed freely. She ran a finger along the mirror's surface. It stayed perfectly normal—no tingling at all. Maybe it wasn't working.

Alex used a thumb to brush a tear away from Iona's cheek. "I'm so sorry to tell you this. I know how much you loved them."

The mirror stung her hand—a lie. Alex wasn't sorry at all. And it proved that the mirror worked. Did it mean Ben and Kat were dead? Could Alex simply be wrong? She once said that the mirror detected falsehoods even if the speaker wasn't aware a statement was false. That meant her story had to be true. And now she had no violinist to play *The Eternity Psalm*. Ben and Kat were dead, their plans ruined.

"And I have more bad news. I heard from one of my influencers who sent a team to follow Jack and Trudy to a museum in Jerusalem. According to the museum curator, the team ambushed your friends. Jack was shot and badly wounded, and Trudy now has to care for him. They will be of no help to you."

The mirror stayed quiet. More truth. She spoke again with faltering breaths, trying desperately not to break out in sobs. "Why ... are you ... telling me ... this?"

"As you might expect, I want you to fully cooperate with me, and the best way for me to get your cooperation is to show you that you have no hope of rescue. You are completely on your own."

Again the mirror proved Alex's words. "Why ... do you ... need me?"

"I don't. Not at all. You were leverage to keep your allies at bay. Now they have been conquered. They cannot help you."

The mirror stung. Something that she said wasn't true. Maybe Alex did need her, and Leo was obviously still around. She had one ally who might help. And maybe Caligar would step in, but without Ben's leadership, would they know what to do?

Alex gave her a knowing nod. "I can guess what you're thinking. You're counting on your faithful friend, Leo. I saw him down there, stumbling around in the snow. Nothing could stop him from trying to rescue you, but he is in bad shape. His recovery from being restored is far from complete. Any attempt to stop me would end in failure, perhaps his death. I'm sure you wouldn't want that to happen."

Iona shook her head. "No. I wouldn't."

"I thought not. The mirror in the abyss revealed that you two are related. Have you learned how?"

Iona kept her mouth shut. Alex didn't need to know. She would just use it against them.

"He's your father, isn't he?" Alex peered closely at her. "Yes. I see it in your eyes. Even your soulless body couldn't hide it. And the age difference between the two of you makes that relationship quite possible."

Again Iona stayed quiet.

"Then here is my proposal. I will give you two options. One is to leave you here right now. Leo will collect you and take you home. You will not be restored, of course, but this ordeal will be over for you. The other option is for you to come to Viridi with me. I will restore you to your body there, and when my one hundred influencers come, I will put you in charge of them. You will be second in command in the entire world."

Iona felt the mirror. Every word Alex spoke was true. She forced out a labored, "Why?"

"To tell you the truth …" Alex leaned closer, her steely eyes glimmering. "To keep Caligar from trying to stop me. I hope to continue using you as leverage. Your reward for faithfully accepting that role will be power and prestige in my new world. If Caligar accosts me, I will pretend to threaten you, but, of course, I won't want to do you harm because of your value to me."

Once again, Iona felt the mirror, still stable. Iona turned her head. She had to escape from those penetrating eyes and concentrate on this new dilemma. Getting off the cruiser and running into Leo's arms sounded wonderful, but then who would stop Alex from conquering Viridi? And who would keep her from a further path of destruction? She had mentioned destroying hell, but that didn't matter so much. God could always create it again. That was his business. But might she still destroy Earth out of spite?

Iona again spoke in halting phrases. "What will ... you do ... to Earth?"

"Nothing. With either choice, Earth will be safe. Once I am on Viridi, the events on Earth will mean nothing to me."

The mirror stung Iona's palm, hard this time. She tried to keep her face from reacting, but she wasn't sure if she had succeeded. She regained eye contact and spoke more forcefully. "You're lying."

Alex cocked her head. "What are you up to, you clever conniver?"

"What ... do you mean?"

"Stop pretending." Alex grabbed Iona's arm and jerked her hand out of her pocket, though the mirror stayed inside. "What do you have in there?"

"Nothing."

Alex slapped Iona's face. "Liar." She pushed a hand into Iona's pocket and pulled the mirror square out. "Aha! You're using this as a lie detector."

Iona looked directly into Alex's eyes. She had to keep her composure, steel herself. There was no use denying the purpose of the mirror. It would expose any lie she told. "It's true. It's a ... lie detector."

"So now you know that I really do plan to destroy Earth. That means I can't let you stay. You're coming with me." Alex slid the mirror into her pocket. "I plan to use this to interrogate you further. I'll find out if you're hiding any other secrets."

Iona kept her face slack. She couldn't afford to give away any further information, especially the presence of the transmitter. Losing that would mean losing everything.

"Stand up." Alex pulled Iona to her feet. "Pull your pants pockets inside out."

Iona reached into her pockets, palmed the transmitter, and pulled the pockets out, but someone as smart as Alex probably wouldn't be fooled.

The cruiser rocked hard, tossing both Alex and Iona to the floor. Iona used her co-pilot's chair to climb to her feet and pushed the transmitter under the cushion on the way up. Alex rose as well and looked at Iona's open hands and dangling pockets. "Okay. Apparently, you're clean. I'll check you more thoroughly later." She snatched the radio handset from the console and pressed the button. "What hit the cruiser?"

A gruff voice replied, "A man is dangling from one of the ship's landing runners. When we started the tower network energy, he jumped from the platform. He's a madman!"

Iona suppressed a smile. The man had to be Leo.

Alex barked into the handset, "I didn't tell you to start the network."

"I … I assumed you would be leaving soon. It takes a few minutes for everything to get up to full power."

"Very well. Then accelerate the process. I'm leaving as soon as possible."

"But your entourage isn't here yet. I got word that they're only a few minutes away, flying in the SkySweep drones."

"Then they can follow me later. I need to teach that huntsman and his devious daughter a lesson."

Ben ran up the tower's steps, a new switchback stairway instead of a ladder. Above, Leo dangled from the cruiser's left runner, hanging on desperately with both hands. When the tower energy turned on,

280

he probably thought Alex was about to leave with Iona, and leaping to catch the cruiser was his only chance.

Since the usual quake had already begun, the tower shuddered, but not as badly as the older one did. Whoever erected this one used sturdier materials. It could easily withstand the initial tremors.

With a final jump, Ben surged onto the platform. Five people stood near the edge, looking up at the hovering cruiser, yelling at Leo to drop, but the ship began rising. In seconds, the fall would be too far to survive.

"Leo!" Ben shouted. "Let go! You're not too high yet."

Leo didn't seem to hear, his body and mind apparently unable to do anything but hang on for dear life and try to save Iona. The five people on the platform watched, mesmerized. Maybe they were zombies, purged of their souls.

Ben shouted again, "We have it all planned. Iona will be all right. Just let go."

The cruiser zoomed away, Leo still hanging on, too high to drop. Now the only way to save him was to shut everything down before the cruiser could enter the Oculus Gate.

A series of pops sounded, followed by a loud buzzing noise. Bright streams of light shot out from the tower's antennas and wriggled through the sky, following the Arctic Circle around the globe. Soon streams from the three other towers would unite with these and create the conduit north of the line. Someone had to stop the process. Without a parachute, Leo couldn't possibly survive the transport to Viridi, unless, of course, he could continue hanging on until the cruiser landed, but that seemed highly unlikely considering the speed the cruiser would soon be traveling.

Ben rushed to one of the antennas and pushed the pole holding it in place, but it proved much sturdier than the original ones. He looked up. The cruiser was now flying north into the launch zone. Alex could leave in a matter of moments.

"Hey!" A man strode toward him, a pistol in hand. "Get away from that."

Ben lunged, knocked the gun from the man's grip, and punched him across the jaw. He staggered back and fell off the platform, screaming as he plunged. Ben scooped up the gun and fired it at the antenna. Each bullet pinged off the metal but seemed to do no damage.

He spun toward the other four on the platform and aimed the gun at them. They raised their hands, shivering, both from cold and fear.

Above, the streams now appeared to be connected. The conduit was forming. "Stop the process!" Ben shouted.

One of the four, a woman in a parka, called out, "Impossible from here. Once we started the process, it switched to an automatic timer. I would have to go to the underground chamber to stop it now."

"Kat," Ben called through his earbud, "are you in position?"

"Yes. And so is Caligar. Are you all right? You sound—"

"Just listen. Blow the machinery up now. Hurry. If you don't, Leo's dead."

"I'm putting the last bomb in place. Once I set them, I'll have two minutes to get out."

"Can you get out in one minute?"

"Probably. The path is clear."

"Then set the timers for one minute and run." Ben waved toward the four. "Get off the tower! Or you're dead." He sprinted down the stairs three steps at a time, now glad for a nearly empty backpack. Behind him, the pounding of feet followed. Even zombies still knew to save themselves.

When Ben reached the bottom, he ran away from the tower with a limping stride while looking to the north. The cruiser zoomed upward toward the Oculus Gate at lightning speed. With the mooring lights still illuminated, Leo was easy to see as he hung on. Then, he dropped, but his plunge slowed, and he followed the ship upward. They were both being sucked into the conduit, but would they make it through the Gate before—

A boom thundered. The ground shook harder than ever. To the rear, the ground erupted under the tower, sending a fountain of snow, dirt, and rocks up into the framework. The larger rocks fractured some of the beams, but after the explosion settled, the tower remained upright, though the energy streams sputtered and crackled, likely no longer able to create a conduit. If the conduit was still there, it would weaken soon.

Ice pellets and pebbles rained for several more seconds as Ben continued looking northward, breathless as he hobbled on. The angel cruiser was nowhere in sight, nor were Leo or Caligar.

He halted and gazed at the Oculus Gate, as clear as ever, like a gaping maw waiting to devour. If the cruiser successfully flew through the Gate, Alex and Iona would probably be able to land safely. And if Caligar also rose into that maw, he could parachute to the ground. But what about Leo? The only chance he had to survive would be for Caligar to grab him in freefall, but the odds of that happening had to be microscopically small.

A drone landed near the tower, and the door opened. Three men and a woman stepped out, all dressed in parkas, visible in the tower's dying streams. Ben eyed the drone. It might be his only hope … Leo's only hope.

He hustled toward the craft, his foot again aching with every step. Beyond it, Kat ran toward it as well, an empty backpack in one hand. Ben dodged the new arrivals, hopped into the drone, and shouted to Kat, "Get in!"

When she leaped in behind him, he sat at the controls and started the props. The drone lifted into the air. He pushed the throttle and zoomed north and upward, aiming directly at the Oculus Gate. "I'm going to try to save Leo."

"I know," Kat said from behind the pilot's chair. "I figured that out."

"Let's hope the conduit is still intact, or this is going to be a short ride."

283

Kat touched her earbud. "Caligar, this is Kat. Are you still on Earth?"

Ben held his breath, hoping for no reply. They needed their giant friend on Viridi. He might be Iona's only hope.

Kat breathed a sigh of relief. "No answer. He must've made it through."

The drone surged upward, faster and faster.

"Did you hit the throttle?" Kat asked.

"No." Ben lifted his hands from the control panel. "The conduit has us. The drone is no longer in my control."

Kat stood next to him and held his hand. After a few quiet seconds, she whispered, "We'll find her, Ben."

"I know, but right now I have to focus on Leo. He lost his grip on the cruiser. The moment we get into Viridi's atmosphere, we'll look for him and for Caligar's parachute. Catching Leo might be impossible, but we have to try."

"And knocking the tower out made things worse. There's nothing to pull Leo back toward the Gate, nothing to slow him down. He'll drop like a rock."

Heat surged into Ben's ears. "Yeah. Don't remind me."

As they zoomed onward, the Oculus Gate drew closer and closer, the outline of the eye growing wider by the second, more like a ravenous maw than ever.

Ben buckled the seatbelt, pulled Kat into his lap, and wrapped both arms around her. "Hang on. Here we go!"

Like being shot out of a cannon, they zipped inside, and everything fell dark.

Iona leaped off the co-pilot's chair, ran to the side door, and slapped the open button. The door slid to the side. Air rushed out.

Alex screamed, "What do you think you're doing?"

"Saving my father's life!" Iona threw Charlie's cloak off and climbed down from the cruiser, hanging on to the bottom of the doorway, her feet on a landing runner. As thin air rushed downward, she held her breath and looked all around. Below, Leo flew spread-eagle at the same speed they were hurtling upward, maybe thirty feet away, his cloak flapping at his sides.

Not wanting to shout and lose her air, she clenched her jaw shut. She grabbed the runner with both hands, curled her legs around it, and hung upside down, reaching for Leo, but he was still much too far away, his eyes wide and his fingers groping. Thirty feet grew to forty, fifty, sixty.

As she stretched with all her might, her cross dropped out from behind her shirt and whipped in the furious wind, like a tiny bird battling a gale. Iona bit her lip hard. Was this a sign? A reminder? Gasping for breath, she whispered, "God, help me. I can't do this without you."

Seconds later, Leo began drawing closer. Within seconds, their fingers touched. Iona stretched and latched on to his wrist. Finally, she let out a grunted, "I've got you!"

As she pulled, his weight seemed like almost nothing, as if he were a disembodied soul again. The beating wind had settled. Iona's head pounded like it was about to explode. Had they flown into a vacuum?

Something jerked her body and slung her and Leo into the cruiser. They tumbled to the floor and rolled to the opposite side of the ship.

The door slid closed, and Alex stood in front of it, a fist on her hip and Charlie's cloak in the other fist as air hissed all around, maybe an emergency supply refilling the cruiser. "Care to explain yourself?" Alex asked, her eyes like boiling silver.

Iona tucked her cross away, rolled to a sitting position, and glared at her. Would it do any good to try the halting words trick? Probably not. She took on a matter-of-fact tone. "I had to save my father's life."

Leo sat next to her and laid an arm around her shoulders. "And I thank you for that, though the dangling daughter maneuver nearly put me back in my grave."

"I see." Alex tossed the cloak into Iona's lap. "How did you get restored? And don't lie." Alex showed her the mirror square. "I'll know if your words are true or not."

Iona crossed her arms over her chest. "I'm not telling you anything."

"Really?" Alex set a hand close to the door's open button. "Do you think I am incapable of throwing your father out of this cruiser, especially considering his poor physical condition? Who do you think hauled you both in?"

Iona continued glaring at Alex. Although she had saved their lives by pulling them to safety, she didn't do it out of the kindness of her heart. Something sinister drove her, but what could it be?

Iona broke her stare and looked at Leo. With a pale face and bloodshot eyes, he seemed ready to keel over. Even though he was too weak to help battle Alex, at least he could provide information. "Are Ben and Kat dead?"

Leo sighed. "I'm afraid so. I found their charred bones at the Russia tower site. It looks like a bomb went off under the tower and burned their bodies."

A sob tried to erupt from Iona's gut, but she forced it back down. She couldn't lose control. Too much was at stake.

Alex looked at the mirror square and murmured, "Very interesting."

"What's interesting?" Iona asked, heat and prickles crawling across her neck.

"Nothing that I wish to tell you." Alex fixed her stare on Iona. "Now tell me, how did you get restored? If you refuse to answer, I will cast Leo out, and he will die in a cold vacuum. Since we are now on the Viridi side of the Gate, his body will crash to the planet, and his soul will wander on that world for all eternity."

Iona glared again at Alex, her vision blurred with tears. "If you throw Leo out, I'm going with him. Kill him, kill me. We live or die together. I would rather wander for eternity with him than give you a single scrap of information, you cold, calculating witch. You might think you're winning, but I promise you, you're going to die a violent death, and everyone on Earth and Viridi will celebrate the day you get thrown into the Lake of Fire forever."

Alex slid the mirror into her pocket and began a slow clap. "Brava, Iona. Brava. You have convinced me of your value. How could I go on without such passionate entertainment?"

Iona frowned. "What's that supposed to mean?"

"It means that both you and Leo will join me on Viridi. There I will establish communications with Lucifer, and he will decide what to do with you after he has had the chance to convince you of his own purpose."

Iona concealed a shudder and kept a hot glare locked on Alex. As she inhaled to shout, Leo clasped her hand and let out a low shushing sound. The sensation cooled her rage. He was right. Screaming at this witch would've been a waste of time, something the childish Iona would have done. Watching and learning would be a better strategy.

"It's time to check for weapons." Alex stepped toward Leo, bent over, and pushed a hand into one cloak pocket, then the other. Her brow shot upward. "What's this?" She withdrew a violin and bow and straightened. "I thought I noticed a lump earlier. Hiding weapons from the person who rescued you is poor behavior, Leo."

"That's not a weapon," Iona said, her tone calm.

"How little you know." Alex set the violin and bow on a passenger's seat. "And now ..." She snatched Charlie's cloak from Iona's lap and put it on. "I'm going to probe these fibers and see what I can find. Maybe a bit more leverage will help me gain what I want."

"What do you want?" Iona asked.

Alex strode toward the pilot's chair. "You will see, Iona. You will see."

When Alex seated herself, Iona looked at Leo and whispered, "Are you all right?"

He winced. "I am feeling as good as can be expected. Considering what we both have suffered, I would say that we are faring quite well. Yet, the situation could be better. We have been alone together in hell, but being alone together with Alex might be worse, especially since you have an appointment with Satan on the horizon, or so I heard from Damien."

"You heard right. And since Ben and Kat are ..." New tears welled, and her throat narrowed. She swallowed and continued at a higher pitch. "Since they're dead, everything's a whole lot worse." She blinked away the tears and gazed into Leo's eyes. "But we're not alone. You know Jack and Trudy won't give up, and Caligar's probably on our side." She lowered her voice further. "And I think Charlie might still be in the cloak. We've got some assets."

"If Alex doesn't find her." Leo nodded toward the violin. "And our so-called weapon might come in handy, assuming we can find a player." He slid his arm around her again and pulled her close. "And we have each other. We're already a formidable team."

"Yep. We'll figure out how to whip that witch." Iona glanced at Alex in the pilot seat, flying the cruiser toward a safe landing on Viridi, too distracted to pay attention to her captives at the moment. Iona withdrew the transmitter from her pocket, recently retrieved from the copilot's chair, and set it on her palm.

Her voice lower than ever, she whispered, "And this might be just the weapon we need to get it done."

CPSIA information can be obtained
at www.ICGtesting.com
Printed in the USA
BVHW042351290322
632740BV00028B/572